D0070170

In the City

of

Dark Waters

By Jane Jakeman

IN THE KINGDOM OF MISTS
IN THE CITY OF DARK WATERS

The Lord Ambrose Mysteries

LET THERE BE BLOOD
THE EGYPTIAN COFFIN
FOOL'S GOLD

62421332

M

In the City

of

Dark Waters

Fic
Jakeman,
Jane

JANE JAKEMAN

BERKLEY PRIME CRIME, NEW YORK

East Baton Rouge Parish Library
Baton Rouge, Louisiana

THE BERKLEY PUBLISHING GROUP
Published by the Penguin Group
Penguin Group (USA) Inc.
375 Hudson Street, New York, New York 10014, USA
Penguin Group (Canada), 90 Eglinton Avenue East, Suite 700, Toronto, Ontario M4P 2Y3, Canada
(a division of Pearson Penguin Canada Inc.)
Penguin Books Ltd., 80 Strand, London WC2R 0RL, England
Penguin Group Ireland, 25 St. Stephen's Green, Dublin 2, Ireland (a division of Penguin Books Ltd.)
Penguin Group (Australia), 250 Camberwell Road, Camberwell, Victoria 3124, Australia
(a division of Pearson Australia Group Pty. Ltd.)
Penguin Books India Pvt. Ltd., 11 Community Centre, Panchsheel Park, New Delhi—110 017, India
Penguin Group (NZ), Cnr. Airborne and Rosedale Roads, Albany, Auckland 1310, New Zealand
(a division of Pearson New Zealand Ltd.)
Penguin Books (South Africa) (Pty.) Ltd., 24 Sturdee Avenue, Rosebank, Johannesburg 2196, South
Africa

Penguin Books Ltd., Registered Offices: 80 Strand, London WC2R 0RL, England

This is an original publication of The Berkley Publishing Group.

This is a work of fiction. Names, characters, places, and incidents either are the product of the author's
imagination or are used fictitiously, and any resemblance to actual persons, living or dead, business es-
tablishments, events, or locales is entirely coincidental. The publisher does not have any control over
and does not assume any responsibility for author or third-party websites or their content.

Copyright © 2006 by Jane Jakeman.
Cover illustration © Claude Monet.
Cover design by Pyrographx / David S. Rheinhardt.

All rights reserved.
No part of this book may be reproduced, scanned, or distributed in any printed or electronic from without permission. Please do not participate in or encourage piracy of copyrighted materials in violation of
the author's rights. Purchase only authorized editions.
BERKLEY PRIME CRIME is an imprint of The Berkley Publishing Group.
The name BERKLEY PRIME CRIME and the BERKLEY PRIME CRIME design are trademarks belonging to Penguin Group (USA) Inc.

First edition: May 2006

Library of Congress Cataloging-in-Publication Data

Jakeman, Jane.
    In the city of dark waters / by Jane Jakeman.—1st ed.
        p. cm.
    ISBN 0-425-20981-4
    1. Monet, Claude, 1840–1926—Fiction. 2. English—Italy—Fiction. 3. Venice (Italy)—Fiction.
I. Title.

PR6060.A435I49 2006
823'.92—dc22

                                                                                2005057225

PRINTED IN THE UNITED STATES OF AMERICA

10   9   8   7   6   5   4   3   2   1

Last Baton Rouge Parish Library
Baton Rouge, Louisiana

*In affectionate memory of
Leona Nevler,
editor and friend*

1

VENICE 1908

PARTS OF A GONDOLA: ferro: *the iron beak at the prow;* poppa: *the platform at the stern where the gondolier stands;* forcola: *carved walnut oar rest;* felze: *a discreet curtained cabin for passengers. Gondolas were used in Venice as far back as the eleventh century. An edict passed in 1562 made it compulsory to paint them black.*

The green canal water shivers in the morning breeze. The sun is shining on a long façade of dappled pink marble and a deserted balcony. Set rhythmically along the front of the building are doors and windows with Gothic pediments, arches, and black interiors like strange-lipped mouths. There has been a high tide and here, where we can glimpse it through the entrance, the marble floor of the palazzo is one long perspective of wet gleams and shadows.

Someone is moving deep inside, seen first as a faint, pale glimmer shimmering towards us. Then after a few moments our eyes can make sense of the shape floating through the dimness of the interior. It resolves itself into the form of a young woman, who enters at the far end of the hall, pulling a cream-colored wrapper round her shoulders, and picks her way through the puddles in her satin slippers, carefully carrying a bowl of figs.

We are in one of the palaces lining the Grand Canal. Uninvited, of course. This crumbling baroque riot of brick and marble belongs to the Casimiri, one of Venice's oldest families, whose name is inscribed in the *Libro d'Oro,* the Golden Book. These families were once permitted to marry only among themselves, and still do not welcome outsiders. So watch and listen very quietly as Clara Casimiri walks through the columned hall of Palazzo Casimiri. This is the *androne,* the long, water-level floor of the old Venetian palaces, reaching back into the depths of the building from the Grand Canal portico, into which the salt spray blows as casually as dust in other climates.

Clara goes towards a small door which is almost concealed among the carved window arches and plasterwork. She has dark blonde hair and a long, graceful neck, clearly a tall and healthy young woman, an unusual specimen in a city where damp and inbreeding have reduced much of the population to pale and stunted creatures. The Venetian nobility, in particular, take no exercise whatsoever. They have no opportunity to ride or hunt, they cannot walk any distance, obviously, and they are conveyed around the waters of their city like an exotic species of crippled wildfowl. Clara Casimiri is a healthful exception. Her animal strength raises the spirits just to see it, to witness the strong movement of her legs under the silk skirt that blows against them, the upright back.

Inside the door in the wall, Clara sets her foot on the first of a flight of stone steps, calling out, "Tanta, Tanta," as she mounts the stairs. There is no reply, but this does not seem to surprise her, and she pushes open the door at the top unconcernedly. The small salon beyond is in a state of disorder, a mandolin with broken strings lying on a table, some loose pieces of silk on the floor, a browned and half-eaten peach on an old blue and white plate, and she adds her bowl of figs to the chaos on the table.

"Ah, Daniella!" sighs Clara, but she is still not much concerned. This state of affairs, things half-finished, half-eaten, half-mended, is not unusual in Tanta's apartments, nor is it unusual for Daniella to fail in her duties of clearing up the mess. Tanta's life is confined to this small space, these rooms which she can never leave. Nevertheless, in spite of the disorder, Clara usually feels a sense of safety here, at the top of that little staircase. These untidy chambers have been a refuge for her on many occasions. They had never thought of looking for her in Tanta's rooms.

Something does give Clara cause for alarm. Again she calls out, "Tanta!" The disturbing peculiarity is the unusual behavior of a small dog with a fluffy ring of white fur surrounding its babyish face, which rushes out of the bedroom beyond and dashes across the room to Clara, whining anxiously. Clara crosses to the half-open bedroom door. The dog anticipates her movements and is standing there now, turning its head nervously from her towards the next room and back again.

The door whispers over the carpet as Clara pushes it open. Inside, the bedroom is still in darkness, and she crosses to a window closed by a shutter, which when opened lets in a greenish undulating light reflected from the waters of the canal. The center of the room is occupied by a vast tester bed draped with crimson velvet curtains and swags suspended from a baldachin, and opposite the foot of the bed a long, tarnished, silver-framed mirror hangs at an angle of forty-five degrees from the wall, reflecting the drawn curtains and the black and brown depths of their folds. Beside the bed a night table holds yet more random objects: a blue and silver decanter with a small glass next to it, a box of Turkish Delight, a stained face flannel.

Clara now has to gather up her courage. She pulls back the bed curtain with a rattle of the ivory rings running along the poles.

The small face that lies on the heap of pillows is crumpled with age, and the mouth and chin are stained with thin vomit that has cascaded down the satin valance at the side of the bed. The body lies on its side, with the knees pulled up to the chin as if in some final agony.

Clara cries out, a sharp sound muffled in the wood and draperies of the room, and backs away, and as she turns to leave, she encounters another woman, middle-aged, dressed in black, big and broad, with a gray sash around her waist.

"*Dio,* Daniella, I think she's . . . I think she's gone!"

The other woman pushes quickly past her and goes up to the bed, where she peers down at the dead face. She does not cross herself: Daniella is not one of those devout old women who always have a crucifix at their throats or a rosary in their hands. She bends down, puts her ear to the mouth, slips her hand under the sheet, and lays her fingers on the side of the neck. She looks at Clara and nods. *"La poveretta,"* she whispers. "Poor little thing."

"Are you sure?" asks Clara softly.

"I've seen it often enough!"

"I'd better tell my father."

Daniella looks at her for a few moments without speaking. Then she nods and takes up the flannel. She is wiping the dead mouth as Clara leaves the room.

COUNT Roberto Casimiri is standing waiting for his valet to shave him, towels, silver basin, and shaving stick at the ready, as Clara bangs on the door of his dressing room. A big, good-looking man with red gold hair and a complexion veined with grenadine crimson, the count is wondering if he could have a system for heating water installed in his apartments. But his daughter puts this scheme entirely out of his mind as she rushes in calling, "Papa! Oh, Papa, Tanta is dead."

"What, just now? Have you seen her?"

"Yes, there's no doubt. I went to her room, and she's lying there, in the bed. Quite gone. And Daniella was sure of it."

The count utters an exclamation. Only now does Clara feel the shock and tears start coming to her eyes. The valet, Tommaso, with the gesture of a near-perfect servant, swiftly hands her a big, white man's handkerchief, shaking out its folds as he does so, and she buries her nose in the damask crest.

"Clara, go and tell Claudio, and let me get dressed. Tell Pietro we want a fire lit in the drawing room, will you?"

"Shall I call Dr. Albrizzi?"

"Not right away. There's not much point, after all."

Clara knows her father would not go to see the dead woman for him-self. He has always avoided her living presence. Why should he be inter-ested in her corpse? Except, perhaps, to make sure of something.

He is looking at Clara now, and she tries to make her mind as empty as possible in case he reads her thoughts. In this place, it is not merely a question of keeping secrets. Sometimes the only safe thing is not to have them at all.

SOME members of the Casimiri family are assembled in the long draw-ing room on the first floor of the palazzo, before a huge fireplace riotous with cherubs and goddesses in various rusty shades of marble, figures ex-ecuted by a rather heavy-handed sculptor. Along the room runs a series of pointed window arches with lacy stone embrasures. Before the fire-place are arrayed several heavy chairs with cut velvet cushions, and in the grate on this chilly autumn morning there burns a small fire. A manser-vant, Pietro, stands beside the door awaiting further orders.

Smoke billows into the room and drifts along its length in black clouds. "Pietro," exclaims the count, "go and see about having this chim-ney swept. Right away!"

Pietro knows that this will be an utterly fruitless errand, knows that there is no way of telling which, among all the mazes and nests of an-cient pipes and ducts that constitute the Palazzo Casimiri's haphazard chimney system, serves to ventilate the smoke from this particular fire-place, and that a chimney sweep once sent up to investigate was alleged to have been utterly lost and never seen again except as a small black ghost occasionally emerging into bedchambers. Nevertheless, the errand will allow Pietro some respite in the warmth of the kitchens. He bows and departs. The story of the chimney ghost is not the only secret he has learned during his service with the family, and sometimes he feels a great sensation of relief when he quits their presence, as though he has left some darkness at his back. At least, Pietro thinks, at least his conscience is clear. That morning he had refused to help Rinaldo with a certain assignment. He had not liked the look of it at all, nor the things they were supposed to put in that secret place.

Claudio, only son of Count Casimiri, has now joined Clara, the count, and his second wife. Clara's fiancé, Principe Antonio Prepiani, usually included in family councils, has not yet arrived. Claudio's hair is the same dark gold as Clara's, but he has nut-brown skin, which the Casimiri account as evidence of their descent from some oriental ancestor who joined Doge Dandolo of Venice at the sack of Constantinople over six centuries previously.

He is shaking his head before he says, "Will we have to inform the English consul, do you think?"

There is a long pause. Claudio looks round in case he has said something wrong.

The count, who has been standing before the fireplace gazing up at the worn paint, the small blind eyes and bulging cheeks of his cherubs, sinks into his chair before he says, "Yes, I suppose so. However, the English are a practical people. We must make the funeral arrangements, of course, but I do not think they will raise any difficulties. And the marriage was so long ago that I don't think any of the family will want to come. There will be no need to delay matters. After all, it was not so sudden—Tanta has been ill."

Beside the fire there is a movement as the Contessa Mariella shrinks further down into her deep-sided chair. She is a natural watcher who has played no part in this conversation and will not expect to do so, although there is a certain look in her pale face which suggests that she is not as passive as she seems. It is not a fiery or rebellious expression, but more as if she were carefully considering the outcome of the latest development in the history of the Casimiri family. Her expression is evidence of a weak but manipulative personality, some might think, as she turns her gaze from one to another and assesses the effect of the principessa's death.

"I will go to Marzano," says the count.

The Casimiri look at one another. Pietro comes back into the room. Silence reigns.

ON the steps of a humble house, a tall thin building in the Giudecca overlooking the water, Revel Callender was standing with his landlady, Signora Amalia, when they saw a long black boat hung with faded canopies and ancient shields gliding past. If there were any passengers, they were seated beneath the *felze,* for no one was visible except for the boatmen, who were clad in livery and whose slow strokes carried the vessel silently along.

Amalia crossed herself, staring out over the water.

"What is it?" asked Callender, surprised by the expression of fear on her face.

"It's the Casimiri boat. Something must be happening. They're one of the oldest families in Venice, with a palazzo on the Grand Canal."

"But what is frightening you?" He could see only that the boat looked old and somber, the gilding worn off the ornate decoration at the prow, the mottoes on the shields along the sides illegible with age. All the same, there was a presence about it: the very stillness on its deck made him uneasy.

He was slightly amused when, as well as the sign of the cross, she made the ancient gesture against the evil eye and touched an amulet she wore on a chain round her neck. *Venice, where all beliefs meet,* he thought to himself, *and its citizens call on the protection of them all.*

"It's not just the boat," she said, turning to him, and he could see that her black, bright eyes were rounded with alarm, shiny as little berries in her plump, pale face. "Their house has a bad reputation, Signor Callender."

He was fascinated and at the same time irritated by her Venetian taste for intrigue, for sniffing out drama. So often, he had come to learn, it was mere gossip, smoke without fire. "Bad reputation—for what?" he said now, quite brusquely. "What's this about?"

"Oh, you know what they are saying!"

"No, signora, I don't, as a matter of fact. Tell me about it."

"Oh, you English, you always have to have explanations! Well, the Casimiri have never been liked—put it that way. Most of their servants come from outside Venice, so you can tell something by that."

"Yes, I suppose so, but is that all you have against them?"

She put a finger to her nose in the ancient gesture of one imparting a secret. "No, signor—something happened only recently. There was a maid who went to work in their kitchens—and she has never been seen again."

Callender laughed skeptically, which to Amalia was almost unforgivable.

"What an absurd rumor!"

"*Si, signor,*" she said crossly. "Ginevra Rocalle, the butcher's daughter. One day she was stuffing sausages in her father's shop. The next, he sent her for a job in the Palazzo Casimiri and—pouf!" She clapped her hands together. "Like that, she vanished!"

"She had a lover, I'm sure! What do you think really happened, Amalia?"

But she was offended and wouldn't tell him anything more.

This was a pity, because a clear warning would have been timely. The journey which was to take Callender into darkness and danger had begun.

2

That journey had an unexpected beginning.

"No, Miss Marshall. I assure you, there is not the slightest chance of redress."

He was speaking patiently to the girl opposite him, sighing inwardly at the familiar narrative which he had just heard from her pretty little mouth. She could not be more than eighteen and was classically English in appearance, with her upright posture and fair hair piled tightly on top of her head, her innocent pink skin a trifle roughened by the Italian sun. Her blue eyes were at present very damp and reddened by tears.

Best to be direct, he thought to himself. *She will recover all the sooner.*

"But he *promised* me!" the girl wailed.

"And then you never saw him again. Yes, I know."

The small brown-clad woman sitting on the other available chair in Callender's tiny study said anxiously, "It was not my fault, I assure you, that Clementine became acquainted with him." She turned an accusatory gaze on the girl.

"I wasn't blaming you, Miss Tenbaker!" wailed Clementine.

"You slipped out of the hotel without me—I would never have permitted you to speak to a total stranger who merely approached you in the piazza in the first place."

She turned back to Callender and said meaningfully, "I made sure she was never alone with him again. I was always in the room, though sometimes I could not hear their conversation, of course. But he was very . . ." She sought for a word. "He was extremely plausible."

Extremely good-looking, thought Callender. *That's what she means. They all are; that's how they do it.* Aloud, he said, "I can only advise you to return to Wiltshire and forget about this man. An action for breach of promise would not be at all feasible."

"But you're an Englishman!" sobbed Clementine. "Surely you could do *something.*"

"Call him out in a duel? Horsewhip him? My dear Miss Marshall, this is the modern age! Believe me, your best chance of happiness is to get over this incident."

Had he been too sharp? She had so obviously been utterly smitten by the dashing Venetian "nobleman" who had promised her marriage and taken her jewelry, but it was an old, old story. At least the man probably hadn't taken her virtue—the companion would have guarded that like a tweedy dragon huffing and puffing over its treasure. Callender sighed. He felt sorry for her, too. The companion had failed to properly protect her charge and would probably be dismissed when Clementine's family came to hear about their daughter's misadventure.

Clementine was getting quite angry now, which at least brought her sobbing to an end. She stood up, wielding her parasol about with a surprisingly firm grasp, directing it in the direction of the few accoutrements of Callender's "study," his two shelves of law books and the somewhat battered table, in order to make her point. "I thought as soon as I saw this room it would be useless," she said. "I can't imagine why that man at the consulate recommended you."

Because he himself has more important matters to attend to, and because you might need legal advice, was the obvious answer. *And there are few British residents in Venice who are legally qualified, and fewer still who are honest, many of them being renegades or rogues, and I happen to be one of the most presentable.*

But he said nothing and let Clementine have her head.

"A proper British lawyer wouldn't have such a tiny little box of a place," she raged.

The companion, Miss Tenbaker, meanwhile attacked on another front: She peered at an object lying on the desk in front of her and said with some disgust, "Why, that's a book of poetry!" Turning to Callender, she whispered, her round mouth forming the words with exaggerated disgust as if it were uttering an obscenity that it was obliged to relay, the words *"Shelley!* That dreadful man who wrote about such shocking things!"

Her diatribe was interrupted by the rich baritone song of a gondolier, which came echoing across the canal outside. There was a pause, during which all parties silently acknowledged the absurd magnificence of Venice.

"I assure you, ladies," said Callender, putting on some indignation, though part of it was perfectly genuine, "I am perfectly well qualified as a lawyer. I do not practice here—I am endeavoring to assist a fellow citizen, as I do from time to time when legal questions arise. Now, I have explained that you have no redress, and I am afraid there is obviously nothing more I can do for you. Miss Marshall, I suggest that you put all this behind you and return to your family."

"And I'm a pompous ass," he added under his breath, but it was good advice, and the companion seemed to realize this. In fact, rather surprisingly, she backed him up.

"Yes, Clementine, it would do not any good to make a fuss here. I am sure we must not create any kind of scandal, please remember that. The less said the better in these matters; that is always the best policy." She stood up purposefully, and Callender gave her credit for having more backbone than he had thought.

Clementine was dabbing at her eyes again, but her passion seemed to have been spent for the moment, and when her companion took her by the hand, she allowed herself to be led away. She gave one last glance at Callender, who was a handsome man, and managed a smile.

Callender rose to open the door, and as the ladies squeezed out past him, he murmured, "The jewelry might always have been taken from your room. By some anonymous thief."

Miss Tenbaker, at least, took his hint. Her eyes were really quite shrewd behind her neat, round, wire spectacles, and she nodded in acknowledgment as the two ladies passed him. A story of some unknown thief in the night would be sufficient explanation for the family at home. Nothing more need be said in Wiltshire, if only Clementine could contain herself. It was the best possible counsel, positively fatherly, and his own consultation fee had been settled in advance, so as far as he was concerned, his duties were completed.

IT was an interest in art that had actually formed the basis of his acquaintance with the British consul, Theseus Barton, though they had studied law at the same Oxford college, which already provided a bond. There, Callender had been considered a brilliant outsider and Barton a steady and reliable all-rounder, but their characters had become more alike during the eight years since those days. Barton had lived abroad and widened his mental horizons, and Callender had been constrained financially to make a career after college.

In London, Callender was a junior partner in a legal practice representing an affluent clientele drawn from the best ranks of society. This year abroad, now but three months advanced, had been intended as an interlude, a brief escape before the iron gates of obligation finally clanged shut upon Revel Callender's life and he devoted the rest of his existence to legal practice. His family, though they were of an old lineage which could trace their descent back in the same house for some four hundred years, was not rich; indeed, their fortunes had recently taken a turn for the worse. Callender would have to make a successful career for himself, a prospect which no member of his family had faced for centuries. But among their traditions had been that of the grand tour, whereby a young man would travel through Europe and pick up some culture and polish, and quite possibly the pox as well. On the walls of the dining room at Damson Castle hung a few misty landscapes brought back from these expeditions a couple of centuries previously, pictures which had enchanted Callender as a boy. They made him long to visit the places they depicted, Italy especially, the gardens of Tivoli, the Bay of Naples, and above all, Venice.

When Revel Callender was a grown man, he realized that the grand tour was no longer fashionable, and travel had lost much of its appeal, now at the beginning of the twentieth century. The world was full of steam engines and telegraphs. Even so, he had never entirely given up on the life of the imagination. Revel had assessed his precarious finances carefully and decided that some time abroad was a possibility, especially if he could earn some money giving legal advice to English travelers. He had actually intended this one year mainly as a breathing space from law: as an opportunity to learn Italian, to study the galleries, to perhaps experiment in art himself, before his return to London. It was out of necessity that he advised Miss Marshall and her like. Ancient lineage and a tumbledown castle might mean a great deal when it came to the social pecking order, but the Callenders of the past had been notorious spendthrifts, and it was generally known that there was little left for the present son and heir. Hence his humble lodgings with Signora Amalia. At least, he consoled himself when some dubious piece of anglerfish was yet again dished up at her table, he was in the misty golden city of Titian, of Canaletto, wrapped in sea mists and open to the spicy airs of the Orient.

And this was a fine morning, the salty air of the Adriatic blowing inland out of a pearly sky. Callender stepped out onto Signora Amalia's balcony and began his belated breakfast, but a second intervention promised to spoil his day. Not ten minutes after the departure of the English ladies, a messenger was hurrying through a narrow *calle*, zigzagging through groups of tourists, panting with exertion.

Such haste was most unusual in Venice, and Revel, with his long legs now propped up on the balcony railings and breakfast dishes of coffee, figs, and peaches in front of him, had noticed the agitated movements even before the flunkey turned aside and rapped on the door below.

"Eh, signor!"

Amalia's voice called up to him, after barking out the usual watchdog challenge which she always offered to callers. Reluctantly, Callender got up and leaned over the balcony. Amalia and the messenger were standing below, the one with hands on her hips, the other flourishing a document, like figures from an operetta, but to his surprise the messenger looked up and addressed him in English.

"Mr. Callender?" The stranger was holding a letter which Callender could see was sealed with a large official-looking blob of red wax. His heart sank at the thought of officialdom finding him out this morning.

"Yes, all right, let him bring it up, Amalia."

There was some bowing and scraping performed in a narrow compass, which inhibited some of the flourishes when the man emerged onto the balcony and put Revel in a better mood: the sound of his own language had almost driven away the pleasure with which he was anticipating the day, which he had intended to spend at liberty, wandering through the art galleries on his own. At least, that was his plan. But when he took receipt of the letter and nodded at the messenger to indicate he could leave, the man said stubbornly, "No, sir, I have to wait for an answer."

Revel looked at him with surprise but ripped the envelope open, tearing disrespectfully at the lion and the unicorn impressed on the flap. Crumbs of orange pink wax showered down in the dusty air.

The contents were in the hand of the British consul, the man to whom he owed the visit of Miss Marshall and her companion. Yet another favor? The day stretched before him still, and he wanted to make the remainder of it his own. He said reluctantly, "Tell Mr. Barton I shall be there."

The man declined the coins which Revel pulled from his pocket in order to conclude the conversation. "I must take back a written answer, sir."

Callender sighed as he went inside out of the sunshine. The bright-
ness of the morning already seemed to have gone off, the best part of the
day was slipping past him, and the bedroom, which last night had
seemed quite luxurious and exotic when he and Mira had fallen onto the
couch, now seemed rather shabby. It was fortunate that Clementine
Marshall and Miss Tenbaker had contented themselves with inspecting
his study and not penetrated farther into his apartments—otherwise
they would probably have gone instantly shrieking down the stairs, and
even more fortunate that Mira, a casual and cheerful acquaintance, had
departed to her oyster stall on the Rialto, where Callender had first fallen
into conversation with her. It had been followed rapidly by falling into
much else. The Turkish rug in his room was marked with peculiar
tracks, and there were stains on the fraying blue silk cushions. Damn, old
Amalia would undoubtedly put it all on the bill! With a sudden flash of
memory, Callender remembered that he and Mira had filled their
mouths with wine and spurted it out over their naked flesh, a thought
which made him laugh out loud with a renewal of pleasure, though a
cough from the respectful official messenger waiting outside the door of
the bedroom made him return all too quickly to the present. He walked
over to his night table and, straight-faced with an effort, wrote out a brief
note, which he handed to the man waiting outside.

Reluctantly, he changed into his only decent suit. He gazed at his
crop of curly dark hair in the mirror and smoothed it down with the pair
of silver hairbrushes which had belonged to his grandfather. Then he
asked Amalia to summon a gondola, having rummaged in his trouser
pockets to ensure that he had the fare. As he waited at the modest house
on the Giudecca, he almost had second thoughts and was wondering if
he could still bow out, perhaps sending a message to the consulate an-
nouncing a sudden fever or the death of a long-lost relative.

He was considering the wording in his mind when he saw that he
might have yet more visitors that morning. Clambering purposefully out
of a boat and pointing towards his residence was another young, fair-
haired female clad in a light dress, already holding up a parasol against

any attack by the morning sunshine. A rotund elderly person, this one dressed in slate gray, trailed along behind.

The gentlemen of Venice had clearly been very busy of late.

But at that moment a gondola drew alongside the quay, and Callender stepped quickly aboard.

In the boat, he took Barton's letter out of his pocket and reread it.

"There is a task which a lawyer would be best equipped to perform, and of course since this is a confidential matter, it goes without saying that the person concerned must be a British subject. I have suggested to His Excellency that there is an entirely suitable British resident here in Venice who could perfectly be charged with this undertaking. I should like you to call on me this morning at eleven o'clock."

3

"Mesdames, messieurs, the Simplon Orient Express is about to depart!" There was a long hoot of joy from the whistle, and the carriage jolted slightly.

Fifteen stab wounds! The papers were still mulling over the horrible details that had been made public at the trial. A platform vendor had thrust the newspaper at him as the train pulled out, and Claude Monet hid it under his overcoat. He would make sure it was thrown away before his wife could see it.

Alice didn't notice. She was sitting opposite him as they started through the suburbs of Paris, wearing the intent expression of the traveler embarking on a long journey. They could hear the cry of the guard as he passed along the corridor calling out the stops. *"Genève, Lausanne, Milan, Venise, Trieste, Stamboul . . ."* The man had a mournful air, and he seemed to make even the place-names sound like sad cries.

There was a jolt, and they began to move, with a burst of steam and a spray of smuts flying past the window of their plush-lined compartment. His wife was spreading out various bags and smoothing her layers of skirts. She had removed her feathered hat, carefully taking out the pearl-headed hatpins, and it now sat in the woven string rack above her head, perched there like some absurd huge bird caught in a net. They could afford the space and comfort of a first-class carriage to themselves, though sometimes he felt nostalgic for the old days when they had to travel in the horse cart from Mantes, the time when they were poor and the world had been full of sharp sensations, blunted now, though he tried to preserve them amid the engulfing spread of middle age. And amid success, which was also taking its toll on once-youthful eagerness and energy. He had no doubt that Venice would be full of society ladies, who would seek to put him on show at their dances and tea parties as the famous artist, a captured star brought down from the heavens to cast its luster on their gatherings. Once Monet had sought their patronage, would have scraped their boots for a commission in the days of desperate poverty. Once, indeed, Alice had been one of them before she joined him in poverty. Now, successful, he merely resented all interruptions to his work.

"I hope we can make it clear to Mrs. Hunter that I am coming to Venice to paint," he said.

Alice nodded, settled herself, and then very carefully, her shoulders hunched protectively as if someone were looking over her shoulder, although they were quite alone in the compartment, she opened her smallest case, a silk-lined affair in burgundy morocco with a silver clasp and key, unlocked it, and took out a letter. "This came from Cecile just before we left. I didn't have time to read it."

Inwardly, his spirits sank at the sight of Cecile's handwriting sprawling across the black-edged notepaper appropriate to a recent widow in deep mourning. A letter from Alice's sister seemed always to be a source of anxiety these days, and inevitably it would contain more about that terrible affair in Paris. He had so hoped it could be forgotten during this stay in Venice.

Fifteen wounds! Even the powerful influence of Alice's family could not entirely keep such details out of the newspapers. This was what Paris was avid for; under all the songs and music of the halls, under the civilized living of restaurants and opera, was a longing for blood and cruelty, for the stripping naked, whether in soul or body, of just such plump and pompous creatures as his late brother-in-law.

Alice read through the first page, and he saw that her forehead was already wrinkling with anxiety. She looked up sharply. "Cecile says there is a possibility that the investigation may take a new course."

"What sort of course?"

"There is to be an appeal hearing," she answered. "It will all be gone through again. The servants were clearly convicted at the trial, though personally I would never have believed Renard was involved. He's got a good background, a respectable middle-aged man."

"From whom are they taking statements?" asked Monet. He meant, *Do they know about Léon?* He didn't want to upset her, but she understood what he was saying.

She answered carefully, "Cecile thinks the course of the investigation won't concern Léon. Not in any way."

"But Léon was there. He was right there on the night when it happened."

"Ah, but he wasn't able to give a description—you know how shaken he was."

Yes, he did remember that. Alice's seventeen-year-old nephew Léon Raingo sprawled in a chair, his whole thin body trembling with shock, Cecile forcing sips of brandy down him, and the Raingo family, Alice's relatives, arrayed around, closing ranks already, before they even knew any of the details.

"No, darling boy, don't say anything. You need to rest." Claude Monet, who had been summoned to this family crisis, remembered Cecile's voice and glimpsing, through the partly open doors of the salon, the faces of the gendarmes kept out by the servants.

This trip to Venice would, he hoped, take Alice away from the consequences of those events in Paris, coming as it did while the police investigations were still going on in France, and he was glad of the steady rattling on the tracks as the engine gathered speed, passing through suburbs on the way out of the city. He looked at his wife, and it occurred to him as significant that she was wearing a light-colored dress and dark blue jacket.

"I'm glad you're not wearing mourning, at any rate, like the rest of the family."

"It was very suitable for Cecile," Alice replied. "It's what a widow is expected to wear—at least, someone with a position in society."

"She has always done her best to remind you of it."

"That's unkind, Claude. If it hadn't been for Cecile, we would have starved in Vétheuil or frozen to death in that terrible winter. There weren't even boots for the children, don't you remember?"

The river had frozen over after Camille's death. Alice had come to live with him, leaving her bankrupt and good-for-nothing husband, Ernest, and she had brought their five children with her. Claude had written begging letters to everyone who might help, to every acquaintance in the art world, to their families, the respectable Monets and the wealthy Raingos. Every penny of the small dowry that his first wife, Camille, had brought with her had been spent. They lived from hand to mouth, no bills paid, everything sold or pawned. Even her favorite locket had been pawned, so that he had been obliged to ask for a loan to get it back in order to place it around her neck before she was lowered into the grave.

Alice, still jealous of her dead rival, had destroyed all photographs of Camille and almost all her letters and papers. Little of their own mother survived for Camille's own two sons, Jean and Michel Monet, to inherit. They called Alice "mother."

Sighing, he thought about it now. He had long recognized that Alice had a passionate and vindictive side to her nature. The fires had not entirely died down with age, and he still feared her storms and tempests, white-haired though she had become. Nevertheless, he wanted to protect her from the horrible business of her brother-in-law's death. And it was true that the dead man, Auguste, and his wife, Cecile, had been the only relatives who had helped them, though it had been with a bad grace on Auguste's part. He had sent Alice some very unpleasant letters along with the money.

Claude Monet recalled with pain their groveling abasement of any vestiges of pride, just so that they could stay alive. No, so that he could paint; he must acknowledge that. To buy canvas and oils, and to keep him from the fate that would await him if he gave up art and became reconciled with his family: going to work in the family's drapery business in the provincial town of Le Havre.

"Well, your sister did help us, it's true. But I don't think Auguste liked it."

It was an odd thing, he thought, that Cecile had not been in the house on the night when Auguste had been killed. She had gone to spend the weekend at their country house.

"Poor Auguste! We mustn't speak ill of the dead."

"He can't have been easy to live with, though."

Alice looked agitated, and he regretted voicing this truth, though it had given him some satisfaction to do so. He was, though it was impossible to say, so sick of the way in which the late Auguste Rémy, loud-voiced banker and undisputed master of his household, had been treated as some species of martyr since meeting his violent and unexplained death. He didn't go down the path of speaking directly about the sainted Auguste, but found that he couldn't leave the topic, as though it were preying on his mind as well as hers.

"I thought Cecile looked absurd at the funeral," he said, "like something out of a harem, shrouded in black from head to foot, with that monstrous veil over her face." He remembered a mass of satin ribbons falling like black waterfalls over Cecile's stout, middle-aged figure and shuddered.

Alice didn't respond with a quick and vocal defense of her sister, as he expected; it would have put their conversation back on a normal track and somehow taken the pain out of the recollections of that June day a few months ago, in the cemetery of Montmartre, those sooty bundles with living human beings somewhere inside the garments, the mourners around the neat, dark pit. Instead, she said carefully, "Claude, something happened at Auguste's funeral. At the graveside, it seems."

The train lurched as it shunted through the suburbs. *Good-bye, Paris,* he thought.

"Alice, let's leave all that behind."

"I must tell you this—it's something I hadn't heard of before. Cecile mentions it in her letter."

He sighed, leaned across, and took her hand, as always after they had argued. It was smooth now, no longer roughened by housework, though the fingers were stiff and thick.

"Very well, tell me."

"It seems the police received an anonymous letter the day after the funeral. The writer of the letter claimed to have overheard something that was said to young Léon at the graveside. Apparently the words were, 'The old man is dead. He can't keep us apart now.'"

Monet gazed in horror at his wife as the implications sank in. "This was in an unsigned letter?"

She nodded. There was a pause. He didn't want to ask the next question, but there was no going back now.

"And who spoke those words?"

It took a long time for Alice to answer this. Eventually, she said, "According to the writer of the letter, it was the butler, Renard. That's why the police are so convinced of his guilt."

"He and Léon? But he's a man of forty odd . . . he's got white hair, for God's sake!" Husband and wife stared at each other across the dusty gulf, the tiny space of their compartment, as the long express swayed along the track that was taking them away from Paris.

THE luggage, the bags and boxes and easels, had been loaded on to the gondola, and he forgot the awkwardness of it all, contented to have arrived in Venice at this moment, as they slid through the orange light of the dying sun, which was reflected in the water as if another sun were burning beneath the surface. In the walls of the palaces along the Grand Canal were rows of arched windows traced with indigo, lit with gleams of mother-of-pearl and orpiment that framed enticing darkness. Leading off from the main channel were shadowy alleys and waterways, where an occasional figure flitted from a doorway into a black skiff, which slipped away into the approaching night. His sense of mounting excitement overcame his anxieties; indeed, Monet had become almost oblivious of Alice, huddled beside him, but as they neared a landing stage flanked by poles twisted like sugar-candy sticks, he looked at her and saw pityingly the heavy drooping curve of her neck and shoulders and her rather absurd fashionable feathered hat.

The landing stage was wet, fringed with juicy green weeds. The gondolier helped them out, and there was a great shouting in Italian as servants appeared and started unloading their possessions. At the top of a sweeping staircase was a tall, gowned figure descending the steps, holding out her hands as she cried, "My dear M. and Mme Monet—welcome to the Palazzo Barbaro!"

This was their hostess, Mrs. Charles Hunter, patron of the arts, a lover of painting and music—indeed, her sister was the composer, Ethel Smyth. Her salons, at which she gathered together the rich and the famous along with the occasional struggling painter or writer, were celebrated throughout "La Serenissima."

Monet was under no illusions as to the luster which his name now conferred. From a youth of poverty, grinding yet deliberately chosen, he had become one of the most famous artists in Europe. Even as he greeted Mrs. Hunter, he was wondering how much time he would have to allocate to the process of being lionized.

"I thought you would want a quiet evening to recover from the journey," Mrs. Hunter was exclaiming, and he began to hope that perhaps it would be easier with her than he had thought. "Let me take you to your rooms right away."

They followed her up the staircase.

Their rooms were on the first floor. The first was a bedroom, lined with so many dark old wooden screens, cupboards, and armoires that the windows and walls were scarcely visible, but the bed looked new and comfortable and was heaped with pillows, and a fire burned in the grate.

"Dear Mme Monet, you have your own bathroom," said Mrs. Hunter, pushing open a door at the far end, which gave a glimpse of a modern bath and basin and emitted an odor compounded of some powerful disinfectant and lavender borne on an undercurrent which brought back an instant memory of Parisian sewers. Mrs. Hunter shut the bathroom door quickly.

"M. Monet has a room through here." It was more sparsely furnished, not exactly a separate room, though it had another bed, made up ready. Mrs. Hunter drew aside a curtain that served to divide them. "I'll send a maid to unpack—and perhaps you would like a tisane, madame?" She was turning back to where Alice was surveying her room, smiling politely but in a way which suggested to Monet that his wife was covering up her exhaustion. "I'll leave you to rest a little, shall I? We are not entertaining tonight, so you need not fear any disturbance. Just tell the maid if there is anything at all you require. Dinner is at eight. Will that be convenient?" She had some tact, after all.

When she had finally left them, and the maid had squirreled their possessions away into so many obscure cupboards and drawers that they would probably never find anything again, he helped Alice off with her hat and cloak and unclipped her heavy silver necklace. Then he unlaced the back of her dress and her corset, a service he often performed for her, enjoying the act of releasing her white, still-velvety flesh from its constraints. As she pushed down the long-sleeved bodice, he saw a long bruise down one arm and recalled that she had knocked it against the door of the carriage as they had left the train. She seemed to bruise at a touch these days, but he did not want to mention it for fear of worrying her, and went into his own room, or rather the curtained-off part of their room. He couldn't help saying as he did so, "I hope Mrs. Hunter doesn't make a lot of arrangements for parties and so on. I'm here to work."

"We have to show that we are not ashamed. The gossip will certainly have reached Venice; I have no doubt of that."

"You have nothing with which to reproach yourself," he answered, feeling impelled to come back and touch her neck gently. "Nothing at all. We could not have saved him. He made his own way to destruction."

Her face was square and heavy now, the skin thickened, its fine tracery of quick-flushing veins now destroyed and defeated, though her eyes kept a certain splendor, and the line of the jaw could still be traced in all its delicacy beneath a padding of fat. "They will all be whispering," she said.

"Let them talk. It doesn't matter."

She was suddenly fierce. "Yes, it does, Claude. It matters to me and my family."

"Your family? When I was a penniless artist, they scarcely wanted to have anything to do with you!"

She smiled for almost the first time since they had arrived in Venice.

"Ah, but I knew you would be a success! We have a place in society now."

He didn't answer. Opposite Alice's chair there was a heavy wooden shutter covering a window. Pulling it open, he saw that it overlooked the Grand Canal. A silvery moonlight ran and pooled like mercury on the surface of the water. Forgetting their conversation and with an immense and deep delight of anticipation, he stared out for a while and then turned to fetch a small printed map of the city from his pocketbook and, as Alice kept silent, he began to plan where he would set up his easel at first light.

Revel always found it difficult to believe in the sight before his eyes when he contemplated this city: the unreal beauty of the sweep of green water as the Grand Canal opened out into the Adriatic, the dome and tower of San Giorgio Maggiore floating above it, the sugar pink and white icing of the Doge's Palace, the curves and points and curlicues of San Marco, and all so animated, enlivened by white-tipped waves and fluttering birds, not still and pickled in the past, as it so often appeared on canvas.

Theseus Barton, the British consul, was a small, dark-haired man with monkeyish brown eyes set in big, round sockets, whom Revel found hunched over a heap of accounts, perusing them carefully line after spidery line. "If we're to have any influence at all here, we have to know what their mercantile situation is in regard to Turkey. I've got a set of customs figures to break down here. Make yourself comfortable for a few minutes, would you? I'll get through this as fast as possible. They are supposed to be sending me an assistant from Rome, but I'm single-handed here at the moment, except for a secretary who comes in to deal with routine correspondence. Nevertheless, I want to get your business settled without delay, I assure you."

He clapped his small hands, and a young man with a turban appeared. He had an unnerving combination of brown skin and blue eyes.

"What would you like, Callender? I usually have sherbet; it's most refreshing at this time of day, I find, but of course you can have some tea if you would prefer . . ."

"No, no, I should like to try the sherbet."

It came in a tall iced glass, and he sipped it, looking out at the Accademia gallery nearby, while Barton rustled away at his accounts, occasionally making a penciled note. Finally, the consul dropped the last quire and threw the heap aside, stretching and yawning as if worn out by the effort. But he seemed able to come back to a state of instant alertness, sitting up and giving Revel his full attention.

"Have you heard of the Casimiri family?"

Callender was startled. "The Casimiri?"

He remembered Amalia's reaction to the black boat that had slid past the house on the Giudecca, how she had crossed herself. Aloud, he said to Barton, "Merely some gossip, nothing of any real importance."

Barton said, "Did you know that there is a member of the Casimiri family who is British?"

"No, I did not." Callender was surprised. He thought he was familiar with the names of the prominent British citizens permanently resident here.

"The principessa is very elderly and never leaves the Palazzo Casimiri. She is, however, a member of the Maloney banking family."

Barton spoke the name of one of the richest families of financiers in Europe with due reverence, and Callender understood why the matter should be of importance to His Majesty's Consulate. Where the name of Maloney was mentioned, large sums of money were also sure to be under discussion.

"I understand the old lady is very ill indeed, and I have heard from the ambassador in Rome that HMG desires us to keep a watching brief on this matter. To be blunt, the king has borrowed money from the Maloneys, as he has from many financiers—the Rothschilds, for example. His extravagances seem to be limitless."

Yes, mistresses, luxuries, gambling—all the vices that Edward VII's mama, Victoria, had attempted to suppress in her son, and in which he now indulged to the full. Sometimes Callender had a powerful feeling of sympathy for a man who made no secret of his pleasures.

But Barton was continuing, "Anything that affects the finances of the Maloneys concerns HMG, you see. At the moment, they are being generous in extending credit, but we want to know whether they might call in their loan. That, of course, would have serious repercussions—a huge scandal, at the very least. So even the death of this old lady in Venice might affect matters."

"An inquiry into her finances? Surely, no noble family would permit that."

"Nothing official, obviously. But I believe we can act on an informal basis," said Barton carefully. "I suggest you simply call on the count, offer your services in case you can be of assistance, ask if they wish you to deal with any documents in English, that sort of thing. I will furnish you with a letter of introduction."

"But I'm just an English lawyer who happens to be in Venice!"

"No," and Barton was flourishing a piece of paper. "You are now formally appointed my temporary attaché. All taken care of, dear boy. We're a long way from Rome and rather a rule unto ourselves here." Barton offered him a small black cheroot. "Remember, there will also be a fee from the Maloney family, a very generous fee, if you are also acting privately on their behalf. Which of course, you may do. In addition to your official capacity."

Callender declined the cheroot and sat back in his chair, aghast at what had been arranged for him without his knowledge or consent, but also aware of the enormous possible advantages to his career of acting as the Maloneys lawyer in this case.

"I suppose they may not let me see the old lady, if she is so ill."

"Very possible. There is no need for you to do so. She never went out into society and would probably not welcome it now."

"Shouldn't I try to have a word with her? She might welcome the presence of someone who speaks English . . . a person from home."

Barton looked at him with an odd sideways glance. "Follow the count's wishes in this matter. If he does not desire you to see her, do not attempt to do so."

THE gondolier stared and then nodded his head silently when Revel asked to be taken to the Palazzo Casimiri. The pole swished and dripped rhythmically, and there was no conversation. Revel assumed the man was naturally silent. They glided up towards the Rialto Bridge.

On a balcony with crimson velvet padding on the balustrade a woman cushioned her white forearms as she leaned over to stare boldly down at Callender. Others, dark figures, moved through long galleries behind her. All the length of the canal he had the strange sensation that flitting eyes were monitoring his progress, some with the hard, assessing glances of prostitutes or touts, but others with different purposes, intentions of their own, unfathomable, perhaps malevolent.

The Palazzo Casimiri stood on a corner of the Grand Canal, one façade stretching along a *rio,* a smaller tributary canal that led off the major one. The building seemed to Callender's eyes like a rich old patchwork carried out in stone, something that many ages had added to, repaired, or let pieces fall off, as the fancy took them. It looked as if it could even have been several buildings with uneven rooftops, cobbled together over the centuries. The expanses of wall on the *rio* side were covered with patterns and stretches worked in narrow old bricks, blood-colored and soft-surfaced as suede. Along the canal façade were huge pockmarked blocks of pink marble that looked as though they had belonged to some much older building, and whose coral and rose reflections danced and swayed in the water below. Above these appeared an unexpectedly rhythmic row of elegant windows flanked by carved white columns that looked as if they had been looted from some Byzantine palace, perhaps by some Crusader ancestor. Between the windows, yet not placed centrally so that the effect was somewhat disorienting, was an elaborate balcony with a long gold brocade curtain flapping out like a flag from the long window behind. Callender had the impression that some smoke blew out with the gold curtain, rising high up into the blue air.

The balcony overlooked the main stretch of water so as to command the long bend that led beyond the Rialto, and in front of it was the Casimiri landing stage, marked by red and white poles and a huge stone shield with worn carved heraldry. It looked to Callender like some rough representation of Saint George killing the dragon, the same crest, he thought, that had appeared on the prow of the boat which he had seen sliding past Signora Amalia's house on the Giudecca. At any rate, there was an armored knight, his face worn to a featureless blank, who seemed to be thrusting a spear at some contorted, scaly beast.

As it drew closer, the gondola bobbed awkwardly in the wash of larger craft passing along, and a servant in some outlandish suit of sea-green velvet ran forward to help Revel get out onto the slimy wooden planks of the landing stage. Looking straight down as he stepped across, he could see the massive black piles going down deep beneath the water, the precarious splitting and waterlogged foundations that shored up all this ancient grandeur. The wood beneath his feet was slippery, and he took the arm which the man held out to him, which was clad in the slashed and padded sleeve of some Renaissance-style servitor's uniform. A ray of sunshine showed that the handsome livery had faded to chartreuse yellow in places and was worn down to the nubble of the fabric.

Within the water entrance a glistening marble floor of soft wet ochreous colors stretched towards a long staircase, and the servant ushered Revel towards it, but as he put his foot on the first stair, there was a movement in a far wall. He stopped in midstride as an unexpected door was opened in a shadowy archway.

A young woman came out and moved towards the entrance.

Her face was serious, sad, and beautiful. Her hair, dark blonde, the color of sandalwood, was hanging carelessly down her back. She seemed caught in some private deeper world, and Revel felt a totally unexpected intense moment of feeling, a sensation almost of being physically magnetized, tilted suddenly towards some newfound compass point.

She looked up and saw him, and with an exclamation of surprise and a quick gesture pulled a scarf over her hair, then vanished again through the door in the wall.

Revel forced his foot onto the next stair, hoping that his features had remained impassive.

There was a faint sound of a dog barking in the distance: something had taken note of his intrusion, at any rate.

The velvet-clad servant had paused behind him, but the man appeared to have noticed nothing of the young woman's presence, and Revel felt already, at these very first moments of his arrival at Palazzo Casimiri, that he could not ask directly who she might be.

This was a place of questions that could perhaps only be whispered, of answers that might drift in soft, murmured echoes through the halls and loggias, as if the stains in the very blocks of marble and its crumbling carvings were part of a perpetual state of conspiracy in which this household must have its being, as if those within were swimming like fishes in a secretive essence that was both surrounding and penetrating, threatening and yet elemental.

He handed his letters of introduction to another silent servant, also clad in pale green livery with gilt froggings across his chest, and was asked to wait. His shoes became uncomfortably wet, and he realized the lower steps had been slopping with water, of which he had not been aware when he ascended the staircase.

Shown into a small and windowless lobby where the walls were inset with roundels of some speckled starling-breast purple stone, Revel felt a sense of relief when, after a short delay, he was conducted into a long room filled with a watery light, which he realized must lie behind the row of white columns which he had seen from the canal The gold brocade curtain was still flapping out onto the balcony, and gusts of smoke from an elaborately carved fireplace billowed out with it. Revel advanced midway down the *salone* to where a bulky middle-aged man stood before a huge fireplace.

Count Roberto Casimiri did not have the thin, pallid face one might expect of the descendant of an ancient and inbred family. He had a strong, big jaw, and though he was short in stature he had the breadth of shoulder and chest, and that wide-legged straddling stance which reminded Revel of Holbein's paintings of Henry VIII.

In spite of this appearance of physical toughness, he spoke an elegant Italian, and not the Venetian dialect heard elsewhere. Revel responded carefully with the courtesies he had learned. Small clouded glasses of a clear syrupy fluid awash with drifting flakes of some glittering substance were served, and the visitor was surprised by its alcoholic fire. "It's an old Venetian concoction," said the count. "They crumble gold leaf into the flask. It's said to be very good for boneache and rheumatism. People believe that the gold forms a coating in the joints."

Old bones, old decaying hips, with streaks of gold lining the sockets.

Revel forced his mind back to his instructions and felt it was his duty to make an inquiry. He was encouraged by the count's affability, in spite of the way in which these old walls seemed to resist intrusion. "I wonder, sir, if perhaps the principessa would permit a visit?"

"Ah, Signor Callender, it is with the deepest regret I have to tell you that you have come too late! Poor Tanta—that is how we called her in the family, you understand—poor Tanta died this morning. I trust you will be able to attend the funeral? And as a matter of fact, I wish to call upon your services, if you would be so gracious."

In spite of the softness of the voice, a pleading arm gesture, there could be no denial. "Of course, Count Casimiri, you have only to instruct me."

"Among her possessions there are a good many papers in English, some of which may be significant and should eventually be returned to her family lawyers, though others will be trivial and could simply be destroyed. If you would consent to spend some time sorting through them, we should be in your debt. For matters such as this it is necessary to find a person in whom we can trust, of course, so we would profit by your visit, if you would be so kind."

"Yes, please allow me to assist." Revel remembered further necessary courteous phrases. "And please accept my condolences on this sad family loss." Damn, he supposed he would have to have a suit of mourning and attend the funeral. The Venetian nobility would doubtless be extremely insistent on formalities of dress. Perhaps the costs could be charged to the Foreign Office.

"Tomorrow morning, then, you may begin your work. The funeral will take place on the following day."

There could be no argument, and probably no time to get a black suit made. Maybe Barton or Signora Amalia would help him to borrow one. Though Amalia would want to know what it was for, and all about the funeral, and there would be no point in trying to pull the wool over her eyes, since word would be bound to get back to her that her English lodger had been seen in the entourage of the sinister *famiglia* Casimiri. Better speak to Barton about the mourning. Amalia had looked truly frightened, had crossed herself, had warded off evil, at the thought of the Casimiri.

He shook from his mind the memory of Signora Amalia making the sign of the cross. This was a city full of superstitions, most of which meant nothing.

As he walked down the grand staircase, he saw that the door in the archway, the one where he had seen the girl with dark blonde hair, was open.

Knowing he was being foolish at best, discourteous certainly, Revel yet moved towards it as if pulled on an invisible cord and saw a narrow flight of steps. He hesitated, and would probably have overcome his compulsion, but as he was about to turn away, there came sounds from above, a succession of shrieks and cries, and a thin, dark-haired girl ran out of the door. "No, no, don't ask me!" she shouted, turning her head back, and followed this with a few words which Revel understood, *"Damnata!* Damned!—this thing is of the damned!" Another voice called to her, "Angelina, come back, there is no harm in it," but this persuasion was ineffective, though Angelina delayed long enough to turn, cross herself, and spit very deliberately at the threshold of the small entrance before she ran past Revel and out of sight.

The voice had been young and light. Revel instinctively went up the stairs and found himself in tiny disordered rooms, ending up at the side of an old-fashioned bed with crimson drapes and some absurd tiara-like ornamentation. The bedclothes had been stripped, and a body lay on a sheet. Long tresses of bright yellow red hair had been carefully combed out like a halo around the old face, shockingly bright against the whiteness of the linen. The corpse was naked, wrinkled, and tiny, and as Revel looked down at it he saw that it had breasts with long mole-snout nipples and below them, in a nest of thin gray hair, a shriveled but undoubted penis.

"Yes," said a voice, with a note of defensive anger, "there were many strange things about her." On the opposite side of the bed he saw the girl with dark blonde hair, and the distressed look on her face reminded Revel of the intrusion he had committed. He began to apologize, losing his command of Italian in his unusual anxiety, and to explain who he was.

"Ah, Signor Callender, Papa told us you were coming to see him." She was calmer now, perhaps angry with him, but not allowing it to master her.

"I'm sorry—this is an unforgivable intrusion," he mumbled with deep embarrassment, trying to recover himself.

She pulled the curtains round the bed and moved with him as he attempted to retreat. "Unforgiveable, no. But I hope you will not mention what you have seen. The woman who was laying her out was foolish and ran away when she realized."

"It is—?" He didn't say it, realizing that it must be the old princess, child of the Maloney banking family, sent to Italy and living here for how long? Fifty years, wasn't that what Barton had said?

"My aunt by marriage. I called her Tanta. I had hoped for her sake that she would be in her coffin before anyone came into her apartments."

It was a rebuke but not a harsh one, he felt, and in any case he had no time for further apologies, because the girl introduced herself as Clara Casimiri, and, indicating a jumbled desk, said, "These are the documents which my father wished you to examine. We were intending to sort them out for you. As you can see, things are not exactly in an orderly state here."

"Don't bother; I can organize them."

"Then I'll get a servant to put them into a box ready to be brought to you when you start work here." Going down the stairs, they walked out onto the landing stage. The water was choppy and slapping, the air cold. "We may be having a storm," she said. "You should leave now."

He had to ask her. "Tell me about the princess. Did she keep it a secret all these years?"

She smiled sadly. "She tried to, and if it was a scandal, it was long ago. I believe that, recently at any rate, only the physician and old Daniella, her servant, knew of it. And the family, of course, but her husband died many years ago. You are the first outsider to learn of it in this way . . . that is, to actually"—she searched for a word—"to actually witness it, let me put it like that."

Revel knew that he had burst into a world where he was not meant to intrude, yet could not prevent himself even in these grotesque circumstances from feeling a deep, warm pleasure at the sensation of sharing a secret with this beautiful woman. At the same time, he doubted her words. He had learned something about the potential spread of scandals in Italian society, and he doubted this particular one could have been hidden for long.

Before their conversation could go any further, however, he saw her eyes change, starting as though she saw something over his shoulder, and he turned to find a tall man with a somewhat yellow tinge to his skin standing in the entrance to the palazzo, almost behind him. Startled, he looked at Clara Casimiri inquiringly.

"This is Rinaldo, my father's majordomo, our steward, if you like. He runs the household for us. Rinaldo, this is Signor Callender, an English lawyer who has called to examine the principessa's papers. He will be returning to inspect them another time."

The man wore modern dress, a sober dark suit and tie. Rinaldo was certainly the only person Revel had yet seen in this place who looked as if he came from the twentieth century. He bowed in a rather absurdly incongruous way and was standing motionless on the landing stage behind Clara as the gondola slipped away.

Theseus Barton confirmed Revel in his doubts that the bizarre nature of the principessa Casimiri could have been kept secret.

"This is a city where rumors glide out of every door and window," said the consul.

"I had suspected as much."

"Yes, and you were quite right to do so. She was a hermaphrodite who married old Ricardo Casimiri, the present count's uncle. He died many years ago, but she remained here. It was a matter of convenience on both sides, of course. The Maloneys were glad to find a place for her in Venice, since this is a world that does not put too high a value on conventional respectability, and the Casimiri needed the dowry, because their finances didn't live up to their pride. You've seen how their palace is falling into the canal. In any case, the story of the old principessa is one of the vapors that escaped out of the Palazzo Casimiri like wisps of smoke quite soon after the marriage. Impossible to keep such a condition entirely hidden. She, or he, was a vain creature; she loved clothes, and the tailor came. She was sick sometimes, and the physician called."

"So it was generally known?"

"Yes, I believe so, though the Casimiri themselves may have been under the illusion that it was a secret, and she never went out. But there were the questions, early in her married life, which all Venice was asking. Why the marriage was infertile, and why had the Maloneys given her quite such a large dowry, rumored to be ten chests of gold *soldi*, though that, of course, is merely the stuff of romance, the kind of legend that Venetians create to amuse themselves on foggy nights. Nevertheless, my predecessor, old Bingham, said it was an exceptionally large banker's draft that came with the marriage contract. You will probably find all the details when you go through the documents."

"The Maloneys were glad to get rid of her, then?"

"She would undoubtedly have been an embarrassment at home. And a connection in this city would have been extremely useful to them. Venice is still a great center for banking transactions. The Ottoman Bank of Constantinople maintains a representative here. But bankers spend their money wisely, even if it is to hush something up."

The shutters rattled. "Shall I send for a cup of chocolate?" said Barton. "There is a storm out on the lagoon, and the wind often blows cold on nights such as this."

"Thank you. I'll have to attend the funeral. Can you arrange a mourning outfit for me, by the way? I suppose the funeral will be a private affair."

Barton sighed. "Yes, but there may be difficulties in keeping things quiet . . . However, it was all talked of so many years ago that most people in Venice have probably forgotten it."

Callender had picked up a curious emphasis in what Barton had said. "Difficulties?"

"Listen, Callender, you are still a stranger in Venice. You would not believe what I might tell you about this, no one outside the city would credit it, but when the storm has died down tonight, I will take you to a certain place. About two o'clock. You will be woken if you have fallen asleep."

Revel was taken by surprise. The idea of a late-night expedition with His Majesty's representative in the Most Serene City, that they would go off "a-roving / So late into the night," in the words of Lord Byron, astonished him, and though he tried to hide it, Barton saw him shrinking back, and laughed. "Nowhere that will test our virtues, I assure you." His small simian face was creased up into a grin. "Don't go back to your lodgings tonight; stay here. Before we go out, we'll wrap you in a heavy cloak against the cold."

Revel laughed as he took the conspiratorial implication. "No one here knows me, in any case."

Barton put his finger to the side of his nose. "Ah, this is Venice!"

THE young man with the turban called him, bringing in a lighted candle, and he saw by a little silver clock that it was two fifteen. Over one arm the fellow had a cloak, which he offered to Revel, who was about to refuse it as an absurd stage prop when he remembered the storm that had been getting up, and took it.

Barton was downstairs and looked approvingly at his guest's appearance. "Your hair and eyes are very dark, Callender, so fortunately you don't look too out of place, especially with that cloak over your clothes. This is an occasion for Venetians, not for tourists; they would not be pleased if they thought you were British."

A small boat, not a gondola but something lighter and sculled by a silent oarsman, was waiting at the landing stage. They stepped in, and Barton gave some direction which meant nothing to Revel, but the man immediately began to row without question, as if he knew exactly where to take them.

A heavy mist hung over the water, which glimmered jade green in the occasional patches of light from lamps and torches, and Revel pulled the cloak around his shoulders. They swung into a canal so narrow that he could have put out a hand and touched the walls on either side, and here the marble surfacing of the grander houses gave way to decaying bricks broken by dark holes. A rat suddenly splashed through the scum on the surface of the water and slipped with smooth confidence into the brickwork.

The boat pulled up outside a doorway that was little more than a human-sized rat hole, but there was a murmuring of voices and a glow of illumination at the end of a corridor. Theseus Barton said nothing, but looked at Revel and jerked his head over his shoulder in the direction of the light. His small bent figure led the way, obscuring most of the candlelight so that Revel, crouching, was discomfortingly forced to move mainly in the dark.

They came out into an opening, what seemed to be a small vaulted shrine, where a small crowd stood pressed around a central alcove, where a statue was standing on a low altar. The air was dense with scent and candle smoke and the smell of bodies, but the light was brilliant, glittering from banks of candelabra and reflected by the gilding of a half dome over the statue. There was a constant swaying and jostling in the crowd, but they appeared docile, reverential, even. Some of them were holding tapers as if they had just lit them within a church, lighting up faces that were avid in their stares.

"Is it some sort of cult?" whispered Revel.

"Watch!" said Barton.

There was a strange hollow sound, like the distant blowing of a horn, or the bellowing of some creature in a cave beneath the waves. Revel found that he was taller than most of the crowd. Turning his head to the source of the long, soft note, he saw to his astonishment a man standing to one side of the altar, with fat cheeks puffed out and his head leaning backwards as he blew into an upraised conch shell exactly as if he were a personification of the wind in an old Italian painting. Revel had a sudden realization that what he had seen in the galleries of Rome was an Italy that was alive elsewhere, that had gone to ground, perhaps, but still possessed a burning vitality somewhere out beyond the academic canvases and the metropolis.

And now, at the mournful note of the conch, the crowd began to move, to file towards the statue, pushing gently yet with some strange attitude in their faces, a greedy curiosity that looked forward to some fulfilment with the covetous gaze of gamblers. Revel looked at the statue and started as he took in the details of its execution. It was ivory white, naked, and as his eyes traveled over it, he saw that it had the full breasts of a young woman yet between the white thighs was a boy's penis, covered with gold. Traces of gold were on the nipples, the lips, and the eyelids. A man came first out of the crowd and stretched out his hand, touching the gilded breasts and penis in a gesture that was a curious inversion of crossing himself.

Barton and Callender watched for a few more minutes as the crowd patiently filed past, each repeating the movements of the first, and the air grew closer and hotter. The hair of the statue was arranged in ringlets and interwoven with a garland of flowers. Revel saw drops of moisture on the brow, and then the eyelids fluttered slightly, and he perceived a gentle movement of the breast as air was drawn in. Turning to Barton with shock, he saw that the consul was regarding him with a slight smile and nodded as if to say, *Yes, it is true. It is alive.* Yet the small, white-painted face above the malformed body remained impassive, tilted upwards, gazing over the crowd as if it cared nothing. Was it even conscious? Perhaps not; perhaps it was drugged.

REVEL was glad when they had forced their way out into the clean wind that swept along the canal. As they settled into the boat, the newcomer unconsciously beginning to do this in a natural way without anxiety, Barton said quietly, "I wanted you to see for yourself. This is a city that creates myths about itself all the time, but some of the legends, you see, are real."

"It's extraordinary. Was it natural, or is it some sort of trick?"

"In the case of that boy, it is a natural deformity, but sometimes it is faked. Many of the common people of Venice believe that touching a hermaphrodite brings extraordinarily good fortune. That is why the old principessa could not go out when she first came here."

"How did people come to find out about her?"

"The Casimiri servants talked. There are a lot of secrets in this city, but there are some it is impossible to keep, and this was one. When she was young, she—or he, but I'll call her 'she,' for the sake of courtesy—was mobbed every time she left the palazzo. People tried to pull her clothing off and touch her body. It happened even as she was coming out of church once, on the steps of Santa Maria Maggiore. She was half-naked by the time the police pulled her out of the crowd." Barton's ready flow of speech hesitated, for the first time in their acquaintance.

"How horrible," said Revel, looking up at the blackened brickwork that closed them in.

"Yes, it must have been, but I suppose it had a certain aspect of wonderment or worship, as it might have held in antiquity. On the other hand, I have heard that the count, the present count, positively hated being near her, felt disgust in her mere presence, though that may have been aristocratic disdain for what he saw as an object of common superstition."

Revel saw in his imagination the unhappiness of that poor creature's life, forced to take sanctuary within walls where she was an object of repulsion, unable to go out without being surrounded by hands pulling at her clothing, eyes avid to stare at her deformity.

"But so many years have passed since she first came to Venice," Barton continued, "that I think eventually her condition has mostly been forgotten, though doubtless there will be some medical interest now. I should not be surprised if several distinguished physicians request to view the body."

"And the . . . the person that we saw in there? The one who was being, well, I suppose you could call it being worshipped?"

"Yes, I think you could call it that. There is something of an ancient cult about it, didn't you feel? What will become of him, do you mean? I believe they don't usually live long. The principessa was an exception, protected from the world as she was, which perhaps prolonged her existence. Hermaphrodites fetch a fortune in brothels, of course, so the ones from poor families get sold into them, as I hear, though I haven't encountered many personally, I must say. It's pretty rare, even in this city, and Venice is a sort of cabinet of living curiosities. Rome is innocent by

comparison. You'll need a suit of formal mourning clothes for the funeral, by the way. I have nothing that would fit you, but I can get a tailor
to run you something up. I can have a room made ready for you here, if
you want to move out of your lodging house. I suppose it's not that
comfortable."

"Oh, it'll do for the moment." Revel was not sure why he wanted to
keep the modicum of independence afforded him by his small and stuffy
rooms at Signora Amalia's, but he was not willing to give them up.

"Incidentally, there's a message for you," added Barton, and then
said, apparently casually, as if it were the most natural thing in the world,
"The count wishes you to watch the sealing of the coffin."

When Revel arrived at the palazzo, the count did not specify the reason, but, briefed by Barton, the Englishman guessed. The purpose was
so that he could bear witness to the fact that the principessa's body had
been decently committed for burial by the Casimiri family, that it had not
been taken for the purposes of dissection or worse in order to investigate
or profit from her sad condition. Revel wondered at the count's sensitiv-
ity on this point but thought that a sense of family honor and dignity of
the Casimiri might be uppermost in the man's mind. Perhaps, also, the
Maloneys could still exert some financial pressure if decent treatment
had not been accorded to the corpse of one of their relatives.

Callender stood therefore in the water-soaked marble entrance hall
of the Palazzo Casimiri while the small corpse was brought down the
stairs from the principessa's rooms and placed in a short ebony coffin
resting on trestles at the base of the stairs, the lid being propped open.
The undertaker standing by took a screwdriver from a pouch and offered
it to the count, who motioned to Callender. He stepped forward and
looked down on the shriveled little face, framed by a white cloth going
under the jaw and tied on the top of the head. The large eye sockets were
disturbing, blind and rounded by silver coins placed upon them.

Callender was not sure how to proceed with this strange little cere-
mony, but he nodded and then stood back; there was a dull thud as the
prop was taken away and the heavy wooden lid closed over the body, and

the workmen proceeded to screw it down themselves. No other member of the family was present apart from the count, though Revel had hoped to catch a glimpse of the girl who had illuminated this grim place like a descending angel.

6

The funeral took place towards dusk. Revel stood with Theseus Barton on the barge, which was draped in black velvet. The Casimiri shield decorated the prow. In this case the blazon was a painted wooden version, which was recognizably a knight in armor attacking some reptilian monster.

The coffin was brought aboard, followed by the members of the Casimiri family. Clara stepped onto the barge with a sad and tearstained face, as if she truly mourned for the little creature in the coffin. Watching her, Callender saw that she frequently spoke quietly to a redheaded young woman with a black lace headdress and a rather inappropriate, devil-may-care look. She had no family likeness to the Casimiri and Revel wondered who she was: not a servant, by the richness of her dress and the confidence of her stance.

There were two other people who seemed apart from the family group. One was a tall, thin man with silver hair, looking, even though he was dressed in black, somewhat out of place among the Italians. He followed the count aboard. The other was young, with a lively, intent face. "The older fellow is Sullivan, one of the main bankers to the foreign community," whispered Barton. Sullivan stayed apart, but the other stranger came over and nodded to Barton as if they were acquainted.

"Dr. Albrizzi, allow me to present my compatriot, Mr. Revel Callender," said Barton. "Callender, this gentleman's grandfather was physician to the late principessa."

Revel bowed and glanced at the doctor with some surprise. He had expected some coiffed and fur-robed scholar from a Renaissance portrait, or at least a bent, elderly gentleman with pince-nez, but this was a young man with a brisk, fresh face, wearing a plain dark suit and wing collar. Sullivan joined them then, and again Barton introduced Callender.

"And may I ask if you have a connection with the Casimiri family, Mr. Callender?" asked the banker, evidently wondering why a complete stranger should be intruding on such an occasion.

Callender was about to respond sharply, but the consul said smoothly, "Mr. Callender is working on a family archive for the count."

At this, Sullivan smiled slightly, seemed to relax, and stood a little apart from the others as the barge moved on slowly down the Grand Canal to a slow drumbeat. The black-clad drummer boy sat at the prow, behind the family shield. Callender was aware that at the windows and balconies past which they made their slow and stately way, silent crowds were gathering to watch them go past.

"This may be one of the last funerals of its kind," said Albrizzi, who had paused and was standing near them. Callender was surprised that he was speaking in English, and with a decidedly American accent. "Though in my grandfather's day, things were even more spectacular, with hundreds of mourners and black flags flying overhead."

"You are from a Venetian family, then?"

The physician turned his keen face towards them. "Yes, Mr. Callender, and an old medical one. I think the Albrizzi may originally have come from Syria; at least, there is a tradition that they learned their skills from the Arabs at the time of the Crusades."

"Dr. Albrizzi's family have a long tradition as physicians, isn't that right, Doctor?' Theseus Barton had taken up the conversation.

"Yes, though I myself have only recently qualified. I studied medicine at Harvard. Then I came back to spend a year at the University of Padua, where my family had traditionally trained, but now I find myself involved in Venetian affairs, since my grandfather is too ill to attend this funeral. He asked me to come and represent him. I must say, I would never have imagined such a grand spectacle."

"Did your grandfather look after the principessa?"

"Oh, yes, all her life. He was the confidential family physician, and they grew old together."

This conversation was halted when the funeral barge, instead of striking out into deeper water for the cemetery island of San Michele, moored first at another landing stage, where a flag of checkered red and gold fluttered above an awning. As if a signal had been given, the mourners formed themselves into two files, the count at their head on the left-hand side. There was a pause. Then a tall, narrow-shouldered man emerged, stepping slowly forward, a cloak of black velvet swinging from his back. A thick gold chain gleamed across his breast. He stepped onto the barge, strode down between the mourners, and took the count's hands in his. There were murmurs of greeting as he moved along and took a seat at the prow, and Callender noticed that though the men bowed and most of the women curtsied, Clara and her redheaded companion did not.

The mourners settled themselves again, the drum resumed its beat, and the sailors, with their black arm bands, cast off.

"Marzano."

Barton's voice was nearly muffled by the drumbeat, and Callender had to raise his eyebrows in inquiry. "Lorenzo Marzano, the head of the *signori*, chief of the ancient patrician families of Venice," said the consul, indicating the newcomer with a slight nod of the head.

"I thought all that had been abolished," Callender whispered back.

"Officially, yes, but socially they still observe the old rules. Of course, they don't have a doge anymore, but Marzano is the closest they have to such a leader. It's a considerable honor if he's attending the funeral."

Callender watched with fascination. Marzano's bold profile, as he stared out with his face raised to the horizon, was like something on an ancient coin. The man exuded a certain physical confidence; perhaps, thought Revel, a member of the Roman imperial family would have had this bearing, this sense of reserved power.

"Who is the redheaded girl?"

Barton looked at Callender with a flash of amusement. "Taken your eye, has she? Be careful; I understand that one is dangerous! That's Fiammetta Corradini, a close friend of Clara Casimiri, and a totally unsuitable one, according to most people's calculations. She is the orphan daughter of a family with great libertarian ideals, followers of Garibaldi. Count Casimiri was made her guardian recently, when her father died— he and the count were students at Padua together. And a really tricky handful she's supposed to be—not at all the submissive young lady one might desire! But then, neither is Clara Casimiri, by all accounts."

Fiammetta! "Little flame." It seemed appropriate, thought Callender, looking at the fox-red hair and sharp, determined chin.

The consul paused and looked closely at Callender. "Does Signorina Fiammetta interest you, then?"

Callender said lightly, "No, she seems very young. I have more sophisticated tastes."

They ended the conversation there. The barge was rowed slowly out in traditional fashion as the drum thudded out over the water, the sound echoing and carrying strangely through the fog. The coffined body of little Tanta, lying under an elaborate canopy, was given some pomp and dignity at the last.

As they neared the funeral island of San Michele, Clara Casimiri stood beside the coffin, which looked merely an elongated box, it seemed so tiny. One of her hands was touching it as if in a final gesture of affection. Her face was grave, but she was not weeping now. Her hair seemed to be pulled severely back and was covered by a lace veil, through which came occasional glints of gold. The men of the Casimiri family were standing farther back in the stern, their faces giving nothing away. Revel wondered who else was present here, and who besides Clara might care about the little creature in the box before them. Glancing discreetly round, he saw the servant, Daniella, sitting beside a sad-looking woman, delicately boned. He did not know her relationship to the family, yet on her face there were tears, and she dabbed at her eyes with a handkerchief.

Barton saw the direction in which Callender was looking. "The weeping lady is Contessa Mariella, the count's second wife. The mother of Clara and Claudio died some years ago. Don't know why she's looking like the tragic muse—I wouldn't have thought she would be particularly distressed by the death of the principessa. Mariella has only been in the family for a few years, after all. She can't have known her well."

The water was getting rougher now that they were farther out in the Adriatic and nearly at the island where the Venetians had their cemetery and crowded down their corpses into this small patch of overgrown land. "These days they usually have a steamboat for funerals," said Barton. "But the Casimiri are never going to adapt to modern life. They wouldn't exist anywhere else."

Venice is a tropical fish tank in which exotic creatures can survive, thought Revel, but he made no reply. He already had absorbed something of the atmosphere in which this funeral was to be observed when he tried on the suit of mourning clothes, which a tailor had delivered that morning after a brief call to take his measurements on the previous evening. It was not well finished, he discovered when he pulled it on; the seams of the jacket lining seemed to be unravelling already. In England, it would have been considered cobbled together, but it would presumably see him through the occasion so that he would present the desirable appearance of conformity. Except that it would have been thought positively eccentric in most cities, since Revel found himself not merely clad in a mourning suit but in a sort of fancy-dress costume which sported sooty velvet trimmings, a saturnine cravat, and a top hat draped with hastily tacked bands of violet-colored ribbon.

With the other men, led by Marzano, he stepped onto the island, walked through the cemetery, and stood around the mouth of a vault as the small coffin was lowered into it. The women remained on the boat and, looking out towards the lagoon, Revel saw their black-clad figures

outlined against a lavender-colored sky of late evening, the vessel rocking gently on the water. Clara put her arm around her stepmother but
whether to give her physical or emotional support he could not tell. The
service was over quickly, briefly conducted by a priest and terminating
when the count stepped forward and threw a handful of earth into the
grave. This seemed almost abrupt, and Revel wondered if the service
had been deliberately curtailed to avoid attention. But the idea that this
family could avoid attention seemed preposterous: if the count believed
that, then he must move in a rarified air indeed.

There was no equivalent of a wake or any social occurrence afterwards. Callender was invited—instructed might better have described
the tone—to return to Palazzo Casimiri the next morning. The count
was entirely businesslike and showed the visitor to a study which,
though it was grander than Callender's room at Signora Amalia's, was
scarcely better furnished, since it held little more than a desk, a chair, and
some shelves. Pens, ink, and tape lay ready, however.

"I'll have the papers sent up," said the count. "We would prefer you
to go through them here, rather than to take them away with you."

"Yes, of course." Callender saw no particular reason to question this.
Many people might be sensitive about family business papers leaving
their house.

"You may take as long as you like," continued Casimiri. "It may be a
matter of some days, and of course we would normally expect you to
dine with us while you are working here. If there is anything you require, ring this bell."

A long velvet rope hung down beside a grate in which a fire of small
damp coals was sputtering. Revel looked around this little space which was
to be his temporary eyrie, unsure of the room's original purpose. It was
better than he thought, although the furniture was scanty, for the walls
were hung with red-stained leather, flapping loose in places, thin and
cracking, but stamped with shields and roundels.

There was a window with a shallow balcony, the iron fittings loose in
the wall, upon which he did not dare to put his weight. Callender looked

out to see a sight which he knew was most unusual in Venice, where any scrap of space reclaimed from the sea was built upon. The Palazzo Casimiri possessed a garden in a small internal courtyard, though in most places it would not be considered a garden at all. A stone staircase ran down the outside of the building from the first floor of the palace, and there seemed to be an old well with a carved stone wellhead in one corner and planks laid across the mouth. The yard looked scrubby and infertile, overshadowed, and the only plant of any size was a large thorn tree, which seemed almost leafless. Looking down, Callender saw that it had sharp and angular branches crisscrossing one another to make ugly nests, the pointed thorns thrusting out in bunchy spikes. Below the tree was a patch of yellowish grass, and someone had planted a small bed of madonna lilies which had flowered, drooped, and died.

Opposite his own window was another balcony, longer and deeper than his own, and he thought he glimpsed someone moving to and fro in the room behind it. Instinctively, he drew back, and wondered why this place seemed to create within it a compulsion not to be seen. But then the figure emerged onto the balcony, and he recognized it as Antonio Prepiani, Clara's fiancé, to whom he had been introduced at the funeral. Prepiani seemed to be staring down into the courtyard and at the thorn tree beneath, but at what exactly, and why in so fixed a manner, Callender could not make out, and after a few minutes he emerged at the top of the stone staircase and ran quickly down it, crossing the yard below into some place which Callender could not see from his viewpoint.

The young man was a strange creature, he thought: slender, almost frail-looking, but with an almost reptilian speed and ease of movement that had reminded Callender of a lizard flickering across a wall. He found the idea of Prepiani in bed with Clara was deeply unpleasant, and wondered why she was attracted to him. It crossed his mind that she might have little say in the matter; modern customs of marriage, such as the bride's being allowed to make a free choice, had probably not penetrated to Venice, even though some people such as Dr. Albrizzi might have studied in places such as Harvard.

More than ever, Callender felt he was living in the past here, and whereas he had previously rejoiced in that sensation, he now found that it did not seem so attractive.

But there were some surprising modernisms. In spite of the window and the time of day, his room was not well lit, and he had resigned himself to working with the added aid of candlelight when, turning back inside, he noticed to his amazement an electric cord tacked under the door and up across the leather, terminating in a unshaded lightbulb hanging oddly but conveniently on a bracket over the desk. Pushing down a switch beside the door produced a yellowish glow, faint, but the light was definitely the voice of the twentieth century, which lay all around this magical city like a fog. It was a century which was easy to forget once one had become immersed in this strange and watery place, and even deeper within, inside the palace walls lining the canal, walls where there were all kinds of gaps and black spaces, and even more so here, in a room where the walls themselves were covered with a layer of animal hide, so that anything might be behind the leather sheeting. Callender was sufficiently a reader of poetry to explore his own sensations and found that he disliked the idea of the skins of long-dead beasts hanging around him, screening the stones of the palace and whatever they, in turn, might conceal.

Swearing at himself for these disturbing thoughts, he rose and stared around, tempted to pull away the leather in the hope of finding an ordinariness behind, plain solid stone walls such as might be found anywhere, the kind of sensible walls that constituted the solid mansions of London, and would banish these Venetian imaginings. Such thoughts had never occurred to him elsewhere in Italy, certainly not during his visit to Rome, which now seemed to him a bright and sunny land inhabited by human beings doing normal things: making love, stealing purses, eating in the street. He thought affectionately of the Roman love of anything new and lively.

He actually moved forward in order to touch the wall nearest the desk, as if it would somehow give physical proof of solidity to conquer his imaginings, but there was the sound of something heavy being dragged up a staircase, and two footmen appeared pulling and pushing at a huge trunk, blackened with age. "Maloney" was painted in flaking white letters on the lid. The two men placed it before the fireplace, and one of them turned to him with a hand outstretched. Revel stared for a moment, then came back to the world and dropped a couple of coins into the palm. He saw that it was worn and dirty, crisscrossed with black lines. As he dropped the money into it, the man stared at him intently, shook his head in a strange movement, and backed out of the room.

Somehow the incident, the black palm and the intent look, reminded Revel of a fortune-teller he had once seen at a fair. He couldn't remember what had been predicted for him on that occasion. But he realized a moment later that he had been glad of the brief human contact, which recalled him to practicalities. He turned to the trunk.

The lock was broken. Inside was a sea of documents, mostly parchment covered with close lines of old-fashioned scrivener's copperplate, a complex interlacing of twirled letters that would make the task of reading quite painful, even for the experienced eye. Revel was contemplating how to start—whether to simply tip up the trunk and let the papers cascade out—and also wondering how he could contrive to get something to eat in this rambling aristocratic rookery—when there was a knock at the door and the servant, Daniella, whom he had seen on the boat and also in the apartment of the old principessa, came in bearing a tray.

"The family are not lunching at home, sir, but the young mistress thought you might like something to eat." She removed a battered silver lid to reveal a substantial pile of grilled chops.

"Thank you." She had disappeared before he could ask her whether "the young mistress" meant the daughter of the house or her youthful stepmother.

Having demolished the meal and placed the tray at the end of the desk, he knelt on the floor and began pulling out papers, sorting them roughly by type of document. There were bills with engraved headings, receipts, a sea of private letters in English and Italian, and these he put on one side, reserving them for later examination. For immediate scrutiny, he placed some heavy legal papers hung with seals to the forefront of his desk. After about three hours' work, mostly spent on his knees, he had more or less emptied the trunk and decided that his duty for the day had been fulfilled. The room seemed to be growing damp. The little fire had long died down, and he had exhausted the stock of sea coal left in a scuttle beside it. He was about to leave, and had put on his coat, when there came another interruption.

There was a slight footstep on the stairs, and a faint perfume reached the room. *Clara,* he thought and surprised himself with the upsurge of hope, but no, it was the young woman with red hair who had been at Clara's side on the funeral barge.

"Signor Callender, there is something that Donna Clara wanted you to see. She was summoned to visit the Prepiani family today, so she cannot show you personally and asked me to bring it to you. Apparently it was in the old principessa's bedroom, where she died, and not placed with the rest of her papers."

He took the document she held out, a scroll closely covered with lines of legal script, and realized that it was in English. With it was a pile of old bank accounts, unenticing fodder, but they would have to be scrutinized. *Remain hardheaded here,* he told himself. *And follow the story of the money.* Unpoetic though it was, this remained the best maxim he knew for unraveling human affairs.

Fiammetta Corradini did not wait for thanks or comments but slipped out of the room as quickly as she had appeared.

A few moments more were enough for him to see that the scroll was the original marriage contract, made between the principessa's family, the Maloneys, and Ricardo Casimiri, uncle of the present count. Callender sat down again, still in his greatcoat, to look at it further and marked the document down as important for future study.

Deciding he had done enough for the day, he paced the little space for a few moments, then grasped the bell rope. The bell seemed to echo as a faint chime in the distance.

To Revel's embarrassment, the count himself answered the summons, suddenly appearing in the doorway just after the bell had sounded, and escorted him down the stairs to a long hall which lay two floors below. From here he directed Callender to a small staircase which presumably would finally lead to the outside world, or at least, to the dark and enclosed *rio* which flowed alongside Palazzo Casimiri.

"Till tomorrow morning, then, Signor Callender."

CALLENDER dined with Barton that evening. Calling at the consulate to report on the day's events, he found unexpectedly that the consul was about to eat.

"We dine early in Venice, though the rest of the world has a more fashionable hour. Won't you join me? By the way, did you speak to the count after the funeral?"

"Scarcely at all and he was away for most of today, I understand. Don't tell me to accept any invitations to dinner—I don't think I'd care to dine with that family."

Barton laughed. "No, I'm not going to do that. No, I was going to say that if he invites you to stay in the Palazzo—"

"Why should he do that?"

"Oh . . . I don't know, he might want to see how you're getting on. To have you under his roof, as it were." Barton opened a cigar holder and offered it to Callender, who shook his head. "No? Sure? Well, as I was saying, if he does invite you, I think you would do well to refuse."

Callender sat up in surprise. "Why do you say that?"

"Just . . . the stories one hears from time to time, you understand." He closed his long mouth in a tight line, plainly unwilling to say more.

Callender found that he was growing angry at this mystification, and knew also that fear was playing a part in this, though fear of what, he was scarcely able to formulate in his mind.

"Look, I agreed to come here to help out the embassy in a spot of difficulty, that's all. There's no reason why I shouldn't leave the job at any time."

"Quite, quite, of course. But if you do want to move from the Giudecca, then you would be very welcome to stay here. Just bear that in mind. It might help you to answer any invitation from the Casimiri, to say that you are staying here because you and I have some work to do, quite apart from his affairs. In any case, I have another invitation for you. We are invited to a soirée this evening, by Mrs. Charles Hunter. She's a well-known collector of cultural scalps. I'm afraid I took the liberty of informing her that you were an art-loving British citizen temporarily in Venice, and my invitation was immediately extended to include you."

"Ah, I don't think . . ."

"She's connected with all kinds of interesting people, you know. Her sister is the composer, Ethel Smythe, rather a strange creature, masculine sort of personality, if you know what I mean. But I gather the main lion of the evening will be that modern French painter, does rivers and poppy fields, that sort of thing."

"Claude Monet, here in Venice? He's becoming famous."

"Yes, that's it. Used to shock people, I gather, didn't make a penny for years, but now everyone wants to know him. It's an opportunity for you."

Barton was too sophisticated to add, "An opportunity you would not get at home," but Callender was aware that in England he would scarcely get a chance to rub shoulders with the rich, art-loving crowd who would surround someone like Mrs. Hunter. He accepted quickly.

"Thank you for arranging this, and for the dinner."

"Any time, any time." Barton waved the cigar vaguely over the table, as if indicating the sweep of his generosity. Callender felt a liking for the odd little man, who evidently possessed a subtle talent for dealing with difficult situations. He returned to his lodgings to change, and, staring at the blotchy walls, wondered if he should consider Barton's offer to stay at the consulate. It seemed an obvious move, yet he felt an odd sensation of safety in this ordinary, noisy, anonymous lodging house.

5

In the Palazzo Casimiri there was a profound silence. Prince Antonio Prepiani, making his way along the *androne* to the principal staircase, noted it particularly. It formed a great contrast with his own family home, which was just as large and ancient but seemed to be full all the time, indeed bulging at the seams, with the Prepiani family, its dogs, servants, and hangers-on.

Prince Antonio was the eldest of ten children, nine of whom formed a noisy, cheerful gang. Antonio had always been the exception, solitary from birth, physically less strong than his siblings, inclined to be bookish and to shut himself off to read in the library, a place never graced by the presence of any other member of the family. It had been arranged that after their marriage, he and Clara should live with the Casimiri, an arrangement that suited both bride and groom. She had not wanted to leave Tanta, who seemed in good enough health at the time, and as for Antonio, there were things he wished to do that might be easier performed in the silent depths of Palazzo Casimiri than in the chaotic and bustling palace of the Prepiani, where someone was always wanting to know what one was doing. He was in fact well acquainted with the rambling rooms and galleries of Casimiri, since he had played with Claudio since childhood, and they had investigated all its cavernous halls and twisting passages, from the boathouse to the attics. Claudio and he knew each other's tastes.

On this visit to Palazzo Casimiri, Antonio desired particularly to speak with a servant, which galled, but there was no help for it if he was to attain his wishes.

The maid, Daniella, emerged as he passed the door to Tanta's quarters, now emptied of the jumble of things the old creature had treasured.

"I wish to speak to Rinaldo."

She looked surprised but bowed her head in acknowledgment. Antonio felt a great irritation that she did not humble herself further, bend her knee and curtsy. Nevertheless, he showed no sign of anger—that would have been a betrayal of his dignity—and waited as Daniella scurried off. She seemed to conjure the majordomo from a dark corner under a bend in the stair, and he came hurriedly to Prepiani.

Rinaldo's face registered nothing, no reaction of surprise: he seemed to Prepiani the perfect servant, a man with no feelings of his own. Was it possible that a human being should be a mere instrument, he wondered, looking at Rinaldo.

But smiling outwardly, he said to the majordomo, "I wish to make some secret preparations to follow our wedding, as a gift for Donna Clara. These will involve giving access to certain men whom I wish to employ in this business, you understand?"

"When will they be coming, sir?"

"I'm not certain. I'll tell you that later, when I have made the arrangements."

He held out a leather purse, but Rinaldo did not take it immediately. He said, "Prince, I cannot guarantee that I will be present on all occasions when you require it. My master may send me about the city on business."

Prepiani understood. He shook the purse. The coins clinked heavily. "Very well—there will be more."

Rinaldo took the purse.

*   *   *

THE city had fallen quiet, the silence broken only from time to time by the splashing of oars. Venice lay in sleep, a long dream broken by old memories and stirred by the soft, slow noises of decay.

Along the long galleries there moved a grotesque figure, reflected here and there in tarnished glass. The face was as white as death itself, a thick, chalky color, the eyes huge and red-rimmed, and below it the body was enveloped in a heavy cloak so that an onlooker might have wondered to which century this scene belonged.

The cloaked figure slipped to the door of the master bedroom and listened with absolute concentration. The grimy marble floor was cold under the bare feet, but they appeared to feel no discomfort, did not make the slightest shuffle, so absorbed was the concentration of the listener. Within the room, a sleeper turned heavily amid the sheets, and the figure at the door hesitated for a minute: it might almost have moved away, but there were long reserves behind its determination, many hours of hatred, banked up like embers.

There was silence again within the shadowy room.

Then came a long pause, and soft sounds outside the door; the figure started and turned around, its huge, pallid face staring along the gallery to where two more shapes crept towards the door where it waited. The others had arrived, as planned.

They were keeping the pact.

They entered the room and paused for a moment, as if on the threshold of something prodigious. At a sign, they dropped their cloaks and stood naked. Their faces were like that of the first comer: vacant shields that betrayed nothing, no expression, no identity.

But only the first comer held the dagger and was also the first to cross the moonlit expanse of floor and stand beside the bed, looking down on the empty face with its slack, open mouth from which had trickled a snail's trace of spittle. The sleeper had drunk his fill last night and lay now, heavy in sleep.

Gradually, the other two grew more confident and crept across the room till they surrounded the bed. Even then, when all three of them were staring down at him, if the sleeper had awoken they would probably have turned and fled, for he had exercised authority over them for many years, and when he again made a movement in his sleep, they started back.

"Do it!" muttered one of them desperately, knowing that if the victim awoke they were lost, and the first figure raised the dagger, gripping it with both hands, and gazed down for a second, perhaps to perfect its aim, perhaps to imprint the sleeping feature on its mind. Then the dagger plunged down, but maybe there had been some slight hesitation, some trembling just before the descent of the blow, for the point came down a small way to one side of the target and slid into the socket of the right eye just at the outer edge, jarring on the bone as it entered. But the blade went home, deep into the brain.

That eye slipped out of the socket and hung suspended on the cheek by a jerking and twitching nerve. It glistened in the moonlight as blood and matter poured out down the face and across the pillow.

There was a cacophony of noises: a screaming bellow as the victim writhed for a few moments, one of the figures surrounding the bed started to cry out, and the other, the one had who urged "Do it!" said desperately now, "Finish him off! For God's sake, finish him." And the killer with the knife, seeing the victim was not yet dead, raised it again and thrust it as they had planned, into the places they had agreed, but again, its aim was not quite true, and there were stray cuts that had not been anticipated. The murderer who had called out was silent now, listening fearfully. How could the servants not be aroused, how could some passing vessel on the water not have heard the dying shriek? But this was a household that was used to hearing strange sounds, where hearers were fearful of investigating, where merciful intervention never came, and the evil reputation that had spread around the place protected it further. No one raised the alarm.

There was a remaining task, which would be physically the most difficult of all and take the strength of all three of them, but they managed it at last. Blood and brains had sprayed and smeared their flesh, but they could wash that off, and they slipped away to their rooms. This, too, had been planned. But as one of them stood alone before a heavy marble washbasin, the door whispered open, and another figure crept in, still covered in splatters. "Don't wash," it whispered. It threw aside its bloody mask and, clasping its naked bloody fellow conspirator around the waist, fell to its knees and began to rub its face against the other's body.

8

The Palazzo Barbaro was a blaze of orange and yellow light, both the natural flickering flames of torches burning in iron hoops on the walls outside and the harsh yellow glare of electric bulbs in bulbous brass stands that lit up the grand staircase, at the top of which Mrs. Charles Hunter stood resplendently to receive her guests. Below her, ranks of footmen stood positioned at intervals, gazing into space as the guests passed them on their way to do social obeisance. Callender supposed the flunkies were for decoration only.

"Hunter made his money in American mines," whispered Barton as they mounted the carpeted steps.

"They're Americans?"

"No, he's from Northumberland. Family had a lot of wealth from coal. 'To them that hath shall be given,' eh? She's British, too. The sister's a bit of an oddity. You'll see sometime, I expect, though I don't think Ethel Smythe's in Venice at the moment. She's a composer, it appears—writes tunes for the suffragettes, I believe. Ah, here's our hostess now."

Mary Hunter was not by any means beautiful, though she had distinct personality and upright bearing. She had a pale, pointed face, the eyes set too close together, the nose long and thin. She was wearing the most elaborate dress Callender had ever seen, presumably the height of fashion in Venice. His hostess was swathed in what seemed to be layer upon layer of pleated organza, creamy pink and almost transparent in its frailty and lightness, which covered her shoulders and trembled in little ruffles and frills along her arm as she held out her hand during the introductions. It also appeared to be puffed out around her skirts in swags and bows. Callender supposed there must be a solid opaque foundation beneath the gauzy layers, but all he could take note of was some sort of heavy silk bodice and sash. Her neck was clasped with diamond chokers, and the light brown hair piled high on her head was topped with more jewels set into a high comb.

In spite of this impression of glitter and insubstantiality, however, she clasped Callender's hand firmly with white-gloved fingers. He recognized the long jaw and physical strength of someone who came from an English country family, brought up amid hunters and farmers, characteristics which were still there, no matter what polish wealth and sophistication had overlaid them. "I'm so glad you were able to join us, Mr. Callender. Now, I understand that you take a great interest in art, and I have a wonderful treat for all art lovers this evening. What do you think?"

"I hardly dare guess, madam. Mr. Sargent, perhaps?" Callender knew that John Singer Sargent and Mary Hunter, whose portrait the American artist had painted, were on good terms. Mary Hunter collected famous men as a zookeeper collects exotic creatures.

But the great Sargent beast was not on show tonight. Another lion would be paraded before her guests.

"Mr. Claude Monet, the famous French painter!"

Callender could scarcely do anything but make a deep bow and express his delight at being in the same assembly.

"I shall make sure you are introduced to him. And to his wife, of course." Mrs. Hunter turned to Barton. "Theseus, how enchanting of you to come to my little soirée."

Barton bowed in his turn. "My dear Mme Hunter, you look as enchanting as ever. No, forgive me, more so! Tell me, will we have the pleasure of hearing one of your sister's compositions tonight?" There was a subtle undercurrent to this innocent question which seemed to fluster Mary Hunter.

"No, I'm afraid Ethel's music is considered too . . . too modern for most people's tastes." She turned quickly back to Callender. "Do be sure to circulate! We love new company in Venice."

"Her sister is a very strange creature," murmured Barton as they passed on into the salon, assailed on either hand by flunkies holding out trays loaded with glasses of champagne. "Ethel Smythe always wears tweeds, on every occasion. But Mary's friends put up with her eccentricities, though between ourselves, Ethel is much the cleverer. You can have an interesting conversation with Ethel, whatever her proclivities."

"Proclivities?"

"Only rumor, of course, but here in Venice people can indulge as they wish, you see."

Yes, Callender was beginning to see. They were now in a throng of people, most of whom were dressed in a fashion that might be described as richly artistic, the men in velvet smoking jackets, some with cravats, the woman in loose and flowing drapery, heavy rich brocades with threads of gold, or else the kind of meringuelike frills which their hostess was sporting.

"Don't suppose Hunter's anywhere to be seen. He usually makes himself scarce at these gatherings. I'll introduce you to the daughters."

Three young women were seated in the most eye-catching position in the center of the salon on one of those curious triangular seats known as a *confidante*, where all three occupants, almost back-to-back, are facing outwards but may partly see and converse with one another. The arrangement looked carefully managed, as contrived as their white silk dresses with organdy fichus, less elaborate than that of their mother, but surely from the same fashion house. Kathleen and Sylvia had their mother's thin nose and long face. Cary was perhaps more like her father, her face rounder and more animated, and Revel came to a halt in front of her. Conversation would be nevertheless difficult: the Misses Hunter remained seated, waving their fans modestly before their faces, and he discovered that the seating arrangement made it possible for anyone standing before them to converse with only one of the ladies at a time; whichever one he spoke to, the others were always at a slight angle, which he found disconcerting. It was a relief, after he had answered questions about how he liked Venice, had he been to the Accademia, didn't the canals smell frightful, when two young men who were evidently friends of the family came up and began to be chaffed and joked with in an easy sort of way. Callender found that it was possible to slip farther and farther away, noting that Barton had done the same, and was now in deep conversation with a middle-aged man on the other side of the room.

Callender drew an inward sigh of relief and contemplated retreating out onto a nearby balcony. The rippling indigo sweep of the Grand Canal at night, with great windows lit up along its length as one palazzo after another entertained its guests, the beaked gondolas gliding towards landing stages, the yellow lights reflected in the swelling water, all these amounted to a spectacle in which he could delight, if he were not forced to make conversation.

But as he was turning towards the balcony he was aware of a renewed buzz in the room and looked back to see his hostess bearing down towards him. Behind her came two people, a middle-aged man, powerfully built like a farmer, with a full belly and a long white beard. The eyebrows were still black and strongly marked, and although the eyes peered from behind thick, round lenses, the overall impression this man made was one still of vigor and strength. On his arm was a white-haired woman.

"Monsieur, Mme Monet, may I present a British art lover, Mr. Revel Callender?"

Revel had the presence of mind to bow, take the hand of the artist which was held out to him, and kiss the fingers of Mme Monet. "Mr. Callender is in Venice to appreciate some of the great paintings here, the works of Titian and Tintoretto, isn't that so, Mr. Callender. M. and Mme Monet are my guests here in the Palazzo Barbaro."

Revel murmured a few conventional phrases in French, and the

Monets seemed to relax. They smiled at him, and he was able to see that Mme Monet, though she seemed much older than her husband, had fine brown eyes in a ruined and wrinkled face that must once have had tremendous charm. She was wearing an utterly absurd hat with bright hummingbird feathers attached. Their hostess excused herself and bustled off to speak to a group of people nearby, and he asked the Monets something commonplace about visiting the Accademia.

"Ah, yes, but it is the air outside that I need to see," said the artist. "This famous Venetian light on water and marble. There can't be anything like it in the world."

"Do you paint every day, sir?"

"At every opportunity I am given, yes."

Was there a slight bitterness on his tone? Revel felt a little uncomfortable, but in any case Mme Monet put an end to the conversation by saying, "M. Callender, I hope you will forgive me—I cannot stand for long at my age. Claude, could you help me to a seat, please?"

"Yes, of course, my dear. M. Callender, another time, I hope."

He watched them as they made their way through the throng, forced to pause and accept interruptions at every turn as people came up to them.

"The world is anxious to know them now."

It was a soft voice at his shoulder. Turning, he saw a woman dressed in dark red that sheathed her body like the calyx of a flower. Her neck and shoulders were white and unadorned, and her black hair was dressed up around a filigree silver headband from which a few fine curls and tendrils escaped to brush her cheeks. Her eyes were huge, velvet-brown, and her upper lip had a distinct cupid's bow. He thought she was probably about thirty years old, but it was difficult to tell. The other women in the room suddenly seemed to be attired in some sort of conspiratorial semi-historic fancy dress. The city itself must have some kind of atmospheric effect on what people wore and how they behaved, he decided. This woman was resistant to influence. But he felt a certain current between them which was unmistakable.

She pulled out a cigarette case and screwed a cigarette into an ivory holder. "Do you mind?"

"Er, no, of course not."

He found some vestas in his pocket case and lit her cigarette.

"Helena Marino."

"Revel Callender."

"Yes, I caught your name as our hostess was introducing you." She had a pleasant voice, quite deep, with an English accent.

"You were saying—about Mme Monet?"

"Oh yes, they were very poor not so many years ago. When she was his mistress. This is his second wife, you know."

"As a matter of fact, I didn't."

"Yes, Alice went to live with Monet when his first wife was still alive. It caused a frightful scandal—her family would barely have anything to do with her."

"Really? She doesn't look—" He stopped, conscious that he was about to make a faux pas, indeed, probably had already done so, since this woman looked quick-witted.

"Oh, she was a beauty once, I believe. You wouldn't believe she was once a lovely creature and became his mistress. She's aged prematurely, poor thing."

Helena Marino had lowered her voice, and he had to lean closer over her bosom and shoulders, from which arose a delicious scent. There were traces of powder on her shoulders and the warm skin between her breasts, at least, he fancied he could sense its warmth arising with her perfume. Her rather malicious conversation, the apparent satisfied amusement in her face, should have repelled him, but it had the opposite effect. She continued, "And of course, the dreadful business that happened a few months ago will have made things much worse. Didn't you know?"

Providentially, a piano started tinkling nearby, and somewhere behind him a soprano launched into an aria.

"No, I don't, whatever it was. I'm sorry, I can't hear you now—look, shall we step out onto this balcony and then you can tell me about it?"

As they moved out of the salon, he caught a glimpse of Theseus Barton looking at him from the other side of the room, his eyebrows raised. "Damn it, why should I care?" he muttered. "I don't have to be continually in the service of His Majesty's government."

Helena Marino saw the direction of his gaze.

"I beg your pardon? Are you connected with the consulate? I saw you talking to Mr. Barton earlier on."

"No, I'm nothing to do with it. I'm sorry about what I was saying—it doesn't matter."

Scented plants in tubs had been placed out on the landing stage of Mrs. Hunter's domain, and the perfume of carnations and gardenias mingled with the watery, salty sea air that blew towards them from the Adriatic. Boats floated past beneath their balcony, with murmuring voices and music drifting along the water. A gondola eased its way close to the wall of the Palazzo Barbaro, the occupants invisible save for a glittering braceleted arm trailing from the protective *felze*. From somewhere there came a long, sharp cry that suddenly stopped. It set his nerves on edge and broke the mood of the moment.

"What were you going to say about the Monets?" he asked. "Do you know them well?"

"No, but I don't live in Venice, you see, I live in Paris. I stay here from time to time, and I only arrived yesterday on this occasion, so I can tell you all the latest French gossip. It seems Alice Monet's brother-in-law, Auguste Rémy, was murdered. He was a frightfully respectable stockbroker, quite an old man."

"Robbery, I suppose."

"You would suppose wrongly, almost certainly. He kept rather a strange household, it appears, although he had been married to Alice's sister, Cecile, for many years."

"What do you mean?"

"Oh, you know, this and that," she said vaguely. "But two of the servants, the butler and a valet, were convicted of the murder, though there are rumors going round Paris."

He laughed. "You can't tantalize me like this."

"Can't I? I suppose not. There was a young man, Léon Raingo, in the household, seventeen years old. Alice Monet's nephew, her brother's son. His father died years ago, and he was living with old Auguste and Cecile. It's not clear at all what happened to the boy on the night of the murder. It seemed that the old man put up a real fight, but no one heard a struggle—not Léon, not the other servants."

He thought about this, as a puzzle that he might have found in the amusement column of a newspaper. "What about the butler? What did he have to say for himself?"

"He claimed that he heard nothing and that he had gone into his master's room as usual in the morning, drew back the curtains, and then turned and saw the old man lying on the bed. Quite dead, and everything was covered in blood."

"Good God! How was he killed?"

"He was stabbed. They said there were many wounds on the body." She stopped, blinking her eyes, like someone trying to banish an image, as if she had said too much for her own imagination to cope with. "Look, it was a mistake to begin talking to you about it. I'm sorry, I'd really rather forget it. Let's go back in. I shouldn't have said anything. Please don't tell anyone I mentioned it, will you?"

He was annoyed both by her taste for scandal and her hypocrisy. He would have liked to think better of Helena Marino, but she attracted him, there was no doubt about it. This woman was a part of a different world, a modern life which was easy to forget among the crumbling marble glories of Venice, that self-absorbed little kingdom lost in the past. The Palazzo Casimiri seemed a long distance away, the count's daughter Clara to be a creature from another age, certainly not of his own time.

"May I call on you?"

"I'm staying at the Danieli," Helena said as she stepped back from the balcony.

★   ★   ★

CALLENDER woke slowly, becoming aware that the morning sun was shining on his eyes. He cursed himself for having not drawn the blinds before he went to bed, and then as he turned over and saw the half-naked female form beside him, recalled there had been no time to spare.

Helena murmured something in her sleep and stirred her long legs, entangled in the sheet. Her white shoulders and heavy breasts with full, dark nipples rose out of a swathe of some silken garment around her waist. Raising himself on one elbow, he saw a silver wine cooler stood on an ormolu table. Scents of sperm, patchouli, and female body hung in the air over the rumpled bed.

"May I escort you to your hotel?" Yes, that moment last night had been quite clear, as was her smile.

He had awoken in her suite at the Danieli, and on the other side of the bedroom was a door that led to a splendid bathroom with a flotilla of white towels. He definitely recalled kneeling among them, yes, he certainly remembered that.

And remembered also his task at the Palazzo Casimiri, work which he had agreeably forgotten. He got out of bed and crossed to the window. From the window of the hotel room he could see the blackened tints of the leads of San Marco, and beyond the turquoise water of the Adriatic, stretching to misty blue distance. It would be a fine morning for exploring, if he had not been required to attend at the Palazzo Casimiri.

He thought of the tiny room to which he would be confined and the dusty pile of papers within it, and was almost on the point of sending the count a message that he had suddenly been called away, but other considerations prevailed, two of which seemed inextricably entwined. One was that he would soon feel obliged in reality to leave Venice, since he had no doubt that his stay here would be noted by many eyes and he could not prowl the narrow *calli* and the crumbling churches without his movements being reported back to Palazzo Casimiri. The other was that he would forgo any chance of meeting Clara Casimiri again. Puzzled by his own thoughts, he found that she was still preoccupying his mind, even when there was another woman lying naked in the very same room. He had to admit that Clara interested him far more than any of the well-dressed and conventional young women he had seen at Mrs. Hunter's, even more than Helena Marino. He recalled the independent way she had stood on the deck of the principessa's funeral galley with her head held high, slightly apart from the rest of the family. Clara, he felt, had emotional depth and individuality, a brain which would be interesting, and this was an intriguing sensation for Callender in relation to his dealings with women.

Perhaps it was not entirely new; perhaps he had felt such a curiosity as a schoolboy. He remembered wondering at the age of sixteen about how women thought and felt, but it had been overlaid, he recognized now, by the sexual and material pragmatism of the adult male moving in a society which expected him to fulfill physical and worldly desires within certain prescribed ways. Venice seemed to license the fusion of emotion and beauty, of intelligence and sensuality.

So he resigned himself to a day working for Clara's father, remembering wryly Jacob's seven years' servitude for Rachel, but guessed that he need not start at this early hour. He had little to drink on the previous evening, but his head still felt slightly muzzy. Mrs. Hunter's rooms, though very grand, had been frowsty with cigar smoke and foggy air, and in Helena Marino's marble-clad bathroom, so absurdly like something from ancient Rome, he stripped and showered, splashing himself fully awake with cold water, glimpsing his reflection in the wide bathroom mirrors as he tipped the water over his black curly head, where the drops hung bluish in the glassy morning light.

As he returned to the bedroom, Helena opened her soft brown eyes and smiled at him again, that charming, lazy, pansy-faced smile that had attracted him so much. It almost performed its magical effect once more, but he resisted, and took her hand, kissing it, and saying, "I hate to go."

"Shall I ring for coffee?"

"No, I'm so sorry. I have a business appointment."

"You look very businesslike!" She burst out laughing. "Better get dressed, then. I'll go back to sleep." And, stretching out lazily, she closed her eyes again.

He dressed quickly, dropped a kiss on her forehead as he left, and stopped at a florist opposite, who was just opening his shutters, the scent of the flowers fresh and sharp in the salt air blowing from the Adriatic. Revel ordered a bunch of lilies to be sent to the suite of Madame Marino at the Danieli. "No, no card." *She will know,* he thought.

An affair with Helena Marino was an attractive prospect, and he felt flattered by her attention. Certainly, it would lend a delightful dimension to his life in Venice and seemed somehow appropriate—long, luxurious, and uncommitted sensuality, as aqueous light played over gilded plaster knotwork on walls and ceilings. But did he want to continue? He realized that certain thoughts were interfering with his pleasant desires. The face of Clara Casimiri came between him and thoughts of Helena.

Why was he still thinking of her? A night with another woman should have banished any dangerous desire for a strange girl in a shadowy, disturbing setting.

Revel Callender found an old saying coming to mind: "A reformed rake makes the best husband." He laughed aloud and continued with his walk, strolling from the Danieli through the pleasures of early morning Venice, where cobbles were being swilled down, boats cleaned out, and bulging nets of quivering, silvery fish were being carried from quays to markets. He returned to his lodgings at Signora Amalia's for a change of clothes, taking some breakfast at a café on the way. The count would surely not expect him to attend before midmorning, and he could take in an hour or so of sightseeing before he need face his temporary imprisonment.

As he walked across Saint Mark's Square he glanced towards the Café Florian, gazing at first casually at the customers seated at the tables outside in the square, and then turning his head and hurrying away quickly as he recognized two of the ladies who were gazing raptly towards Saint Mark's. Too late! He had crossed their line of vision, and one of them was hurrying across to speak to him, a small, brown-clad figure who scattered pigeons in all directions.

"Mr. Callender, why, what a coincidence!"

"Miss Tenbaker!" He bowed politely. "I thought you would have returned to England. How is Miss Marshall? I trust she is quite recovered from her experiences." It was perhaps rather indelicate of him to refer to Clementine Marshall's adventure with the handsome gigolo who had stolen her jewelry, an incident which was doubtless best forgotten, but the companion, whose name he had managed to recall, had taken him by surprise. Miss Tenbaker, however, took it in her stride. Perhaps she was rather glad to see a friendly face, for she rattled on, "Oh, I think she has forgotten that unhappy event, Mr. Callender. She was quite remorseful, you know, to have behaved so foolishly. But you certainly gave us some good advice, and we have done as you said. We just put everything behind us and telegraphed to Clementine's parents about the loss of the jewelry—mentioning that it was the work of some unknown sneak thief."

"And they didn't make you return to. Wiltshire straightaway?"

Miss Tenbaker looked a little shamefaced as she said, "No, on the contrary, they insisted that we should continue to enjoy our visit to Italy. They did not want Clementine to waste anything that might contribute to her education. And the jewelry was insured, after all."

"So you stayed in Venice."

"It was on our itinerary, yes, so we stuck to what we had planned. That is always the best policy, I believe. The unexpected is always to be avoided, in my experience."

It might have been his imagination, but it seemed to him that Miss Tenbaker said this with peculiar meaning as she stared at him earnestly. But he forgot this as she rattled on. "You know, Mr. Callender, I was confined in an office for many years before I obtained my present position with Miss Marshall, and I'm so much enjoying this. I was a lady clerk, and I dreamed of Italy very often, I assure you! But we have already have been here for a week, Mr. Callender. What a shame we did not meet you before, and now we are leaving for Florence very shortly. Won't you come over and take some coffee with us?"

Callender hoped he did not betray his feelings of relief at the news of their imminent departure and forbore to point out that that the last time he had seen Clementine Marshall she had been storming and weeping like a miniature hurricane and would be unlikely to rejoice at seeing him again.

"I'm so sorry, Miss Tenbaker, I'm in something of a hurry—"

She turned her small, round face up to his, and he thought for a moment that her eyes seemed remarkably sharp, but he was able to distract her gaze. On the other side of the square he saw that a dark-haired man with a shiny satin cravat had seated himself at Clementine Marshall's table and was making animated conversation. Evidently, the gigolos of Venice would not desist from their advances to Clementine.

"Ah, I think Miss Marshall is speaking to a gentleman . . ."

"Oh, Mr. Callender, I had better go straightaway!" The companion had turned towards Florian's. With a look of horror she gathered up her heavy skirt and flurried across to her charge, like a small, fussy dog that takes its guard duties very seriously, an irritating but thoroughly ordinary tourist, a creature from a different world to that inside the Palazzo Casimiri. On the way, he called at the British Consulate, where Barton had gone out, but the blue-eyed servant stopped him as he was turning away. "Signor Callender, there is a message for you."

Revel was surprised, but presumed it might be from the count, perhaps altering the arrangements they had made. Instead, he found a brief note in very distinctive thick black handwriting, and glancing first at the signature, saw the words, "Claude Monet." It simply asked him to call upon the artist one evening, at Callender's convenience, adding enigmatically, "I have a request to make of you." In spite of Callender's admiration for the artist's work, his heart sank slightly. The thought that immediately came into his mind was perhaps that he, speaking some French and interested in art, might be put on escort duty for Madame Monet. Given her grim expression, it was a prospect which did not appeal to him. Still, he would have to call on the Monets and at least hear what they wanted.

WHEN he arrived at the palazzo a servant conducted him to the long gallery where he had first met the count. To his surprise, Clara Casimiri, standing near a window and wearing blue silk over which reflections of rippling water flitted like butterflies, received him. "Welcome, Signor Callender. My father says you are to be treated as a guest, so I am here to greet you. Would you like something to drink before you go to the study?"

He had not intended to ask for anything, but he found now that he wanted to prolong the moments of contact. "Thank you, Donna Clara. It's a damp morning. Perhaps something to keep out the cold would be welcome."

She indicated two upright gilt chairs, and they sat down. The old woman who had looked after the principessa was already seated next to the fire. Callender wondered at the privileged position she was assuming, behaving like a member of the family, but probably she was almost that. Clara pulled a bell rope, asking the servant who appeared after a few minutes to bring hot chocolate and cognac.

"Daniella was my nurse," she said. "Now she is my chaperone. My father and brother have gone to do some family business," Clara said as she whisked up froth on top of the chocolate and handed it to him in a rather tarnished silver cup contained in an elaborate filigree holder which also required a good clean. Or did it? Tarnish was natural here, thought Callender, part of the shade and mood of the city, casting a spell which would undoubtedly be broken by brisk housewifery.

Clara continued, "So I may receive you in their absence—provided, of course, I do not do so alone."

"The contessa?"

Clara looked at him sideways from under her long eyelids. "Is ill. Unfortunately. Otherwise, of course, it would have fallen to her to greet visitors."

"Then it is my good fortune," said Revel, "though of course, I am sorry for the contessa's indisposition."

He looked along the gallery and sought a topic of conversation, taking refuge in the first subject that occurred to him. He indicated a dim oil painting hung between two windows and said, "That is a most interesting picture, Donna Clara. Is it an ancestor? Do tell me something of your family history."

He observed with some surprise that her hand trembled as it picked up her own silver cup, but she answered him casually enough, glancing at the stern, beruffed female on the wall.

"That is an ancestress, a Contessa Casimiri of the sixteenth century. We have been here a long time, Signor Callender, always a prominent family in Venetian affairs. A Casimiri stormed the walls of Constantinople with Doge Dandolo, and a Casimiri tried to resist Napoleon's conquest of the city." He sensed that in spite of her pride in it, the subject of her family was perhaps the cause of her nervousness.

"A noble past! And what of the future?" They were gazing intently at each other now, and he sensed an unspoken dialogue between them that had nothing to do with these conversational commonplaces.

"The future? Ah!" She sighed. Her eyes were large and sad. "None of us can see that, can we?"

"But we can decide it, sometimes." He set down his cup and leaned towards her. Tendrils of fine gold hair clung gently around her face, and he wanted to touch them, to brush them back from her cheeks, but did not dare reach out his hand.

Through an open window came the sound of male voices echoing over the water below, the splashing and grinding of a boat mooring at the palazzo landing stage.

"My father and brother have returned," said Clara. Daniella came over to stand beside Clara's chair, and Revel stood up as he heard the sound of footsteps on the stairs.

When the count and Claudio came into the room, they greeted him formally, but Revel sensed a burning irritation in the younger man, who had looked startled to see a stranger in the gallery. The Englishman told the count he wanted to start work without delay. Clara called to Daniella, and the old woman rose stiffly and led Callender out of a side door and by a winding staircase into the leather-hung study, where the parchments and papers lay in their neat and dreary piles as he had left them.

When they got to the room, Daniella, to his surprise, entered it after him and closed the door behind her.

"Signor," she said. "The young lady." Revel found her Venetian dialect difficult to understand, but managed to follow her words.

"What about her?"

"She goes in the afternoons to the gallery. To look at the pictures."

"The gallery? The Accademia?"

"*Si*, signor. By the bridge."

Was she telling him this with Clara's permission, or had she sensed the atmosphere and taken matters into her own hands? The latter would be surprising, that a reliable old family servant should regard a complete stranger, a foreigner to boot, as suitable to be entrusted with Donna Clara's private acquaintance, but Daniella added softly as she closed the door behind her, "This is not a good house, signor. Not at all."

9

The next morning he decided to walk through the narrow streets that lay between the Piazza San Marco and the Accademia Bridge. Usually, when going in this direction, he had taken a *vaporetto*, but this was a pleasant morning, and he plunged into the network of alleyways that lay before him. There were sudden and surprising little openings into small crumbling courtyards or groups of market stalls. Sometimes women leaned over balconies and either smiled down at the passerby or hurled the contents of chamber pots into the street. One pretty girl did both, and then laughed with a good-humored apology.

In a square that was larger than most, he came to a rather grand façade decorated with framed posters, and he realized that he had arrived at the Fenice opera house. Near it was a row of smart shops, evidently aimed at the better class of tourist: a jeweler's, a shop that seemed to specialize in ivory-handled shaving brushes, a bookshop selling works in German and English: Libri Gozzi. Gozzi, presumably, was the proprietor.

Idly, he stopped to look in the bookshop window. The usual guide books of course, Baedeker's and Murray's, the poems of Goethe, *Stories from Italian Opera*—strange, he tried and failed to think of an opera set in Venice, except for *Otello* and that was based on Shakespeare, so perhaps it didn't really count as Italian—these idle ideas were passing through his mind, and he realized that he should move quickly on to attend to his duties at Palazzo Casimiri. But his eye fell on another book in the window: a beautifully bound copy of something by Shelley. He had a book of Shelley's poems in his lodgings. In fact, amusedly, he recalled Miss Tenbaker's shock at seeing it on his desk when she and Miss Marshall had called for his advice. That appallingly rebellious creature, Percy Bysshe Shelley!

Callender decided he had a few minutes to spare. Wandering into the tiny shop, he asked a young man who was in attendance to show him the work. He looked a bit young to be Gozzi himself, as Callender pictured the founder of an antiquarian bookshop such as this, but he took the book from the window gracefully enough. The title, *The Cenci*, was stamped on the spine. It was a rich, soft, green leather binding, and the covers were embellished with gold arabesque designs. When Revel opened the pages, he saw that it was a play, with Italian characters, and glanced down the list of names. Count Francesco Cenci. His daughter, Beatrice. Lucretia, her stepmother.

"Beautiful. Very nice book." The young man was doing his best in English, but another figure came forward, an older man, stooping slightly, whom Revel took to be the owner himself.

"You like the binding?"

"Yes, it's very fine."

"We have them crafted especially for our shop. It is a traditional Venetian pattern; you see these interlacing designs stamped into the leather. Books have been bound in this way for centuries in this city."

Gozzi smiled and moved forward. Now he was in the light, Callender could see that he had a scholarly look, thin-faced and bespectacled, yet still with a handsome quality, fine dark eyes that, like so much else here, had a suggestion of the Orient.

"You see, signor, in Venice, we make everything our own, even an English poet," he said. "Even your Shelley, the advocate of rebellion against tyranny!"

Callender laughed. The book was a beautiful piece of craftsmanship.

Now he had it in his hands, he couldn't resist it, the soft and supple leather binding, the gilt edges to the pages.

"I've read Shelley's poems, of course, but I must confess I don't know this drama."

Signor Gozzi said, "It is set in Italy, signor, but not in our era, of course. In the sixteenth century."

"Really?" The supreme century of Renaissance Italy, and also the era of plots, of poisonings. Callender was intrigued. "What is it about?"

The old man evidently loved a bit of mystery, for he leaned forward and said in a whisper, "About the murder of Count Cenci, signor. But I won't tell you any more—it will spoil the story for you!"

"How fascinating," said Callender, and he wondered why this old story should have intrigued the poet. Clearly, the tale of the murder must have survived for centuries. He looked at the date on the title page again. It was dated 1819.

"A first edition," murmured Gozzi. "One of only two hundred and fifty copies printed in Italy."

"Really?" Callender thought for a moment. Now that he had the book in his hands, he was unwilling to part with it. He couldn't normally afford such a luxury as a first edition of Shelley, but there would be the fee from the Maloneys for working on the old lady's papers, and like most tourists he had secretly wanted to find a treasure in Venice.

"I'll take the book."

Fortunately he had sufficient lire in his pocket, though it would leave him very short, and he would have to make do with a cheap lunch in some trattoria.

"Would you like some bookplates made with your name on them? We can match them to the design on the covers and have them printed within a few hours."

Why not? The extra expense would be trifling: he could rake it up.

Callender chose an ornate bookplate depicting architectural columns holding up a shield on which was engraved "Ex Libris," followed by his name in wiry curlicued script. He gave the address of his lodgings on the Giudecca and paid the sum requested, which turned out, after all, once it had been written down and added up, to be not so inconsiderable as he had thought. He found the Shelley fitted quite snugly into his pocket.

"Are you returning to the Giudecca now, signor?"

"No, as a matter of fact, I'm not."

"Ah, then you will be going to the Palazzo Casimiri."

Callender nodded, somewhat surprised, but resigned to the Venetian information network that seemed to catch his every movement.

As he was leaving Gozzi's, he saw someone evidently making for the shop with a pile of books under his arm, and recognized him. It was the young doctor who had been at the principessa's funeral, Albrizzi, he who had learned his English in America.

"Mr. Callender, how good to see you again." He indicated the book poking out of Callender's pocket. "Have you been buying from Gozzi?"

Callender showed him the Shelley. "I found this, and it seemed a reasonable price."

Albrizzi laughed. "Beautifully bound, but Shelley is rather an unorthodox taste, I think, among the respectable English-speaking community. There are ladies in Boston who won't hear the man's name mentioned—advocate of free love, expelled from Oxford, and all that. Still, it's a fine copy, and Gozzi always has a fair price, I find."

"Do you buy much from him?"

"He's very good at obtaining medical textbooks for me. Indeed, he lets me bring back others when I have finished with them, and takes them in exchange. When I was a student, he almost allowed me to use the shop as a library!"

"Very good of him."

"Indeed. Are you on your way to the Casimiri now?"

"Yes, my work on the princess's papers is not yet finished. In fact, I have barely made a start."

"Then I won't delay you."

Albrizzi made a courteous bow, and Callender went on his way, wondering how it came about that all Venice seemed to know one's movements.

As before, he worked steadily at the documents, classifying and translating what seemed to be the most important financial papers, but was aware that outside the sun was rising high in the sky, and when his pocket watch announced one o'clock, he made his way downstairs. The place seemed to be in a noontide stupor. Slipping out of a side entrance, he found a skiff still doing business and had himself rowed to a point near the Accademia. If his actions should be reported, there would be no cause for suspicion, because it was virtually next to the British Consulate. Even as he thought this, he cursed himself for being so vulnerable to the atmosphere of suspicion and concealment that seemed to be as much in the city as its penetrating sea mists.

There was a small bar at the end of an alleyway where he had some food and a drink, after checking his watch. Then he made his way to the Accademia.

AS Revel walked towards the gallery, Dr. Albrizzi was letting himself into his house on the opposite bank with the enormous key that had served his family for generations, a piece of iron, solid and cold in the hand. There was a familiar smell that he had known all his life, except for his sojourn in America, compounded of beeswax and bergamot, with an occasional chemical whiff of sulfur. Not so noticeable today.

His housekeeper came to greet him. "Ah, *Signor Dottore,* you didn't take your gabardine overcoat? The cold winds will be blowing any day now."

"I forgot, Teresa. I'll get it out of the wardrobe."

"*Si,* and maybe the lining needs mending. I'll have a look."

"Thank you."

"Talking about sewing, *Dottore* . . ." She was hanging up his cloak. Teresa was a large woman who blocked a fair amount of the entrance hall, but her fingers were remarkably small and neat, white against the black fabric.

"What about it?" He was looking at the list kept in the hall, patients who had called or sent messages while he was out. She went on saying something, but he caught only the end of it.

"Mmm. What were you saying—something about sewing?"

"Well, it's just a piece of gossip, really."

She turned her back, but he could tell that something had distressed her. She had gone into the dining room across the hallway from the surgery. Her lower lip was twitching, and those small hands were restlessly brushing imaginary crumbs from the table.

"Teresa?"

She wanted to tell him, and it came bursting out. "I've always done their sewing, for years. Just collected it every so often and did the repairs for them. Of course, after the old principessa died, I didn't expect to have so much, but they still sent me their linen. But now—I don't know."

"Whose linen? Who are you talking about? Ah, the Casimiri. I've just met the Englishman you told me about, the one who is working on the old lady's papers."

She sat down heavily on a stiff-backed dining room chair and said softly, "Yes, Pietro was talking about him. But I don't want to go to that place again."

"Why is that, Teresa?"

"There is a certain atmosphere there—I've felt it before, but now—Ginevra Rocalle, the butcher's daughter—she went there to work in the kitchens. They say she didn't come out again."

"Oh, but surely that's just vicious gossip!"

"Yes, probably." The housekeeper was deferential, not liking to disagree. "But one thing is true—Ginevra Rocalle hasn't been seen for some time. I used to talk to her almost every day, because she helped her father at his stall in the Rialto market. And he is very upset—he thinks she's run away. But I don't think so. She would have told a friend, or someone would have found out, if she had a young man, as her father believes. You know how it is here."

She stopped, paused, as if she didn't want to continue with this topic. Then she said, *"Dottore,* have you ever heard of something called *La Veglia?"*

Albrizzi was puzzled. "What an odd name. 'The Watching,' 'The Vigil,' something like that?"

"I don't know what they meant by it, sir. Only Pietro said he had heard they would be keeping *La Veglia* in the Palazzo Casimiri. I don't think he knows what it means either. He's not a bad sort. But I don't want to go there for the sewing anymore, that's certain."

Albrizzi sat down opposite her and looked straight into her face, as he would into that of a friend, an equal. It was old, anxious, lined. He put a hand over one of hers.

"You don't need the money, Teresa? If you do, I will make it up to you."

She smiled at last, and he felt he had achieved a small victory. 'You are so good, *Dottore*! No, I don't really need the money, that's true. Besides, if Donna Clara asks me, I would do some work for her, in any case. She gave me money for my sister once, when Giulia was desperate and I couldn't help her. You were away in America then."

"Well, then, Teresa, just stay away from Palazzo Casimiri, and if Donna Clara wants you to do any dressmaking, surely she could come here to arrange it? I would have no objections."

Teresa made no reply. And that was how the matter was left.

THERE were few tourists jostling over the bridge that led to the Accademia: Venice was getting colder, and the mists of autumn were deterring all but the most hardy, determined travelers such as Miss Tenbaker. Revel almost expected to see that formidable little figure and her skittish young charge as he entered the Gothic porch and mounted the steps that led into the galleries, but there was no sign of them; in fact, the great rooms seemed almost empty, the paintings speaking to one another in long silent Venetian dialogues of the past.

Callender knew the Accademia well and had spent many afternoons there without ever encountering Donna Clara. If she had taken to coming here, perhaps this was a new interest for her. He walked steadily, his footsteps echoing, through the halls, past pale madonnas and long processions, past gold and indigo and carmine gleaming out of the gray afternoon light. He paused only in front of a magnificent Veronese depicting a feast beneath some splendid marble-columned loggia, and moved rapidly on down the long corridor on the other side of the building. He had nearly returned to his starting point when he found her. Or rather he found her watchdog, Daniella, standing in a doorway. She gave him a nod of acknowledgment as he passed and made no attempt to follow him into the room beyond.

Clara was in the room that contained Carpaccio's long sequence showing the martyrdom of Saint Ursula. They were pictures which he had never studied. Callender preferred the art of the Renaissance and scenes of martyrdom were not to his taste, yet now, surrounded by the story of the saint, he began to feel its power.

Clara was holding a sketchpad as if she had just been copying something and looked up in surprise which he felt was genuine. She had clearly not expected to see him, and he felt obliged to pretend that he had come there by chance. He walked over to her.

"Donna Clara, how fortunate to see you! I am merely a tourist in this wonderful place. Won't you explain to me what all this is about?"

Though he gestured towards the walls around them, he did not entirely mean the paintings, as perhaps she understood, but of course they had to conduct their conversation as if he had. She began to point out details in the Carpaccios.

"You can read the story in the paintings. Saint Ursula was betrothed to an English prince called Hereus—here are the English ambassadors coming to arrange the wedding. And here is Ursula, in her chamber inside the palace. She made her own terms for the marriage—she was to be allowed to make a pilgrimage first."

"Where is it taking place? It looks like Venice." Surely that was the island of San Giorgio Maggiore glimpsed on the left of the painting, still recognizable after more than four hundred years. And looking round at the Carpaccios he saw a city set in a dreamy, magical stillness, a place of white marble and pale golden light, a lighter, richer city, Venice as she must have appeared in the freshness of her glory.

She laughed. "Yes, this is supposed to be Brittany, and that is England in another picture, but all the settings are really Venice. It was the center of the world for Carpaccio."

As she spoke, he glanced down at her notepad and saw that she had sketched Saint Ursula standing gravely in her room behind the throne where the ambassadors were received. It struck him that Ursula was remarkably like Clara, a beautiful, clear face, the gaze direct and thoughtful.

"You are copying the picture?"

"The costumes, yes." She went on, evidently feeling an explanation was needed. "I want to have some of them copied. You see, I am going to be married, and I have a fancy to wear traditional dress—it is so graceful, don't you think? That is why my father allows me to come here to look at the pictures with only Daniella for company."

To cover his feelings at this announcement, Callender turned and examined the saint's garment. It did not look suitable for a joyous celebration: she was wearing a modest gown of silvery gray violet.

"Is this a wedding dress?"

"No, she is wearing something more like that in another picture— here, where she meets her betrothed. There is an undergown of white satin with puffed and slashed sleeves—you can see it beneath these heavy pieces of material on the arms that look almost like men's armor."

Again, he was impressed at the appearance of strength: this was not a vision of shrinking maidenly modesty. Ursula was not averting her eyes like a timid bride-to-be but looking directly at her betrothed, as if calm and considering. On her upper arm was embroidered an elaborate crest, as if it were a soldier's token—the badge of a warrior for Christ, perhaps.

Clara was speaking about the costumes again.

"The scarlet cloak hanging down her back—that would look very fine over a white satin gown, don't you agree? And her attendant has a cloak of that clear emerald color—it would suit Fiammetta so well."

He could not refrain from asking the question that had been in his mind since she had first spoken of her marriage, and found he could no longer speak through allusion to the paintings.

"And your bridegroom, Donna Clara. Who will that be?"

"Prince Antonio Prepiani. One of our leading nobles."

She moved abruptly away as if to examine another detail, and added, "He has been a friend of my brother's since childhood. It is a very suitable match."

Callender thought he had never heard a woman speak so coldly of her own marriage and could not refrain from saying, "But you—do you truly want this?"

She did not answer—perhaps she was too unaccustomed to speaking of her desires—but he saw the look in her face. Instead, she said, "And this is the last picture. It shows the death of the saint."

He looked close-up at the picture which she indicated, and saw that what seemed to be a confused jumble of limbs and cloth resolved itself into the depiction of a massacre. "Ursula and her attendants were killed at Cologne, after she had made a pilgrimage to Rome, as she requested under the terms of the marriage contract. The soldiers killed the virgins who accompanied her, and here, this is Ursula facing her murderer."

He followed her gaze and saw the martyrdom of the innocent: women falling beneath the swords of armed men. A severed head lay upside down before him, and to the left of that a soldier was hewing at the neck of another woman in what looked like a horribly businesslike way. A great cloth was discolored with the dark red of blood, hanging heavily, sopping with it. He felt its weight. To the right of this hideous scene, in front of her dying attendants, knelt Ursula. She was looking her killer unflinchingly in the face. He was an archer, drawing back his bow to take aim directly at her. The bow seemed massive, the arrow long and thick enough to kill a bear. Her eyes were wide open.

Callender could not help shuddering. Clara said, "I have to try not to feel too much when I see them."

He understood.

There was a sound at the doorway, and Daniella was there, shifting restlessly from foot to foot. In the distance a clock chimed: it might almost have been the clock in one of the paintings, so perfect was the silent illusion.

"I have to return, Signor Callender. Thank you for your company."

"We'll meet again, Donna Clara."

She nodded silently, seriously, before they vanished through the doorway. He crossed to a window and, looking down, saw them going away. He watched till Clara was out of sight, with mixed feelings. She was going to make a marriage that was quite possibly not of her choosing, yet one which was obviously eminently suitable for her class and family. Had there been coercion? He recalled the trembling of her hand as she talked of her family, and yet he felt that Clara had a determination and willpower of her own and was a person who would combat her own fear. He stared at the painted perfection of Saint Ursula, in whom innocence and strength were one. Choices were so clear in that world.

Revel suspected that he might begin to love Clara Casimiri, yet his mind was full of doubt. He lived in a different world, of modern complexities and gray moral areas, and as he walked out of the Accademia he plunged back into that existence.

10

When he reached the Palazzo Casimiri on the following morning, the atmosphere seemed curiously heavy, as if thundery weather lay along its waterfront. There were no gondoliers lounging beside the landing stage, no servants hanging round the chipped marble pillars of the entrance. Callender seemed to be unexpected, and no one came to greet him. He had hoped that Clara might welcome him as before, but not even the sound of a barking dog echoed through the long entrance loggia, as it had done on his previous visit. The heavy entrance doors were closed, and a huge black sash had been draped over them as a sign that the family was still in mourning. Callender banged on the sodden wood, which gave out dull thuds.

He heard heavy footsteps within, and one of the servants whom he had seen on his previous visit—Pietro, he thought the man's name—swung one of the doors open on its hinges. He recognized the visitor and gave a bow and a polite greeting.

"The count asked me to return and work on some documents," said Callender.

Pietro seemed at a loss. "He did not mention it to me, sir, but I'll announce you."

Callender hesitated for a moment. On the one hand, perhaps the count should be informed of his presence. On the other, he did not wish to disturb him unnecessarily again so soon after a family funeral, and besides, Callender knew perfectly well what work he was expected to do.

"No need to ask the count to see me now," he said to Pietro. "If you will just show me to the room where I was working on the principessa's papers, and you could perhaps inform him that I am here."

"Very good, sir."

Pietro led the way. Callender was glad he had a guide, for he was at a loss after mounting the grand staircase to the principal rooms. Pietro paused at the top, giving Callender time to note as landmarks the faintly absurd marble urns at the top of the stairs and the long, cool halls that stretched off to right and left. He knew that the room that had been allotted to him was on a higher level but had no way of remembering how to reach it; there had been all manner of twisting staircases, some of them contained in cupboards.

He was led on, through a tortuous passageway. It opened out here and there into darkened rooms, one with pierced window screens through which tiny patches of light fell across the floor, and led at last to a door that was familiar. Here the servant left him, and Callender surveyed the jumble of papers which he had removed the previous day from the old principessa's trunk. Opposite the door, the shutters were pulled back from the window, as he had left them. One of them was swinging slightly: he moved across and hooked it back against the wall. A sudden gust of wind swirled into the room and lifted the leather hangings, which bellied out slightly and creaked as they settled against the wall. Callender hadn't looked down into the courtyard.

He set to determinedly and continued to sort the documents systematically. Then he began making chronological piles of such routine matters as bank statements and receipts. Scraps of material occasionally fell out from tailor's jottings or upholsterer's bills: a bit of crimson satin which had kept its bright coloring within an envelope, a swatch of brocade samples; once he even found the long-lost pearly lid of a pomade jar. It seemed still to exude a scent of violets. The principessa had magpie tastes, he thought, as he made a scrap heap of these fragments, setting aside an ivory prayer book that was probably valuable, yet he liked her for them.

IN the long gallery, Pietro bowed to Claudio Casimiri, who stood in front of the famous fireplace, turning his hands towards the coals.

"What is it, Pietro?"

Claudio sounded impatient, but that was not unusual.

"The Englishman is here, sir. The one who is working on the papers."

"Oh, hell—what is the man doing, calling on us a couple of days after a funeral? Doesn't he know we're officially in mourning?"

"I understand that it was not a social call. He just wanted to work on some papers, sir. So I showed him straight up to the room."

Pietro was anxious that he had acted wrongly, but he saw that the young master's mood had softened.

Claudio Casimiri said softly, "You did well, Pietro. Fetch Rinaldo to me now."

AFTER an hour or so of his work on the documents, Callender had begun to feel the heat of noon was approaching. The air in the room had grown stale: There seemed to be no breeze coming from outside now, and the dust from the papers was making his mouth dry. He pulled on his velvet bell rope and heard a jangling somewhere in the depths of the palazzo, but no servant appeared, though there seemed to be the sound of shouting echoing in the distance.

He stood in the middle of the room for a few moments, and then decided that he would find his own way down in order to get something to drink. At this point, which he would ever afterwards remember, as one does sometimes capriciously recollect those circumstances surrounding a terrible event more clearly than the event itself, he paused for a few moments and looked round the leather-hung walls and perceived them as cracked, smelling, redolent of old death and animal pain. But he did not take this sensation as a portent, neither in the moment itself nor in retrospect, because in spite of what was to occur in the next few minutes, Revel Callender, who was a rational man, succeeded in the end in holding on to this rationality.

He hesitated for a few moments more, then crossed to the window, partly to orient himself with regard to the topography of the place, partly because he suddenly and urgently wanted to look at something beyond the walls of the room, even if it were an enclosed courtyard, though he was not sure why.

It was as if at that moment his mind had been stunned by the brilliant midday light that poured down into the courtyard outside, and refused to make sense of what it saw. He seemed to be faced with some absurd fragmented puzzle.

THE thorn tree in the courtyard was still there, stark in the noonday sun, but, looking down on it from above, he thought it had suddenly sprouted with some monstrous new entanglements. The white branches still bore their spikes of thorn, black and curved like animal claws, but in addition there was something white twisting among them, part of which was hanging straight down towards the ground. It took several moments more—Callender was never afterwards sure quite how long it was—to recognize the secondary, bulging white growth. It was, as Callender's mind reluctantly accepted, a human being, naked, sprawled and caught in the branches, the thighs and buttocks upmost. The head, as in a medieval painting of some grotesque martyrdom, was hanging down from the broad and muscled shoulders, which twisted among outcrops of thorn, and though he could not see the face, by the straight fall of down-plunging reddish hair, Callender was able to identify the inert body of Count Casimiri.

He turned away in horror and heard the sound of his own voice calling out, shouting down the staircase outside the room, and a few moments later, the majordomo, Rinaldo, came running into the courtyard.

IT took the servants a full hour or so to disentangle the body from the thorn tree. Callender watched from the window of his room, and he was aware that at all the small, dark window loops across the courtyard there appeared pale glimpses of faces. He thought of Clara Casimiri and wanted to find her, but where she might be in all this rambling building was a mystery, and he remained watching as her father was brought down from the tree. He himself stood well back inside the window, as if he feared eyes peering from behind the black openings at the back of the balcony in the opposite wall. Suspicion, he realized, had become his habit in this household.

It was a painful process, even though the men armed themselves with axes and chopped down the lower branches that impeded their work. Then they shouted for ladders, which were eventually found somewhere, and wedged, rickety and lashed with thongs as they were, against the trunk of the tree. Sweating, two of them pulled off their velvet coats, and their hands and arms rapidly became streaked with blood as the thorns ripped their skin. They called for gloves, and old leather gauntlets were brought, but curses continued to echo up from the little courtyard as they labored to tug down the strange fruit. The body of the count became more torn as they pulled at the limbs. Long rips and scrapes, triangular tatters of skin, were made by the thorns along the back and thighs. Eventually, two interlacing branches were sawn off, and the count fell to the earth. Panting, the men allowed the body to lie there in a heap for some minutes, staring down. Then slowly, as if reluctant, one of them bent over and turned the body onto its back and straightened the limbs. Another one fetched his jacket and draped it like a loincloth over the genitals. They squatted down beside the corpse as if the end of their initiative had been reached.

One of them brought out a packet of cigarettes, and the blue smoke curled up into the dusty air, adding to smells of freshly broken wood and stale blood entrapped between the four walls.

This commonplace action somehow signaled an alteration in the nature of events, a dispensation from concentration, like a change of scene at the theater. Callender found that his mental processes were operating once more: the condition of passive spectatordom at a drama, perhaps created by the shock of the situation, had passed. He hurried out of his room and down the steep flight of stairs.

He made several misjudgments of direction, striking out along passages that proved to be blind alleys, once disturbing a frightened maid, another time causing a small white dog to start barking furiously. At last he found he had returned to the main staircase, regained the principal floor of the palazzo, and recognized the long, noble salon where he had first been introduced to the Casimiri.

The body of the count had preceded him thither. It had been laid outstretched on top of a long chest. There had been no time to cover it, and seen close up it was truly an object of horror, covered in deep scratches, some encrusted with blood, others mere rents as if the skin had been cured leather. The right eye seemed almost to have been torn out: it was hanging like a lump of jelly beside the socket, suspended by a fiber, and patches of the skin below the ribs were scraped almost raw.

There were sudden footsteps in the room, and the yellow-faced majordomo, Rinaldo, entered. He reached up and tore down a curtain from a window. The old brocade sent puffs of unclean dust into the air as it came down. Rinaldo shook it out and spread it over the body, pulling it up to hide the face. Callender found himself staring at Rinaldo, unable and unwilling to find anything to say. What absurd commonplace might be possible? Rinaldo stared back at him across the body of his employer, giving nothing away, his earthy skin stretched tightly over the cheekbones, so that Callender wondered if the majordomo was sick, and, looking down, saw that the man's hands were shaking.

A thought flashed into Callender's head. Supposing this were murder—supposing the count had not had an accidental fall. Why should the murderer (or murderers, for it would probably have required more than one person to tip the heavily built victim over the balustrade) have taken this course? Surely it would have been far safer to dispose of the body by tipping it into the water? The palazzo had the Grand Canal in front, and two small, dark tributaries at either side. But no, the count's body lay in broad daylight, caught in the branches for all to see.

His train of thought was broken when there was a sudden disturbance at the far end of the gallery, and a man came into the room, a man whom Callender recognized from the principessa's funeral. It was Marzano, unacknowledged successor to the doges, whom he had last seen at old Tanta's funeral.

"They sent for me," he said as he strode along the room, and to Callender's amazement Rinaldo fell on his knees.

"Thank God you have come, Excellency!"

Marzano looked down at the body of Count Casimiri for a few moments. His face and bearing gave nothing away. Then he turned to Callender. "Ah, yes, you are the Englishman looking after the principessa's documents. You were engaged by the count, I think."

"Yes, and I raised the alarm when I looked out of the window and saw his body in . . ." Callender was uncertain how to describe the horrifying picture that had met his eyes and continued, ". . . when I saw him in that grotesque position."

He supposed that this would be of some importance, that he might have to give some sort of evidence or make a statement. There must surely be some sort of formal inquiry into how the count had met his end, even if it was accidental.

But Marzano said coldly, "I am taking charge here now, upon the death of the head of the family."

It was undoubtedly a dismissal. Callender received it with a sense of shock, but he clearly had no choice and turned to leave. Marzano added, "Of course, your task is at an end for the moment, Signor Callender. You will regard all the matters here, whether to do with the principessa or with the Casimiri family, as absolutely confidential."

In the momentary pause that followed, they heard a woman's cry somewhere in the distance, sounding through the stone and marble depths of the building as a series of echoes, and with every resonance Callender knew in the depths of his heart something that his conscious mind was resisting. It was an expression of the most real and powerful emotion, but if he had to put a name to the passion expressed in that long, open-throated cry, he would not have called it grief. It reminded him of birdsong, of the blackbird's call in the early morning. If he had to put a name to it, he would have said it was a cry of joy.

Callender did not want to encounter the source of that sound. He backed away from the body, retreating slowly to the door, and went away without saying a word. As he left, Marzano and Rinaldo were saying something indistinct, but he thought he heard the words, "Fetch the old man," with an odd emphasis on *old*.

As he reached the foot of the staircase he heard a rustling sound behind him. A voice called after him softly, "Signor Callender!" and he turned to see Clara Casimiri, clinging to a marble post above him. She was pale and trembling, and her arms, bared by a loose robe, were actually shaking.

There seemed to be no gap in time, no hesitation at all, between the moment when Callender saw this and the moment when he had leapt up the steps and put his arms around her. He realized that her lips as he kissed them, and indeed her whole body as he clasped it, were actually quivering. They said nothing for a few moments but stayed together in an embrace that seemed out of time and place, as if they were the center of a world spinning wildly around them. Her trembling stopped, and he was certain that she was returning his urgency, but she pulled away and looked searchingly into his face. The remoteness and defensive formality that she had displayed in their meeting at the Accademia had vanished.

"Did you see—you know about my poor father?" she began.

"Yes," he said. "Yes, it's terrible, I'm so sorry," hearing and knowing these were trite things but unable to enunciate anything more, all other thoughts driven out of his mind by the kiss. She broke away and turned her head, looking into the shadows behind him. Callender suddenly knew with absolute certainty, had sensed it in Clara Casimiri as he held her, that this was a house built on danger and secrets, that it had harbored them for centuries. His next words were spoken out of an inner presentiment.

"Come out of here with me. I'll take you to the consulate. No one could touch you there."

Her eyes were frightened, huge, but she drew away a little and said, "No, no, I can't do that," and then added hastily, "They have sent for Antonio."

He had forgotten her fiancé, that feeble-looking specimen he had encountered at the funeral of the princess. He said urgently, "He's no good for you, I know it. Come with me. Now."

"It's all arranged," she answered reluctantly, and now she was peering about her like a fearful creature, as if someone might appear out of the recesses of the stairs and arches.

"That's absurd! That kind of arrangement belongs to the Middle Ages!"

He understood as if it had come to him in a lightning flash that her sketches in the Accademia, her adoption of old costumes, had been a way of expressing this: that her intended marriage belonged to the past and not to the present. Callender drew her further into the shadows but with a shock felt something soft brushing at his back, and turning round, he saw that they were in small antechamber of some sort. From hooks on the wall behind him were hanging old cloaks bunched together, and over them appeared a sight that made him pull her tightly to him: a bunch of white vacant faces staring out, surmounted by tattered plumes and wisps of horsehair.

"For the carnival," she whispered, seeing him looking upwards. "This is where they used to keep the carnival masks and cloaks. Of course, they haven't been used for years. The carnival is over, with everything else here."

He didn't answer but caught her again and kissed her. This time he undoubtedly felt a surging response in her flesh, but she pulled her mouth away from his, saying, "No, you must go now," and he released her reluctantly.

"Daniella told me she had spoken to you," she said. "And I was angry with her at first, but then I realized she had understood something not said aloud."

"Something passing between us, you and me?"

"I think so," and the way she studied his face made him think of Ursula's direct and open gaze. "But promise me," she said, "promise me you won't come here again," and now he could see tears in her eyes.

"No, I can't do that!" he said, but she said again, "Please, it would be unsafe for you," and now she seemed so intense that he said, "Very well, I promise."

"You give me your word?"

"I give you my word: I will only come to this place again if I think you are in danger. I just feel that's possible."

He scarcely knew why he had said this, staring at her across the few feet between them, which now seemed a huge gulf.

Clara looked at him, twisting her hands together, and said, almost despairingly, "Very well, but go now, just leave, quickly."

He tried to bridge the gulf, with words, at least. "Have you some reason to ask me to leave like this?" he said gently. "Any particular reason, I mean?"

"Yes!" she said forcefully, and then added, less certainly, "I . . . I can't say. I can't speak of it just now." She added urgently, "If I send you a message, it will be by Fiammetta Corradini or Daniella. Don't trust anyone else."

She turned and moved up the staircase, clinging to the banisters, her long gown trailing from step to step.

Revel Callender watched her go for a few moments, and then when she had vanished at the top of the staircase he turned and slipped down to the side entrance, which emerged out onto a shadowy, narrow *rio*. A small boat was sculling past. He hailed it and gave the boatman a few coins to take him to the Piazza San Marco, cursing himself all the way for his contamination by the world and his involvement with Helena Marino. "Clara's probably heard about it already. Even the gondolas gossip to one another, in this city."

"THERE will have to be legal formalities," said Barton. "From what you say, it sounds as if he fell from a balcony and unfortunately tumbled into the branches of the tree. It may have been a heart attack or something similar."

"He was naked," said Callender. "Would he have been out on the balcony in such a state?"

There was a pause. "Last night was very warm." Barton was rubbing his cheek with the end of his pencil, a blank sheet of paper lying before him, as if making up his mind how to begin something.

"Yes, but even so!"

Barton's bright, round eyes looked at Callender with an expression which the latter could not read. He said, "You seem to have been the first person to see the body, and may have to make an official statement, so you might prepare yourself for questions."

It had somehow not occurred to Callender, so much had he been drawn back into the past by the fabric and occupants of the Palazzo Casimiri, that a death should be attended by judicial business and investigation, but he now remembered that Venice was not some kind of floating pearly capsule suspended outside all limits, that it was actually part of the modern world, like Rome or even London. He recalled now seeing a *vaporetto* with *Polizia* marked along its side, and uniformed men climbing onto a landing stage as it moored. Yes, this was after all a city with laws and magistrates, and no doubt courts and prisons, modern places, not just the picturesque hellholes that lay on the wrong side of the Bridge of Sighs.

"I suppose the Casimiri family will inevitably be involved."

Barton said smoothly, "No doubt they will be inconvenienced as little as possible. There need not be much intrusion into their lives. These

accidents do happen, unfortunately. Drowning is, of course, the commonest form of accidental death here. If the count had fallen from a canalside window, now, that would not be considered terribly unusual."
He unlocked a drawer and took out a document which looked familiar.

"This was delivered to me from the Maloney family. They sent it to Sullivan, the banker, who put it into my hands."

Callender realized why he thought he had seen it before. It was a copy of the principessa's marriage contract.

"I've already had a look through it," said the consul. "There was an unusual provision: an allowance was paid, not only to the principessa for personal expenses, but to the head of the Casimiri family, as long as the principessa should reside under their roof. It looks as if the Maloneys were trying to guard against the poor thing's rejection, against her being returned to Ireland as unwanted goods, so to speak. Of course, it all lapsed with her death."

"I've seen it." Callender walked to the window and looked out at the midday haze over the canal. There was an unpleasant sulfurous smell. A cloud of midges arose, and he flapped them away, considering what to say next. What he said might be of immense significance, but in its way it would merely be an experiment, a kind of dress rehearsal for what he should say at the proper time to the proper authorities. Looking across the canal, he saw all kinds of small windows and entrances, like rat holes diving in and out of spongy stone, sunk upon weed-covered foundations that seemed almost like some natural growth. Who knew what might resound through these warrens, whose ears any sounds might reach?

Barton seemed to realize that Callender was weighing something in the balance. He leaned back in his chair, as if waiting. "Well?"

"Come out here with me, would you?"

"Oh, Lord, it stinks out there!" Nevertheless, Barton, as if he realized the purpose of the request, rose and came out to stand at Callender's side. It was midday, and there was no one on the water near them.

Callender spoke slowly and carefully. "The body was covered in wounds."

"That is as one would expect. It fell into a thorn tree, after all."

"Yes, it's true that the skin was covered in small scratches, the arms and legs, the face: even one of the eyes had been almost torn out. But I saw the body close to, after it had been taken down, before that man— the majordomo—"

"Rinaldo?"

"Yes, before Rinaldo covered it up." He turned away from the canal and inclined his head downwards so that he was looking the consul in the face, into the clever eyes in their round, monkeylike sockets. "Barton, there were other wounds."

"What do you mean?"

"Wounds that could not have been made by thorns. Around the mouth, deep into the lips. Several clean cuts, an inch or so across."

Barton stared at him, and his brown eyes grew larger with horror. "You can't be certain! Look here, Callender, if you're not sure of that, it would be better not to say anything. There would be no need at all to do so, not if you aren't absolutely certain of what you saw. After all, in the circumstances, anyone would have been shocked, it would be easy to be confused!"

That would be the easy path, the way that was being offered to him. The two men stared at each other, looking down different futures, different possibilities, depending on the outcome of what Callender might say next.

He said quietly, "They were stab wounds. I don't think I was mistaken."

Barton waited for a long moment, as if revolving possibilities in his mind. Then he said, "I think it would be a good idea if you moved to the consulate. The police can interview you here."

There was no good argument for resisting this course.

"I'll go to the Giudecca now and get my things sent over."

PIETRO stood uncertainly in the long attic room beneath the roof of Palazzo Casimiri. Three narrow truckle beds and one, much bigger but so battered it was sagging in the middle and all four legs were splayed out like those of an old dog, furnished the living quarters of the male servants. The aged bed, which had been in such a state of collapse it was deemed unsuitable even for a member of the Casimiri family, was the prerogative of the most senior servant, who was the majordomo, Rinaldo. Rinaldo, however, rarely graced it with his person, preferring to sleep downstairs, where he had put a mattress and some coverlets in a kind of nest created under the turning of a first-floor staircase. Pietro had too much pride to dream of sleeping in such a corner, just like some animal, but he knew why Rinaldo did so. The family bedrooms were on the floor above and the long gallery of the palazzo on the floor below. Movements, conversations, orders, all were close by, and Rinaldo was a prime eavesdropper. Of course, it was necessary for a good servant to keep a fairly close watch on the family in order to anticipate orders, but Rinaldo excelled at this. Sometimes it crossed Pietro's mind that Rinaldo got certain particular satisfactions from his silent and solitary watching.

The attic had been whitewashed at some time in the past, but the walls were reverting to flaking stone, and birds had nested in the gaps between the eaves and the tiles. The rough floor was unstained and splintered. Yet here and there were patches of luxury, bits and pieces "borrowed" from the family quarters—a fat red velvet cushion on one of the beds, a walnut clothespress, and beside the window hung one of the faded suits of livery, its gilt tassels tarnished and missing some of their threads. At the far end was a wall with a different surface, smoother and cleaner than the rest. Pietro looked nervously in its direction. That was where, he had heard, they would keep *"La Veglia."* He didn't know what it meant, but from the look on the face of the person who had told him, an intense, gloating smile, Pietro didn't want to keep that particular vigil, whatever it was.

Nevertheless, he was in a state of great uncertainty. Beneath his bed lay a bag which held his few possessions, and tied inside a slit in a corner of his pillow was a small canvas roll containing some money. All he had to do was to pick them up and leave the palazzo, and he would be far from this menacing place and the fearful sense that the darkness that reigned perpetually inside Palazzo Casmiri would soon be exposed to the light of day.

And who would get the blame? Who always got the blame? He hadn't wanted to do anything against the family, but now he was fearful. Since the dreadful death of the count, he had felt that he was being entangled in some deep game he did not understand.

Pietro was lifting his pillow to retrieve his savings when Matteo, one of the footmen, came into the room.

Pietro could tell by his face that Matteo was very scared indeed. Matteo crossed straight to his bed and began to roll his few clothes into a ball.

"We've got to get out of here!" he said urgently. "If they find out what happened—what really happened—then they'll come for us. God, I wish I'd never come here. And as for that—"

He nodded meaningfully in the direction of the very smooth, clean wall.

Pietro was resistant for the moment. "Why should they come for us? We're only servants."

"Because, if they need to find the murderers, they'll get us."

"Murder!"

"I saw the wounds, I tell you."

Pietro had worked for the Casimiri family for some years, yet he was still clutching on to hope. "Even if—why should we be fearful, if we're innocent?"

"Don't be a fool! Who else are they going to blame?"

Matteo wasn't from Venice. He was from Padua; he didn't have the strange lagoon dialect, nor the deference which might be taken for granted in a native-born Venetian. "Think about it, Pietro. No one could have broken into the palazzo, killed him, and thrown the body into the courtyard without anyone noticing!"

"Killed him? You're sure?"

Matteo thrust his face, urgent and sweating, into that of his fellow servant as he said, "I saw the body, close to, as Rinaldo and I were getting him down, and he'd been stabbed before he was thrown out into the yard. They won't be able to cover it up forever. It must have been someone in the house. And of course, it couldn't possibly have been any of the Casimiri—they are one of the oldest families in Venice! That's the way the world goes, believe me, my friend. Listen to me, Pietro, face reality, you must know your place here! Do you have any ancestors in the Golden Book? No. Can you afford to pay a lawyer? No, of course you can't!"

"But if we leave suddenly, won't they say we must be guilty, that's why we've run away?"

"Yes, and maybe we'll have to hide somewhere, maybe we'll have to leave Italy, but at least we'd be alive!"

He swung round and pointed to the end of the room. "Look, you've seen the sort of things Rinaldo took there—you must guess what that is for. If they search the place, no one's going to believe we didn't know anything about it. Come on, for God's sake." Matteo was tearing off his servant's uniform as he spoke and grabbing a change of clothes.

Pietro was galvanized into action. He drew out his knife and cut the canvas roll of money from his pillow, then took his bag from under the bed. He took out a shirt and trousers and pulled off the Casimiri livery. The two of them vanished through the door and down a back staircase. The velvet costumes lay on the attic floor in a patch of dusty sunlight like discarded fancy dress.

11

When Callender got back to his lodgings, he looked around at the faded curtains and the green-striped bed cover in his room, at the neutrality of it, the absence of any personality or history that could be read by the next occupant. Signora Amalia had cleaned the room and efficiently removed any trace of his indulgences.

He packed up his few possessions without much trouble. The heaviest thing was a box of law books, but those could be sent on after him. Then he went in search of his landlady. He was dreading this moment, sensing that she would be distressed, and was determined to say nothing about the death of Count Casimiri, remembering her superstitious fear at the very name.

Amalia was in the stone-flagged kitchen ladling pasta into a huge vat of boiling water. A fragrant smell of olive oil and herbs, along with a pleasant drift of cinnamon, reached his nostrils.

"Signora Amalia, I have to leave you," he said. "I'm sorry about this, but I have to go."

She was shocked and upset, wiping her hands on her big apron in agitation. "But, Signor Callender, you don't like it here? You don't like my food, perhaps? What is it, where are you going?"

"Signora, I'll explain another time, truly I will. I can't tell you now, but I'm moving into the British Consulate in the Quirinale."

This mollified her to some extent. "It is something official, then? You are not leaving for some other lodgings?"

"No, no," he soothed her. "I assure you, I would prefer to stay here. But I have been asked to help with . . . with some work there. I expect I will often have to work late, so it is better if I sleep there, too. Don't worry, I'll settle up the account to date," said Callender, "and I'll pay you for the room for another week."

He could manage it, just about, thanks to Miss Clementine Marshall and her fee.

Before he left, released from a long embrace by a tearful Amalia and furnished with a jar of her special cherries preserved in grappa, he remembered the message from Claude Monet. "Signora, I have to visit someone this afternoon," he said. "I'll call back for my bags later on."

Visiting the artist would be a trivial matter in comparison with what he had been through that morning at the Palazzo Casimiri, yet Revel wanted to be for a while in the company of someone who would see Venice though quite different eyes, someone who sought light and openness in this city full of narrow alleys and canals that twisted in and out like arteries carrying dark silts.

Callender took a small fast-sculled *sandolo* from San Marco to the Palazzo Barbara, where he saw some distance before they reached it that the main entrance and the grandiose landing stage were under water.

"*Acqua alta, signor,*" said the boatman, pulling up beside a quay, and Callender realized that Venice was being washed by the high tides of autumn.

He walked through several alleyways in what he presumed was the right direction, and found himself at what must be the rear entrance of the Palazzo Barbaro. Here he presented his compliments and, asking for Signor Monet, was invited to ascend into a reception room lined with gilded console tables. But after a few minutes instead of the painter, there appeared a female figure, and he recognized Mme Monet, stiff and dark clad, a woman with eyes that must once have had laughter lines around them but were now sad and somber as they gazed at him.

"M. Callender, what did you wish to see my husband about?"

Revel felt embarrassed. Clearly, Monet had not told his wife about this business, whatever it might be.

"I'm sorry, Madame, I don't know. I received a note asking me to call on him: that is all I can tell you."

"He took out his easel this morning, just along to the left, where there is another entrance onto the Grand Canal, a smaller one. I think you will find him there still. He wants to capture the light on the water at noon, when the sun is at its highest."

"Thank you, madame."

She seemed preoccupied, melancholic.

The tide had not reached to the top of this small flight of steps at the side entrance, and there, perched as if marooned on a desert island, the water lapping at his feet, Callender saw a black outline shimmering in the vaporous heat. Drawing nearer, he recognized the bulky figure of the artist, wearing a straw Panama hat and seated before an easel so that his view was angled down the Grand Canal towards the dome of Santa Maria della Salute on Dorsoduro, which floated a pale creamy mauve in the center of their vision above opalescent reflections in tints of violet and pale turquoise. Immediately to their left, the reddish brown poles in front of the main landing stage of the Barbaro were streaked a bright viridian green with algae and slime. Looking at the canvas, Callender saw them reflected there, in fresh, glistening strokes, shimmering downwards, and wondered how the surface of the water was somehow present and indicated, yet transparent at the same time.

"M. Monet?"

Callender felt somewhat awkward at interrupting the artist's concentration, but after all, he reasoned, Monet had written to him and wanted to speak to him. "M. Monet? I'm Revel Callender."

The old shoulders gave a start. "Oh, forgive me, M. Callender. I was quite lost. I was trying to capture that pattern of shadows there, see, like the colors of lilac branches almost, on the surface of the water . . ."

"Sir, your shoes . . ."

"Good God! I hadn't noticed. Perhaps I should move my easel." The water was swirling around the artist's feet, and seaweed was clinging to the sole of one shoe.

"I think the tide is going down now, sir."

Monet laughed, his mouth still red and zestful above his long white beard. "We should retreat for the moment, anyway, in this heat. Yes, I do want to speak to you. Would you help me to pick up my things?"

Callender was impressed at the methodical way in which the artist carefully cleaned his palette and brushes and put them into cases. Together, they folded up his stool and easel. Monet lifted the canvas himself as Callender carried the rest of the paraphernalia and they entered the Palazzo Barbara, where the artist asked a servant to get it all carried up his apartments.

"Come, there is a small bar at the end of the *calle* here. We can relax there."

It was quite a luxurious little place, intended for the well-heeled visitors who frequented this stretch of the canal, with a fine array of liqueurs behind the bar. Monet ordered a bottle which turned out to be a good champagne, misted with condensation on the green sides of the bottle. "I enjoy being rich," he said to Callender, unabashed, as he lifted the glass of white and gold froth to his mouth. "I am not ashamed to admit that in the past I have been very poor, and I like the good things now that I can afford them."

"For myself, I hope the good things are still to come," said Revel, and the artist smiled. "Excellent. I am glad you are not one of those pious Englishmen who hate the pleasures of life. Now, I wanted to talk about something not at all enjoyable, I'm afraid."

Revel waited, sipping at the champagne which was chill and fizzing in his mouth.

"I understand that you give some assistance to people in difficulties."

"How did you—?"

"Ah, some English visitors have been speaking of you. A young lady, particularly."

Revel immediately remembered Clementine Marshall and her trailing companion, Miss Tenbaker. No doubt they had whispered their breathy contributions to the miasma of gossip spreading along the canals.

"Our family has suffered a terrible event in Paris. When I say 'our family,' I mean Alice's relatives, but I am very concerned on her behalf. Her health is not good, M. Callender, and what happened in the Rue de la Pépinière has been very distressing."

The artist turned away and stroked his beard, a nervous gesture that made Revel realize that he was evidently finding it difficult to continue. This must be the business that Helena Marino had been speaking about, the gossip about the Monets which had traveled from Paris. Something about a very lurid murder? Not the sort of thing one would have expected at all. He tried to recall the details. Best not to let the old man know that his family affairs were the talk of Venice.

"Ah, perhaps you could tell me something about it, sir? If it is not too distressing for you."

Monet took a long sip of his wine, set the glass down, and said reluctantly, "Very well, I must do that, I know. A few months ago, in June, Alice's brother-in-law, Auguste Rémy, was found dead in his bedroom. He had a mansion in Rue de la Pépinière in Paris."

There was a pause. Callender knew what must come next, had heard it from Helena Marino, but he thought it prudent to feign ignorance and tried to project sympathetic quizzicality. He appeared to succeed, for Monet explained, "It wasn't a natural death, I'm afraid, though he was an old man. He had been stabbed, many times. The police have been investigating the matter, but my wife wants to know what is going on in Paris and how the investigation is likely to turn out. She is fretting here in Venice. Auguste's widow, Cecile, is Alice's favorite sister."

Callender had a premonition of what would follow. "And you are telling me this, sir, because—?"

"Because I want someone trustworthy to go to Paris and let us know how the situation is developing. And you, I understand, are an English lawyer, a friend of the consul here—you would be objective in this matter, dispassionate as the English always are."

Not always, thought Callender. He said aloud, "So you want me to take a trip to Paris? Acting on your behalf?"

"Yes, yes, just a brief visit, and then you would return and report back to us here, so it need not disturb your stay in Venice much. I understand you have handled matters that require great discretion concerning ladies' reputations. Alice is very sensitive to . . . to family matters being brought into the light . . . unnecessarily."

"I understand." Probably it was the old, old story: The murdered Auguste had been involved with a woman, and perhaps there was a jealous rival, a youngster, no doubt, who had no longer been able to restrain himself. Auguste might not have been a young man, given that the Monets themselves were middle-aged, but still, in matters of passion, the French were notoriously unceasing, so that probably hadn't made any difference.

He thought carefully about the situation. On the one hand, it meant leaving Clara Casimiri for a few days, but after all, she had her brother to protect her. And also that little fiancé Prepiani, though he would not be much good in a scrap. Nevertheless, after he had considered carefully, he did not feel there would be much risk in her position, and besides, such a mission would get him away from the threatening atmosphere of Venice, away from all entanglements. It was, in chess terms, the knight's move, the sideways leap that would take him out of danger. The thought of Clara tugged at his mind, but he made himself put reason before feeling.

Accepting, he was agreeably surprised when the artist offered him a very generous fee. "But of course, M. Callender. I expect to receive a fair price for my pictures, and to make similar arrangements for those who do me a service."

12

The easel was set up with a direct view of the Doge's Palace, the gondola having taken the artist early in the morning to the island of San Giorgio Maggiore. He took folded easels, which stood up in the boat like some strange scaffolding outlined against the dawn, and attracted curiosity from a few fishing-boat boys who were already at work coiling ropes. He had the boat moored against the quay: This painting would be from close to the water level, in the same way as he had worked on the Normandy coast where he had braved the waves and the spume, experiencing the elemental with his body as well as his eyes. Claude Monet prepared his palette carefully, squinting out with his troubled vision towards the glimmering expanse of water and stone.

The light was sweet this morning, and the distant expanse of pink marble was wrapped in a pale bluish haze so that it took on the tints of amaranth or foxglove, yet the fine, emergent day already appeared in the foreground as gleams of buttery-yellow sunshine on the reflective ripples of water. From his position here, the column topped by that absurd yet magnificently triumphant Venetian winged lion would be on the left of the composition. The wall beyond it was already a mass of jeweled amethyst light. The Bridge of Straw on the Riva degli Schiavoni was just visible to the right of the Doge's Palace. Beyond the Schiavoni he did not care to think. There, he knew, lay the prisons, the hellholes of the Most Serene Republic, places where men could rot and die without ever seeing the light in perpetual imprisonment, worse than age, worse than blindness, even than this malign obscuring of sight which was descending on him. Leave them out of the picture, or swallow them up in a narrow pool of indigo, which would darken a patch of the canvas.

As the day advanced, movement began along the façade opposite him: distant figures were strolling up and down. The pale dresses of the women and dark clothes of the men were small, mothlike creatures floating behind the arches, teeming like ants across the bridge, and along the quayside slid the thin shapes of gondolas, black and purple in the shadows.

Gradually, the seaborne traffic passing between the painter and the shore became more and more frequent, till at last, exasperated by the continual flitting back and forth of watercraft, little skiffs, chugging *vaporetti*, he abandoned his work for the day.

That afternoon, he and Alice walked in the Piazza San Marco like any tourists. She seemed happier and was wearing a new blouse with long, pleated ruffles down the front, he noticed. "From Fortuny. I went shopping with Madame Hunter this morning."

"It's charming." And she was wearing her favorite hat, set with tall, curving lyrebird feathers. Alice had always loved fashionable clothes: before her first husband, Ernest, had lost all his money, she had a wardrobe worth a fortune, all from the finest couturiers in Paris. Then, after Ernest's bankruptcy, after Alice had fled to be with Monet, almost every item she possessed had been sold, including those grand, trailing dresses. He pushed away an uneasy memory of the two women: his first wife, Camille, and her rival, Alice, who had come to live in their house when Camille was already sick, though she could still go out of doors sometimes. The two women had only one decent dress between them. It had been Alice's. He remembered her saying, "If you insist on going out, Camille dearest, you can wear my dress," and his heart turned over as he recalled the look on Camille's face. "Thank you, Alice," she had said with dignity. "Yes, I do want to go into the village."

That seemingly innocent statement contained its own riposte. Alice hadn't liked going into Vétheuil. The locals knew that she was living with the Monets and suspected her role in the household. Some made a point of saying, *"Bonjour, Mme Monet,"* to Camille, ignoring Alice.

Looking at Alice now, as she gave a street vendor a few lire for a packet of corn and tossed it to the pigeons who fanned around her in a blur of pink and gray, he realized that her reception in Vétheuil must have hurt Alice badly. She had such an impossible contradiction in her nature: passionate feelings combined with a longing for respectability. Yes, she had been through a hard time, and he feared that worse was to come. The doctors had not been optimistic about her present state of health. They feared an illness of the blood, and her pallor and exhaustion were so unfamiliar, so unlike the Alice of old, who had always been a bustling center of energy, that Monet suspected their diagnosis was correct. He felt a tenderness towards her that he had not sensed for many years, not since their days of youthful poverty.

They wandered through the piazza to where the two columns stood on the *Molo*, the quayside looking out to the Adriatic, where the Venetian argosies and warships had returned from far expeditions to pour in their silks and spices and taxes and tributes as if the city were a great basin to be filled to the brim with treasure. The two columns looked out to sea, one bearing the winged lion whose outline he had painted that morning, and another which had not come within the framework of the picture, with a figure of a man and some sort of creature at his feet: he peered up but could not make out what it was.

"San Teodoro, signor." A man in a cream suit made of some cheap material with an absurd purple and white tie had approached them. He was evidently one of the touts with which the city abounded, yet it seemed pleasant, made it a holiday, just to do the ordinary tourist things, to hold conversation with a man such as this, a man so different from the socialites who tried to scrape their acquaintance at Mrs. Hunter's. This man's greed would be simple, straightforward, and innocent in comparison.

The newcomer was thin-faced, rapacious looking, yet he bent towards Alice in a deep and graceful bow. He assessed her with the quickest of glances and addressed them in French. "I see you are looking at the column of Saint Theodore, Monsieur, Madame."

"Is that what it's called?" Alice seemed pleased at the distraction. "And who was Saint Theodore, pray?"

"Ah, he was a wonder, even here where there are so many. He is the oldest saint of Venice, you know, older even than Saint Mark himself! The first patron of the city, a Greek saint."

"What is that creature there?" asked Monet, peering up to the top of the column where he thought he could make out a scaly tail.

"Ah, well now, a lot of ignorant people would tell you that is a dragon, but that is not at all true, for it was Saint George who killed the dragon. No, that, *monsieur et madam*, that is a crocodile! You see, I am a reliable guide, I know things, I know the history." The man smiled widely, showing a mouthful of yellow and brown teeth, but there was a genuine pride in his expression, pride that seemed to encompass both himself and Saint Theodore. "This was where they kill people," he said.

"Kill people?"

"Yes, sir, in the old days, they execute criminals here. And then they leave their heads just on this spot, at the bottom of Saint Theodore's column. Imagine it!"

Alice said rapidly, "Claude, let's go back." She was holding her scarf up to her mouth. Damn it, why had the man embarked on these horrors? As Alice turned hurriedly away, Monet pressed a few coins into the man's hand and went after her, hearing the voice following him, calling out, "But sir, it's history. Just old things, that's all."

The two French visitors did not give a backwards glance, and the Venetian stood staring after them. He saw two more middle-aged tourists, overdressed in heavy clothes. But the man had been interesting. His eyes were a warm brown, like chestnut, and though there was the kind of film over them that old people got sometimes, they had been very intent, like the sailors who came back after a long voyage spent watching the horizon as far as the eye could see. A man developed a particular look that way. The woman seemed aged, her face lined, with a big square jaw, a really tough sort, if you asked him. You never got much out of people like that. He had smelled illness near her.

The Venetian shivered. His suit was thin, and a chilly wind was blowing off the sea.

13

They were in Theseus Barton's office at the consulate. The air indoors was hot and humid; electric fans were turning rhythmically overhead with a slow drone.

"I myself have become acclimatized," Barton had said as he switched the fans on, "but they really are a necessity here for some people."

The commissioner of police who sat opposite Callender was presumably one such, for he had been perspiring heavily when he entered and was still passing a white handkerchief across his brow. He wore an elaborate blue uniform with silver buttons and epaulettes. Beside him a clerk sat with pencil and notepad ready.

"Signor Callender? I must formally state that I am investigating into the death of the late Count Roberto Casimiri. I understand that you saw the body and raised the alarm."

"Yes, that is quite correct. I had been working for the count, in a confidential capacity."

"What was that, may I ask?"

Callender hesitated but then decided it would do no harm to give the bare facts. "I was working on some papers in English. That is all I am prepared to say."

"Quite, quite, that is perfectly acceptable." The commissioner gestured towards his clerk, who duly made some notes. "Please proceed, Signor Callender."

"Yes, well, I suppose you want me to describe . . ." What would a British policeman have expected in the circumstances? No guidance seemed to be forthcoming as to what was required here. The commissario and his clerk seemed poised to listen intently.

"I was in the palazzo, going through the papers in a small room which overlooks a courtyard. At about midday, I got up and went to the window and I saw . . . something hanging in the branches of a tree in the courtyard."

The commissario's eyes seemed to be bulging. Was Callender imagining it, or was there an odd flicker of the eyelids. The man said nothing.

"It was a body."

"Did you recognize the person?"

"Yes, but not immediately, you understand." He found he was reliving the moment, could see again that white spreadeagled corpse, feel the midday heat that had poured directly down into the yard. The spittle seemed to have dried in his mouth.

"D'you want a drink?" Barton had noticed something; he was pouring from a decanter of water and pushed the glass over to him.

"Yes, as a matter of fact, my mouth is rather dry. Thanks, Barton." He took a sip and started again. "Commissario, the body was that of Count Casimiri."

"Were there any other persons present?"

The clerk was taking notes.

"No." He didn't mention his feeling that there had been faces moving behind the balcony opposite his window. It had been a fleeting impression, after all; he couldn't be certain of anything.

"And what action did you take, signor?"

"Well, nothing, immediately, though I called out, and then some servants came and . . ." He sought for a word that would euphemize the horrible process of tearing the count from the impaling hooks of the thorn tree. ". . . detached the body."

"Did you see any other persons while you were in the Palazzo Casimiri?"

"I saw Rinaldo, the majordomo. And somebody else came, after the body had been taken into the *salone*. It was Signor Marzano."

The name seemed to introduce a new atmosphere. Barton stood up and turned to gaze out of the window, so that his expression could not be observed. The commissario glanced across at the clerk, who had stopped making notes and lifted up his pen.

"Prince Marzano," he corrected Callender. "Yes. Well, I think that is all I need to ask you. The count evidently died as the result of an unfortunate fall. A statement will be prepared for you to sign in due course, and thank you for your help."

The clerk was putting away his documents, the commissario standing up and extending a hand. There was something more Callender had to tell them, and this was the moment to do so; he knew it. Otherwise, he could say nothing, sign the statement, and have a quiet life. Barton was turning back towards him, staring across the room, giving a slight shake of the head as if to deter him from any further comments.

"There is something else," said Callender quickly, before he could regret opening his mouth.

The commissario paused, his heavy mouth open, but he said nothing.

"I saw the count's body after it had been taken down from the tree."

"Yes, you have already said that, Signor Callender."

"There were marks on it. Not just scratches from the thorns. Cuts. Clean cuts, around the lips."

The commissario opened and closed his mouth several times. Then he said, an idea evidently coming to his rescue, his eyes blinking rapidly, "Shaving cuts, no doubt. Well, you have a very observant eye, Signor Callender, thank you, but they need not trouble us."

"They weren't shaving cuts!" said Revel scornfully.

Barton intervened. "I am sure we can leave such matters to the police, Callender."

Callender could not prevent himself saying something, although he sensed at the time that his words might as well be uttered into thin air. Yet there was something fateful about the way he felt compelled to speak them. "Someone else would have seen the wounds at the same time as myself."

"Ah, that would have been Rinaldo and the others! One cannot place any reliance on the evidence of servants!" The commissario was pompously scornful, a stimulus which irritated Callender still further into his pursuit of truth.

"Not just the servants," he said angrily. "Your Prince Marzano, too!" He would have mentioned the doctor, but he thought Marzano would carry more weight.

But the name seemed to fall into a deep well. It was almost as if he had not spoken, except that no one moved for a long, silent moment.

"A few minor marks are not going to be of any significance, I am sure," said Barton eventually, and the sigh of relief given by the policeman was audible. "Thank you, Commissario," the consul continued. "If you would be so kind as to send the statement here for Signor Callender's signature, there will be no difficulty. I am sure Signor Callender was mistaken in what he saw."

As soon as they had gone, Barton turned to Callender. "Are you mad? Do you realize what you were implying?"

Revel felt an anger that surprised him. He had never thought of himself as a soldier for truth, nor did he want to be. It seemed to him that he been put in this position, and some people were trying to distort the experience which he had undergone.

"I don't know if those cuts killed him; quite possibly not," he said, "but he was attacked before he was thrown into the thorn tree. Why even the British consul should be willing to go along with some story about an accident, I have no idea, but I know what I saw."

Barton's small face, normally so good-tempered, was distorted by open anger. He was almost hissing at Callender as he said, "It is not our business, as foreigners, to meddle in something that concerns only Venetians. Don't expect the consulate to protect you if you won't cooperate!"

Callender was stunned. He felt as if he were caught in a mesh, threatened, yet unable to discern where the threat might come from. "Are you warning me about something?"

Barton didn't answer directly. He sat down again and rubbed his hands over his face. "Well, we must do our best at the moment, I suppose," he said. "You will spend the night here, at any rate. Have you had your luggage sent over from your lodgings?"

"I asked them to bring it here, but I don't know if it's arrived."

Barton summoned the turbaned, blue-eyed servant, who seemed to act as general factotum. "No, Signor Callender's luggage has not arrived," he pronounced confidently. "I'll go personally to the Giudecca and fetch it for you, signor."

Callender suddenly felt that he desperately needed some fresh air. "It's all right. I'll go myself. The walk will do me good."

"Very well," said Barton. "Go by water if you like. It will be quicker."

Callender suddenly had a longing to feel solid ground under his feet.

He left the consul unceremoniously, and as he walked out, the turbaned servant followed and opened the outer door for him. As he passed the man, he caught a murmur so low that he might almost have imagined it.

"Return before dark, signor. Venice is not always safe at night."

Startled, Callender turned to stare at the man, but his face was impassive, and he glided away into the depths of the consulate.

Callender did not return straightaway to his lodgings to collect his bags. He stopped at a narrow little bar that stretched back from a small square. There were no tourists around, and the few faces that looked at him from the gloomy interior all looked like locals, probably workmen, judging by their clothes. He ordered a grappa and drank the fiery, clear spirits down in one gulp. He gestured for another, conscious that he hadn't eaten and that he was beginning to feel light-headed, but the grappa seemed to settle his turmoil, a mixture of the aftermath of shock and his anger at the travesty of an investigation that seemed to be going on. The second grappa brought hunger, and the bar was able to supply a plate of *fritto misto*, which satisfied his stomach. The men around him were talking in a relaxed, jovial way, but they were speaking in the Venetian dialect, so that he could just occasionally pick up the gist of what they were saying and sometimes couldn't follow it at all. They brought out a pack of cards, and one of them began to deal out hands around an iron-topped table.

Callender wanted to stay there, in that ordinary world with these quiet, good-tempered people who had presumably just done a good morning's work and could go home to their wives in the evening and continue their lives unperturbed. For a moment he toyed with a fantasy of asking them if he could work with them, on whatever manual labor it was that they did—bricklaying, maybe, judging by the red dust on their clothes. Was another life ever truly possible?

Sighing, he knew there were things he had to do, and began walking towards Saint Mark's Square to get a *vaporetto* to the Giudecca.

The narrow *calle* in which Signora Amalia's premises were situated seemed full of people, and at first he could not make out what was happening at all. As well as people in ordinary clothes thronging the street, there were two policemen at the entrance from the San Marco side. He went up to them and was barred from going through.

"But I live there—at least, I did," he said, pointing to the house.

"*Passaporto, signor?*" One of the policemen was being officious, holding out his hand to stop Callender.

He was relieved that he had his passport in his jacket pocket and brought it out for the official, who glanced at it and then reluctantly let Callender through.

Lying on the cobbles, just beyond the police barrier, was a young man. There could be no doubt about the cause of death in this case: blood flowing from a wound in the man's chest had poured out over the stones, making in slow runnels for the channel in the middle, creating a pattern of brilliant scarlet lines that seemed as random and jagged and violent as lightning.

Callender stood in the middle of the *calle*, stunned by the sight.

Suddenly an agitated figure popped out of the back entrance of the house like a scared jack-in-the-box. It was Amalia, her hands twisting in her white apron, her plump face marked with tears and shock.

"Ah, Signor Callender—there you are! To think, if only you had been here—the thieves who must have attacked this poor young man—it was just his evil chance to come out then—maybe a few minutes later, if he had only seen you . . ."

"What are you talking about, Amalia?" Callender managed to say, standing bewildered, with the harsh smell of blood in his nostrils.

"He was coming to see you, signor. He was bringing you something."

She held out something carefully, holding it between finger and thumb. It was a white envelope addressed in large flowing handwriting: "Signor Revel Callender." Wet and sticky bloodstains were plastered over it.

"He came in and asked for you, and I said you weren't here. He was going to leave it with me, but then he said no, he'd wait for you. I heard the commotion outside and ran out. I picked this up from the ground."

Revel stared uncomprehendingly. Then gingerly, avoiding the bloody areas as much as he could, he opened the envelope. A neat packet fell out, with an elegant leather box inside. He opened it, wondering, and then realized what it contained: his engraved bookplates, ordered that very morning, before all the business at the Palazzo Casimiri and the consulate. That very morning was a time that seemed so long ago that it belonged to another era, let alone another day.

There was a loose bookplate in the envelope, and a letter as well.

"Esteemed Signor, I beg to inform you that a small error was made in our account this morning and to present you with the correct bill. Regretfully, as you will see, it comes to a trifle more than the sum which you gave us this morning, as we have had to pay the engraver his charges. I would be most grateful if you would please settle your account with my son, by whom I send this message and your bookplates. Your obedient servant, Antonio Gozzi."

Callender sighed, folded up the letter, and stepped over to the body. He gazed down at the dead face of the bookseller's son. It was drained of all energy and wearing an expression only of some shock or surprise. What lay in the mind at that last instant? For a few moments, he contemplated his own death, and wondered how it would come.

Then he turned to Amalia. "It was nothing valuable, after all. Just someone bringing me some items I had ordered, with a bill to settle. I suppose he waited for the money."

"*Si,* Signor Callender, he stood waiting outside the door for a while with the envelope under his arm—and then I heard him crying out, but all I saw were shadows on the wall, before I ran out into the street."

Revel stared at the bookplates in his hand.

"Perhaps they thought he was carrying something of value," said Amalia sadly, looking down at them.

It seemed utterly ridiculous that a man had died for these, or for the few coins which were probably all the boy had in his pockets.

There was something strange about the loose plate. He hadn't noticed it before, but it was not the design he had chosen. Quickly, he flipped through the ones in the box. Yes, they showed his chosen engraving of the pillars, and had his own name printed upon them. But this loose bookplate bore the design of a shield, and on it a helmeted figure astride a horse. One arm was jabbing at a coiled creature on the ground whose fanged head reared up.

Callender had the sense of taking part in a maddening dialogue, where he could not understand the messages coming from the other side. He had seen this bookplate, with this very design upon it, somewhere else. Casting his mind back, he recalled the claustrophobia-inducing little room in the Palazzo Casimiri and the principessa's turbulent confusion of possessions. There had been a prayer book with an ivory cover, and inside that . . . yes, Revel had a very good eye for these artistic details. He could visualize the elaborate engraved image now, with one word below it: the family name.

This was their bookplate. It was recognizable enough. The shield of the Casimiri family, which he had seen so recently borne on their funeral barge: the knight slaying the dragon.

★   ★   ★

CALLENDER was allowed to pass through the police barrier at the end of the *calle* after assuring them that he could be contacted at the British Consulate. The policemen seemed to accept that he was an innocent visitor caught up in all this and asked him merely a few questions which were easy enough to answer. Yes, the boy had happened to be delivering a packet to him; no, he could not think of any explanation for the killing: a feud, perhaps? But he knew nothing at all about the boy or his family, apart from the fact that he had bought a book from them, a book by an English poet, and at the same time had ordered these with his own name upon them.

He did not show them the bloodstained bookplate of the Casimir, which he had slipped back in the envelope. Callender was uncertain why he did this, except that he thought somehow about Clara, and how she might become involved if the police went to the Palazzo Casimiri. But he did fetch the copy of Shelley's play which he had bought from Gozzi from his room and gazed at the book for a few minutes, as if it were the answer to some riddle, before putting it into his pocket.

When the police let him pass, he walked to the quay on the piazza and took a *vaporetto* to the Accademia landing stage near the consulate. There was a small queue waiting for the boat, a few who looked like Venetians, with shopping baskets or business suits, and a bunch of German tourists. Still in a state of semishock at his closeness to death, he boarded the boat, watching as the sailors clanked the chains to cast off.

Was that a figure running along the quayside, a man with a hand shading his eyes, peering at the passengers? Some instinct made Callender slip into the saloon among a knot of German tourists. Some instinct also made the back of his neck prickle, and he hurried over the bridge when he disembarked. Fortunately, he was among a party of art lovers bound for the Accademia. The doors of the consulate were open, and he slipped in and stood within the shadow inside, watching out, feeling that he was somehow becoming part of the life of Venice with this mysterious tension, nerve-racking though it was. It seemed to him this was a city of eyes gleaming in alleyways and black or sepia shadows passing behind galleries.

The art lovers had all disappeared, and so had the few other passengers who had disembarked with him. An old woman with a straw basket had been swallowed up by the porch of a church, and only a schoolboy in a neat sailor suit and boater was walking across his line of vision. Callender was beginning to relax the instinctive defenses aroused in him by proximity to murder when he jumped at a touch on his shoulder.

It was Barton's servant, the man who wore a turban, yet had light blue eyes that suggested that he was a Turk of mixed blood.

"Damn it, man!"

"I'm sorry, sir. Please come further inside."

Was the gesture merely inviting, or was there a suggestion of urgency? The door to Theseus Barton's office was open, and the consul swung round on his chair as Callender stood in the doorway. He was beginning to feel the aftereffects of shock and leaned against the doorpost. Barton's big, round monkey eyes were full of astonishment as he looked at him.

"What is it, Callender? Zayed, get some brandy, will you?"

But Callender was recovering. Waving away the glass which the turbaned servant swiftly produced from a fretted ebony wall cupboard, he said lightly enough, "I seem to be prone to finding dead bodies in your city, Barton. Perhaps for all our sakes I should have stayed in England."

"Why, what has happened?"

"A man was stabbed to death—a boy, I mean. It was at my lodgings, or rather, in the street outside."

Callender walked across the room as the consul uttered an exclamation, and lifted one of the blinds. The window was on the street side: All looked deserted except for where a woman was flinging out some liquid from an upper story.

Barton got up from his chair and said anxiously, "But you were not involved in any way in this, surely?"

"No, no, of course not."

Barton seemed to relax. "It was a complete stranger, then."

"Well, not exactly, no."

"What do you mean by that?" The consul's tone had become tense.

"I don't know his name, but I had seen him before, in a bookshop. He was bringing me these." Without thinking, Callender withdrew the packet and held it out. Barton took it and saw the bloodstains, smeared and drying but unmistakable. With a horrified expression, he took out the contents.

"That crest—"

"Is the shield of the Casimiri family. Yes, I know. I can't explain it. The rest are exactly as I ordered them."

Barton sank back into his chair, frowning and troubled. There was a silence. Callender fancied he could smell a sickly scent of stale blood arising from the packet of bookplates.

Finally, Barton said slowly, "I think you should go away from Venice, for a while at any rate. The principessa's papers will keep. Leave Venice for a few days while the matter is being investigated, and in the meantime I will make whatever statements are necessary to the police on your behalf. If they want to see this envelope and all the contents, we'll assume there was some confusion in the bookshop, and somehow a different bookplate became mixed up with yours."

Callender burst out, "But that would be an absurd coincidence!"

Barton looked up with his round, brown eyes and said in a tone that was soft yet somehow unanswerable, "Many strange coincidences do happen and must be accepted."

"Very well, if that is your considered advice." *He knows Venice,* thought Callender. *He must know what is acceptable here in the way of judicial fictions.* He said aloud, "As it happens, I have some business in Paris."

"Not a certain lady whom we met at the Hunters'?"

So his adventure with Helena Marino had not been overlooked, but his feelings for Clara Casimiri had remained hidden. That was the way he wanted things to remain. Callender said calmly, unembarrassed, "No, I understand she will be staying in Venice for the autumn."

Barton said, "Well, whatever your concerns there, I think you should leave today. There is a train at five o'clock—you will be in Paris by tomorrow morning. Send me your address, and I'll keep you informed of any developments."

IN the consulate boat, on the way to the station, Callender looked up as they passed the Grand Canal frontage of Palazzo Casimiri. Black banners hung from the windows and were draped over the balcony. The palazzo was in silent mourning for its master, and there was no sign of any of the inhabitants.

At the post office near the station, Callender placed a call through to the Hotel Danieli. "I have to go away for a few days—I'm so sorry. Thank you for that wonderful night."

Her voice was slow and amused. "And where do you have to go, my prince? Tell Helena everything."

"To Paris, and not for pleasure, I'm afraid."

"I won't ask any indiscreet questions. Here am I, alone in the Danieli, waiting for some boring relations to descend on me! They insisted on holidaying in Venice. But listen, while I am here, you could borrow my little house in Paris. It's in Montmartre, Rue de la Galette, right in the artists' *quartier*. You know, I have the most artistic tastes!"

"Thank you, darling, but I've booked into a hotel. It's a most generous offer, though." It was, and he might well have accepted, but he didn't want any complications. He told himself that this was because he was going to Paris on business, but had to admit, as he put the telephone down, that perhaps it might have something to do with Clara Casimiri.

He looked down at the receiver for a few moments, then picked it up again. There was one final call he had to make. Yes, the operator had a number for Doctor Albrizzi. A rapid and brief conversation followed, ending with Albrizzi saying, "You are wise to leave the city, Signor Callender."

14

Ippolito Albrizzi was standing in the office of the commissioner for police under the slow-moving electric fan. His muscles were taut and his shoulders tense. Now that he had decided not to play the game anymore, the old Venetian game of deception and intrigue, the doctor had found a new strength and anger.

Perhaps his change of heart owed something to his experiences in the New World.

"I tell you, Commissario, I saw the body. So did Signor Callender. He told me so. And the count was murdered."

The heavy eyes of the police chief looked up from the other side of the desk. "He fell over the balcony. That is the official conclusion. As for Signor Callender, the evidence of a foreigner must be treated with suspicion, and in any case, I understand he is leaving Venice."

Albrizzi felt his impatience growing.

"And the wounds on the body?"

"Lacerations, merely." The commissario's eyes were steady, but his mouth was jerking slightly under his mustaches. He added, "I advise you, *Dottore*, to accept this conclusion."

Albrizzi felt a new surge of anger. He leaned over the desk. "Count

Casimiri was stabbed! There were wounds to his face—I was a witness, I tell you!"

He expected bluster, perhaps denial.

The commissario said nothing. He took a sip of the grappa set before him in a tiny glass with wet, misty sides, held precariously in his meaty fingers. Albrizzi had already refused to join him in this autumnal corrective against the heavy, damp air that filled the building.

"Winter is on the way," the head of police observed as if this were a perfectly ordinary conversation, though the doctor had the feeling that the commissario's mind was working away busily. Perhaps the man was not as stupid as he looked.

"Damn the weather!" But Albrizzi sat down and felt his anger subsiding. *I'll go straight to the point,* he thought, and said, "I will take the matter further—to Rome, if necessary. Marzano cannot influence promotions in this city forever."

It was as if speaking the name aloud had broken a spell. The policeman put down his glass with a wet click onto the mahogany desk, damp with the sea air like every other surface in this city. He was slow and ponderous, but his thoughts seemed to have reached a conclusion.

"To Rome, eh?" He leaned towards Albrizzi, his heavy stomach rolling at the waist where it pressed against the edge of the desk.

"Yes."

"Our difficulty," he continued, "is that if the count was murdered, then there must have been a murderer. Or murderers."

Albrizzi pressed on. "Probably there were two of them. It would have taken some strength to get the body down into the courtyard."

The commissario spelled it out. "And the murderers would in all probability have been members of the household."

The doctor was not deterred.

"You will investigate on that basis, then? You will not simply call it an accident and close your file?"

The commissario sighed heavily. "No, *Dottore*. I assure you. I will consider whether this is a case of unlawful homicide. And if it is, then I will find the murderers."

Albrizzi left the police station feeling that perhaps he had achieved something, some small step towards justice. But as he walked out towards San Marco, he turned round and saw a policeman following him. The man was making no effort to hide his presence; indeed, his garish uniform was positively advertising it.

Albrizzi turned towards him.

"What do you think you're doing?"

The man was muttering something. "*Scusi, Signor Dottore.* The commissario's orders."

"He ordered you to follow me. Well, you're making a most incompetent job of it! Anyone could spot you in a crowd." Albrizzi began to laugh.

The man said earnestly, "No, signor, not to spy on you. To keep you safe. Those are my orders."

Albrizzi stopped laughing.

AT the railway station, Revel Callender saw a commotion outside the ticket office. Two shabbily dressed men, protesting violently, were surrounded by a group of police officers, who had hold of their arms.

He looked inquiringly at the booking-office clerk.

"They are arresting them, signor—I don't know why. Best not to ask. Perhaps they were trying to get away, who knows? You are traveling to Paris, sir?"

They were interrupted as one of the men broke free. He ran over to Callender, who thought there was something familiar about his face. The man was beseeching, staring at him. "It's Signor Callender, isn't it? I'm Pietro, sir. We're innocent, signor, innocent!"

The policemen had seized the man's arms again in a tight, cruel grip and were dragging him away. He called out something, twisting his head around to shout to Callender, "Signor, *'La Veglia!'* For God's sake, signor, help me!"

"What was that?"

But Pietro had been pulled away and out of hearing. The struggling group moved out of the station. Callender stared after them.

"Sir? A ticket to Paris?"

The booking clerk was behaving as if the brief episode of human agony they had witnessed had never taken place. Perhaps there were some things it was better not to have seen. Callender returned abruptly to the business before him.

"Yes, please. I'm not sure when I'll be returning." He was only half attending to the business of handing over a thick wedge of *lira* notes and receiving an elaborately printed ticket.

Later, seated in the Orient Express and contemplating the luncheon menu, he realized where he had seen the man who had pleaded with him. On that occasion the fellow hadn't been in ordinary street clothes. He'd been dressed up like something out of a play, in the uniform of an eighteenth-century flunkey.

It was definitely one of the servants from Palazzo Casimiri.

15

Paris was having a warm autumn. All along the Boulevard Haussmann the sunshine glowed through the trees, their leaves turning
with the season to shades of honey and umber.

Revel Callender did not know Paris well, but he had a rough idea of
the location where the murdered man had lived, and he booked into a
hotel near the Place Saint Auguste, close to the street where the Rémy
town house stood. On the first day after his arrival, he telegraphed the
address of the hotel to the consulate in Venice, in case Barton should
need to contact him, and decided to commence his mission for Claude
Monet by reconnoitering the ground where the death of Auguste Rémy
had taken place. Later on, he would use the letter of introduction which
Monet had given him to Alice's sister, Cecile, but for the moment he was
content to walk around the area, sensing the atmosphere.

The Rémy house straddled the corner of a triangle where the Rue de
la Pépinière met the wide Boulevard Haussmann, and had entrances
onto both streets. It was in truth a magnificent bourgeois mansion, all of
five stories in height and massively built, but there was something rather
odd about the character of the Rue de la Pépinière, which ran eastwards
from the Boulevard Haussmann towards the massive bulk of the Gare
Saint-Lazare, one of the biggest railway stations in Europe.

The Boulevard Haussmann end of the street was a series of utterly respectable large dwellings, and the few people visible at eleven o'clock in the morning were those one might correspondingly expect. A woman with an elaborate gown and a huge feathered hat emerged from a grandiose porch, her high-heeled shoes tapping softly on the steps, and settled herself and a small, fussy dog into a barouche. They set off at a trot, the horse's well-groomed coat gleaming in the sunlight. In a house nearby, a small maid in a white gown with a broad apron was flicking around the inside of a bay window with a feather duster, and a grocer's van delivered a crate of fruit to the back entrance of the house next door.

Such mundane comings and goings signaled the nature of the place. Secrets might lie behind these façades, but they would be very well hidden, Revel was sure. And they might be more innocent. Unlike the crumbling palaces of Venice, these were new dwellings, with fresh brickwork and immaculate paint behind which one did not imagine acts of darkness taking place, buildings that were not worn by the rub and soil of centuries of human existence.

Yet the other end of the street seemed to have a different character. It was not so much that the houses were smaller, but they were of a different nature, split up into apartments and allowed to decline into shabbiness here and there. This, of course, was the end of the street that lay near the Gare Saint-Lazare, and like the districts around all great railway termini, the area had its seedy side. Here drifted the chancers and the beggars, the poverty-stricken and the confidence tricksters come to make their fortune in Paris, the unfortunates who had emerged from the maw of the Gare Saint-Lazare and been spewed out into the city streets. There were those who could make it no farther than the steps of the station, some who simply lay there with a hand outstretched, hoping for some unknown and impossible salvation, or in a drunken stupor, all hope obliterated, and every other feeling, too. Here, too, came those on legitimate business, the nervous Normandy farmers who occasionally might have dealings in the capital, and the students with their way to make in the world. Here once had arrived the penniless artist, Claude Monet, for the railway lines from the Gare Saint-Lazare stretched westward to his hometown, the port of Le Havre. And, of course, around the Gare Saint-Lazare were those who lived by preying on the new arrivals.

Walking around, Callender saw for himself the processes of human life in operation. A heavy-faced man with a flashy tie pin followed a young woman as she left the main entrance to the Gare Saint-Lazare and caught her up just outside. There had been a look of hopelessness on her features as she emerged from the canopy in front of the station: she wandered around as if bewildered and seemed to have no particular destination and no friends to meet her. She seemed to have no possessions except for a carpetbag, and her dress was poor, though her face was fresh and clean and her light brown hair neatly pinned up. Callender judged that she would be some country maidservant turned out of her place.

The heavy-faced man started off his place as soon as he saw her. He had marked her down as a beast of prey scents a quarry: She was a bird with an injured wing, and he would snatch it up. He circled round, stopped her, and began a conversation. She looked puzzled at first, but she seemed willing, even relieved, to speak to someone who was not unfriendly, among all these indifferent Parisians passing by. They began to move along the pavement together.

On an impulse, Callender went after them and walked boldly up.

"Our new maid, I believe," he said authoritatively. "The groom will collect your box. Where have you left it?"

The girl opened her mouth and gasped at the apparently insane intervention of this complete stranger with his foreign accent, and Callender thought she would make some exclamation that would give the game away. Fortunately, she seemed too overwhelmed to say anything, and the man, as he had hoped, made off immediately, the moment he saw that his supposed quarry was apparently in the hands of a respectable personage.

"Where did you come from?" asked Callender.

She was still staring in astonishment, but managed to say, "From Normandy." Tears formed in her big gray country girl's eyes, whether through shock at the madman who appeared to confront her as soon as she set foot in Paris, or because she had a sudden surge of homesickness at the thought of her own countryside.

"Go back!" said Callender. He fished in his pocket and found her some francs. "This city is no place for you. Go back, I beg you, to anything in Normandy, rather than staying here."

The girl looked down, amazed at her hand which now held probably more money that she had ever had in her life.

"Go on!" he cried, shooing her back to the station as one flaps a chicken away in the yard, and she turned obediently on her heel, her mouth still open in an O of astonishment.

She might board the next express for Rouen or Le Havre; she might not.

Cursing himself for being a fool whose quixotic action would probably achieve precisely nothing, he watched her enter the station and saw the man who had tried to accost her slip away towards the Rue de la Pépinière, a furious expression on his face. Yes, Callender could see very well the kind of house that the girl would have been taken into: one of those big shabby buildings with rubbish overflowing untidily onto neglected gravel. Yet after dark it might serve quite discriminating customers, even gentlemen from the Boulevard Haussmann. At night, all cats were gray.

At Number Twenty-five, the Rémy residence, the brass bellpull shone brightly beside a heavy front door. The blinds were all drawn. Auguste Rémy's widow, Cecile, and their son Georges, were probably away at their country château, Mont Ganelon, trying to avoid the publicity which Auguste's death had brought. He rang the doorbell. There was no response, but he saw a curtain twitch down at a basement window and tugged again on the bellpull. After a few minutes a wizened old man appeared and peered at Callender.

"I am a friend of the family and would like to express my condolences to Madame Rémy."

The concierge regarded him suspiciously. "The family is not here. Would Monsieur like to leave a card?"

"I'll call again. When do you expect them back?"

Now the old man was definitely hostile. "You're not from the newspapers?"

"No, I assure you." But the door was already closing.

As Callender turned to leave, he saw the little maid who had been dusting away at the window of the house next door. She was walking out into the street and called to him as the door closed, "They're not very friendly there!"

"I suppose it's natural after what happened."

"They were like that anyway, before. A sour lot in that house, for all their money and the way they spent it. You haven't seen a baker's van, have you, Monsieur? The chef told me to look out for it, and he'll be furious if I miss it."

"No, I haven't. But what did you mean, 'The way they spent it'?"

"On high living, in spite of all his age, old M. Rémy liked his pleasures still."

"Did he now? Was there a lot of gossip about him?"

"Him, and the rest." A voice inside the house was shouting, "Lisa, Lisa! Come here, girl, I want you! Now!"

Lisa made a face. "Old cow," she said and ran inside.

16

Monet had given Revel Callender several letters of introduction, including one to Hamard, chief of police at the Sûreté, but he determined to begin his investigations lower down in the ranks, where greater friendliness, or less resistance to bribery, might be expected. In the meantime, he put together a picture of events on the night of June 6, based on the version given him by Monet himself.

The first strange fact was the age of the victim. Auguste was no less than seventy-eight years of age; he must have been considerably older than Alice Monet's sister, Cecile, when they had married in 1870. There had been a few newspaper reports of the case, and the cuttings were included among the papers Monet had given him. A photograph of Auguste showed a portly elderly gentleman, leaning on a walking stick, with thick white eyebrows, a neatly trimmed white beard and mustache.

The other two males of the family were his son Georges, who looked to be in his thirties and descending rapidly into middle-aged pomposity, and his nephew, young Léon Raingo, aged only seventeen. Léon's own father was dead, and Auguste had more or less taken his place: The boy and his sister, Suzanne, lived in the Rue de la Pépinière with Cecile and Auguste. Léon's mother remained with her own family. Auguste and Cecile were in the roles of the boy's parents.

The family had maintained considerable style. There was a list of the servants present in the house on the night of the murder: an elderly janitor and his wife, a junior valet, a footman, a chambermaid, a cook. Another valet, the senior of the two, had been away visiting his family that night. They were all overseen by the man who appeared to have really run this household, the butler, Pierre Renard, and this was the character who most interested Callender. There was a photograph of him at the funeral marching behind the coffin with the other mourners, top hat in hand, an immaculately groomed man in his forties, still handsome and strong-featured. He was marching towards his own misfortune, for it was at the funeral, at the very graveside, in fact, that he allegedly whispered to young Léon the fatal words, "The old man is dead! He can never separate us again."

The implications of these two brief sentences, if they were true, were profound and damning, utterly sinister in the eyes of respectable society. Of course the homosexual underworld existed, in certain bars and cafés, in some theaters and music halls, but here it had entered within the very citadel of the bourgeois family, the household of a rich banker, and corrupted an innocent youngster—these were the shocking inferences drawn from the flimsy testimony of an anonymous letter. Paris might have a reputation as the most tolerant of cities, but it was just as capable of an orgy of self-righteousness as London had shown itself to be during the trials of Oscar Wilde. There was no doubt that the prison sentence Wilde had received was the result of virulent prejudice. Callender wondered if Renard would fare any better in Paris.

The immediate question was how to get some further information, given the fact that Number Twenty-five Rue de la Pépinière seemed almost as impenetrable as a castle. Monet had furnished Callender with a note to Cecile, widow of Auguste and sister to Alice, but she was outside Paris at Mont Ganelon, near Annel, a recently fashionable village in Picardy favored by the rich bourgeoisie.

Callender did not relish approaching the bereaved widow and supposed that he would be treated by her only to long eulogies of the deceased. But as he set out in the direction of the Gare Saint-Lazare to inquire about trains, he saw a man descending from a cab outside the Rémy mansion. He was neatly but unostentatiously dressed, and he did not make for the imposing front porch but was walking round the side of the house, where the servants' entrance would probably be. Callender followed him quickly and called after him. The man turned abruptly.

"I have come on behalf of M. Claude Monet," began Callender. The name was evidently familiar.

"Yes, sir, what can I do for you?"

This man was deferential, more compliant than the old concierge who had opened the front door.

"You are a member of the household?"

"Thomassin, sir, senior valet." The man's eyes looked red and watery, but not by grief. An odor of brandy was detectable when Callender moved closer.

"Do you have time for a few words?"

"Not if you're from the papers, sir. I would lose my place if I talked to one of them."

"I give you my word that I have no connection with the press. Would one of those little bars near the station suit you?"

The valet hesitated. "Sir, I have to collect some clothes for M. Georges. He sent me to fetch his evening dress suits for him."

Callender said pleasantly, "Well, you can always do that later, and I am sure he won't be needing them for the moment." He jingled some money in his pocket. "I could stand you a spot of lunch, too, before you have to go back to Mont Ganelon. In the bar, of course."

Thomassin nodded. He was a fairly well-built man, on whose appearance the habit of drinking had not yet made any serious impression. When they reached one of the brasseries around the square at the end of the street, he accepted a brandy at the zinc counter, and seemed to relax as he drank. "I was badly shocked, sir, by that business. Can't seem to get over it."

Callender looked at him sharply. Was it hypocritical? The man's tone had sounded sincere enough. "You were not in the house when it happened, I understand. You were away visiting your relations."

"No, sir, but it were terrible all the same. And what happened after, I feel awful about it."

"You can tell me about it over a sandwich."

They ordered *rosbif* sandwiches and adjourned to a table. Thomassin asked for beer to drink with the meal, since it was a warm day, and Callender followed suit. Callender found his thoughts intrigued by a question that one of Thomassin's comments had aroused.

"You were away that night, but what about the rest of the household? Madame Rémy?" Surely the dead man's wife had slept either in the same room or close at hand.

"She were away, sir, that night, out at Mont Ganelon. She took Mademoiselle Suzanne with her."

"That still leaves Monsieur Georges and Monsieur Léon? The other servants?"

"They was all there, sir. But none of them heard a thing."

It was pleasant sitting there in the café with the awnings flapping over the tables in a gentle breeze. But the thoughts that were coming into his head were anything but pleasant. Callender was silent, running over the picture of the Rémy house at night.

He remembered quite clearly the details in the newspaper cuttings that Monet had given him. Old Auguste Rémy had put up one hell of a fight. Callender knew that the police theory at first had been that the murder was the result of a break-in, because a drawer and a desk had been forced open, some banknotes and some of Cecile's jewels stolen, but then the evidence against this grew incontestably. The murder weapon had been extraordinary: a dessert knife with a rounded tip, such a feeble instrument that it scarcely seemed possible it could have killed a man. And it had not been brought from outside: it had come from the Rémy household. This had also been the source of the chisel used to break open the drawer and the desk, and there was no sign of a forced entry. Some linen had been strewn around, an armchair overturned, but there had been no ransacking, no real burglary by professional thieves. Auguste Rémy's personal safe remained untouched. And, if the attack had come from strangers, why had the old man not raised the alarm, called for help from his nephew, his son, his servants, as he struggled?

Rémy's shirt had been torn, there were marks and scratches all over his throat where he had struggled with the murderer, as well as the wounds on his body. He appeared to have been attacked in his bed and had dragged himself out to die on the carpet. So it had not by any means been a rapid murder nor the case of a passive victim who had not put up a fight, yet no one, not his son Georges, not his nephew Léon, nor any of the domestics in that lavishly served household had admitted to hearing anything.

"You mean to say that as well as the two young men of the family there were—what, a footman, the old couple downstairs, a cook, a maid, the other valet, what was his name—Courtois?—and Renard, the butler, and they all claimed not to have heard a sound?" Callender said incredulously.

"That's right, sir. Of course, the police arrested Renard and Courtois, so they must have been lying, those two, anyway. But their rooms were two floors above the old man's, anyway, so anyone up there might not have heard him crying out. If he did, that is—easy enough to shove a gag in his mouth."

The man leaned back expansively, self-importantly, from the café table. A motorcar swept past between the clopping horse-drawn traffic, making a roar around the square.

It seemed a familiar story, as Callender recalled the scene he had witnessed at the station in Venice just as he was leaving. The head of the household had been murdered, servants were being arrested. . . . How often did this sort of thing happen? When there might be some sort of scandal involved, presumably, and the blame would be thrown on the weakest and least able to defend themselves. Arresting the servants would be so very convenient to any powerful family that was faced with unwelcome inquiries into its secrets.

"It was on account of what I found, sir."

The white-aproned waiter appeared, and Callender signaled for Thomassin to be brought another drink.

"I'll tell you the story, sir, just like I told the police."

"Go on."

Thomassin took a swallow of the beer which had just been brought and ran his tongue around his lips. "It was in July, a full six weeks after the murder. It was a hot day, sir. We menservants used to hang up our waistcoats and jackets in a little cloakroom when we didn't need to be serving. I had taken my waistcoat off because of the heat. Courtois had the same kind of jacket as me, because he was a valet, too, though he were my junior, of course."

"And?"

"Master Georges rang for me, sir, and I went to put my jacket on in a hurry. And there was something in the pocket. A hard object, something small. I took it out, and it was a little jewelry case, and in it was the jewelry that had been stolen from Madame's room. I'd picked up the wrong jacket, you see, sir. It belonged to Courtois."

Callender was astonished. "This was six weeks after the murder, you say?"

"Yes, sir. Oh, Courtois denied having anything to do with it, said he didn't know how it got there and all that. But he confessed, in the end, and said it was Renard who had talked him into murdering the old man."

"But how did it come to be in his pocket all that time after the murder, if he had stolen it that night?"

Thomassin shrugged. "He said they'd hidden the jewels in the coal cellar, on the night of the crime. I suppose he was going to try and sell them, but I don't know why he brought them to Mont Ganelon."

"I beg your pardon? I thought this discovery of the jewels had happened in the house in Paris."

"No sir, the family all moved out to Mont Ganelon afterwards, and we went with them, except for a couple of servants left behind here in Paris to look after the place. Anyway, according to Courtois, Renard took the money they had found, so Courtois thought the jewels were his fair share. He'd been flashing a bit of money round, had a new suit, took some girls out to supper."

Callender said, "But if he hadn't taken any of the cash, and he still hadn't sold the jewels because you found them in his pocket, how come he had any money to flash around? And surely, to leave the jewel case in his pocket, to take it out to the château in the country—that was a huge risk!"

Thomassin said deferentially, "It's not my place to speculate, sir." Then, as if perhaps perturbed by this questioning of the evidence which he had been responsible for finding, he added, "Would you excuse me now, sir? Only I got a lot of things to do."

"Oh, yes, of course," said Callender, still distracted by details. "I suppose you are acting as M. Georges's valet now?"

"Not only that, sir, I'm the butler now, in charge of the household," said Thomassin, standing up and pushing back his chair. "I've been given Renard's job. The family has a lot of trust in me, you see."

Callender remained staring after him. It seemed so blatant, the way in which Thomassin, the lower-ranking servant, had benefited by the imprisonment of Renard, yet Thomassin had appeared not to realize what an independent mind might make of his story.

If there was one thing which Callender possessed, it was an independent mind, and he found, as he rose from the table and settled the bill, that he was becoming engaged in this business, not simply to report on the state of affairs as he had been charged by Monet, but because of the extraordinary and puzzling characteristics that surrounded the murder.

He looked at his pocket watch. It was only midday. There would be plenty of time to go along to the station and inquire about trains to Compiègne, near to where the Rémys had their country house. There were some things he very much wanted to ask Cecile Rémy, the grieving widow, if she would condescend to see him the following day.

That evening he had intended to dine at one of the restaurants near the Opéra. The Café de la Paix, where Rémy's son Georges, accompanied by two male cousins, had gone to "take the air" on the terrace on the night of the old man's murder, would probably be out of his reach, even though this visit would be funded by the artist rather than being paid for out of his own thin wallet, but he determined to call in there after a meal elsewhere, for a liqueur or a cognac.

According to the newspaper accounts, the family party had all enjoyed an excellent dinner at home on the evening of the murder. At ten o'clock, Georges and the cousins had gone out to the Café de la Paix; Léon and old Rémy had stayed at home. Léon had been described in the newspaper accounts as *légèrement souffrant*, which probably meant something like "out of sorts," or "a bit under the weather." It could also have meant that he was somewhat the worse for drink. Georges did not return till a little after midnight.

It was a family that seemed to stick together, but how far along the line would its members go? Would they lie for one another?

Callender pondered the question of family ties and what role the desperate desire for respectability might play in such a household. The alliances of blood might be all-powerful among the older families of Europe, from the aristocracy of Venice to the humble families of Sicily, but the urge to keep the family dirt to themselves was also a powerful motive for secrecy and mutual support, an *omerta* code of the bourgeoisie, the families that had got newly rich through trade or the stock exchange.

When Georges had come back, the whole household appeared to be asleep. Where had he been in the meantime? Perhaps to a cabaret or a whorehouse. Either the police had not demanded to know his movements, or they had not been made public. Georges was divorced, so there had been no wife to corroborate the time of his return or reproach him for staying out so late. At any rate, there had apparently been no cause for Georges to have any suspicions, and he had retired to bed. It was not till Renard entered the old man's room the next morning with his usual breakfast tray that the alarm had been raised.

But Callender's visit to the Café de la Paix was somewhat delayed. As he crossed the Rue de la Pépinière, he saw emerging from a side entrance of one of the houses a small female figure who seemed to be following his movements from the opposite side of the road. She waited till he had gained the pavement before asking him, "Sir, are you the gentleman that Thomassin was speaking with earlier on?"

Callender recognized the maid whom he had seen brandishing a feather duster at a window. She was an anxious little thing, a long shabby coat around her shoulders, trying to keep close to an overhanging hedge so as not to be seen.

"Yes, if you mean the valet—I mean, the butler—from Number Twenty-five."

"Yes, sir, that's what I do mean."

Callender was curious. The girl seemed sincere, and she went on to say, "Your pardon, sir, but would you let me speak with you for a few moments? Somewhere else, not just here." And she glanced up at the windows behind her, as if fearful that someone from the household that employed her might be watching.

He drew her into a side street.

"You want to tell me something."

"Yes sir, you see, there's some of us think it's not fair at all, what happened to Renard, the butler to Monsieur Rèmy. Not fair at all. And Thomassin said you had come from the artist gentleman. And he was always real kind when he came along this way. I think he'd want to know."

"To know what?"

"What I saw, on the night the old man were killed."

Callender looked down into her face, which was small and thin, but the eyes were bright and intelligent and looking straight into his.

"I want to hear it."

"I saw someone, sir. It was a real hot night, you see, and I couldn't sleep, not up in the attic. That's where they put us maids, of course, and we only has little windows that don't get a breath of air some nights. So I crept down and—well, I shouldn't have gone in, but you see, sir, the mistress was away, and her room has these beautiful big windows, and it's really lovely there on a warm night, so fresh and cool."

"So you were watching at the window?" Perhaps she had a lover for whom she was waiting, thought Callender, but if he showed his suspicions, she might not say anything more. She surely came from the sort of household where maids were forbidden to have "followers." He thought of the girl outside the station, the country lass whom he had so precipitately told to go home. This maid was another who would lose her place and be turned out of the house if she put a foot wrong.

"Yes, sir, I was looking out over the street, some time after midnight. And I saw someone watching from the side door of Number Twenty-five."

"Someone you recognized?"

"No, sir. The shadows were too deep. It was a man, though, that's all I can say."

Callender turned this over in his mind, but it did not seem to point towards anything in particular, though it added to the mysterious nature of the activities in the Rue de la Pépinière that night.

"Is that all?"

She was hesitant but seemed to get some more courage, perhaps even sounded slightly upset that he should think that she had only such a trivial incident to report.

"No, sir. Not long after that, a *fiacre* came along, must have been one of them late cabs returning from the Opéra or somewhere like that. I saw someone running out into the street and stopping the cab. The cabbie was fair amazed, sir; I reckon he'd been nodding off and letting the old horse find the way home."

"Did you see where this person came from?"

"Not exactly, sir, only that it were the Boulevard Haussmann end of the road."

That was the closest end to the Rémy household.

"But sir, I could see it were a lady. She had on a long white dress, all frills and flounces. And, sir, it had stains on it."

"What do you mean?"

"Dark stains, all down the front. It were a fine moonlit night."

Callender stared at her.

"Did you say anything to the police?"

The girl was rubbing a fold of her dress between her hands in agitation, in a compulsive movement.

"Don't be nervous," he said.

"Yes, I told the police. I told the inspector about it. They came to all the houses in the street and asked us to say if we'd seen anything on that night. I told him, just as I've told you." She paused. "Except for one thing, sir, and please don't say anything about that. I said I was looking out of the attic window, because I didn't want to admit having been in Madame's room. The inspector listened at first and wrote it down. But then the big boss came in—the superintendent, I think it was. And he said to ignore it all. Just silly fantasies and that I was a wicked girl to make such things up. I was very upset by it because I've never told tales in my life, so I was crying, and of course that made him think I was sillier than ever, and he shouted at me some more. And he tore up the paper that the inspector had been writing on."

"Can you remember their names, these policemen?"

She paused, trying to consider. "Not the superintendent, sir, no, I don't think I ever heard it. But the inspector, yes, because it's a silly name, though he were quite a decent sort, I think. Inspector Blot."

Real life does it to you every time, thought Callender. *Comedy of the macabre, Inspector Blot and the appalling murder mystery.* Somehow it made him think of the music hall, of the semisinister underworld that surrounded it, lurid, absurd, yet at the same time savage, the underbelly of polite society.

The girl was already edging away down the side street, as if anxious to get back. "They might miss me if I'm out any longer, sir."

He had one more thing to ask her.

"Can you describe the woman that you saw? Was there anything you might recognize if you saw her again?"

"No, sir, I just saw her outline. I couldn't see her face. She was thin, that's all I recollect. Just a thin figure standing there, in a white dress, with all them dark patches on the front. I don't know why, but it was horrible even then, when I didn't know what was going on. I still see it in dreams sometimes. It was a moment . . ." She struggled for words. Callender did not prompt her. "Sometimes, you just feel that you see something that's wrong, something really important, but you don't know why, and it sort of sticks in your mind like a picture. That's what I feel about that night: I was watching from the window, and she was standing there in the road, and then the old horse came along, all slowly, clip-clop, clip-clop . . ."

"The woman must have given the cabbie some directions."

"I didn't hear what she said, sir. Look, I must go now. I really must. If I get sent back home, my dad will kill me."

Callender found some money in his pocket, but she pushed it away. "No sir, I'm that angry with the police boss, the one who thought I was making it all up. It was the truth, and I'm not taking money for it."

"Well, thank you. What's your name, by the way?"

"Bernadette, sir. Bernadette Montpellier. But you tell M. Monet there's more to it than the police are letting on. When you see him, sir, tell him that, please." And she ran away and turned the corner of the street.

THE next day he set off for Compiègne. There was a regular service to the railway station, and from there it was quite close to the Rémys' country house at Mont Ganelon. But there was an hour or so to wait before the next train, and he took out the copy of The Cenci, which he had bought at the Gozzi's shop in Venice. The gilt ornament on the rich green leather binding had a flamboyance, almost an absurdity of excess, which spoke clearly of Venice, and he felt chilly as he recalled the death of the boy, Gozzi's son, murdered on his way to bring Callender the bookplates he had ordered. But he opened the book. There was an introduction by the poet, but he decided to go straight into the play.

It was about an Italian murder.

17

The journey to Compiègne was pleasant enough, the train passing through rich green countryside with towers and spires tucked into small valleys.

He had taken the precaution of telephoning Cecile Rémy in advance. It was quite possible the grieving widow would refuse to see anyone: he knew these bourgeois women made a great show of deep mourning, almost putting themselves into a state of purdah. Cecile and Alice came from a family with humble origins, small shopkeepers who had made their way up the ladder, but they would have certainly adopted the ways of the wealthy.

A servant had answered. Madame Rémy was unable to come to the telephone at present.

"My name is Callender. Please tell her I have recently spoken to M. and Mme Monet in Venice and hope to call on her tomorrow."

"*Oui, Monsieur.*"

That had been all, but Callender hoped it was sufficient for Cecile to be willing to meet him. At Compiègne, stepping out and enjoying the sight of the great spreading chestnut and beech woods that lay around the little town, he found a cab with a sturdy little pony and a driver who knew Mont Ganelon.

The mansion lay below a hillside. It possessed sweeping, manicured lawns and wrought-iron gates leading up to a long, modern house of heavy architecture, with a graveled drive curving around in front of the porch and rose beds in front, a few late autumnal roses still in bloom. He knew that Auguste Rémy was a rich man, had seen for himself the imposing bulk of the house in the Rue de la Pépinière, but he had not appreciated the extent of the man's wealth till he saw this country retreat. It was huge, new, and showy. It made him crave the subtle atmosphere of Venice, where all walls were decayed and seemed to be slowly crumbling into the water, yet inside lay warmth and drama, even if it were as extreme and ill-suited for the modern world as those carnival masks hanging in the Palazzo Casimiri.

The door was opened by a maid who was wearing a frilled white cap trimmed with a black bow, presumably in token of mourning for her late master. Callender gave her his card, which she duly received onto a silver tray, and showed him into a long drawing room, obviously freshly painted and papered, the walls hung with indifferent landscapes and a few sentimental watercolors of little girls and puppies. How on earth did such a society nourish a great painter, how could their eyes look on the work of Claude Monet and be so blind as to chose these dreary things, he wondered as he gazed out over the gardens at the rear of the house, where a fountain played over heavy-limbed stone cherubs in a sort of minor imitation of the gardens of Versailles.

These thoughts were interrupted, and he was indeed wondering how much they were motivated by envy, when a large lady in black silk entered the room. He could immediately see her resemblance to Alice Monet, but Cecile's face lacked the traces of charm and animation that he had detected in Alice. However, she crossed the room to greet him agreeably enough and without affectation.

"Monsieur Callender? I understand you have seen my sister just recently. How is she?"

"She seemed well, Madame, and I thought her quite cheerful."

"I'm so glad. She has been ill, you know, and now this dreadful business has upset us all so much."

"Yes, Madame, may I express my condolences. Evidently it was a most tragic loss."

"Horrible, Monsieur, and I blame myself, you know . . . if I had been there, if I hadn't returned here . . ."

"No, Madame! You yourself might have been in danger if you had stayed in Paris."

She seemed to consider this a new thought, though surely it was obvious that the presence of a murderer, perhaps two, stalking through the house at night would have put all the inhabitants in danger, and especially the wife of the murdered man, whose bedroom was next to the one in which his murdered corpse was found. It was Cecile's own jewelry that had been stolen by the killers and hidden in the coal cellar, if the reports were true.

"Yes, you may be right, Monsieur." She sank into a chair and indicated to Callender to do the same. "I've asked the maid to bring us morning coffee. I hope that is acceptable."

"You are most kind, Madame."

"Now, tell me about Venice. Have you met dear Mrs. Hunter?"

The conversation continued along these lines, discussing what Callender had seen of smart society in Venice, which was really little enough. Tiny gilded cups were brought, and coffee and small cakes served, though Callender, who had left Paris early that morning, could really have done with something more substantial. After about half an hour, Cecile Rémy seemed tired, and he felt he should leave. But he was unwilling not to have discovered anything more about the strange events in the Rue de la Pépinière. Just before he rose to go, he said, "Madame, forgive me, but M. Monet asked me to report back on any developments in the case. Do you have any information you could give me?"

"You heard they have convicted those two devils—Renard and Courtois? And now, it seems, they are appealing—the murderers! I had a telephone call from M. Hamard, the head of the Sûreté, himself."

"Yes, Madame. Evidently, as head of the special investigations section, M. Hamard must be the most senior police officer in Paris."

"Yes, indeed. Dear Auguste, my husband, was always so kind to all of the servants, you know. What a dreadful way to repay his goodness! I warned Auguste about the vices, I suspected them, you know, but Auguste would do nothing. 'Let him be,' he said. 'Renard is a good butler, and that is all I care about!' "

"What vices, Madame?"

Cecile stood up, as if she had said too much and wanted to draw the encounter to a close. She tapped her foot nervously as she said, "Never mind, M. Callender, never mind. It is all in the evidence, I am sure. At the appeal, there are going to be more legal proceedings. They will confirm everything."

The atmosphere had gone chilly, and Callender felt, as Cecile rang the bell for the maid to show him out, that he had gone too far in discussing the subject with her. He sensed that it would not be prudent to ask her about the strange discovery of the jewel case, supposedly brought by Courtois to Mont Ganelon and found in his jacket pocket by the other valet, Thomassin. But some warmth came into her voice as she accompanied him to the door of the drawing room.

"Please tell my sister not to worry in the slightest on my account. We have always been on the most affectionate terms, you know."

Callender recalled the story told him by Barton. It had been handouts from Cecile that had sustained the entire Monet family when they were in direst poverty, and Rémy had been the richest member of the family, though Alice had once, in her marriage to Ernest Hoschedé, been the mistress of just such a country house as this, surrounded by grand grounds and shooting drives. But Ernest had gone bankrupt, spending all his money on such foolish foibles as Impressionist paintings instead of attending to business, and Alice had ended up with a penniless artist.

"Old Rémy thought she was a fool," Barton had said back in Venice. "That's the story, anyway. The family felt she had disgraced them, and only Cecile supported her. Auguste agreed to send Alice money, but he wrote her cruel letters to accompany the checks."

There had obviously been a special bond between the two sisters, and Callender was aware of the gentleness that broke through Cecile's icy expression when she mentioned Alice. He took the hand which she held out to him, small, wrinkled, and covered with rings. "Thank you for seeing me, Madame. I shall return to Venice in a few days."

"Good-bye, M. Callender. Elisabeth will show you out. There is a door just along the passage here, and a path that leads around the house, if you would care to look at the view while you are here. Henri, the coachman, will be waiting at the front to take you to the station, that is, unless you want to go elsewhere."

She seemed to imply that this was a most gracious concession, and Callender was not sorry when the heavy doors of the Rémy mansion closed behind him. He found himself looking out onto a formal garden at the back of the house, with woods beyond, and behind them the view was indeed magnificent. The hill of Mont Ganelon arose ahead of him, clad with gold and blue, the shades of turning leaves, gorse, and bracken, and the misty haze of a day that held the promise of autumn.

He was standing contemplating this scene when there was a young voice behind him.

"Are you the man from Venice, from Aunt Alice and Uncle Claude?"

She had long, fair hair held back with a band and big, rounded blue eyes, a girl of about fifteen or sixteen, as he could judge. She wore black, which seemed a harsh imposition, but had put a blue scarf around her shoulders. Her question had the bright, uninhibited directness of youth.

"Yes, my name is Callender. I'm English, but I met them in Venice."

"I bet it's about what happened to Uncle Auguste?" Her eyes were bigger than ever, fixed on his, and her tone held a note of horrified fascination. "They won't tell me things, you know. It's so mean, I don't know anything about it, and I wasn't even in the house at the time. Aunt Cecile brought me here with her, when she came to Mont Ganelon after the row."

Callender worked out the ramifications of the Monet family. "So you are Mademoiselle Suzanne?"

Suzanne would be the daughter of Amédée Raingo, the brother of

Cecile and Alice. He had died some years ago. "Yes, and Léon is my brother. He was there in the house in Rue de la Pépinière when the murder happened. But Aunt Cecile won't tell us anything about it, except that she says Renard and Courtois are very wicked men, worse than just murderers, but when I asked her what she meant by that, she didn't answer. How are you getting back?"

"Your coachman will take me to the station, I believe."

"Oh, we'll walk together round to the front, then."

Suzanne, self-possessed and determined, was walking beside him. He was aware of the heaviness of the black crepe in which her legs were swathed and she noticed him glancing at her. She was just at the age when she was going to notice men's glances.

"Are you looking at my dress?"

"Well, Mademoiselle—"

"You must be looking either at my dress or me!" Her voice was sweet and silvery. He felt slightly embarrassed, but she went on to say, "I don't mind wearing black, if you must know. It's quite like being in a play, isn't it?"

"Don't you miss your uncle Auguste?"

"Oh, of course, but I never really had much to do with him. He was so *old*! He saw more of Léon."

Callender stopped and looked out over the soft and lovely landscape that lay before them. They had turned the corner of the house now, and he saw that the carriage to take him to the station was standing ready in front of the porch.

"Suzanne, if I may call you so?—good—Suzanne, there was something you said a moment ago. 'Before the row.' What row was that?"

He felt this was unfair, that he was looking down into a pair of very innocent eyes, but the truth was that he felt very drawn into this matter now, and the whole atmosphere here out at Mont Ganelon suggested the sanctimoniousness which wealth can create. This young creature still had a lack of reticence about her, very different from the cautious and withdrawn attitude of her aunt Cecile.

Suzanne said with relish, "Oh, it was a simply *dreadful* row! Uncle Auguste was going to send Léon away, to our grandmother's house in the country. You know, that's just dreadfully dull, worse even than here. Grandmother doesn't see anyone from one year's end to the next. Léon would have gone crazy there. And Aunt Cecile took his side."

Callender said, conscious that he might be treading on difficult ground, "But why did your uncle want to send him away?"

There was a pause. Suzanne looked down, and he saw that her eyelashes were thick and blonde. She twiddled with a ribbon on her dress. "I don't know, really," she said. "I didn't understand it. He said Léon was 'depraved.' I don't really know what that means. Léon had been naughty—he got drunk sometimes."

"He's—how old?"

"Seventeen. Can you really do anything so wrong at seventeen?"

He didn't answer. She looked at him again, out of those big blue eyes, and went on, "Anyway, it was something to do with Renard, the butler, I don't know exactly what. But that was what Aunt Cecile got upset about—I mean, what Uncle Auguste was saying about Léon, not just that he was going to send him away. Uncle Auguste said, 'I'm not having that boy under my roof any longer! There's something about him I don't like at all.' But he didn't say what it was. It was more than Léon just getting drunk, though. Aunt Cecile burst into tears, it was such a bad quarrel, and she got up from the table and said, 'Come, Suzanne!' Just like that! And then she said, 'We're not staying in this house a moment longer. It's no place for a young girl with that sort of talk going on.' She made her maid pack us a few things, and then we came here."

"What, straightaway?"

"Oh, yes, we were out of the house within an hour."

"And Léon?"

"We left him behind. He and Uncle Auguste and my cousin Georges, that's Uncle Auguste's son, they went out to dinner that night, all the men, if you can count Léon as a man. And, of course, that was the very night that . . . the burglars broke in and killed poor Uncle Auguste."

So that was the story that the girl had been told, impossible though the idea of an outside intruder had become once the evidence had been considered. However, Callender did not want to implant doubts into the head of Suzanne, little more than a child. Instead, he changed the subject and asked, "Where is Léon now?"

"Here, at Mont Ganelon. Aunt Cecile insisted he should come back with us after the funeral. She doesn't like him to see anyone, though. He stays in his room most of the time. His nerves are in such a state, you know." Her tone was adult, knowing, as though she had picked this up from adult conversation.

"I see." The carriage horses were shifting restlessly on the drive. Callender thought he saw a curtain moving at one of the great windows in the front of the house. Time to go.

"Well, good-bye, Mlle Suzanne, and I wish you every happiness in life."

"Thank you, Monsieur," she said with a serious expression. "Oh, M. Callender?"

"Yes, what is it?"

"Give my love to my aunt Alice and uncle Claude when you go back to Venice. Uncle Claude is very kind, you know."

But Alice, thought Callender, *is made of tougher stuff. Yes, I'm inclined to agree with you, Mlle Suzanne.* Aloud, he said, "Of course I will! Good-bye."

She was a small black figure with a touch of sky blue around the shoulders, waving good-bye to him over the great sweep of the drive as the carriage rolled away.

18

Revel Callender, as he took a simple café lunch of thick slices of smoked salmon overlapping a piece of crusty buttered bread, thought of Shelley's play lying on the table here in his Paris hotel room. He had barely started it, though he felt that it stirred an uneasiness, would say something particular that he did not quite as yet understand.

Shelley could wait. His business in Paris was more pressing now, and he ran over the situation in his mind. He wanted to make a full report to the Monets, and he was conscious of needing to make notes of the information he had received so far. And yet it seemed so insubstantial, so much a tissue of innuendo and gossip. The most obvious course was to resort to the hard facts, and this would involve the police reports, and undoubtedly would entail speaking to the inspector who had been immediately involved, the unfortunately named Inspector Blot.

The day had changed, and a bright shower had passed over Paris, so that the shiny wet pavements of the boulevards reflected shop windows and carriages. Passersby, just finishing lunch or hurrying to the shops, were shaking their still-wet umbrellas or laughing in little groups under trees where they had taken shelter. A stylish woman with an hourglass figure and a deep blue dress that fell in tiers to the ground gave him a very special smile as she held up her skirts and dashed for shelter in the silvery rain. She had dark curls and a pretty cherub's face with a small red mouth, but Callender resisted. For some reason he thought of sea-stained aquamarine skies and long strands of blonde hair.

He had decided to walk to the police headquarters on the Île de la Cité in the middle of the Seine, and did not regret it, though he had to take temporary shelter from the rain in a café on the Rue de Rivoli, where the harassed waiter was hastily collecting up outside tables and chairs. The Seine flowed with a platinum gleam, with facets of light here and there where the reemerging sun caught the final cascades of rain-drops as they fell into the river, sparkling through the air against the vast black towers of the cathedral of Notre-Dame in the background.

He crossed by the Pont-Neuf onto the tip of the Île de la Cité, paus-ing on the bridge to look upriver with pleasure at the elegant expanse of gray buildings and green gardens of the Quai du Louvre. On the island, he turned left along the Quai des Orfèvres, where the goldsmiths of the city had once had their shops, past the Sainte-Chapelle, and into iron gates set into the forbidding, heavy stonework of the prefecture. The courtyard was full of gendarmes in swinging capes who seemed to be coming and going according to predestined patterns. Making his way through them into the building, he gave his name at an inquiry desk and asked to speak to Hamard, head of the Sûreté, the criminal investigation department. At first he was given to understand that M. Hamard was far too important to be troubled in this way, but when Callender produced the letter of recommendation from Monet, the police officer manning the re-ception bureau changed his attitude and asked him to take a seat.

Callender was in luck, he was told after about twenty minutes of pe-rusing a two-day-old copy of *The Times*, which he had purchased from a kiosk. M. Hamard was in his office, and would receive him.

It was a wooden-paneled office with heavy mahogany furniture. Above the chief's chair hung a tricolor French flag, and over this were the words *"Liberté, Egalité, Fraternité."*

Not that there seemed to be much in the way of liberty, equality, or fraternity hanging about Chief Hamard. He was immaculately dressed, with a stiff wing collar, and a face so smoothly shaved that his skin looked positively polished, an illusion enhanced by his shining bald head. He had a long, thin black mustache that reminded Callender vaguely of cartoons of Chinamen. Waving the visitor to a chair, he immediately took charge of the conversation.

"I understand you have come to Paris on behalf of M. Claude Monet about this sad affair of M. Auguste Rémy."

Callender let the interview flow Hamard's way. "Yes, I am returning to Venice in a day or two, and will be seeing M. and Mme Monet again then."

There was a slight smile on Hamard's lips. "They are appealing against the convictions, but the evidence against them is very solid. The valet, Courtois, has confessed."

"But is there any other evidence against them?"

Hamard sat up stiffly and tugged on a bell rope behind his chair. When a uniformed policeman arrived, he said peremptorily, "Bring Blot to us." He turned to Callender.

"Blot is the inspector in charge of this case. He will tell you of the evidence."

Hamard spoke as if mere evidence was beneath him.

A minute or two later, there entered a tall, shambling man who had a big, round face with heavy spectacles. Callender guessed that he would normally be a cheerful fellow who liked his food and drink, perhaps a good fat *cassoulet* with duck and Toulouse sausage, something that really lined the stomach, washed down with a heavy red wine. But he was looking tense and responded cautiously when Hamard said, "Blot, this gentleman has come on behalf of the Monets to inquire about developments in the Rémy case. Tell him of the discovery which proves the guilt of Courtois and Renard."

"There is the jewelry which they stole from Madame Rémy's room, as well as the confession of Courtois," said Blot, who had not been invited to sit down, in spite of the number of empty chairs around the table. He had a provincial accent, thought Callender, not from Paris, maybe from the south.

He was about to say, "But anyone could have put the jewelry in Courtois's pocket." However, he thought better of it. He didn't want them to clam up. Nevertheless, he was puzzled to the extent of risking a question.

"The press reported that there were no bloodstains on the servants' clothes. Yet there must have been a great deal of blood around, surely?"

Hamard pressed his lips into a line. His small, black eyes suddenly looked like those of a predatory animal, looking out for the attack. He had evidently decided to answer this himself.

"M. Callender, there is something in Courtois's statement that will not be released to the press, but I will tell you now so that you understand this point clearly. They were naked when they committed the murder."

"Naked?"

Hamard tapped his fingers on the mahogany tabletop. "You must understand, these were creatures of the most depraved habits."

"You mean they were . . . ?"

"There is no doubt they had the most disgusting and perverted relationship."

Callender thought of the newspaper reports. From the newspaper photographs, Courtois looked to be about twenty or less, whereas Renard the butler was a man in middle age, and, according to the reports, was married with children.

Hamard mistook the source of the doubtful look on his face.

"You may well be horrified, Monsieur, that such appalling events occurred in the home of one of our leading citizens. Renard was undoubtedly the ringleader and the—er—the dominant party. It was he who persuaded Courtois into the crime. And I have no doubt that they were entrapping young Léon, the nephew of M. Rémy, into their foul practices."

Callender remembered the anonymous letter that claimed to have heard Renard pronounce those fatal words at the graveside, "He can never separate us again."

"I heard there was an anonymous letter . . ."

"There have been many," Blot interrupted. "All accusing Renard. We have never discovered their source."

"So what about the appeal hearing?"

"Undoubtedly, Monsieur, we consider the conviction will not be overturned. Not unless someone comes forward—with new evidence, and that seems extremely improbable," Hamard responded. He rose and walked to the door. Clearly, the interview was at an end. "You can report our progress to M. Monet. Please give him our regards."

It was politely phrased but undoubtedly an order.

Blot had said very little, thought Callender as he walked down the staircase. Somehow, he was not too surprised when he heard footsteps following him, and the big inspector caught up with him as he crossed the courtyard.

"We wanted to keep this case out of the newspapers, of course," he began.

"Because of M. Monet's fame?" said Callender innocently.

"Well, not only that, the Rémy family is very well known, and so are the family of Mme Rémy, the Raingos. They are among our leading citizens."

"M. Blot, I came from Venice on behalf of M. and Mme Monet to inquire about progress in the case—"

This was the wrong course, for Blot instantly took this as criticism, and his red cheeks bulged out indignantly as he said, "Of course, we have made excellent progress! Why, it is practically solved! And in any case, the papers have picked up some of the story—we could not help that."

Callender changed tack. No matter how hollow this sounded, he wanted to get some information from this man. *"You can open any lock with a golden key,"* he remembered his governess saying so many years ago, urging a small boy that politeness paid off.

"Congratulations on your progress, Inspector. I'm delighted to hear it! Your superiors must be pleased with your work in such a delicate case."

Click! The gold key turned in the lock. Blot subsided. "Yes, delicate isn't the word, I can assure you, Monsieur. Combustible, that's what it was. Combustible!" He seemed to be proud of the word, and less harassed, but continued, "The fact is, Monsieur, I'm pressed for time just now. I have another investigation in the Boulevard Malesherbes."

Callender realized that the Boulevard Malesherbes intersected with the Boulevard Haussmann, just south of the Rue de la Pépinière. "That is your particular area of Paris, Inspector?"

"The Eighth *Arrondissement*? Yes, sir, and believe me, there's all sorts there, rogues and rich, and some rich rogues, I shouldn't wonder."

He stopped, as though perhaps he had gone too far, but Callender laughed easily, and Blot relaxed.

"I'm staying near there, Inspector, as it happens." Blot nodded, as though this was no surprise. "Perhaps we might take a cab together?" Callender added.

The inspector gave the cabby some quick instruction, and they set off, jolting through the rain, which had begun to fall again. The cab got held up in a long stream of carriages trying to cross the Seine, when it seemed natural to make conversation, though Callender carefully did not mention the Rémy case again for the moment. "May I ask what sort of business you are going to now, Inspector?"

The man sighed. "A nasty matter, sir. I don't see why I shouldn't tell you, for there's nothing special about this one. Just an ordinary case—a prostitute murdered by a pimp. Only thing that's a bit different about this case is that the prostitute wasn't a woman. Of course, you get that from time to time—in fact, I would say passions run higher amongst that lot than in the regular brothels. The clients are very choosy about their favorite boys, and so on."

"But isn't . . . that sort of thing . . . isn't it illegal?"

"Oh, yes sir, of course it is, but if we tried to arrest everyone involved, the prisons wouldn't hold them all, and as you will have learned from M. Hamard, the most respected households in Paris can be involved."

Was he being given a hint? wondered Callender.

"So we turn a blind eye," continued Blot. "But most nights you can see them lined up in the Place Pigalle, women on one side, boys on the other. We just step in when there's a case like this one I'm on my way to attend just now, some serious crime."

The cab jolted on along the Rue de Rivoli, the blinkered, steaming horse moving patiently through the screaming of drivers, the abuse of passersby who were splashed by the wheels of carriages, and the screeching of the occasional motorcar—one was a De Dion Bouton as Callender noted with pleasure and awe. They passed the smart shops, La Samaritaine, Galeries Lafayette, where uniformed commissionaires struggled on the pavement to summon carriages for their wealthy customers. One, with absurd gold epaulettes that would have put a general to shame, even had the temerity to pull open the door of their cab, but Blot growled, "Police!" and it was slammed shut again.

The rain beat down steadily, drumming on the roof, their small square of protection against the elements. A warm smell arose from Callender's companion, an odor of damp wool and wine. It joined the animal smell of damp leather that filled the cab and seemed to be part of a natural and constant state of affairs within this little world.

They seemed to be irretrievably stuck in a line of carriages moving westwards towards the Arc de Triomphe. Blot fumbled in the pocket of his overcoat, opened a case of small cigars, and offered one to Callender, who shook his head. The policeman produced a small silver match case and struck a light. It was a strong, cheap tobacco, yet Callender found it pleasant. He took up the conversation they had been having earlier, scarcely knowing why, sensing there had been something there.

"You say you turn a blind eye to prostitution. But what do you do when there are children involved?"

Blot gave a sigh and drew in heavily on his cigar. "We don't like it sir, not one bit. But what can we do? There are a few charity orphanages for the girls, but if the boys have been guilty of some offense, if someone complains they've been robbed or solicited, well then, we have to take them into custody. And then, I'm afraid, there's only one place where they're likely to end up."

The man's expression was so serious that Callender forgot about the crazy wet city that was dashing about outside this enclosed space.

"And where's that?"

The man answered slowly, as if unwilling to say the words. "You don't know, sir? They're taken to La Petite Roquette."

As he spoke the name, he made a curious gesture. He shifted his cigar to the other hand, moved his right arm, and Callender realized that he was actually crossing himself.

What this might be, Callender had no idea, only that the notion of the place seemed to horrify even this hard-bitten French policeman.

"Are you really interested, sir?"

"I'm not sure, to tell you the truth. Is it a prison?"

Blot spat out a shred of tobacco into a dusty yellow handkerchief, which he tucked back into his waistcoat pocket. He seemed to be considering something. Afterwards, when Callender had the time to contemplate this conversation, he wondered whether the man was much cleverer than he thought, whether he had deliberately led the conversation in a certain direction and wanted Callender to take up his hints. When Callender came to know Paris better, he realized that the cab had, in fact, gone quite a distance out of their way.

In any event, Blot's answer came sounding full of caution.

"Yes, La Petite Roquette is a prison, sir, in the Rue de la Roquette. I don't think I can describe it for you."

Callender leaned forward. "Why not?"

The cab turned off to the right. Blot didn't answer the question. "We're in the Boulevard des Malesherbes, Monsieur Callender. Didn't you say your hotel was somewhere near here?"

"Yes, in the Place Saint Auguste. What were you saying about the prison—La Petite Roquette, was it?"

But the inspector was calling to the cabbie to stop. Callender saw that there would be nothing more forthcoming and reluctantly climbed into the drizzling rain. "Can I speak to you again, Blot?"

The policeman merely tipped his hat in acknowledgment.

*   *   *

THE line to Venice was a constant crackle, like the subdued mad laughter of pantomime demons, and the elderly voice that responded to the rusty-sounding bell ringing at the end of the line did not promise any great efficiency.

"*Allo,* Palazzo Barbaro?"

"Signor Monet, *per favore.*"

"*Uno momento, signor, momento.*"

But one moment slipped into another, and they ticked away, though Callender thought he could hear the sounds of Venice along the wires, the calling of gondoliers, the splashing of oars . . . no, those must be fantasies, surely. Odd that the noises, real or imagined, made him long for that decayed old city, a place half-phosphorescent with rot. And it was not the Barbaro that came into his mind, but the Palazzo Casimiri, and the long staircase down which Clara would descend when he called there on his return. . . . At last there came along the telephone line some sounds which he was sure he could identify, the sound of footsteps on marble floors. Nostalgia for a place one scarcely knows—is it possible?

"*Allo?*"

"M. Monet? It's Revel Callender here."

"Ah, M. Callender. Do you have any news for us?"

"The police do not expect the appeal to succeed. No one has come forward with any other evidence to support it. They are facing the guillotine."

There was a long pause, as if Monet were trying to assess this. Callender felt it would be too complex to try to convey the other issues over this crackling line, the picture of violent homosexual decadence that Hamard had evidently been careful to create in their conversation.

"I was astonished when I first learned of their guilt, I must admit. Courtois is a very weak personality; I sensed that when I went to Auguste's house. He might be led astray—but surely not to do such a dreadful thing! And Renard, he was always so polite, so efficient—no, one could never have imagined how much the two of them must have hated Auguste. You would think that hatred like that would be—I don't know, almost an extra presence in the place, M. Callender. How could I not have felt it?"

The voice seemed to be breaking with feeling. Callender changed the topic, so that the old man might not dwell too long on this horrible idea of a family household full of secret loathings. "I've been to Mont Ganelon and seen Mme Cecile," he said quickly, "and she's well, at any rate, considering the situation."

"That's good to hear. Have you spoken to anyone else in the family?"

Callender hesitated for a moment and then decided not to mention his meeting with young Suzanne. After all, she was barely more than a child.

"No, I haven't."

Monet's voice came again, faintly along the line, emerging from the black receiver as though made tiny by distance.

"Would you do something more for us, Callender? Go and see Georges, Auguste's son. Alice is very fond of him, and she's been worrying about how he would react to it all."

"Yes, of course." Callender wasn't sure what made him add, "And young Léon? What about him?" It did strike him as odd that the family should seem to be more concerned about the adult and self-confident Georges than about the nervous adolescent, Léon, who was apparently not well enough to see any visitors to Mont Ganelon. Léon, like Georges, had been in the house on the night of the murder, after all. He might have his own story to contribute, especially in view of what had allegedly been said to him in the cemetery.

Claude Monet did not answer straightaway. He said, after a pause, "No, I don't think you need see Léon. He's barely out of school, after all. But talk to Georges, please."

The Monets were paying Callender's train fares and hotel bill. He would act as they wished.

"Very well, Monsieur. I'll arrange to see him."

And so he had, sending a message to Georges care of his mother Cecile at Mont Ganelon, and receiving a stiff note that invited him to call on Georges at his club.

"I'm very anxious about Cecile."

Alice Monet was looking out over the water with a silver-framed photograph in her hand. She never traveled without these small sepia icons of her family. Now she was gazing at a miniature studio portrait of her sister Cecile, whose charm had been overtaken by the fleshy heaviness of middle age.

They were still in Venice, staying in the Grand Hotel Britannia, to which they had removed from the Palazzo Barbaro, making their apologies to their hostess, Mrs. Hunter, as best they could. Monet had insisted on the transition, partly because his work was being constantly interrupted by the round of parties and lunches which Mrs. Hunter arranged for them, but partly also because he was growing more anxious than ever about Alice's health. She had endured several attacks of bitter vomiting, her skin turning a jaundiced color. He wanted her in comfortable surroundings, and grand though the Palazzo Barbaro might be, it could not provide the comforts with which the Britannia furnished its guests, such as central heating and elevators. It reminded him of the Savoy Hotel, where he had stayed on his visits to London at the turn of the century, and gave him a feeling of greater safety than the old Barbaro mansion. It was part of the modern world, where illnesses could be diagnosed and treated by up-to-date means. The old places of Venice spoke of superstitious practices, of leeches, bloodletting, and old apothecaries in grubby robes.

He turned from assembling his brushes in preparation for another painting expedition. They had taken a light luncheon of *omelette aux fines herbes* and white wine in their rooms.

"Yes, it's a terrible business," he answered. "But don't let what's happening in Paris trouble you too much. The servants are guilty, and that's all there is to it."

He spoke confidently but hoped she could not catch his true feeling, which was one of deep unease. Supposing the servants were not guilty, after all? Who then would be accused? He had never particularly liked Auguste, a bullying old man. God knew, there had been enough people with cause to hate him—Cecile herself, if she did not seem to be determined to play the part of grieving widow.

"I think your sister may be happier . . . once she has got over the shock . . ." he began.

Alice's mood turned to a spark of anger. "That's a dreadful thing to say! I suppose you mean because of the disagreements she and Auguste had in the past," she said.

"You know as well as I do that they had some terrible rows over his mistresses," said Monet.

"He hadn't had any affairs for a long time," said Alice. "Besides, all the men in his circle do that sort of thing. Cecile more or less expected it."

"Yes, those rich bankers who think they're just being a man of the world in keeping a mistress. Men who justify their adultery by saying, 'Everyone does it.' Don't you despise them, Alice?"

She sighed heavily and sat down on a cane chair on their balcony, rubbing her eyes with a handkerchief. "Ah, well, it's the way of the world."

"Not my world," he said. "And Georges may not be unhappy at his father's passing, if the truth be told."

"Georges!" she said, and the name was an exclamation which conveyed anxiety and despair. "Cecile spoiled him, that's the truth, and he has always done as he liked. Yes, he and Auguste quarreled—but what are you saying, Claude?"

The parchment color of her face was striking, shocking, as the sun fell on it. Such a terrible death, the guillotine, but at least it was quick. There were certain diseases, on the other hand . . .

He suddenly realized where their conversation might have been leading and left off the subject. There would be plenty of time to consider matters in Paris after he had a final report from the Englishman, Callender.

"How are you feeling now?" he said anxiously. "Would you rather I didn't go out?"

Alice smiled at him again, and said, "No, of course not! You must carry on with your work—that is the reason we came to Venice. I shall be perfectly all right. Mrs. Hunter has offered to take me to the Lido this afternoon. I think she has forgiven us for moving here, after all. We shall walk a little on the beach, and the air will do me a great deal of good.

"Let me get a doctor to see you. People were speaking last night at dinner of an excellent man here. I understand he has trained in the States."

But his wife refused, saying that she was already feeling better than when they had arrived, that Venice was doing her good. In fact, they both knew that it would probably make little difference whatever the doctor said. Within Alice, in her very blood, lay something that would not be denied, and their understanding of this was at a deep physical level of perception that went beyond the formal terms of diagnosis. Something was happening to Alice beyond the normal changes of age.

He said nothing at that moment. Husband and wife had momentarily entered an unspoken conspiracy to deny the future. She stood up and said, "You must get outside, Claude. You can't work indoors."

It was true: he approached his painting like military campaigns conducted outdoors, among the elements themselves, working under sun or rain, squinting painfully at light cast on water.

★   ★   ★

THE afternoon sun was almost setting when he put up his easel. It was a view of the Grand Canal on which he had been working the previous day, seen from the spot close to the landing stage of the Palazzo Barbaro where Callender had encountered him. Tints of carmine and violet streaked the sky and seemed to be bathing the ancient brickwork in a veil that lay darker towards the west. Gradually, as he dabbed and tipped bright slicks of oil, chasing opal and iris, a dark grayish purple light sank over the sky of Venice. The painter turned away from the subject of his canvas and glanced farther along the stretch of water, wondering whether the light was fading too fast for him to continue. Twilight had fallen more quickly than he thought possible. Away from the sea, the Grand Canal was already shrouded in dusk.

His head moved in sudden surprise as he tried to focus better on something. Sometimes, as now, he mistrusted his aging eyes, especially when he was gazing farther away. There was a tall building on the opposite side, farther along the water's edge, a grand but crumbling place doubtless occupied by some old family that had let it go to rack and ruin, and he seemed to see something strange there, outlined on the roof. He had thought for a moment it was a statue, but surely it was moving: a human figure, thin and black against the faint remaining light, that seemed to be bending down and pulling something up.

But he could no longer see with any certainty. The artist began to pack up and prepared to leave. The scene was overtaken by night.

20

Georges Rémy sat in a wing chair at his English-style club on the Boulevard Haussmann. This heavy, ornate fashion, all mahogany and dull brocade, was the rage among Georges's acquaintance. Callender, who would not have dreamed of setting foot in such an institution back home in London, where they were the lairs of the most stifling elderly bores, guessed this, and wondered why a youngish man should be so willing to give up what one might expect to be the pleasures of a city like Paris. Georges Rémy had a plump and friendly face, with a neat black beard and mustache, but he seemed shy and older than his years, greeting Callender with stiff politeness. Perhaps this club was a refuge from publicity and the world outside. Callender was received hospitably and offered drinks, which he declined, though he appreciated Georges's affability. Outwardly a pleasant man, he thought. A waiter brought him something that looked like a bill for signature, apologizing for the interruption, and Georges perused the paper carefully before appending his name in neat handwriting.

Why had Georges got divorced? Callender found himself wondering. Divorce was something quite rare in this Catholic country, where the principle of keeping up appearances also helped to preserve many a marriage, no matter what the truth behind the façade.

"M. Callender, it's very kind of you to give up your time for our family in this way," he began, when the waiter had departed with his piece of paper.

"I believe my uncle and aunt know about most of the developments in this dreadful business, though I quite appreciate they wanted someone to make personal inquiries," said Georges. "So much more reassuring than the official channels. But they may not know of the latest development in the case: that Courtois and Renard are appealing against conviction."

"Yes, they do. I discussed it with M. Monet by telephone."

"Ah, yes, of course, there are Mme Hunter's American connections, so no doubt the Palazzo Barbaro will have some conveniences of modern life, in spite of its antiquity. Good. I must say I am truly shocked at Courtois and Renard; you know, we were always a very kind and generous household. My father paid the servants well, and I think it's true to say that we looked on them like friends."

Georges looked sanctimoniously down his nose.

"They were of good character?"

"Oh, yes, it would have been impossible to believe the things that have occurred, the charges made against them if we had not known . . ." Georges looked around the room. No one was sitting within ten feet of them, but nevertheless he lowered his voice and said almost in a whisper, "I understand the police made some discoveries in Renard's room in Paris that prove he had the most debauched tastes."

Callender was confused for a few moments. "You mean, his room in your father's house?"

"No, he rented a place of his own. He said his wife suggested it, but I suppose he wanted somewhere to conceal the evidence of his unnatural tastes. There were photographs of young men, photographs which prove beyond doubt that the man was a homosexual pervert."

"But had you seen nothing of this tendency while he was in your father's service? He was married?"

"Yes, but his wife is a lady's maid, so perhaps it was a marriage of convenience, just something that suited them both. Of course, neither Renard nor Courtois had been with us long, Renard only two years, but he came with a marvelous reference, and as for young Courtois, he was being trained up to be a first-rate gentleman's valet. I would never have believed they could do this to us! But the evidence is there, Monsieur Callender, before our eyes."

"Renard has never confessed?"

"No, he has not, at least, that's what I understand from the police. The two murderers haven't had a chance to coordinate their stories, evidently. They're being held in separate prisons."

"Really? Is that usual?"

"I couldn't say," said Georges. "I'm afraid I know so little about this sort of thing. All I know is that Renard is in the Concièrgerie."

"And Courtois?"

Georges Rémy looked around the room again, this time as if quite perturbed, but his eyes eventually returned to Callender, and the man seemed to stumble over the words as he said, reluctantly, "Courtois is in La Petite Roquette."

THEY were rolling round the Place de la Bastille, past the slender column that marked the towering fortress where the kings of France held their prisoners, and which the revolutionary citizens of Paris had stormed on that momentous day in 1789. Then the cab began moving uphill, away from the direction of the river. "This is the Rue de la Roquette," said Blot. "There may be some delays here, I had better warn you."

"I am grateful that you were willing to accompany me, Inspector."

"Well, when you rang up to ask if you could visit—I was in two minds to say no, to tell you the truth. But anyway, you would never get in on your own, not even past the entrance." He shifted his big buttocks on the seat.

The cab stopped. Callender put his head out of the window. An extraordinary sight was moving along the road, coming downhill towards them: a black hearse pulled by black horses who were being whipped along at full gallop. The hearse bounced lightly at top speed over the uneven cobbles of the street as though it were empty. There was no sign of any mourners.

Blot laughed at Callender's expression. "This is the road they take to Père Lachaise, the cemetery up at the top of the street. Of course, the hearses go up the hill really slowly and reverently. But then they tear back down after the funeral, to be ready for the next bit of business. We'll be stopping a few times to let the funeral processions go past to the cemetery."

And indeed, they did so. Callender observed with fascination the elaborate trappings of the horses, their nodding black plumes, the gondola-like carriages on which the coffin lay, and the long rows of coaches behind, some with crests on the doors indicating the presence of a noble household, some containing heavily veiled women.

A sickly scent of tuberoses and gardenias drifted down the hill as the processions passed. Death could be made as formal here as it was in Venice, yet somehow it lacked the brooding presence of that antique funerary boat that had headed out towards the Adriatic bearing the body of Count Casimiri.

The cab pulled up suddenly, and at first Callender thought it was to allow another funeral procession to pass, but Blot, who was on the pavement side, pulled open the door and dismounted. "Here we are," he called.

"We're not going as far as Père Lachaise?"

"No, the prison we're going to is here, on this side of the road, sir," said the policeman. "It's for boys, kids between six and sixteen."

"But surely, Courtois, the valet, is a grown man? Why was he brought here?"

Blot said nothing. He turned away, as if determined not to give an answer. Then he said, "I think you should see the place for yourself. Before we go in, take a look, there, though."

He was pointing across the road to an undistinguished plot of empty ground. "That's where they used to have the men's prison, the Grande Roquette. They used to bring the guillotine and set it up in the street outside."

Callender stared in horror. "I didn't realize they moved the guillotine round."

"Yes, Monsieur Callender, they used to bring it to the prisons where there were condemned prisoners and set it up in the street outside. This was one of the places. There used to be crowds gathering around, drunk and screaming when they brought the men out. I remember it, when I was a young policeman and I was on duty round here. They had to drag the prisoners up on to the platform, then the blade fell down and took the head off, cleanly enough, though I remember one big man with a neck like a bull . . ."

He stopped as if visualizing a scene of horror. "A big, thick neck. I won't tell you about that one. And sometimes there would be a number of executions to be carried out, and the blood would be running in the middle of the street, down the hill. A few years ago they stopped those executions in the streets, thank God, and pulled this place down. They've put the grown men in a different prison now—and the guillotine, too. Anyway, this prison across the road, La Petite Roquette, this is still standing." He led the way to the other side of the street.

Courtois, the young valet, was confined in a grim enough building. It had a stone frontage along the street with an iron door. Blot rapped on the door, and a small window in it slid open. There was a grunt of recognition when Blot put his face up close to the window grille and the door swung slowly open. They passed through a tunnel-like entrance into a courtyard, and the entrance clanged shut behind them. Callender, looking round, saw tiny windows studding the high walls. He felt a breeze on his face and shivered. The air was cold and wet, yet there was nothing refreshing about it: instead it smelled of urine and stale food, and under that was the sour stink of mold, which hung in black patches on the stonework.

"The smell of La Petite Roquette," said Blot somberly, seeing Callender raise a handkerchief to his mouth.

The jailer fumbled with a huge bunch of keys. "If it weren't for Monsieur Blot, you wouldn't be let in here at all, sir," he said. "There's no visitors but priests allowed."

He took them inside a corridor that led into the depths of the prison, past an endless series of iron doors with sliding observation windows set into them. Sounds came from within, sometimes of weeping and shouting, once a breathless sobbing that chilled Callender to the bone. At that point the guard flung back the shutter of the observation window and signaled to Callender to look inside.

The cell was bare, completely empty except for a narrow bed on which sat a small figure clutching a torn and dirty blanket, and a chamber pot underneath it. It was a tiny space, which Callender estimated at being six feet in width and a little more, perhaps seven or eight, in length. The boy looked up as he heard movement at the door, and there was no hope on his face, only a dreadful adult despair, though he was sobbing in gasps like a small child. Callender thought he would be about eight years of age, though it was hard to tell.

"He looks so thin," whispered Callender.

"Aye, I think he won't last long," said the jailer. "They can't eat the food, very often."

"What about his parents?"

"No, sir, we don't allow any visits from parents. These boys are here to be reformed, and how can that happen if their filthy, thieving rogues of families are allowed to come and see them and make trouble? In fact, we don't allow any visiting, except once a week the priest speaks to them. He doesn't go into the cell, though. They has to recite their prayers aloud so he can hear them through the grille. Solitary confinement, sir, that's the rule here."

"They don't talk to anyone? No one at all?"

"No sir, not allowed."

The smells of La Petite Roquette were beginning to get deep into

Callender's lungs, so that he began to feel that the miasma of mold and piss was choking him.

"Is there no fresh air? Do the prisoners get no exercise?"

"No, sir, we never lets 'em out, except sometimes they can take a turn in the yard. One at a time, of course, so they can't speak to each other."

Inspector Blot had been walking silently beside them, his head sunk over his chest as though he were trying to avoid the foul air. He said, "They used not to allow them out at all. But the rate was so high . . ."

Callender stared at him in horror. "Rate of what? You mean it was only because so many of the children were . . ."

"Were dying, yes. The authorities thought they could have a little exercise now and again."

Callender had glimpsed a few faces through open grilles. "But some of these are so young!"

"Yes, sir. Later on, if they survive, the authorities set them to work, but they teach them solitary trades, engraving or carpentry. Here we are."

The jailer walked up to the next cell door.

"You're not to speak to the prisoner Courtois, sir. That's understood?"

Callender turned to Blot. "Is a man accused of murder not allowed to receive any visitors at all?"

"No one in La Petite Roquette may have any visitors. That's the rule here." The policeman's voice was careful, neutral, his face impassive, as if he were reciting from a rulebook.

The hatch in the cell door slid back. The occupant did not move, did not appear to hear it, though he was looking straight at the door. Callender was transfixed by a thin white face and fair hair plastered down with damp or sweat. Courtois, formerly well-clad servitor in that opulent mansion on the Rue de la Pépinière, was reduced to a walking skeleton, his head skull-like and his eyes sunk into their sockets. As Callender gazed into the cell, the prisoner doubled up in a fit of coughing that seemed to shake his entire body. He held a filthy handkerchief to his mouth and spat out some dark substance. Sweat glistened on his forehead in spite of the cold atmosphere.

Callender turned away, feeling profoundly disgusted, not least with himself for staring at the prisoner. "He is sick, I can see that."

"They all have the lung trouble, sir. It's nothing out of the ordinary in La Petite Roquette. We gets it ourselves, from time to time."

"But that is no ordinary cough! He needs a doctor!"

"And what would a doctor say, sir, except to take him out of here? Which cannot be done."

They walked back to the entrance in silence broken only by faint cries and coughs that were like voices echoing up from the mouth of a well. Callender thought of Dante and the souls in hell, clamoring in despair.

At the entrance, Blot took some coins out of his pocket and gave them to the jailer, who fumbled them into a waistcoat pocket. "You understand, gentlemen, I dared not let you say anything to him," he said. "That was as much as I can do." He stretched out a palm to Callender, but Blot said, sharply, "No, you've had enough!" and the hand was withdrawn.

Callender had rarely been so glad to walk out into a street. One thing puzzled him.

"Since we couldn't speak to Courtois, why did you agree to take me to him?"

Blot rubbed his face with his hand. It was a crumpled face, with deep bulldog creases from nose to chin, and badly shaven, the sort of face that turns out of bed to look reluctantly at another day. The policeman answered slowly and carefully, "Well, sir, put it like this. I wanted you to see it."

"Merely to see Courtois?"

"No, sir, not just the man." Blot waved a hand to indicate the whole monstrous edifice that stood behind them. "This, the prison, La Petite Roquette. He confessed, you see, sir, after he had been brought here. There are many—circumstances, shall we say?"

Callender said carefully, "Inspector, I have been reading a play."

The other man turned a wondering face towards him. Callender realized the name of Shelley would probably mean nothing to him, and went on, "The author doesn't matter. The play is about tyranny in the home—that's what matters. An old man is murdered because of the way he treats his family. At first, the servants are arrested, but in fact the murder was instigated by the old man's children. They're the guilty ones."

Blot was silent, and Callender wondered if he had made a mistake, pushed the policeman too far. But then Blot said slowly, "Monsieur Léon was like a son to old Rémy."

Callender understood. The policeman added, "There are many forms of tyranny, Monsieur. There is the political kind, of course, and then the tyranny you have mentioned, which reigns secretly in some respectable households. But then there is also a special kind, the bureaucratic tyranny, one might call it. The authority of men sitting in offices and issuing orders. Men willing to protect the rich and respectable."

Callender thought of Hamard, Blot's arrogant superior at the prefecture. No doubt he would be only too ready to protect the rich and respectable. Yes, that, too, was a form of tyranny.

He said, "I talked to a maidservant in a nearby house who said she had seen someone in a woman's dress getting into a cab outside the house late that night."

"Yes, a hysterical girl. Her evidence is of no account."

"She was not called as a witness?"

"Certainly not. It would have been a waste of time."

A few minutes later, Callender decided to get out. "I feel like a walk," he said to Blot. "Alone."

As he got out of the carriage, the policeman's heavy face appeared at the window for a moment. "Monsieur Callender!" he called after him.

"Yes, what is it?"

Blot looked like a sad bloodhound. "Do you have a family?" he asked.

"No, as a matter of fact."

"I have a wife and child, Monsieur."

The cab rolled away. The cemetery of Père Lachaise lay a short distance uphill, and Callender decided to go in that direction. At that moment, he felt despairing of humanity, and the company of the dead seemed preferable to that of the living.

When he got back, there was a telegram waiting for him at the hotel. "ARRIVE PARIS TUESDAY MORNING STOP DO CALL STOP MARINO."

"Thank you," he said automatically, taking the piece of paper from the reception clerk. Helena Marino would evidently be returning to her house in Montmartre the following morning, and the telegram was the clearest of invitations.

He thought of the things he missed during this stay in Paris, not just the sexual pleasures he had enjoyed with Helena but such matters as being in charming and intelligent company and dining in a home, even premises as humble as Signora Amalia's, instead of being forced to eat always in cafés and restaurants. And, after the experience of La Roquette, he had a longing to remind himself that the pleasant side of life still existed, that there were pretty women, fine restaurants, things that would banish the haunting memories of the prison. Furthermore, Helena would have news of Venice, and he found himself longing for that city in a way that seemed absurd. "Can one fall in love with a place at such short notice?" he asked himself.

It was quite easy to check the timetables of the Orient Express arriving from Venice, and he met Helena's train at the Gare de l'Est, where she alighted in a whirl of parcels and packages. She seemed delighted to see him and kissed him on both cheeks. He breathed in her fresh perfumes, freesias and sweetgrass, maybe.

"Revel, darling, thanks for coming. It's always so nice to be met."

"Let me take that hand luggage."

"No, I'll give it to my maid. Celestine, will you see these are all loaded into the carriage?"

"*Oui, madame.*" A plump woman with a red curly hair plucked the small valise from his hand and whisked off. She wore high-heeled shoes that clicked along the platform, turning the heads of the porters as she went.

"Oh, she has good ankles, and she knows it!" exclaimed Helena. "Never mind, it means she always gets a porter for us. Darling, I'm famished, and I don't think there'll be anything ready in my house. Shall we have lunch somewhere and let Celestine go ahead and fix things up?"

"Yes, of course! Let me take you to lunch. Where would you like to go?"

"Oh, I don't know, I feel like somewhere light and fashionable—somewhere that feels like the smartest place in Paris, after being so out of the way."

"Venice is out of the way?"

"Yes, you know, Revel, it really is a provincial place. Everyone there is so taken with it, so wrapped up in themselves, that they forget what's happening in the world. Now, where shall we go?"

Without thinking, he said, "What about the Café de la Paix?" As soon as he had said it, he had a pang of anxiety about the expense, but then thought, *Hang it! I need some enjoyment!*

"Wonderful!"

They arrived in time to have a choice of tables, and Revel saw that there were seats on the terrace overlooking Opera Square. He gestured towards them inquiringly, but Helena giggled.

"No, not there, I can see you don't know Paris very well!"

Callender was rather piqued by this. "I would say I know it pretty well, as a matter of fact."

She laughed. "Darling, this terrace is where the marmosets parade up and down."

"The marmosets?" It was a term Callender was not familiar with.

"Yes, sweetheart, marmosets are the pretty boys. This is where they stroll around to catch the eyes of rich old men at the tables."

"Really?" He was not truly shocked, just surprised that it should be such an open trade here in one of the most expensive places in Paris.

"Yes, haven't you heard of it? You know, there's said to be one of them who has a kind of baton, like a marshal in the French army, only instead of battles written all over it, it has the names of his clients in gold. And their crests, too, because most of them are from the nobility."

"Good God!"

"So you see, I'd rather stay inside, if that suits you."

"Absolutely!" Revel sounded almost embarrassingly English, even to his own ears.

He couldn't help remembering, as the waiter came to take their order, something he had read about the Café de la Paix. Surely it was in the newspaper reports? Yes, that was it. Georges Rémy had come here after dinner on the night of his father's murder, and walked on the terrace to take the air. Where, presumably, the marmosets had been prowling. Did Georges's inclinations lie that way?

"I beg your pardon?" Helena Marino had been saying something to him as they studied the menu.

"I said, I think I'll have the *suprême de volaille*," she answered. "It's always good here."

"Certainly. And would you like some wine?"

She tapped on the gigantic fan-shaped menu. "Just champagne, thank you, my angel. Perrier-Jouet for preference."

He could not resist an indirect inquiry about the Casimiri, ungallant though it seemed to be thinking about another woman while he was talking to this delightful creature. Still, he did not mention Clara by name.

"I suppose I missed a great occasion in Venice. Casimiri, the count who died just before I came away, must have had a magnificent funeral."

Helena frowned, trying to recollect something. "Casimiri? Oh, no, I remember someone mentioning that he was being given a very quiet, private burial. Apparently there was a lot of disappointment—you know how those old families normally put on these great occasions, with funeral barges going out to San Michele and so on."

"Really? How surprising!" He thought of the dramatic burial of the old principessa; surely the head of the family would normally have been given a splendid send-off. The black-plumed horses in the Rue de la Roquette would have nothing on it.

"It seems the family were grief-stricken and just wanted privacy. Not the way Venice usually does things, but never mind. This sauce is heavenly."

The food was light but delicious, the champagne airy and transform-
ing. Callender forgot his anxiety about the bill. There are some experiences
in life that are worth every penny, he thought as the waiter brought a dish
of fresh hothouse peaches, and lunching in one of the finest restaurants in
the world with a pretty woman is one of them. The gilded interior of the
restaurant took on a small aspect of paradise, so that he found himself enjoying an absurd fantasy along these lines, where the attendant servitors
were transformed into black-and-white guardian angels fluttering around,
and the rainy glass skylights overhead became so many windows into
heaven. He did not concentrate greatly on what Helena was saying, until
she mentioned the name of Monet, which brought him back to reality.

"I hear they have moved from the Palazzo Barbaro."

"Oh, yes?"

"Apparently Mrs. Hunter was too keen on getting him to socialize—
she wanted to introduce all her guests to the famous French painter and
so forth. All he wanted to do was to concentrate on his canvases, so they
have moved into a hotel. It's the Grand Hotel Britannia, I believe, between the Barbaro and the Doge's Palace."

Callender deduced that Helena knew nothing of his message from
Monet, and therefore probably nothing of his special commission here in
Paris. In spite of the effects of the champagne, he was cautious in his re-
sponse and merely asked, "And what does Mme Monet think of that?"

Helena Marino laid down a silver fork and twirled her champagne
glass. Her long black hair seemed to be more loosely done than he remembered, perhaps in a new style, that parted in the middle of her brow
and fell in curves along her cheeks. It was very becoming, at any rate.

"I have the impression that Mme Monet quite likes going out into society and being deferred to by rich Americans, in spite of her poor
health," she said. "Of course, she originally belonged to the wealthy
classes herself, didn't she? I'm sure one develops a taste for deference—
and she now is entitled to it all over again, as the wife of one of the greatest living artists. Though I understand they went through a very hard
time before he gained recognition."

"I believe so. I should think Mrs. Hunter is not terribly pleased to have her leading lion escape from the social zoo!"

Helena laughed. "Rather an unkind way of putting it, but it's probably the case. I would have offered to convey the news to you, by the way, when I told the Monets I was coming to Paris."

"Oh?"

She leaned towards him. "But I wanted to be discreet!" She was definitely flirting, her cheeks slightly flushed. Her huge, dark brown eyes were very bright. "Odd," she went on. "Very strange!"

"What is?"

She smiled in a certain, unmistakable way.

"How much I missed you." She sat suddenly back in her seat, leaning against the carved and gilded paneling behind.

"I'd like to go home now," she said. "Would you call for the bill?"

The invitation was clear. Would they renew the passionate encounter they had experienced in Venice?

Callender surprised himself by the consideration that he seemed still able to bring to this question, in spite of the champagne. In England, he had naturally accepted the customs of his class, the aristocratic attitude set by the courtiers surrounding the king towards sexual encounters, which were unrestrained in private provided that no public scandals were caused. Edward VII was celebrated for his mistresses, women of considerable beauty and intelligence who hung on his arm at private parties with ropes of royal pearls around their necks. In this world it was the normal thing for a man to have a mistress, and for a married woman to take a lover, after she had provided her husband with the required son and heir.

Callender had had several mistresses, mostly older women, for whom he had felt friendship and attachment but no great passion. During his stay in Venice, there had been a woman, a jeweler's wife, with whom he had enjoyed considerable passion until he found out that she expected him to direct all English visitors to her husband's shop, which mercenary piece of calculation partly amused, partly disgusted him, but disgust proved dominant in the end, and he terminated the affair. And then there was Mira—but no, that had not been at all serious on either side, he was sure. Signora Amalia had been amused and complaisant, turning a deaf ear to unusual sounds in the night and laughing when once she found hairpins in his bed. "You have taken to doing your hair a different way, Signor Callender!" she exclaimed with laughter, holding up the gilded pins, and he had smiled, remembering the joyless land-ladies of London.

The night with Helena in Venice had been intensely pleasurable, there was no denying that, and normally he would have seized this op-portunity to repeat it, but he found himself wondering if he really felt for her on any level that would run deeper than a brief liaison, although she was part of the life that he led, and Clara Casimiri was not.

This doubt was in itself a new sensation to him. He almost mocked himself for his restraint as he said, "Dearest Helena, please let me take you to your door, but forgive me, I have to return to Venice very soon, and I have a great deal to do beforehand."

She responded, slightly petulantly, "Well, it seems that you and I are always traveling in opposite directions," but then recovered her good hu-mor. "Very well, Revel, but you are an English innocent in Paris, you know! Let me know if I can help you while you are here."

The carriage took them from the Place de l'Opéra up to the narrow streets of Montmartre, past open-air markets and shops selling artist's supplies, past bright little paintings hanging on railings, with hopeful vendors sitting nearby, and the whole pleasant life of café lounging spreading out on the pavements before their eyes.

High up on the hill was a charming yellow-washed house with bougainvillea climbing over the front walls.

"Thank you, Revel," she said, and he kissed her cheek gently. "Friends?" he said, and she nodded, smiling.

On an impulse, he decided to confide in her. He knew no one else in Paris society, no one who would be outside the Monet circle and indepen-dent of the investigation. She would make a good ally, he thought. "Helena, can I ask you something? If you hear anything about the Rémy family, about the murder in the Rue de la Pépinière, will you tell me about it?"

She said thoughtfully, "Well, that's very intriguing, but I thought the matter had been settled."

"The servants are appealing against the convictions."

"So there's still a chance? I'll put out some soundings, if you like. I suppose you know you're using me dreadfully, but I rather like it, I must confess. You're really a very good-looking man!"

She laughed and waved at him as her maid opened the front door and the carriage clattered off, giving him a glorious bright glimpse of the roofs and spires of Paris spread out below.

For the pleasure of traveling around Paris as the locals did, he dismissed the cab at the foot of the hill of Montmartre and took the Metro. In his compartment there were three smartly dressed girls, their mouths brightened with cosmetics and their hair and clothes infinitely smarter than he could recall seeing in the Underground in London. Along with them were a businessman reading *Le Figaro*, an elderly man who just escaped trampdom and was exhaling powerful fumes of some raw spirits, and a young soldier in uniform. Callender enjoyed the little scene enacted by this sextet as if he were at a play. One of the girls was laughing excessively in the ear of the businessman, who remained imperviously reading his paper. Also watching the businessman was the tramp, whose gaze slid down to the other man's pockets, as if spying out the location of his wallet. Meantime, the soldier was eyeing one of the other girls . . .

It was Revel's stop. He was sorry to leave the small human dramas of his Parisian fellow passengers, but as he walked up out of the underground he realized that he had been giving them only a small part of his attention. Instead of going straight to his hotel near Place Saint Auguste, he made a detour to the Gare de l'Est railway station.

"I shall be leaving for Venice tomorrow night," he told the clerk when he had finally got back to the hotel. Once in his room, he began to sort out his papers and his luggage ready for departure. There would be, however, one last duty to perform before he took the Orient Express.

21

The Concièrgerie prison appalled Callender at first, but then he began to recognize that it was not perhaps as dreadful a place as La Petite Roquette. It was an ancient prison, dating from the Middle Ages, but the horrors of solitary confinement and total inaccessibility were absent. It was in fact at the center of a bustling kind of legal vitality, next to the courtrooms where serious trials were held. Its reputation was gruesome, for here during the French Revolution Queen Marie Antoinette and other members of the royal family had been imprisoned until their execution, but the present-day reality did not seem so bad.

Callender had requested the interview "on behalf of M. Claude Monet." He was shown into a room furnished somewhat like a sparse office, with a warder in attendance, and after a considerable wait there came the sound of footsteps on the flagstones of the corridor outside and a man entered, in middle age but still handsome and with a strong frame and an upright bearing. His black clothes were rubbed and creased, but they had been carefully brushed, and his face and thick white hair were neat and clean.

"*Quinze minutes,*" said the jailer who had followed Renard into the room.

Callender stood up. "Pierre Renard?"

The man nodded, and a ray of hope came into his expression. "You have come on behalf of M. Claude? He was always good to us."

It was the same refrain as the little housemaid's; she, too, had commented on how kind Claude Monet had been to the servants. Callender felt unhappy at the optimism in the man's voice, since there might be little that kindness could do in the face of all the official cards that seemed to be piled up against this man.

Callender nodded and indicated that Renard should sit down. The warder remained in the room with them but did not interfere with the conversation, which began immediately with the butler leaning across the table and saying, with a deep earnestness, "Monsieur, I am truly innocent!"

Callender paused before he responded, so powerful was the man's personality, which even here seemed to carry a natural authority. Renard had been in charge of all the staff at the Rue de la Pépinière, dominating the household below stairs, according to all accounts Callender had read. Courtois had claimed that Renard had been the dominant partner in the murder, that he had suggested it to the younger man and instructed him in how to carry it out. Callender tried to imagine their actions that night as Courtois had described them: this man, stripping alongside the adolescent Courtois, and then the two of them creeping about the house and into old Rémy's chamber . . . then, their naked bodies covered in blood, they had washed in the bathroom attached to the master bedroom . . .

That had been Courtois's detailed version, according to his confession. The fault had all been Renard's, and the disturbed and frightened boy merely an instrument for an infinitely more powerful personality.

Callender took his time assessing the man seated across the table from him.

At last he said, experimentally, "The valet, Courtois, has stated that you planned the whole thing."

This seemed to break through the man's self-control. Renard became agitated at this. "Yes, M. Callender, and they brought him here to confront me, but it is all lies! How could they believe him? He was always drinking—I had to reprimand him for it, he is a fantasist, he will say any-thing people put into his head. When I saw him, he was sobbing all the time—he could scarcely speak!"

"So you will not change your statement of innocence?"

Renard's strong voice filled the room with passion. "No, of course not! Because it is the truth. Why should I want to kill M. Rémy? He was always a good master to me—I had the best of positions. Courtois says I killed him for a few thousand francs—a paltry amount of money!"

Callender thought about this. On the surface, it sounded plausible. If Renard was all-powerful among the servants, if he had things all his own way, as Courtois had alleged, why should he want to say good-bye to this state of affairs? Why kill the goose that was laying the golden eggs, the employer who trusted him? On the other hand, there had been evidence at the trial that on the very morning of the murder Renard had been go-ing for an interview for another position in a different household. He de-cided to challenge the man and see what account he gave of himself.

"If things were going so well for you in the Rémy household, why did you inquire for another position?"

"Because it was near my father's home, and my little girl would be living there. I wanted to be able to see her. That was all, Monsieur."

It seemed a good answer. But Renard was speaking again. "Please, Monsieur, give my good wishes to M. and Mme Monet, and I beg them to help my appeal if they can."

Another warder came into the room. The fifteen minutes was up. The prisoner's face, previously composed, suddenly contorted into a fearful expression of despair. "Please, Monsieur," he was saying as the warders pulled him away, "Please!"

Callender sat in a shocked silence. He had never heard such a plea be-fore, not the mutterings of someone close to the borders of insanity, like Courtois, but the despairing voice of a rational man who knows he has been caught in the most terrible trap. After a few minutes, one of the warders returned and silently tapped him on the shoulder, and he rose slowly and walked out into the autumn sunshine.

★　　★　　★

HE returned to the hotel and was packing when he had an unexpected visitor. "I gather you have seen Renard at the Concièrgerie," said Inspector Blot.

"Yes. I wanted to hear what he had to say from his own lips, to form my own impression of the man."

Blot didn't ask what that impression might have been, and it was a significant omission. *He doesn't want to know,* thought Callender, *and he doesn't want to know because he guesses that I think Renard is an innocent man.*

The police inspector went on, "You realize that the evidence found in his rented room was very damaging. It will inevitably prejudice the court against him at the trial."

"Yes, I see that. Paris is like London, there is an enormous amount of prejudice against homosexuality. But isn't it strange—"

"That he was married? But there are many cases of married homosexuals."

"Not just that. Why didn't he get rid of those pornographic homosexual photographs after the old man had been killed?"

"You are suggesting they didn't belong to him? But Monsieur, where would they have come from?" Blot's voice was very careful.

Callender said slowly, feeling his way, "That case you were investigating—that of the homosexual who was assassinated. No doubt the police often have to raid illicit premises?"

The policeman nodded. Their eyes met in mutual understanding.

Callender pressed his point.

"Surely Renard must have realized that everyone in the house would come under suspicion. And he didn't try to keep the existence of his rented room a secret—his wife knew all about it, after all. Wasn't she the one who suggested he should rent it in the first place?"

"Maybe she advised him to keep his . . . indulgences away from the house in the Rue de la Pépinière. If she knew about them, and wanted to preserve their marriage, that is. If he lost his job or went to prison, what security would she have, after all?"

"But taking that room could have had a perfectly innocent explanation. She just wanted somewhere they could call their own from time to time, have their own things, instead of continually living as servants in other people's houses. In which case, how do we account for the photographs?"

Callender turned and looked directly at the policeman as he asked this question.

Blot said, "I know nothing of any other explanation for the photographs being found in Renard's room. Believe me, Monsieur, I know nothing about it."

"Is that what you came to tell me?"

Blot did not answer. Callender felt he had almost had an admission that the evidence might have been planted, and that Blot was covertly trying to protest his own innocence in any such complicity, but there were obviously limits as to how far he could go, beyond hints and suggestions. And they would not save Renard from the guillotine. He tried something else that occurred to him, something he recalled reading about in the English newspapers.

"I believe in England the police have introduced a system of identifying criminals through what is called their fingerprints. You take the prints by pressing the suspect's fingertips into a pad of ink and . . ."

"I know how it is done, sir. We have the same system in France."

"And could it not be applied here? Were there no prints on the murder weapon, or on the stolen jewelry?"

Blot said, turning his big, heavy face towards Callender, "It was not considered suitable in this case."

"Not suitable? What does that mean?"

But the policeman did not answer and, walking to the door, took his leave.

Callender sat up late into the night with Shelley's play. He became more restless than ever and, looking out at the wet dawn, felt a huge anxiety that was driving him back to Venice. The following morning, with a couple of hours to spare, he studied the newspaper cuttings Monet had given him. The reporter from *Le Figaro* seemed to have obtained a great deal of information, and the thought occurred to Callender that perhaps the paper had an ally within the ranks of the police. The thought of Inspector Blot came to mind.

It was with a sense of relief that, a couple of hours later, Callender boarded the train for Venice. Yet he could not stop thinking about the wretched prisoners in Paris, and jotted down notes until he had arrived at some disturbing conclusions.

The women had all left the house for the night. The valet Thomassin was away. There remained on the five floors of the house in the Rue de la Pépinière the janitors, the elderly couple in the basement with the other servants, and the male members of the family on the floors above. In the attic: Renard the butler and Courtois the valet. Mme Renard had left with her mistress. Below them was young Léon's room. Then under that in the principal bedroom was old Auguste, and below that was the semi-independent bachelor suite set up for Georges after his divorce.

There had been no break-in. The janitors were a frail and elderly couple, with no known motive. We must therefore seek the murderers among the family or the other servants.

There must have been more than one murderer. Probably two did the actual killing, because there were light cuts on the front of the face and body, but a blow to the back that penetrated the lung and actually killed Auguste. At least one of these people had an extremely unstable mind and a powerful hatred of the old man—evidenced by the number of unnecessary superficial cuts on the face, which are indicative of a personal emotional outburst.

And then after the murder a cool and orderly mind was involved, someone who tried to make it look like a break-in. Someone who did not panic, who had control of the situation. This person might, of course, have also been one of the killers, the one who delivered the mortal blow from behind. Or it could have been a third individual who discovered or was called in to the scene of the crime after it had been committed.

There were two orderly minds in the household, Renard and Georges, both probably capable of organizing the cover-up. Georges's divorce had caused bitter conflict between Georges and his father, who disapproved and sided with his daughter-in-law. Renard had no reason to attack the old man or to help his killer or killers.

As for the psychological or emotional motives attributed to Renard at the trial, they seem very slight. It emerged in court that Auguste was going to send away the Renards' little girl, who lived in the house, and she would go to live with her grandparents. But Renard had already applied, and indeed had just had an interview, for another job near his father's home, where his wife and daughter could also live.

The death of Auguste would also have meant that Léon would stay in the house, and his sexual relationship with Renard could continue—this was suggested by the words attributed to Renard at the graveside, "He can never separate us again." But both parties stated this affair had finished some months previously. Léon in fact had acquired a mistress, in true family tradition, with whom he had already quarreled.

There were two very unstable mentalities present in the house, Léon and Courtois, adolescents close in age. Both drank heavily, both had homosexual experience, in Léon's case, the previous sexual relationship with Renard. So there were similarities between the two young men, but Courtois had no reason for the personal hatred of the old man demonstrated by the blows to the face. Whereas Léon had been involved in a blazing row the previous evening, was to be sent away in disgrace, and probably believed he had lost the inheritance he expected to get from his rich uncle Auguste.

Psychologically, the evidence points away from the servants and towards the family.

But who had to gain materially from the murder?

Georges inherited—but he would have had to wait only a few years anyway. Léon gained in that he would not be sent away from this very comfortable home if Auguste died: Cecile would not have done this to her adored nephew. Léon would be left a substantial trust by Cecile and Auguste, but it operated only if Cecile died first. However, he may not have appreciated this legal technicality, and in any case, if Cecile were the survivor, she would have probably favored Léon.

The valet Thomassin got Renard's job after his arrest, so, although he was not present in the house on the night of the murder, he did benefit subsequently.

What of the jewels and cash allegedly stolen by Renard and Courtois? Courtois was alleged to have spent money on suits and women (in spite of his homosexual inclinations), but this is vague evidence. Courtois was alleged to have taken the jewels, which were subsequently found in his pocket by Thomassin, not in Paris but in the country house. There is no evidence showing that Renard had any of the cash or jewelry. Madame Renard stated at the trial that their entire savings amounted to little more than one month's wages, and she had to take in sewing to support herself and their daughter.

As to the jewels: assume they were not deliberately planted in Courtois's pocket at Mont Ganelon by someone else: this means Courtois was taking the huge risk of carrying them from Paris to a remote spot in the country where he would have stood no chance of selling them. It seemed an absurd proposition.

Assume therefore the jewels were stolen at the time of the murder and planted at Mont Ganelon, then:

This means the person(s) who planted them must have been present at the scene of the murder and at Mont Ganelon six weeks later when the jewels were discovered. The women were not in the house at the time of the murder. Of the servants, Renard was not at Mont Ganelon when the jewels were discovered—he had already been arrested. Courtois was not taken into custody till after the jewels had been found, so he was both at the house in Paris at the time of the murder and at Mont Ganelon at the time of the discovery. The other valet, Thomassin, was not in Paris at the time of the murder.

Those who fit the bill are therefore Georges, Courtois, and Léon, the only three who were present at both times. Courtois would hardly have planted evidence against himself. Georges, who tends to get overlooked in the judicial ac-

counts, had the clearest mind. If he had arranged the scene after the murder, he would have been in a good position to bring the jewels to Mont Ganelon and plant them. As for Léon, it seemed totally unlikely that he would have been able to plan or execute such a long-term cold-blooded maneuver.

Who made the remark at the graveside: "He can never separate us again," which caused the police to arrest Renard? It was normal in society at the time for men only to go to the actual interment. Presumably the servants would have been standing close together: Renard and Courtois are walking together in the photograph of the funeral procession. This remark can't have been made loudly. Would it have been made to a boy of seventeen by a man in his forties who seems to have been calm and sensible? If there was a current homosexual liaison, it is much more likely to have been between the two adolescents, Léon and Courtois. There is a slight confirmation of this: the police found a suit of Léon's clothes in Courtois's wardrobe.

Who then wrote the anonymous letter claiming it was Renard who made the damning comment in the cemetery at Montmartre? Possibly Courtois, trying to pin the blame on him? Or Thomassin, wanting Renard's job? It seems psychologically much more likely that Courtois made the remark, realized it would be damning if overheard, and attributed it to Renard.

Bearing in mind the evidence of the witness who claimed to have seen a woman in bloodstained dress and a man on the lookout in the street: A possible scenario is:

Auguste interrupted some scene with Courtois where Léon was wearing a dress. Both boys were drunk. He threatened them, and someone seized a knife. This is rather mysterious: the only knife mentioned in the report is a fruit knife, which could have inflicted the cuts to the face but is unlikely to have delivered the fatal blow in the back. One of them inflicted the blows to the face—probably the nephew, motivated by fury and grudges. The other finished the job, either with a lucky blow inflicted by the same small knife or by fetching another which was never found. (The number of stab wounds varies with different accounts. The Gazette des Tribuneaux, an official legal journal that reported the case and probably the most reliable account, says one blow that pierced a lung actually killed old Auguste. There were four stab wounds to the face. The discrepancies between the different numbers of wounds were probably caused because some were very minor, perhaps just scratches.)

The disposition of the blows does not necessarily imply two attackers: the blow to the back could have been delivered after those to the face, if the old man fell forward at his attacker's feet. But a person acting alone would have found it difficult to silence the old man, as apparently happened.

At this point, just after the murder, Georges returned from his evening out. He saw the dreadful potential scandal that would overwhelm the family and initiated a cover-up. He bundled Léon out of the house, just as he was in the blood-stained dress, looked out for a carriage, and sent him away, perhaps to a hotel or a male brothel for the night, somewhere in the shady quarter near the Gare Saint-Lazare where no questions would be asked if the money was right. Georges took Cecile's jewel case from her room and took the key to a desk containing cash from the old man's watch chain. (This was a giveaway—no casual thief would have known where to find that particular key.)

Georges would surely not have done all this for anyone but Léon, who was a member of the family. But there remained the problem of the unstable Courtois, who might easily confess.

Courtois would have been an obvious suspect once the police had stopped looking outside the house. And Renard was the accomplice on whom the blame could most safely be pinned, assuming, as the police did, that two people were involved. The alternative was to involve a family member, Georges or Léon.

Possibly, the homosexual material found in the room the Renards rented elsewhere in Paris, and put forward as evidence that it was Renard who spoke the fatal words at the graveside, was planted by the police. Surely, if Renard really kept erotic photographs of boys in this room, unknown to his wife, he would have had ample opportunity to destroy them.

In any case, a way had to be found of making the suspects, Courtois and Renard, confess. Renard was already in custody but denied everything. Courtois was placed in the terrible environment of La Petite Roquette prison, where he gave a confession that was so circumstantial, that covered so many details, that even at the time it was hinted that it had been dictated by the police. Renard has never confessed to the murder, though he did acknowledge the sexual relationship with Léon. ·

Callender read through his notes. It was a difficult conclusion, but the only one he could come to.

He added,

Renard may have been involved sexually with Léon, but he is almost certainly innocent of murder. However, the only way of proving it would be for a member of the family to come forward at the appeal hearing and tell the truth. Cecile Rémy will not do so—her manner made that quite clear. And neither will Georges or Léon, since they would be inculpated. Furthermore, it is possible that Georges, who frequented the terrace at the Café de la Paix where the marmosets or male prostitutes are on the prowl, also had some homosexual involvement which he would be desperate to keep secret, so he would not want his movements that evening to be inquired into.

The police failure to take fingerprints in the course of their investigations seems to deprive the prisoners of any material proof of innocence. It is quite possible that the evidence—the knife, the "stolen" jewels—have now received so much handling that it would not be possible to get prints with any clarity.

But someone outside this immediate family group could tell the truth to the world. M. and Mme Monet are no doubt aware of the secrets within their brother-in-law's house. An innocent man stands to be condemned unless they speak out.

He saw through the window of the train that they were passing through the wild mountain scenery of northern Italy, and closed the notebook.

22

Venice was agog.

There was such a strange spectacle on the Rialto. A tall young woman in full mourning had dashed through the crowds in the markets and was running over the Rialto Bridge, her black satin skirts flying, jostling the crowds peering into tiny jewelry shops.

They stared and some muttered angrily, but most took note of her garments and drew aside to let her through with instinctive respect.

"You know, people can go crazy with grief!" said one woman with a stout shopping basket, and her sister, standing beside her, nodded wisely. Rumors flew back and forth like the pigeons in Saint Mark's Square.

The truth was that Clara had made a decision and felt that she must act on it straightaway. Hesitation would be fatal, could only undermine her purpose. She paused and looked quickly down the length of the Grand Canal, and then ran on over the arch and down along the quay on the other side.

If they had followed her, she had lost them. She was close to her goal now.

The police station was quiet, dealing only with an American tourist who wanted to know the proper fare for hiring a gondola.

"But you must agree to it in advance," the policeman was saying. "Before you step into the boat!"

They were interrupted as the young woman swept in and said imperiously, "Are you holding two of our servants prisoner?"

"Signorina?"

She was not the least intimidated by the sharp tone of his voice, and said, with her chin held high, "I am Clara Casimiri. Look, there's been a very serious mistake. I want to speak to the commissario. Immediately, if you please."

"Please, signorina—" But Clara had burst into a corridor, looked about for a moment, and then flung herself through a door that was marked in heavy gold lettering, Commissario G. Benedetti.

The commissario was lighting one of his cigars. He threw down his match case in amazement.

"Donna Clara! Whatever brings you here?"

"Two of our servants have been arrested."

Clara's hair had tumbled down, and her skirts were muddy and damp where she had splashed them in puddles in her haste, but she was still a Casimiri. The commissario got up, came round to her side of his enormous desk, and pulled out a chair.

"My dear young lady, please take a seat and tell me what this is about." His cigar was going out, and he laid it carefully in an ashtray, trying to exude a heavy masculine calm. "Oil on troubled waters," he said to himself. "That's the first thing."

Clara refused the offer of a chair. "No, I just want to know where Pietro and Matteo are. Have they been taken to prison?"

"Please, calm yourself, there is no reason for agitation—"

"Don't treat me as if I were a child, Commissario. Just answer my question."

"They are under arrest." He lifted his chin pompously, trying to retrieve some authority.

"For the murder of my father! That's what I have heard. Is it correct?"

"Well . . ."

"Don't play games with me, Commissario."

"Yes, it is right. They have been charged with the murder of Count Casimiri and with trying to conceal it by throwing his body into a tree."

"But why? What motive could they have?"

"Theft," said the commissario with an air of satisfaction. "I am afraid there is proof that they were quite untrustworthy. A necklace belonging to the Contessa Mariella has been found in the attic which they shared."

"What necklace?"

For answer, the commissario unlocked a drawer in his desk and opened a purple leather case that lay inside. On a bed of white velvet lay a necklace of balas rubies, big and smooth as blood blisters.

"This was under Pietro's bed," said the policeman.

"In the case, like that?"

"No, covered in a cloth. We put it in back in its case for safety. Of course, it will be returned to the contessa once the trial is over."

She did sink into the chair then, as if she had exhausted all the breath in her body.

"No, I don't believe it, even so! I am sure they are innocent. I want to make a statement."

She was very pale but obviously determined.

The commissario said carefully, "The necklace was found by your brother himself. Are you sure you want to defend the servants' innocence?"

She looked up at him. "I've thought about it for many hours. All night, in fact. So you see, I have made the decision, and I am not going to change it because of some business about a necklace." She was about to say more, but he held his hand up.

"Very well, would you wait here, please, while I ask someone to come in and record it in due form."

He closed the door behind him, and Clara was left staring at the desk. A trail of blue smoke was still arising from the cigar in the ashtray. It spiraled up and out of the open window.

★   ★   ★

THE cigar had stopped smoldering when the door opened again. She swung round to see a tall, thin figure entering ahead of the commissario.

"Prince Marzano! What are you doing here?"

"I might ask the same of you, Clara."

It was preposterous, his unctuous voice, his assumption of the role of some caring uncle, yet the commissario was looking on approvingly.

Clara found a great depth of anger within her and used it to answer boldly. "They have arrested our servants, quite wrongly, for the murder of my father, and I have come to tell the commissario that an appalling injustice is being done."

Marzano walked around the desk and seemed to fill the room with his presence as he towered over her, tall though she was for a woman.

She spoke out nevertheless. "And I have come to—"

But Marzano was talking loudly, his voice drowning hers.

"Let me tell you, as a friend and an adviser, dear Clara, that I am not going to allow you to say any more just now."

"But—"

She could not go on. The commissario was speaking now alongside Marzano, their voices a drowning chorus of bass and baritone. "You are evidently distressed, dear signorina . . . Clara, let me speak to you as a father . . . Please allow me to call you an escort . . ."

And suddenly there were two sergeants outside the door, and the commissario was saying, "I shall send for Count Claudio also. He is the head of the family now. It must have been an accident that the telegram was delivered to her."

Clara slumped down into her chair. When Claudio walked in a few minutes later, she was too distressed to wonder how he had known where to find her so quickly.

23

The traveller can still stand upon the marble balcony in the soft summer air, and feel its smooth surface, warm from the noontide as he leans on it in the twilight; he can still see the strong sweep of the unruined traceries drawn on the deep serenity of the starry sky, and watch the fantastic shadows of the clustered arches shorten in the moonlight on the chequered floor.

John Ruskin, *The Stones of Venice*

The sky of Venice was charcoal-colored, the water looked dark green and choppy along the Grand Canal, but even with a storm apparently looming, Callender had a feeling of homecoming to this strange and battered old city as the gondola slipped past a sequence of rose and ochre walls patched and stained by the centuries. The peculiar amused delight he had felt on his first visit at stepping into a boat outside a railway station, instead of an omnibus or a cab, had not left him. Even the sense of apprehension that accompanied his journey in the gondola seemed familiar and expected, almost as if being watched from sundry holes and windows might be a tribute which Venetians paid to their fellow conspirators. In this city, of all places, you were nobody if you were not worth spying upon.

Barton was sitting in his study and lifted his head in surprise as the turbanned servant showed Callender in.

"I did not expect you to return!"

"Why not?"

The consul seemed momentarily at a loss for an answer. Then he said smoothly, "Oh, the fleshpots of Paris, you know!"

Was he alluding to Helena Marino's return to her house in Montmartre? Callender chose to ignore the allusion, if it was indeed the case and said, as Barton called for some wine and cold meat to be brought for his guest, "I still have a duty to perform here. It's a question of going through the old principessa's papers, isn't it? I intend to carry out that obligation and make my report to the ambassador."

"Ah, yes, of course. But I feel that after the death of Count Casimiri, with the family in mourning, your task may be necessarily concluded."

Callender felt that he was being pushed into something, and a corresponding stubborness surged through him. "But it isn't. Concluded, I mean."

Theseus Barton looked up at the sharpness of his tone, and Callender sensed he was being reassessed. Perhaps Barton had not expected this.

"Who is now the head of the family? Young Claudio?" asked Callender. There was a pause as the servant brought in a plate with slices of ham and melon and a pitcher of wine, and cleared an extra place at the cluttered table. Callender added, "I would have thought his sister more capable of dealing with family affairs."

"Undoubtedly, but a woman cannot be the head of the family."

Barton stood up and paced round the table to pour Callender a glass of wine. "It doesn't matter much anyway. Look, there is something you must understand here. Claudio Casimiri may be the male heir, he may be entitled to all the deference that five hundred years of noble inbreeding can command, but in Palazzo Casimiri, he decides nothing. If ever he had aspirations to do so, all power has been taken out of his hands."

The melon was exquisitely moist, its sweetness exactly counterbalancing the spicy flavor of the ham. Callender wiped his mouth on a napkin. Barton's round, brown eyes were staring down at him with an expression of intense seriousness.

"Then who is the real power behind the scenes?"

He felt he knew the answer before it came, spoken reluctantly, in a low voice, as if Barton were afraid that even here in the British Consulate someone might have an ear to the door.

"Marzano."

"Ah, yes!" That was what he had half-expected, recalling the tall, black-clad figure, the powerful deep voice of the man who had taken charge when Count Casimiri's body lay stretched out on a chest in the grand salon of his palace. "Marzano, I suppose, is a great man in Venice, though the rest of the world knows nothing of him."

"You suppose correctly."

"And does"—he didn't want to mention Clara by name—"do the Casimiri accept that?"

Barton resumed his seat and said very seriously, "Oh, yes. They had no choice."

Callender was startled. "He must be very powerful here."

"He is," said the consul simply. He changed the subject. "Look, stay the night at the consulate, and then you can leave Venice as soon as arrangements can be made."

Callender was almost amused at the way he was being hustled off: Barton seemed to have forgotten his customary discretion.

"Perhaps I'll move to a hotel?"

Barton answered quickly, "I don't think that would be advisable."

"Oh?"

"There are things I can't . . ."

"Things you can't tell me," said Callender. "But for some reason you don't want me in a hotel, and I am inclined to accept your advice, since I came across a dead body outside the last Venetian establishment I stayed in. Let me tell you, I intend to call on M. Monet tomorrow, since he asked me to perform a commission for him in Paris. I have that to keep me here, as well as the principessa's papers."

"Does the Casimiri family want you to continue your work on them, assuming Marzano will tolerate it?"

"Why not?"

"I just thought that perhaps you would not wish to do so, in the circumstances."

"I have a strong stomach, if that's what you mean. I have no intention of abandoning ship."

They left the topic at that. However, a little later, as Callender looked down from his window at the square at the back of the consulate, he saw two people walking towards the entrance. There would have been nothing unusual in either of them calling on the British consul, but Callender found it intriguing that they appeared to be deep in conversation. One was the downtrodden companion, Miss Tenbaker, who had accosted him in Saint Mark's Square, and the other was someone whom he racked his brains to remember. Then it came to him. He had seen the man at the old principessa's funeral, on the barge that was taking her body out to San Michele, the cemetery island. He recalled the fellow's name: it was Mr. Sullivan, the banker.

There might be good reasons why the Tenbaker woman should be speaking to Sullivan: she was herself probably penniless or she would not be in such depressing employment, but possibly her charge, the wealthy young Clementine Marshall, required his services. Yet there was something about the way in which they spoke briefly and then separated that made Callender wonder.

A few minutes later, Barton called up to him, "Callender, come here a few moments, there's a good fellow."

He found Sullivan in Barton's study. There was no sign of Miss Tenbaker. The consul introduced the two men, and Sullivan wasted no time.

"Mr. Callender, I am representing the interests of the Maloney family. May I ask if you intend to proceed with your work on the principessa's papers?"

"Sir, I must regard it as a confidential matter," began Revel, but then thought there was no reason why Sullivan should not at least know his intentions. The old lady's family surely had some moral rights in the matter, after all. "However, I see no harm in saying that I expect to return to Palazzo Casimiri and resume my task."

"Thank you, Mr. Callender. I can imagine there is a multitude of documentation to be sorted out."

And not only documentation, thought Revel grimly to himself. What he had read so far of *The Cenci* had put such notions into his head that he was determined to find out what really went on within the walls of Palazzo Casimiri.

24

The easel was set up opposite the Palazzo Dario, on a landing stage lapped by the water of the Grand Canal. Strange, he thought, how these waterways cast their spectral reflected lights, giving the illusion that solid brick and marble were shimmering and veiled, impermanent and changeable as the element of water itself. The instability of this entire city had captivated him, and he could never get enough of coveting it with his eyes, cursing his degenerating sight, yet aware that the haziness with which he now viewed the world spoke to some desire within, so that his outer and inner worlds corresponded. He had lost all interest in the human face: humanity was for him something glimpsed at a distance, tiny streaks upon a canvas.

He loved this city, but there was no doubt that the Dario was a sinister-looking building, its roundels like so many eyes peering out along the canal, the strange leaning and angles of the old walls giving an insecure and unreal effect. Perhaps Alice was right. She didn't enjoy this place of shadows and flickering light: she wanted the solid streets of Paris, or at least the clean country air of Giverny. But at least she had recovered enough to get up and enjoy something of their sightseeing in Venice.

She came hurrying towards him before he had begun to work, a letter in her hand.

"It's just arrived from Cecile. She's seen that fellow of yours, that Englishman. He's been upsetting things all over the place, apparently. I don't know why you had to send him."

He sighed. "Because I wanted an account from someone who was . . ." He hesitated over the word *objective*, which might, by the implication that her family were the opposite, cause her distress. "Someone who was not involved."

"Don't you trust Cecile to tell you the truth?"

"Of course, darling, but you know how much she feels things. Look, we have to go back to Paris, and I want to know what we'll be facing, that's all, for your sake as well as mine." The murder appeal in Paris would not be the only, nor even the major, future ordeal they would have to face, but she must not suspect that. Time enough for her to know later on.

She sat down beside him and put her face in her hands. "I know, Claude, you do think of me, I just can't help feeling so distressed for Cecile. There will be a terrible scandal, but I've been through those in the past. No, it's the evidence in court that will be the hardest to bear, to think of those evil creatures, Renard and Courtois, in Auguste's house, stalking around at night with no clothes on. That's why the police didn't find a speck of blood anywhere on their things. That's what Courtois says in his confession, that Renard was naked himself, dreadful creature, and told Courtois to take off his chemise. Then they got a knife and went for Auguste . . ."

He put out a hand to her. "Listen, my darling, we must try to forget it while we are here. This is to be a holiday for you, a complete change of scene, not just a working expedition for my painting."

She sighed and began now to reproach herself. "I know, I'm spoiling things, and I must let you go back to your canvas." But she could not forbear from one further comment.

"At least, Cecile says they are keeping our name out of the papers."

Poor Alice, he thought, *always so passionate and doomed by her nature to break the bourgeois proprieties, her first husband a man who bought "crazy" pictures and went bankrupt, her second an artist. And yet she always wants to be accepted by society, to be correct and respectable. The two things would always be in conflict.*

"That's good, if they can avoid publicity," he said aloud. He said nothing about the mission with which he had entrusted the English lawyer. He had a premonition that even if Callender found out the truth about who had killed Auguste, it might be better for Alice never to learn it. Another thing to be hidden from her! He wondered if he had the right to do so, and also whether he had the strength. She had always been his support, the background against which his life as an artist had been led. Now their roles were reversed.

Alice kissed him on the cheek and left. He turned back to the Palazzo Dario, gleaming across the water. He glanced down to the building where he had thought he had seen someone on the roof a few days previously. But all was still.

CALLENDER'S room at the consulate was high up, and he was restless that night. Getting up and going to the window, he saw an unusual aspect of the sleeping city, the canals winding their silvery way between domes and spires, bridges that looked like tiny miniatures arching across them at intervals. Occasionally a boat splashed past, its wake forming platinum ripples in the moonlight. There were a few soft sounds from a long distance away within the building, feet shuffling over the floor, perhaps.

He was not sure why he went to the door of his room. It had no lock.

Callender listened intently for a moment. Yes, there it was again, that slight rubbing sound which he had already learned to recognize in Venice, characteristically made by a felt or leather sole moving gently over marble.

He looked around the room. The door was furnished with a doorknob, even if it had no lock. He lifted a chair that stood at the side of his bed and wedged the top of the back under the doorknob. The chair was flimsy, but it would at least delay the entry of anyone who might be ascending the stairs to his room. There seemed to be nothing that would serve as a weapon, but he found something and hefted it up.

The footsteps slowly crept closer, audible only as the slightest sounds, and paused at the door. Callender could hear soft breathing on the other side of the wood, so close he felt a strange intimacy, as if he were sharing a bed with someone. Looking round, he found a makeshift defense and raised it in preparation to strike the preemptive first blow. Getting it in first had always been an essential key to success in the many brutal fights of his public-school childhood. The tactic had been spectacularly successful against the bullying Barrington-Fowles, would-be captain of the cricket team.

Irrelevantly, he wondered what Barrington-Fowles was doing now. Probably a cabinet minister. Some people learned nothing by their mistakes.

His upraised weapon seemed to be getting heavier as his unseen opponent delayed on the other side of the door.

Then suddenly everything happened with terrific speed, just as in the fights at Eton. The intruder pushed, the door, temporarily jammed by the chair wedged under the knob, failed to yield, the stranger realized that the element of surprise had been lost and hurled himself against the door, the chair flew over, and a man appeared, almost tumbling over. Callender raised the antique mirror he had lifted off the wall and brought it smashing down on the stranger's head as he fell into the room. The glass shattered in pieces around them with a noise that sounded like an explosion.

Only, this was not like the fights at Eton. In his attacker's hand was a long, thin, steel dagger, and the man was turning to strike upwards towards Callender's heart, as though, even when taken by surprise, he knew exactly where to aim. Callender slipped aside in time to avoid the blade and struck again with the frame of the mirror, still grasped in his hands. It was a glancing blow that hit the side of the head, and the Englishman was surprised at the effect it seemed to have. Something flew across the room. There was a scream and dark liquid suddenly poured from the side of his opponent's face.

The attacker was frozen in midriposte, putting one hand to his head. Callender dropped the frame.

Then came a commotion outside, more footsteps, this time pounding up the stairs, and Barton's turbanned servant appeared bearing a lighted candelabra. *Damn it all*, thought Callender as he peered round in the flickering light, *couldn't they get electricity up here, even in the British Consulate? Was this entire city dedicated to living in the past?* Even as this thought passed through his mind, he leaned down and grabbed the knife from his opponent's hand and threw it safely into a corner. Blood seemed to be gushing down onto the man's neck and chest, and he could not make out the source of the wound.

The servant called downstairs, and a boy appeared with more lights, and then Barton himself, carrying a lamp, so that now suddenly all became visible. Kneeling on the floor was a man clad in the green velvet livery of the Casimiri, clutching the side of his head with fingers through which the blood was spurting, and lying on the floor nearby was a severed human ear. Looking from the ear back to the mirror frame, Callender saw that a long bloody shard of glass was still lodged in it, and must have sliced along the side of the man's face. He recognized that face, though it was contorted with pain. That faithful servant of the Casimiri: the majordomo Rinaldo.

Then there came a huge commotion, the stricken intruder shrieking curses, a woman summoned to clean up and screaming as soon as she saw the scene, another calmly sweeping up the ear and mopping the blood, and finally two solemn policemen who had been dragged from their post.

Barton took charge.

"This man came here to burgle us," he told the officers in fluent Venetian dialect, indicating Rinaldo, who was sitting up and swearing continuously under his breath. "He must be charged with attempted theft."

"What are you saying?" protested Callender in English. "He came here to kill me! Look, there's the knife I took off him."

Barton was a small man, but he said with absolute authority, "Shut up and let me handle this."

Callender forced himself to be silent. He had been here long enough to know that intrigue and bribery lay under everything in Venice, but not long enough to know how to operate the system himself. Rinaldo, though his yellow face was twisted with anger, said nothing and let himself be taken away. Presumably he knew that someone of influence would come eventually and obtain his release. He would be unlikely to ever stand trial, and if he were, it would certainly not be on a charge of attempted murder.

After Barton had given substantial tokens of generosity and the policemen had taken the still-bleeding intruder away, after the shards of glass had been swept up, the room set to rights, and a decanter of brandy brought, Barton said, "For God's sake, we'll be lucky to get away with this. Did you have to cut the man up like that?"

"The bastard was trying to stab me!" said Callender indignantly.

"And what witnesses were there to that? The knife was across the other side of the room when I saw it."

"I took it out of his hand."

"Your word alone." Barton raised his hand against further protest, crossed to the window, and looked out at the silent canal below. "Besides," he said, as if it were a final argument, "didn't you see the livery?"

25

"No, Claudio! It must take place as soon as possible."

Claudio Casimiri turned on his lifelong friend, his prospective brother-in-law, Antonio, always the weaker, always trailing along moaning!

He said scornfully, "No one says 'must' to the Casimiri!"

Prepiani hesitated. In some ways, he was still overawed by Claudio. That childhood sense of inferiority would never leave him. Claudio had always humiliated him in their schoolboy fights, and later on women had always clustered round Claudio and ignored Antonio.

Antonio recalled a vivid picture: he and Claudio, aged seventeen or so, standing in a long, shabby room with dirty red plush furniture.

The boys had seen three bare-breasted women hanging out of a window, long, glittering earrings dangling down beside their white throats. The women had waved and smiled and clicked their tongues. It was late morning, and the whores were still not really busy, just spending an idle hour laughing and joking with passersby.

Claudio had turned to his friend and said, "Have you got some money on you?" Antonio had pulled out some coins and held them up to the women, who had laughed and nodded.

So Claudio and Antonio went up into that long room in the brothel—Antonio could recall the smell even now, the musk and the chamber pots—and the women surrounded Claudio. "*Dio,* what a young beauty!" one of them had said, gazing at him. "Turn around, boy! Look how strong his legs are!"

And another called out, "You can have it for free, darling!"

But they had taken Antonio's money and laughed when he couldn't perform. He had told himself it was the stench that had repelled him, but he knew—had seen, since they were all in the one room—that nothing had affected Claudio.

But the woman on whom Antonio was lying had recognized something in his eyes, an anger, something he himself did not know about till he felt it overcome him suddenly and raised his hand instinctively.

She writhed out from underneath him, stared for a long moment and said, "You need something else, darling." It wasn't even a question.

He turned his head away from her, and yet he knew she was right and there was an indescribable longing within him.

"Come back tonight," she said. And when he returned, alone, they were ready for him. There had been a different girl, with shackles round her ankles, standing in the shadows.

He hesitated. The brothel keeper came up and thought she knew why.

"Don't worry, she's used to it!"

She reached out and pulled the girl around. Her naked back was crossed over and over again with long white lash marks.

"All healed up!"

But as he was beating her, as his excitement climaxed, the thought was hammering in his mind all the time. *Claudio can do it without this. Claudio just does it naturally, like an animal.*

HIS resentment had grown steadily ever since that time, though he felt that he had since discovered a way to get around it, to bring the Casimiri down to a different level.

That would have to wait, however. His impatience would have to be contained, because Claudio was the nominal head of the family since his father's death and his consent would now be needed to the proposal of marriage with his sister.

"Agreed, of course, I'm not trying to insist on hurrying the wedding," he said to placate his potential brother-in-law. "But it's quite natural that I should be impatient; your sister is a beautiful woman."

And Claudio was as good-looking as his sister. Antonio, jealous all his life of those who were handsome by nature, recognized the family likeness of the Casimiri, the strong features and deep gold hair, even the contemptuous expressions on their faces when they looked at him.

Claudio stared at him in that way now. "You're the groom. I suppose you want to claim your bride?"

"Of course I do."

Claudio gave a sharp dog-bark of laughter. It echoed in the long gallery on the principal floor of the Casimiri palace, where the two of them were standing behind the balcony. The gallery was lit with a spectral green tone, an effect of the light gleaming off the water, as it did at this particular moment of early evening on an autumnal day.

Antonio flinched at Claudio's laugh. He had always been secretly afraid of this family. They all seemed so charismatic and confident. In fact, if it hadn't been for what he knew, he might have asked Clara to allow him to withdraw from the marriage. Antonio had kept strong creatures in cages and knew the restlessness of something that turned and turned in search of release.

But they should go through with it. There was the marriage settlement promised by the count, which would surely still be honored and which he knew to be based on the substantial dowry that would have derived from the dreadful old creature, their aunt or whatever it called itself, who had died only recently. Furthermore, the disgrace of rejection could not be faced; such a thing had never before befallen a member of the Prepiani family. And no one would believe that he, Antonio Prepiani of the weak thighs and the thin chest, had rejected Clara Casimiri of the rich, gold hair. No, all Venice would know it must have been the other way round.

Besides, there were other reasons why he desired this marriage, reasons that lay unvoiced within his secret inner mind, and Prepiani was a student of a certain kind of history.

Claudio was speaking again.

"What an ardent suitor! Still, we none of us have much real choice in what we do, it seems!"

He opened the door leading onto the staircase and called for his sister.

Clara came down from her bedroom and turned with surprise to see Prepiani at the end of the room, but as he was about to speak to her, there came a hammering on a door in the depths of the palazzo, and the sound of voices as a servant greeted a guest.

"This will be Marzano," said Claudio. "I asked him to call."

"I didn't know he was coming." Clara sounded as though she would not welcome the visit.

Her brother looked into her face for a few long minutes as the footsteps ascended the stairs before he said, "Can we trust you any longer, Clara? Have you gone outside the Golden Book? Something has happened to you."

He came closer until his mouth and nose were almost touching her face and took a deep breath through his nostrils, almost snuffing with his teeth bared like a wolf, before he whispered into her ear, "I can smell it. Smell a stranger on you."

She pulled away.

"Go back upstairs, Sister," said Claudio. "We'll speak later."

Clara said, "I won't object this time, Brother. I detest that man."

She hurried away, and at that moment Prince Marzano entered the room, striding down the length of the gallery. He wore heavy black clothing, rich yet anonymous, ageless, and his voice was very low, but they all fell absolutely silent as he spoke. He wasted no time.

"I must warn you all of a danger that has arisen. I thought that what happened to your father was a piece of antique folly, and I would never have given my approval in advance. Our class has to come into the modern world in order to survive, you should know that, and yet you behave like characters from the past."

"But what were we to do?" burst out Claudio, but Marzano ignored his interruption.

"So we arrive at arrangements of our own," he continued, "and justice is dealt out as always, by the old families. From what you have told me, Claudio, your late father was guilty of a dreadful crime, and the family took revenge and subjected the body to the traditional shame and exposure. My task is to ensure that there are no repercussions, that there is no scandal, and we have contained it among ourselves. But one serious mistake was made: the customary way of dealing with the matter was not known merely to the Golden Book families. You had forgotten that there was an unpredictable outsider, an Englishman, who might understand the meaning of the thorn tree, and the application of a clever mind would soon leap to conclusions. Since Signor Callender went to Gozzi's bookshop, there has always been the danger that he would work the puzzle out, seeing parallels between the deaths of Count Cenci and Count Casimiri. Killing the Gozzi boy made it no less likely. It added to the stupidity of the whole business, and it prevented nothing. You left a calling card, but it didn't frighten Callender away, did it? I believe he understood only too well. He's a stubborn man."

He looked at at Claudio Casimiri and Antonio Prepiani, silently listening to this diatribe. Prepiani said hastily, "I intend to marry Donna Clara in spite of what has happened." He turned hastily towards Claudio. "That is, of course, if the new Count Casimiri will consent."

The two young men recognized that this was merely a formality and that the real power lay with Marzano, who said, "Very well. Donna Clara has the reputation of being a stubborn woman, and it will do no harm to have her married." He continued, "But my advice to both of you is to recognize that times are changing, even in Venice itself. We are part of Italy now, and ruled from Rome. Whoever put the paper with your crest into the packet of bookplates was a fool—it points straight at your family. If it was intended as some kind of warning message, then I must tell you that our class can no longer behave in this way, as if we were omnipotent. Venice is part of a nation and subject to the rule of law."

He stared coldly round. Claudio was starting up indignantly. "Sir, you said yourself that Callender could be dangerous!"

"So you leave him something as good as an open message! I suppose you hired some assassin to do so. No, don't interrupt, I can see it in your face. What do you think, that vendettas and feuds can continue as if nothing had changed?"

A voice sounded from behind the two men.

"We are one of the oldest families in Venice. Our position has not altered, surely."

It was the Contessa Casimiri, who had just entered the gallery behind Marzano. She was still in mourning, a gown of black that fitted closely to her whippet-thin body. Mariella was nervous-seeming as ever, yet an independent observer might have thought it was the alert fear of some feral animal rather than feminine alarm.

Marzano was impatient. "The world has moved on, Contessa. We noble families no longer dominate Venice. We can influence events, apply pressure sometimes, but times have changed. The city has other lawmakers; it has magistrates and officers who are not appointed by us. They are people who are educated and raised outside on the terra firma, who have new ideas . . ."

"And our class no longer rules." Claudio looked scornful and angry.

"Not just that, Count Claudio. No, don't look at me like that, just as one of your ancestors might have done, almost as if you might reach for a dagger because you've taken offense. You must grasp what I'm saying now, because it is vital, not just for the Casimiri, but for the survival of all of us. We no longer have the wealth that we once possessed. Look along the Grand Canal, see for yourself, all the houses that are being renewed or rebuilt are owned by the English or Americans. Our palaces are crumbling into the water. Unless we become part of the modern world, we are going to die out—or have nothing left but worthless titles. That is why I say you cannot conduct yourselves as if you were living in the past."

The contessa spoke again, somewhat enigmatically, but no one appeared to need any explanation. "Perhaps we can get it back from him. From Callender, I mean."

"What good would that do? He has seen the crest already," answered Claudio.

The contessa settled back into her chair, arranging the folds of her skirts. Her pale, thin face was agitated as she said, "I didn't mean the crest. I mean, the other thing."

"I'm not sure, but Callender may know about it already," said Marzano. "Though he is still probably unaware of what it implies. In any event, I understand he is no longer in Paris. He has returned to Venice."

"We can easily find out where he is staying. There still may be time, before he realizes."

"Time to do what, exactly, Count Claudio?" said Marzano quietly.

The violent temperament within Claudio found a sudden physical outlet. He had a small knife in his hand, not exactly a dagger, perhaps something he had taken from the desk in the room, but still with a sharp blade. He turned towards the wall and cut open one of the hangings with a single long slash, as if it were some creature's belly. But it did not appease his inner rage.

PRINCE Marzano regarded Callender as if the Englishman were an insect. He had not consented to receive him in his own *Ca'*, the ancestral home, but had asked for a meeting here, in a private room at the most luxurious hotel in Venice. They were seated in deep leather armchairs, a small crystal table between them. Marzano was wearing a well-cut modern cream linen suit and tie but looked no less intimidating than when he had appeared at the Palazzo Casimiri beside the body of the dead count.

"Perhaps you can guess why I wish to speak to you, signor." His voice was low, yet every syllable cold as a drop of ice falling onto glass.

"I believe you are temporarily acting for the Casimiri family," answered Callender.

"I am accepted as the head of the oldest families of Venice. In that capacity, I have naturally given the benefit of my experience and my best advice to Count Claudio Casimiri since the death of his father."

Callender recalled that intense-looking youth, so like Clara, yet with something far too hasty and hotheaded about him.

"Last night," he said angrily to Marzano, "one of their men tried to kill me. Oh, no—it's no use, signor—" as Marzano looked about to deny the possibility. "You and I both know it, no matter what he may be charged with. Why? That's the reason I asked for this meeting. What have I done to the Casimiri?"

"Rinaldo, their servant, made a serious mistake."

"Damned right he did. Lost an ear through it. But why?"

There was in fact, as Callender knew perfectly well, good reason for the Casimiri to launch an attack against him: if they had found out about Clara, anyone in that household, where eyes watching from behind every screen and every gallery might have witnessed their long embrace. He knew now there had been moments when he had felt his soul changing into something new, and sensed that he would emerge from the Palazzo Casimiri a different man from when he had entered it. He recalled the feeling of her mouth and body, the brushing of old carnival cloaks and masks against his back. He had to find out whether her family knew about their encounter, and Marzano would be the start, the controlling element, the most powerful being in this whole complex and dangerous situation.

"I ask you again, how have I offended the Casimiri?"

Marzano's eyes were the most searching, and at the same time the most confident, that Callender had ever seen. This was the moment, he sensed, when he would be warned off if they suspected anything connected with Clara.

But trouble did not seem to stem from that.

"Signor Callender, the man entered your room in error, and I would advise you to leave it at that. Count Claudio is a very impetuous man. Return to England straightaway."

"I must insist on a reason." Callender was not going to back down easily.

"You have made some perusal of the principessa's papers, and your task is now at an end," said Marzano pompously. "A banker's draft will be sent to the consulate for you; the payment will be generous for the work that you have done."

Callender was about to argue that his task was scarcely begun when Marzano added, "We will, of course, count on your perpetual discretion." He stood up to indicate the meeting was over.

Dismissed like a servant! But at least, it seemed to be something to do with the papers of the old hermaphrodite which he had come here in the first place to sort out, not to do with Clara. Something in him had changed since he met her.

The old Revel Callender would undoubtedly have taken the money and left Venice discreetly.

The new Revel Callender set out immediately for the Palazzo Casimiri.

26

The palazzo seemed deserted as the gondola moored at the landing stage. As Callender gave the man his fee and stepped into the entrance hall, he called out and looked about for the servants in green velvet livery who were usually nearby, but saw no one. The long marble floor seemed verdant with some damp slime, and in a cold shaft of sunlight he could see great cracks in the yellowish plaster of the walls. A marble cherub seemed to have fallen from a pedestal, and its wings lay in sharp broken pieces near the door by which Clara had reached old Tanta's rooms.

The sweep of the staircase lay ahead, ascending to the grand rooms which he knew were above, but he hesitated, wondering in which direction to go. Clara could be anywhere in this gorgeous rotting rats' nest, possibly in Tanta's rooms, perhaps even in the place with the old masks, the carnival dressing room where generations of Casimiri, and their servitors had donned cloaks and masks before venturing out to take part, hidden in the traditional disguise, in the wild licentiousness of the festival.

He found the room again, pushing open the door and hearing the soft brushing sounds as the cloaks swung on their hooks with the movement of the air. The same scents of musk, sweat, and powder rose to meet him, and as the cloaks swayed a tiny silver box fell to the floor. He picked it up and opened it: a tiny round mirror was fitted in the lid, and he saw the box contained a few black patches that might once in a previous century have adorned a beautiful cheek or covered up pockmarks. Putting it on a shelf, he left the little room. He didn't want to indulge in fantasies of the past: he wanted the real, a living, present woman.

At the top of the grand staircase, he again called out, and this time heard an answering voice. It was Claudio Casimiri, who came to greet him, emerging from the long gallery that ran behind the canal façade.

"Signor Callender! How good of you to come to see us. I'm sorry there seem to be no servants about. Allow me to offer you something to drink—some wine, perhaps."

The gallery seemed to echo as they walked along to the gilt tables and chairs in front of the fireplace. "Are you cold? I trust not. We must apologize for the lack of fire. The servants have been very remiss this morning—or possibly the supply of coal has run out. But let me give you some taste of hospitality at any rate." Claudio poured out two glasses of a white wine which proved to be vinegary in taste. Callender drank it, nevertheless, and said, "I have been away, and I thought I would call and present my compliments to your family on my return."

There was no doubt that Claudio took the point that Callender was not going to cut and run. He ran a hand through his hair and said thoughtfully, "How like an English gentleman." It was a remark that could be taken several ways.

"I trust the contessa is well?" Callender continued to play his role of courteous visitor.

"Oh, yes, thank you." If this was a game, Claudio was evidently good at it. He could exchange polite inanities with the best of them. "She is with my sister upstairs, as a matter of fact. I'm afraid Clara is ill."

Callender felt a deep stab of anxiety but forced himself not to show it and continued calmly, "And what of Signorina Fiammetta, is she staying with your family?"

Claudio was still unperturbed. "She has left us, of course. For fear of infection, you understand."

Callender understood he would get nowhere with this direct approach. "I'm sorry to hear it," he said pleasantly. "I had hoped to have the pleasure of meeting the ladies again."

"That won't be possible, I'm afraid, at least, not for some time. How long is your stay in Venice, Signor Callender?"

Callender was certain that, however long the stay, Clara's illness would last longer still. In addition to his beautiful manners, Casimiri was a good verbal fencer. In another era, he would have made an excellent swordsman.

"I'm not sure when I shall leave Venice. Well, thank you for your hospitality, Count."

ON the way back, he entered the square where he had found the bookshop, the place where he had bought his copy of Shelley, with the gilt lettering, Libri Gozzi, above the door. He hesitated at the threshold: the old man who kept the shop might not welcome his presence, since Callender had been associated with the death of his son, felled by an assassin within a few yards of the Englishman's hotel and bearing the bookplates Callender had ordered. It might be that this was connected with the recent attack on Callender himself, but whether to raise this with the father of the dead man was something about which the Englishman was uncertain.

He peered into the depths of the shop and the shelves with their dusty cargoes of books and prints. Someone seemed to be moving about in the dim interior, and in a moment the proprietor himself appeared and opened the door a narrow crack. Though his face was grave, his greeting was not unfriendly.

"Signor Callender! I did not expect you to return to Venice."

His tone seemed positively nervous.

"May I come in, Signor Gozzi?"

Callender felt that he did not want to linger in the street and slipped through the door when Gozzi, without speaking, held it open wider.

The man's face, now that he could see more through the gloom, was still marked by grief, the eyelids swollen and reddened, the cheeks thin.

"I don't know how to express my sympathy on the loss of your son." It was the inadequate best that he could do. Gozzi received it with dignity, inclining his head in acknowledgment. "Thank you, signor. Will you take something, a coffee or a *fino*, perhaps?"

"No, thank you. But there is something I wanted to ask you. Last night, I stayed at the British Consulate and—" It would sound melodramatic, but this was a melodramatic place, where the operatic was the ordinary. "And I was attacked by a man who came to my room. He was carrying a knife."

The eyes flickered, and the old man sighed. "Ah, Signor Callender, there are so many thieves in this city of ours! How regrettable."

"The man was caught."

"Really? That is quite unusual. They are very skilled, these people."

He would have to come to the point, and even then Gozzi might say nothing, or know nothing. Was Callender taking a risk by even mentioning it?

"The man was wearing the livery of the servants of Palazzo Casimiri."

There was an immediate change in the man's carefully preserved bearing. It was as if Gozzi crumpled at the name. He slid into a chair that stood behind the counter.

"Signor Gozzi? Can I help you?"

Gozzi shook his head. He took a deep, wheezing breath before he said, "In that case, it is as I feared, then." Looking up, gazing intently into Callender's face, he said, "You must leave Venice, sir. You should not have returned."

"But what is it? What have I done to create this . . . this enmity that they have for me?"

"Done? You have not done anything, Signor Callender. You know something. Not even that. You have the means to know it, that is all."

Callender said, "Has it, by any chance, something to do with this?"

He produced from his pocket the slim gold and green book he had purchased in that very shop. "I didn't bother with the preface when I read the play. But last night I turned back the pages and started reading what Shelley himself said was his inspiration for the story. He was sent a manuscript containing the history of an Italian family."

Callender opened the book and began to read, " 'The story is, that an old man, having spent his life in debauchery and wickedness, conceived at length an implacable hatred towards his children; which showed itself—' "

"No, please, signor, don't go on!"

" 'Which showed itself towards one daughter under the form of an incestuous passion, aggravated by every circumstance of cruelty and violence.' "

He knew by the look on the old man's face that he understood.

"How did they know I bought this book?"

"It was just a casual thing, signor, I had no intention . . . Prince Prepiani asked me to obtain certain . . . works which I did not want to have in my shop. At the time, my boy was ordering the printing of your bookplates and mentioned to the printer that an Englishman connected with the consulate had purchased a copy of *The Cenci* . . ."

"So that was how they knew?" Callender shook inwardly with rage, that such a trivial moment had led to terrible consequences, but there was nothing to be done, no one to be blamed.

"I still have a wife and a daughter, signor, and this shop, which is my livelihood." Gozzi was begging him now. "I won't say anything more to you, except for your own safety you should go away immediately."

Damn it, thought Callender. *I'm sick to death of people telling me to leave Venice.*

27

I'm going to get you a doctor here, in Venice."

Alice was lying in bed, heaped up on pillows. "No, Claude, please, I shall be quite all right in a few days." Her mouth had a thin line of green bile trailing down from one corner. She had just vomited again and was lying back on the pillows as if exhausted.

He was taking matters into his own hands, telephoning first the reception desk downstairs. "Hello, yes, I would like some information, please. I believe you have a doctor in the city who has trained abroad—in America, I understand. Do you by any chance know his name? Oh, and his number, thank you, that's excellent."

Monet scribbled something down and called the operator to ask for another number. A minute or two later he said in rather slow and careful Italian, "Yes, I should like to speak to Dr. Albrizzi, please."

There was a brief conversation, and the painter turned to his wife.

"He can call round to see you this morning, darling. I don't want you to wait till we get back to Paris."

THE young doctor was slim and brisk. He had what Monet thought of as a Venetian face: a fine, intelligent oval with a closed, discreet expression.

He examined Alice carefully and asked for her recent history, noting the details impassively. Exhaustion, bilious attacks. "Crises of the liver, that's what they say in Paris," said her husband, standing anxiously in the sitting room afterwards. The doctor said nothing and waited for the painter to continue. There was something about Albrizzi that persuaded Monet to go on, to mention the other, puzzling signs which the Monets had scarcely allowed within their conscious thoughts.

"Well, there is the bruising," Monet said slowly.

"She bruises easily?"

"At a touch. And besides there are—I don't know what the other things mean?"

"What other things, sir? You know, if we are to make a correct diagnosis, we need to have the full picture."

Monet stroked his heavy beard, as if trying to assess the other man, who was conscious of his remarkable eyes: they were filmy with cataract, and yet gave the impression of seeing with an inner perception, as if with a particular vision of their own. Albrizzi could not remember when he had been subjected to such a scrutiny. Finally, the painter answered him.

"Yes, Doctor, there have been other symptoms. There is the constant weakness, the exhaustion. My wife has also suffered inexplicable bleeding from the gums. And from the vagina."

There was a long pause. Monet had not dared to admit the totality of these things before, not even to himself, the unavoidable implication that the very tissues of that body which he loved so much were breaking down. Had he and Alice once been young, passionate lovers, risking everything, both their marriages, lying together in delicious snatched moments of intimacy?

"Please sit down, sir."

The young doctor had assumed authority suddenly, as if he knew that he had to take charge at this moment, no matter how eminent the patient's husband might be.

Monet sank his heavy body into a chair, as if weakened by foreknowledge of what was to come. Albrizzi said quietly, "I think I should warn you that these symptoms add up to the indications of a very serious condition. The vomiting and yellowish skin colour—yes those may well stem from malfunction of the liver. But the other signs—well, we must look at the whole picture, and at what might be causing the problem with the liver. And I have to tell, you, sir, that the likeliest explanation is a disease of the blood."

Monet clutched at what small medical knowledge he had.

"Hepatitis?"

The doctor looked pityingly down at the artist, who had suddenly seemed to have become an old man.

"Sir, do you want the truth?"

The old eyes looked up at him from under the bushy gray brows. Monet gave a long sigh, and then said, "If it must be faced, then the sooner the better."

"Very well. I believe your wife is suffering from leukemia."

There was a dazed expression on the painter's face. "I believe I have heard of that. Indeed, Doctor, I have to say, I feared it. The reduction of the red blood cells, is that not it?"

"Yes, sir. The white cells take over the blood more and more as the disease progresses, so the red cells can no longer maintain the normal processes of the body, nor help it recover from injury where needed. That would account for the problems with the liver and the tissues."

"And the bruising?"

"Yes, that also. But, sir, when you return to Paris, there are some excellent medical men there."

The painter's face looked up like that of a drowning man sighting a raft. For fear of raising false hopes, Albrizzi said, "I beg you, do not let yourself be deceived."

"They will not be able to cure her?"

Albrizzi had not encountered this moment sufficiently often in his medical career to become hardened to it, and there was great pity in his voice as he said, "No. It is incurable." Then he added quickly, "But she may continue as she is for quite a while, and there is a new treatment which is said to be very helpful, called radiotherapy, administered by means of X rays. It seems to check the progress of the disease."

Monet asked, with bowed head, as if he could not bear to look into the doctor's face, "How . . . ?"

Albrizzi understood. "It's hard to tell. The course of the illness varies from one patient to another, but with good care we may be hopeful."

"Of what?"

"A year or two. That is, if the radiotherapy can be administered." Moving forward, he said with concern, "Monsieur, is there anyone you would like me to contact for you? A friend or relative, perhaps."

"Doctor, I believe there is a small decanter of cognac on the side there. I should be grateful if you would pour me a small glass." He added with his habitual courtesy, as Albrizzi moved towards the sideboard, "And please pour a glass for yourself, naturally." But Albrizzi declined and put the glass into the arthritic hand, which was suddenly shaky and grasped it clumsily. After a sip or two, the older man seemed to have recovered slightly.

"No, I don't wish anyone to know of this yet, at least, not till we return to Paris."

"Your wife?"

But Monet became agitated. "Please say nothing to her! Her spirits have been so low recently, I am sure she would despair. When we are in our own home, with our family around us, that will be the time."

"Very well, sir. I assure you I will not mention this to anyone at all."

Albrizzi saw himself out. His diagnosis would remain a secret, even in Venice.

"FIAMMETTA, please don't press me further on this!"

Fiammetta stood like a small red-haired terrier determined not to move away from its quarry, at the entrance to Clara's bedroom. Her friend was sitting perched up on the high old carved bedstead, watching the dying light over the canal as evening fell.

"Look, I don't know what you're worrying about. I assure you, there's no danger, none at all," she answered, without turning her head from the sunset.

But Clara's statement did not ring true, and she was not looking at Fiammetta.

I've never thought of her as a liar, considered Fiammetta silently, *but now I think she's concealing things from me.*

She knew the story of her friend's motherless childhood, had indeed witnessed much of it herself, when she was an outsider permitted to enter the Palazzo Casimiri as a member of the family. Little notice had been taken of the small girl who had stood and watched, and to whose house her friend ran on many occasions.

"But Mama, can't you stop them?" she had said once when a weeping Clara had run into their courtyard and been taken in by Fiammetta's mother.

"No, darling."

"But why?" said the bewildered child, looking up at her mother's face.

"Because we are among the Families of the Golden Book, and we must keep matters to ourselves."

"But couldn't we tell someone?"

Her mother had stood there in the courtyard with the weeping Clara clinging to the folds of her skirts and said, "I'll try. But I don't think he'll do anything."

And she had tried. Fiammetta knew that now. Her mother had gone, abased herself, and begged.

"I will consider speaking to him. That is all I have to say."

That was all Marzano would say, and then he held out his hand and gave the woman his ring to kiss, just as the doges of Venice had done for centuries, for he was doge in all but name.

That haughty voice! Her mother had never forgotten that, the way she had been treated as a creature of no account.

"This is a city that once was a great republic, but these days it keeps its misdeeds to itself, Fiammetta, and that includes treating women worse than whelping bitches," she said angrily. "Italy is in the twentieth century now. You must never, ever think of yourself as an inferior, as a servant to men."

And Fiammetta's childhood had given her an upbringing that accorded with her rebellious temperament.

But her parents had both died when she was in her early teens, and her home could no longer be a refuge. After that, as Clara told Fiammetta, she went to Tanta, and found sanctuary there.

When she was young, Fiammetta had not understood how it was that Tanta had been able to exert such power. How could a frail old woman prevent it? Later, as Fiammetta grew up, she had come to understand the power of money. Once, handing out sugared almonds to both girls as they sat on a little satin couch in her tiny salon, listening to the pounding feet on the staircase, Tanta had said, "Don't be frightened, don't worry, they know what would stop if anything happened to me."

Fiammetta was puzzled, but Clara said afterwards, "My family is paid by her family, the Maloneys, you see. It's a kind of pension."

"Does it go on forever?" asked Fiammetta, her eyes round with surprise, and she pictured gold coins mounting up, year after year, birthday after birthday. The old principessa must already have had more birthdays than Fiammetta could imagine.

"The money stops when she dies," said Clara. "I've heard my father say so."

WHEN had things changed? Fiammetta was not certain, though she thought it was soon after the remarriage of the count, when Mariella, Clara's young stepmother, had come to live in Palazzo Casimiri.

"But is it really over?" she asked her friend now. "Truly, are you sure?"

Clara turned towards her, and Fiammetta gazed at her cool, classical face: the perfect oval which would have been beloved of Raphael, the large, heavy-lidded brown eyes, the red mouth smiling gently. *She was always far more beautiful than me,* thought Fiammetta, who herself possessed great energy, even a certain brilliance like a sharp-cut stone, but could never have been called lovely. But Fiammetta was not envious. What good did beauty ever do to its possessor, she wondered? And her friend's expression now seemed strange, unreadable: Clara Casimiri seemed to be telling her nothing, to be hiding layer upon layer of feeling and knowledge, to be someone she scarcely knew, might not be able to trust.

"Fiammetta," said Clara unexpectedly, almost as if she had read the other woman's thoughts, "Would you take a message for me, if ever I asked you, without any questions, without telling anyone?"

"Yes, of course," said Fiammetta without thinking, without even reconsidering the doubts that had passed through her mind.

28

"Mr. Callender, you will think I am intruding into areas which do not concern me."

Yes, Callender thought, *Miss Leonora Tenbaker, you are certainly doing that, and in England it would be a case of politely telling you to "mind your own business," that phrase so beloved of the English middle classes.* He looked out over the sunlit canal, where two boats had pulled alongside one another and were transferring some cargo—it looked like a heap of yellow and green melons that bounced around in unruly fashion—while the boatmen called out jokes and curses and family insults.

"Ah, Grigorio, you're not a Venetian—your mother fucked half the Austrian army!"

"Yours had it off with an eel! That's why you stink of fish!"

But here, thought Callender, hoping Miss Tenbaker's knowledge of Italian was decently limited, *minding one's own business is a ridiculous concept.*

He said aloud, "Miss Tenbaker, please come to the point. Has Miss Marshall become . . . er . . . involved with another Italian gentleman?"

Leonora Tenbaker drew herself up with a quick reaction and smoothed the collar of her lavender-colored coat as though calming her own ruffled feelings. "Oh no, Mr. Callender, that is a shocking idea. I have been most vigilant, I assure you. No, I am here on an entirely different errand. To warn you, that is the fact of the matter."

"To warn me, Miss Tenbaker?" He looked at the innocent pink face on the other side of the table. She had asked for a discreet meeting, and this upper room in the consulate was the best he could offer.

She took off her glasses and looked directly at him. The sharp blue eyes had their effect. He began to take notice as she spoke.

"Signor Callender, I have to tell you that my presence in Italy is not merely to act as a chaperone to Miss Marshall. Let me come straight to the point. I understand that you are well acquainted with the affairs of the late Principessa Casimiri. Her marriage contract, in particular."

"Yes." He was startled that she should have called about the affairs of the Casimiri, for anxieties about Clara had preoccupied him, but then he recollected that there were other reasons why people might be interested in that family.

"I have seen the document," he added, wondering what was coming next.

"Then you will be aware of the clause which granted the Casimiri family an annual sum during the lifetime of the princess?"

"Yes, I am. Are you implying—?"

But her mind was as quick as his. "No, not that they have been planning to continue to claim it. But rather, that the money should have been paid over to the princess's bank account directly, during her lifetime. And latterly, over a period of some fifteen years, that was not done—or at least, only partially. She had apparently signed an order permitting this."

Miss Tenbaker opened her bag and took out a piece of paper which she passed across to Callender. He examined it carefully.

"This does not look like her signature to me—I have seen it many times on various documents."

"No, Mr. Callender, I believe it is a forgery. For many years, the poor old thing was cheated of most of her funds and at her death there was nothing at all in her account. This very morning I have spoken to Mr. Sullivan, the banker, who had suspicions some time ago and is the Maloney family's financial agent in Venice. He was reluctant to tell me anything at first, but then he realized my . . . true position, you might say. He, too, fears that this signature is false."

Callender was realizing that the small figure before him was not merely a companion or governess with a brighter-than-average brain.

He looked seriously into her small, intense face as she said, "And I fear for the future, because, you see, the principessa left all her money to her niece, Clara. Mr. Sullivan has assured me privately that this is the case. Her will was lodged with the bank, and Mr. Sullivan is the executor. She must have believed her account was accumulating steadily, because she spent very little of it as she grew older, so there should be a very substantial amount left to bequeath."

"But, from what you say, there is no money?" Callender remembered the papers which had been brought to him by Fiammetta, papers which had not been among those in the box to which Count Casimiri had conducted him. They had been sent him by Clara, who had found them among old Tanta's possessions in her rooms.

They were bank statements. *Follow the money,* he had told himself, and had failed to do that simple thing, amid all the heady atmosphere of violent feeling and intrigue. All the time, the evidence had been lying under his nose in the form of those straightforward accounts. He had little doubt as to what they would tell him.

"It was all gone?"

"Exactly so, Mr. Callender. And I have been asking myself what will happen if Donna Clara Casimiri tries to claim her inheritance."

They gazed at each other for a few moments with a new mutual understanding.

"What exactly is your true position, Miss Tenbaker?" he asked slowly.

She said diffidently, "I have no official role, Mr. Callender. I can only persuade."

"AH, Mr. Barton! Do you have any news of Mr. Callender?" Helena Marino was furling a parasol as she was shown into the consul's drawing room.

"My dear Miss Marino! Have you just returned from France? I'm afraid Mr. Callender went out and hasn't yet returned. What can I offer you? Tea, some iced lemonade?"

"A glass of lemonade would be welcome, thank you."

The consul settled her into a chair, summoned Zayed, and arranged for refreshments to be brought. Barton would not ask the lady any direct question for some time, this being his usual policy. Many years of Venetian diplomacy had taught him that, very often, keeping quiet produced more information than open inquiry. He understood that people liked to be thought of as fountains of information rather than rusty pumps.

Helena was a good fencer. She filled a half hour with small talk, and then only when she was leaving did she say, "He asked me to perform one or two small commissions in Paris. Perhaps you would ask him to call on me at the Danieli when he returns."

A message sent to the Danieli resulted in a meeting on the long terrace of the Hotel Serenissima at the Lido.

Callender greeted Helena Marino as she stepped out of the hotel boat that had brought her across the lagoon.

"You were rather conspiratorial, planning that we should arrive separately, and after dark," she said, smiling at him. "Are you being followed? Perhaps there's an angry woman in the background—or her husband?"

"If only!" He looked at her charming face, her forehead framed by a hat and veil sprinkled with small black sequins. "I've run into something that is a bit out of my usual way. And I'm planning to take you even farther afield—there's an inn on a small island where we can get a marvelous fish supper—better than anything they serve here! I found it by chance—I was passing it one evening and called my boatman to tie up so that I might try out their table."

And, of course, it would be a meal within the reach of his pockets, though Helena Marino was far too tactful to mention this, and merely said, "That would be delightful! I'm so bored with eating in these big hotels—the menus are all the same."

"Good. I thought it would be an attractive place to offer you dinner and listen to anything you have to tell me about Paris."

Callender had found a boatman and asked him to moor it a discreet distance from the hotel, through whose grand public rooms they walked as if intent on spending the evening there. Helena Marino laughed when they emerged on to the quayside and she saw the splintery planks of the boat, but she did not appear to worry, nor to mind getting silvery fish scales on her black suede shoes. "It's a new fashion!" she said, peering down at her feet as the boatman pushed off. "I shall be the envy of Paris when I return!"

She's a good sort, thought Callender. *I wish I was in love with her.* He had arranged to see her to discuss developments in Paris, in which he now felt a quixotic concern, but wanted to keep their feelings on the level of light flirtation and friendship.

The island was tiny. Its only inhabitants appeared to be the family who kept the inn and an aged priest tending a vegetable garden outside a collapsing church whose tower had been patched many times over the centuries, and whose roof was almost in ruins. They settled at a table just outside the door of the inn, apparently the only guests, and the owner came out to greet them. It appeared that there was little choice, so their selection was soon made.

An extraordinary deep silence seemed to be settling on the water with the evening light: occasionally they heard the cry of a seabird that seemed to be carrying a great distance over the sea, or closer at hand the rustling of reeds in dusk breezes that were blowing ashore. Helena looked out across the lagoon at the lights of Venice gleaming against a purplish sky.

"There's quite a lot from Paris to tell you, though some of it is gossip, of course, and I don't know how much of that you can discount. But first, there is the most tremendous pressure on the police to secure a conviction for the murder of Auguste Rémy, partly because they have got nowhere in the Steinheil affair. That happened a few days before the Rémy killing."

"I think I saw something about that in the newspapers when I was there, but I didn't pay much attention, I confess."

"Marguerite Steinheil, the wife of a successful artist, was attacked, and her mother and her husband murdered. Although it can't be publicly admitted, the murderer was probably a jealous lover—she had been the mistress of the president of France, you know, till he died in her arms. And in her bed, as a matter of fact."

"But how does that have a bearing on the Rémy case?"

"The newspapers have been crying out that the police are idle and useless, that stout citizens can be murdered in their beds with impunity—that sort of thing. So a conviction in the Rémy affair is very important to the police."

"They can't think Renard and Courtois committed the Steinheil murders, too?"

"No—I think they have solid enough alibis for that. And Marguerite Steinheil behaved so oddly, it's almost as if she knew who the attacker was, and won't admit it. She made up lots of stories—she even accused the valet of stealing a piece of jewelry and hiding it. The man was able to prove his innocence, of course, and the police had to let him go. It was in all the papers."

"How very curious!" He paused, as food appeared. A young girl was bringing them dishes filled with prawns, calamari, and several sorts of tiny fried fishes coated in crisp spices and golden with saffron, and set these down on the rough planks of their table. Bowls of piquant sauces and wedges of small lemons accompanied them.

"No cutlery, I'm afraid." Callender offered her a slice of lemon as he spoke.

Helena picked up the seafood with her ring-laden fingers and crunched it between her white teeth. "Mmm! It tastes so much better like this!"

"Straight out of the sea, signora," said the girl, handing them white napkins for their hands. The innkeeper, who looked as if he was her father, appeared with a bottle of wine. He poured it into a jug and brought wineglasses to the table. These, surprisingly, were not as rough and ready as everything else on the table, but fine blown goblets from a Murano glass factory. The innkeeper polished the glasses before he set the wine fizzing into them and smiled as they shone in the evening light. The wine was light, refreshing, probably ordinary and young, thought Callender, and all the better for it. One could take deep, refreshing draughts.

"They've kept the wine chilled, somehow." Helena was tasting it appreciatively.

"Perhaps hung in a net in a cold current beneath the waves. That's what they sometimes do."

"What a marvelous thought, nets of wine hanging down into the water like fruit! They need to watch out for mermen."

He looked at her affectionately, relishing her enjoyment, and went on, "Perhaps there are still mermen and mermaids in the lagoon. You can see them in old prints rising from the waves, and Venice is full of antique surprises."

"You sound very enigmatic, Revel."

"Yes—well, there are curiosities enough here. But let's get back to the Rémy murder. You know, it's really very odd, about the valet being accused of stealing jewelry."

"Why so?"

The innkeeper's wife appeared from the kitchen, and there was a quick conference. "I think we might have turbot for the second course," announced Callender. "She bought one at the Rialto fish market today."

"Sounds excellent! I do enjoy food—I suppose I'm just a sensual creature all round." She smiled happily at Callender. He was enjoying the warmth of her companionship, the evident quickness of her mind, and continued, "It is strange, Helena, because a very similar event subsequently happened in the case of the Rémy murder. Some jewelry was found in the possession of the valet, Courtois. And this was six weeks after the crime, when there was not a shred of evidence, and the police, from what you say, would have been desperate for an arrest."

Helena Marino's intelligent brown eyes took the point immediately.

"So do you think that someone got the idea of framing the valet from the Steinheil affair?"

"It is a very odd coincidence otherwise."

She took a sip of wine, considering his comment, rubbing a finger against her velvety cheek as she thought about it. "Yes, indeed. But that is not what *le tout Paris* is gossiping about."

"No? I would have thought that was enough."

"*Non, non, mon chéri!* It's the son, Georges Rémy, who is the subject of all the rumors."

Callender cast his mind back to the interview with that stuffed shirt. If he had ever encountered anyone desperate for respectability, it was Georges Rémy.

"What has he been up to?"

"It's the story behind his divorce."

Callender recalled that Georges had been briefly married and was living in the house in the Rue de la Pépinière because his marriage had broken up.

"What happened?"

"It seems that our Georges is really savage," she answered thoughtfully. "His wife has insisted on the divorce because he beat her brutally when she was in an advanced stage of pregnancy. You know, there are things women just won't accept anymore, and French law gives them the right to a divorce."

There was a pause as a huge fish arrived on a single rounded platter of coarse earthenware. The innkeeper filleted it for them with all the ease of the headwaiter at the Ritz and laid portions reverently on their plates. There was silence for a while as they tasted it. Helena said, "We have to give this the respect it deserves. It comes on that rough plate, in this remote place, yet it's the most delicate thing I've ever tasted."

Callender laid down his fork for a few minutes, the better to savor the experience. He turned back to the subject of the Rémy murder. "So there was at least one person known to have been of a violent nature under the roof of twenty-five Rue de la Pépinière on the night of the murder?"

"Yes, indeed. Two, as a matter of fact."

"Two?"

"Don't look too surprised, Revel. Parisians have got over the stage of saying what a wonderful man old Auguste was, how dignified he was, how generous . . . all that sort of tosh that gets put into the funeral service. Now the truth is coming out. It seems that he was subject to tremendous rages and blew up at the slightest provocation. He had dismissed servants on the slightest pretexts. And when it came to the murder, his wife, you remember, had left the house on the previous evening because they had an argument at dinner."

"Over whether young Léon should be sent away. Yes, I remember that from the reports."

"I get the impression from the gossip that I've heard," said Helena slowly, "that Cecile was actually afraid of his temper, though she tried to turn it into a joke. Apparently she had got so upset on a previous occasion that she threatened to commit suicide."

"What a charming household!" Callender exclaimed. "Georges seems to have been following in his father's footsteps."

"But seriously, it is extraordinary, isn't it, that we have this household where all the members of the family were at loggerheads. You know the reason that the young cousins, the Vialattes, gave as to why there should have been no serious arguments between Auguste and Cecile?"

"I would have thought it was because Auguste and Cecile were an elderly couple who didn't think it worth their while to go on quarreling all their lives."

Helena laughed. "No—is this samphire, by the way? It's wonderful with the turbot."

"Yes—they just collect it from the rocks on this island. It's a speciality. What was the reason why Cecile and Auguste stopped quarreling?"

" 'He no longer kept a mistress.' There, I'm quoting what one of the nephews actually said in his statement to the police."

"Auguste was nearly eighty, for God's sake! But I suppose passions can run high at any age it seems! Here, try the bits around the fins. The Italians think they're the best."

She took a mouthful. "They're right! Anyway, the picture we have of the Rémy household is not a pretty one. The father was a bad-tempered old adulterer, the son was a brute, the nephew a potential alcoholic, the wife had threatened suicide. And of all the people in the house, Renard seems to have had the least reason of any to commit murder. I'm afraid there's one conclusion, and that is that the servants were framed."

Callender leaned back and sighed. "And do you think there's any possibility of proving that?"

She looked sadly at him. "I doubt it. There's an awful lot of money, power, and influence there."

"I think M. Monet—I get the feeling he is an honorable man."

"Yes, in most circumstances, I think he would be. But this is his wife's family we're talking about. If the servants are innocent, then one of Alice Monet's close relations is guilty. And blood is thicker than water—I'm afraid it will be stronger than honor, also."

He said thoughtfully, "But there's not much he could do, in any case. Not in the face of a forced confession and planted evidence. That's what we're dealing with here, I'm sure of it."

There was a long pause, during which the landlady appeared and cleared away the bones and remains of the turbot. Then she brought sweet cheeses, dishes of almonds and candied fruit, and a small flask of golden dessert wine.

"I feel very guilty that we left so much of the turbot, but it's a huge fish!" said Helena.

"Don't worry—it means there's plenty left for the family supper. They probably would be unable to afford to buy one just for themselves."

Helena leaned back in her chair with a huge, comfortable sigh and then looked at Callender curiously. He was staring down at his plate and toying with a few almonds between his fingers. She asked him, "Are you losing your appetite?"

He smiled. "You're very quick!"

She leaned forward and put a hand on his wrist. "You may be drawn into too many battles, Revel. I sense you are fighting already. Don't take on too much. Now, that's good advice—please accept it."

Had he successfully negotiated their brief sexual encounter into a deeper relationship of trust and friendship? Callender felt that he had and looked affectionately at her. "I'm listening to what you say, dear Helena, I promise you."

He sent her back with the innkeeper in the boat belonging to the tavern, and himself followed on after a short delay with the original boatman, who had arrived as planned. Glad of her friendship as he was, this seemed ungallant, but his first concern was her safety, and indeed his fears seemed to be confirmed as they pulled away from the island and through the darkness he saw the shape of a slim prow gliding over the water in their wake. It might be coincidence, of course, but he thought that someone else was silently making the journey back to Venice behind him.

CALLENDER found the consulate not only in darkness, but in complete silence. The eerie quietness of Venice, a city free of the constant rumble of carts and carriages, was most apparent at night. His boatman had deposited him at the landing stage, and looking down the sweep of the Grand Canal, there was no other craft in sight, though at intervals there were the black mouths of all the smaller waterways, and anything might be within those narrow depths. It was impossible to see into the shadows that filled them.

The chinking of coin as he paid the man, the murmured thanks, and the swish of oars as the boat glided away seemed magnified by the night, echoing from the hard marble walls of Venice. The water entrance of the consulate was open, and the staircase to the upper region unbarred.

CLARA Casimiri was at that moment facing her brother and Prepiani over a marble-topped table in the long gallery of the palace.

"But why, Clara?" shouted Prepiani. "Why have you changed your mind now?"

She did not reply with the same anger but spoke steadily, calmly. "Antonio, I will tell you the truth. I have lived most of my life within these walls, and I have accepted it. I was almost like a creature in a harem, although it was voluntary, because I did not see much of value in the modern world. And marriage to you seemed an inevitable part of my existence. But now I have realized that I could not bear it. I will not marry you, Antonio."

Claudio Casimiri stared at her. "What has brought this about? Something must have happened."

Clara said, "Yes, I have become braver. I won't run away anymore, as I did when I was a child. I should have refused this marriage long ago." She stood before Prepiani boldly.

"Go away, Antonio. There is nothing for you here."

Prepiani looked stunned. "Claudio, speak to your sister! Enforce your authority! You brought her back when she tried to go to the police."

But Claudio Casimiri did not answer immediately. Then he said idly, "No, why should I give her to you, Antonio? After all, I'm really not interested in your affairs. It suits me if my sister does not marry. She can stay here and be our housekeeper."

Prepiani was shouting now. "Clara, don't listen to him. He had Gozzi's son killed, just because they had sold the Shelley book to the Englishman. Not even Prince Marzano would have wanted that. It pointed directly at your house. By God, you are all of you crazy as mad dogs."

Claudio's laugh was instantaneous. "You say that, you who tried to buy engravings of tortures from Gozzi? And the evidence of your own insanity has been crying aloud to heaven? Literally, in the case of the kitchen girl. Was that not the case? Be silent, Antonio. There are too many witnesses now."

Antonio Prepiani slammed a fist down on the marble table, where the rings on his hand struck the surface with a clash of metal. He swung round and slammed out of the room.

Outside, on the staircase, where no one could see, he beat his fist against the wall. "But you don't know, Donna Clara, you don't know what I shall do!"

29

It was a clear, bright morning. The Englishman had arrived at the Palazzo Casimiri by a network of back streets and small bridges. There was a visit he wanted to make before he could begin his plan of attack, and he knew that the place he was looking for was somewhere nearby. He went down the length of the *androne* away from the Grand Canal and found a small door opening into a street at the back of the palazzo.

It seemed deserted, but he walked another twenty yards or so, and a maid came out of a doorway carrying a pail of slops.

"Can you tell me where Dr. Albrizzi lives?"

She grinned at him widely with gap-toothed teeth brown as dirty canal water and nodded. A bit of a simpleton, it seemed, but she knew the doctor's name.

It took several twists and turns along narrow alleys between high walls and two more inquiries before Callender emerged into his goal, a small square with a fountain at the center. The water bubbling out of an urn held by a chubby stone nymph looked clear, and he was thirsty, but he did not risk drinking from it. The house of Dr. Albrizzi was evident enough, since it bore a brass plate, newly engraved and polished, beside the door. The doorbell worked, a promising enticement in Venice. However, there was one deterrent: a new iron grille had been secured over the

whole entrance and fastened with padlocks. It was unlocked after an un-
nervingly magnified and distorted eye had scrutinized Callender through
a glass peephole, and a manservant pulled aside the grille.

Callender was shown into a plainly furnished waiting room with
steel engravings depicting an ivy-covered mass, which he identified as
Harvard, and framed medical certificates in Italian and English on the
walls. After a few minutes, Albrizzi himself appeared.

He was evidently surprised to see Callender, but did not hesitate to invite him into a small study furnished mainly with medical texts and a few
objects which looked as if they had been inherited from previous generations. There were some *albarelli*, the big Moorish-style jars decorated with
luster and cobalt, and glass jars with ornate stoppers, the labels round their
necks bearing worn gilded lettering indicative of an antique pharma-
copoeia. A crystal skull lay on a small desk of inlaid work, glittering with
bluish internal refractions in the rays of sunlight that slanted through a
window, which was also barred with a grille. Callender noted in a quick
glance that, like the ironwork over Albrizzi's doorway, it looked new.

The doctor saw Callender's gaze upon the scintillating skull.

"Exquisitely made by our glassmakers in Murano, but I'm afraid
hopelessly inaccurate as far as the lobes of the brain are concerned. I
keep it as a memento. Some of my patients like to see this kind of thing,
these reassuring pieces of tradition. Some of them like old-fashioned
medical remedies as well, of course, though I am trying to introduce
new techniques." He slid open a drawer and took out a green leather
case, flicking the locks open as he did so. On the velvet interior rested a
terrifying-looking display of knives, hooks, and scalpels.

"I inherited the skull with my father's practice, along with his instruments. Imagine operating with these things, yet without anesthetics."

"Horrible idea! The skull is an interesting piece, though. How old is it?"

"Oh, I think eighteenth century." Albrizzi laughed, holding up a long
scalpel and turning over its long, honed blade with a deep slick chased
down the center. "This channel is to allow the blood to run out of the in-
cision, you see."

"Most ingenious."

"I'm glad you appreciate the skill with which it was made, at any rate. You know, it is such a pleasure to see you again, Signor Callender. We had a most interesting telephone conversation before your departure to Pans. Of course, Italian is the most beautiful language in the world, but there are times when I enjoy speaking English again."

Callender felt relief, too, for a slightly different reason. Albrizzi's American accent made him feel he could come straight to the point, without all the elaborate courtesies and preliminaries that Europeans seemed to find necessary.

"Dr. Albrizzi, you're the physician to the Casimiri family, I understand. Have you seen Donna Clara Casimiri recently?"

There was a long pause, and Callender was aware of some feeling generated in that small, dark room, though he could not identify it, could only note the physician's hand tightening on the case of old instruments, the knuckles whitening, and a flinching of the muscles around the mouth that bespoke—what? Fear?

Albrizzi looked at him curiously. "Donna Clara?" he said slowly. "No, I don't think it's breaking a professional confidence to say that I haven't seen her for some days. More than a week, probably. Are you concerned about her?"

"Frankly yes, I am. When I called there I was told she was ill. At first I assumed her brother was merely preventing me from seeing her, but whether she is ill or not, I feel an anxiety."

"It is a strange household, undoubtedly." Albrizzi spoke quietly, rubbing his chin thoughtfully. His eyes were unusual for a Venetian, light gray, though his hair and beard were black. They suggested a profound intelligence, but more than that, there was a directness about his gaze that spoke of an independence of mind that Callender realized he had not much encountered in Venice. If Albrizzi was nervous, he was overcoming it rapidly.

"I went to the Palazzo Casimiri about three or four days ago, to see the contessa," Albrizzi continued. "I'm afraid her nerves are in a very poor state. But I didn't see Donna Clara." He paused for a moment as if considering matters, then opened the door and called out, "Teresa!"

An elderly maid with tiny hands and a white apron came bustling along the passage. *"Si, Dottore?"*

"Teresa, you used to do some sewing for the Casimiri household, didn't you? Have you heard anything of Donna Clara?"

"Oh, *Dottore*, yes, before the old count died I had a message that the ladies wanted me to do some embroidery. I wouldn't have gone, but for Donna Clara. Pietro came to the door and said they wouldn't be able to speak to me after all, and that I was to go away. But Pietro said, 'There'll be plenty of work for you here soon. They'll be sewing Donna Clara's wedding dress!' They might ask me to work on it, perhaps. But I haven't seen Pietro for some time."

"Well, you are a fine embroideress!" commented Albrizzi.

She smiled apologetically, as if she were not being sufficiently modest. "You know, the modern ladies go to the couturiers, and order their dresses from Paris, but the Casimiri, they keep to the old traditions. I expect Donna Clara will have a brocade gown with Venetian embroidery, all worked with gold and silver thread. She has been looking at old pictures for the patterns."

"Has she talked to you about it?" asked Callender. "Donna Clara herself, I mean?"

Teresa turned towards him. "No, signor, not yet. And I don't know if I will do it." Her expression had changed, and Callender exclaimed, "Why not?"

"Pietro seemed different when I last saw him. Now he has disappeared—I can't express it, but he wasn't friendly as he used to be. And then, I don't like the place, signor." She seemed to withdraw into herself, hunching her shoulders as she spoke. "I don't like to go to the Palazzo Casimiri, not now. I said as much to the *dottore*."

Callender asked urgently, "Why, is there something wrong there?"

"Oh, no, signor, I couldn't say, only that it makes me fearful. But I don't know why, only that no one likes to go there. They say the old count walks at night, all bloody and torn by the thorns. But these are the stories that are told by simple people around here, and I don't take any notice of them." She said this too quickly, as if it were a ritual phrase that she used to comfort herself, turned to Albrizzi, and said, "With your permission, *dottore*." He nodded, and she left the room.

There was a long silence. The two men were still standing opposite each other.

"I was watching your face," said Albrizzi. "This marriage of Clara Casimiri means a lot to you, Callender. Am I right?"

"I must see her first, before it happens!" Callender was aware that he had given his feelings away, but he did not care.

"The union with Prepiani was arranged a long time ago, by their parents, I understand," the doctor said. He looked at Callender. "Personally, I believe in freedom of choice, even for women!" He spoke decisively, as if he had come to a conclusion, and added, "There has been enough obscurity there. It's time we stood up to it."

This seemed an odd turn of phrase. "Stood up to what, Doctor? I don't follow."

"There are things I—the truth is, Signor Callender, I have come back into this old world and want to deal with it in the way I learned in the new world. But it needs . . . more courage than I possess." He turned away and gazed at the crystal skull. The glistening eye sockets stared back.

Callender felt he had to put his cards on the table to gain this man's trust. It would be important to do so, Albrizzi would be a good ally, but that trust might not be easily won.

"Albrizzi, I saw something in that place which I myself recall with fear."

"You were the first to see the body of the count, I understand. Yes, it must have been a dreadful sight."

"Not only that. I also saw him immediately after he had been taken down from the thorn tree."

Albrizzi sighed deeply, as if he sensed what was coming. "You told me as much in that telephone call!"

"There were wounds on the body. Not scratches from the thorns."

The Englishman pressed on. "You were summoned to the Palazzo Casimiri after the death. You are a trained physician—surely you could not have overlooked the count's injuries."

As he said it, he recalled the medical evidence in the case of Auguste Rémy, murdered in his mansion in Paris. There, the first three doctors on the scene, one a friend of the family, another his underling, and the third, a society medico, had stated that death was due from apoplexy before the congealed blood had even been washed from the dead man's face. Only after a stranger to the household had summoned the commissioner did a police surgeon examine the body and point out that there were actually stab wounds to the face and the back. Until then, an unofficial conspiracy had evidently prevailed as to the cause of death. Yes, Callender had learned something from that case. For professional men, there was a choice between the way of conformity and the way of truth.

He wondered which path Albrizzi would take.

The pale gray eyes were looking at him cautiously. "We are both outsiders here, Callender," said Albrizzi. "You by birth, and I have made myself so by my training abroad, for the outside world is distrusted here. And by chance two such men as ourselves have witnessed something of the inner secrets of the Casimiri."

He sighed abruptly and brought his fist down on the desk. The glass skull rattled on the wood.

"I should not have done it!" he exclaimed. "I should have been bolder in the first place. I should have taken the matter to Rome, but I didn't carry it out. I merely threatened to do so. All I did was to refuse to make any certification of the cause of the old count's death, and they called in old Gribaldi, who's half-blind anyway. He gave them what they wanted."

" 'They' being the Casimiri?"

"Claudio Casimiri, yes, but not just him. If it had been only Claudio, I might have been braver."

"Who else, then?" Callender felt he could see the answer forming on Albrizzi's lips before the name was uttered.

"Marzano. You know, we doctors must have a license to practice, and his family could get my license revoked."

Callender was beginning to feel that even here, in a professional man educated outside the old closed system of the nobility of the Golden Book, he would find no ally against the overbearing authority which the leader of the aristocracy still commanded. He was surprised when Albrizzi said suddenly, "There have been too many decisions made according to the old traditions. I believe Donna Clara may be forced into marriage against her wishes, and I'll help her if I can." He laughed a little. "That's the bravest I can be. It doesn't lead to heroism, you know, when there is always a dark movement at the end of a *calle*, or an unnamed little vessel bobbing about in the wake of your own boat. I think I am already being followed."

"I believe you. I've been the victim of an attack myself, and the fellow was wearing the Casimiri livery. And poor Gozzi—his son was murdered while delivering a packet to me at my hotel."

"May I ask what was in the packet, signor?"

"Only some bookplates I had ordered."

Albrizzi's intelligent eyes stared at him with amazement, and he went on, "I wandered into his shop on my way to look at the principessa's documents. It was merely a chance encounter."

"But how could anyone have thought there was something sinister in it?" Albrizzi was puzzled and thoughtful.

"It was entirely innocent, of course. I went into the shop in the first place because I happened to see a copy of a play by Shelley in the window."

Albrizzi sank onto a chair. "What was that?"

"Shelley's drama, *The Cenci*. It was a finely bound copy, quite a collector's item, in fact."

Albrizzi said slowly, "Venice conceals a great deal of evil, signor. You must feel yourself under threat."

"What about you?" said Callender, remembering how hard it had been to gain admission to the doctor's house. "The iron grille on your door—that is a recent addition?"

"Yes. Look, Callender, I suggest I begin with a straightforward request to see Donna Clara personally. She is, after all, my patient, and I have heard reports that she is sick."

"When you do that, I shan't be far away."

"If I may say so, you look a useful man in a scrap."

Callender bowed. "Thank you—and you, I take it, did not spend your time at Harvard entirely in the study?"

Albrizzi smiled. "Rugby—I was on the college team. A rough business, even for gentlemen."

"Excellent! And you agree with me that there were stab wounds on the count's body?"

The doctor reached for a book from the shelves before him. It was a fat old thing with a cracked binding, as if it had been well used. He sat down on a high-backed velvet chair and indicated to Callender to do the same.

"Signor Callender, there were stab wounds and thorn scratches. Have you any idea what that signifies?"

"That someone hoped that there would be so many scratches from the thorn tree that the knife wounds would not be noticed."

It seemed pretty obvious to Callender, but Albrizzi clicked his tongue against his lips and shook his head, like a teacher with a disappointing student.

"Not just that. This is Italy."

Callender said with exasperation, "Yes, obviously, but what does that mean, exactly? Surely the evidence of these cuts is the same, whatever the country?"

"No, that is not entirely true. Here, they must be understood in a more subtle way. Let me read something to you. It is the evidence on which your Shelley based his play." As the doctor opened the book which he held, it made a creaking sound, almost as if a door had swung open on its hinges. He began to read aloud. Callender at first had difficulty with the Renaissance Italian in which the document was written, but he began to follow its cadences and had little difficulty in grasping the gist of it.

Count Francesco Cenci was a man of extraordinary brutality and perverted sexual tastes. Even by the standards of the sixteenth century, which gave men almost total power over their families, he was considered to have gone to extremes. His servants testified that Francesco at first satisfied his sexual urges with boys whom he took to the stables, sometimes scratching their faces as he did so. But even a conviction for sodomy, which resulted in his paying a huge fine, did not stop his brutal activities, though these were not confined to boys, and he seemed to get ever more mad and cruel.

His first wife died, and he married again, giving his children a young stepmother. In 1595, he took his second wife, Lucrezia, and daughter, Beatrice, aged eighteen, to a remote fortress in the Abruzzi mountains. There he condemned them to a sadistic imprisonment, locking them into a room with the door nailed up, and only a small opening left through which they could receive food and drink. The windows were also covered, except for small apertures. They had to stand on a chair or a stool to see through them.

Beatrice's spirit was not broken, however. She was determined to get out of this captivity and wrote letters, which were delivered by a sympathetic servant, to relatives in Rome begging for help. But Francesco discovered this and was determined to punish her. He had her dragged out, and waving one of her letters, fetched a bull-pizzle whip and thrashed her horribly with it, like a man out of all control. She managed to protect her face by putting out her hands, but they were badly injured. He locked her up in her room and was her only visitor for several days.

After this, Beatrice was more resolved than ever to defy her father, telling her stepmother, when she emerged from her imprisonment, that she intended to make him sorry for his violence. It was generally assumed this meant he had not only beaten his daughter, but that he had raped her also. There was a strange incident when the distraught stepmother was summoned into the bedroom where Francesco was with Beatrice, and the servants believed that he had enjoyed both women together.

On September 7, 1598, the body of Count Cenci was discovered under a balcony, impaled on a tree. At first, it was thought that the injuries on his body were caused by scratches. But there was a wound to one of his eyes which, when examined more carefully, was too deep to be caused by the branch of a tree. His family all said that he fell by accident. His head had collided with the tree, and one of its great spines must have entered his eye.

At this point, the doctor laid down his book. Callender was staring at him intently, like a man frozen in movement. Albrizzi said, "You see? You know now what the murder of Count Casimiri may have been based upon."

Callender emerged from his horror like a man coming from freezing depths. "You really think that what happened in the Casimiri family had a parallel in the . . . in *The Cenci*? I must confess, it was what I feared."

Albrizzi said gently, "Yes, I'm afraid so. Like Cenci, Count Casimiri remarried. Like him, he had a daughter."

"I saw no sign of anything like that! The count seemed perfectly normal . . ." Callender's voice faded away as the implications came home, and he contemplated the life Clara might have led within the walls of Palazzo Casimiri.

"To outsiders, yes. I'm afraid that is often the case. In America, I had an opportunity to study the works of Dr. Freud of Vienna—but let me tell you that Cenci's body was exhumed, and on closer examination it became apparent that his injuries must have been caused by a deliberate attack. It is said that he was stabbed through the eye and in the mouth, so that no outer marks would be left."

"And Cenci was killed at the instigation of his own family, and his body cast down on to the branches of a tree."

"Yes, Mr. Callender. The Cenci were all condemned to death, in spite of evidence that he was a sexually perverted brute who had forced his wife and daughter into obscene practices. He was a filthy creature, old Cenci. He obviously wanted to humiliate women. There were four of them in his castle, his wife, daughter, and two maids, and evidence was given that he went around clad only in a shirt and a pair of drawers. When he wanted to urinate, he would get one of the women to hold the urinal under his shirt. As for Beatrice, he obviously had strange perversions. She had to scratch his feet and his testicles and rub them with a cloth."

"Good God! How grotesque!"

"When he slept with his wife, he made Beatrice sleep in a bed next to them, divided only by a sheet that had been hung up between the beds. And eventually he had wife and daughter in the bed together."

"But wasn't there anything anyone could do?"

"Beatrice herself didn't make the incest public. It must have been felt too shameful, too much of a family disgrace. The evidence for that eventually emerged from the servants. Beatrice appealed for help against her father's maltreatment generally, but none was forthcoming. Cenci was absolute master of his house in those days. So in the end, it seems his family took the only course open to them. Beatrice's brother, Giacomo, helped in the plot. They killed the count when he was asleep."

Callender was silent, working the scheme of events out, though his mind was recoiling from following the parallels between the Casimiri and the Cenci to their ultimate conclusion. At last he said, "But why should the Casimiri have followed the same course? Surely, we are in the modern age. Clara Casimiri is not Beatrice Cenci. She could have gone to the police."

"And make known a family shame? Besides, she may have feared the same result. That she would try to protest, and no notice would be taken."

"So the Casimiri did what the Cenci family had done all those centuries ago? They took matters into their own hands and killed the father." Was it possible that the woman he had embraced, the lovely and remote creature within the walls of Palazzo Casimiri, had been the victim of her father's incestuous desires? Who knew what went on inside families, especially ones as secretive and enclosed as the Casimiri? Certainly, Clara seemed to have a remoteness about her, a distancing, that was surely more than the result of her birth. He wondered sadly if such suffering as she might have endured could ever be truly resolved.

There came the rushing sound of a slight breeze, and in the distance a voice calling something indistinct. He forced his mind back to the factual details of the count's death.

"But a thorn tree wouldn't really leave marks that would obliterate those deep wounds. They would surely have realized that," he said.

"Yes—but throwing the body into the tree would serve another purpose. It would act as a signal to those who knew the old story. And that would include, of course, the other noble families of Venice."

Callender remembered something that had nagged at the back of his mind. There were surely so many ways of disposing of a body in Venice. Why had the count not been weighted down and slipped into one of the narrow, dark canals, the little *rio* at the side of the palace, for example? Or taken at night to one of the outlying islands in which the lagoon abounded? Throwing the body into the courtyard had seemed too blatantly obvious that the murderer wanted it to be discovered there.

This was the explanation. The thorn tree was a sign.

"So everyone—that is to say, all the aristocratic class—knows the meaning of the place where the corpse was discovered?" Callender asked. "Without anything actually being spoken, or made public."

"Quite. It was as good as saying that the count had committed incest. And the perpetrators could claim justification."

"Because of the cause?"

"Yes."

Callender stared at the doctor, his mind churning desperately round. The woman he had fallen in love with so precipitately, of whose instinctive strength and goodness he had been certain—was it possible that she was not only a victim, but a murderess?

He tried to cling to cold facts in order to banish these nightmarish speculations, the imagining of Clara humbled and outraged, or Clara as a conspirator, perhaps raising a dagger, whispering over the body of her father.

Albrizzi continued, "Furthermore, the rents in the skin caused by the tree would not deceive a careful examination of the body. But they would allow a physician, perhaps a careless or elderly person, to make some sort of semiplausible claim that lacerations were due to the fall into the branches. If that physician were willing to go along with the general idea, of course."

Callender thought of the doctors in the Rue de la Pépinière. No less than three of them had certified that the old man had died of apoplexy, when all the time he had multiple stab wounds, even on his face. Only the police physician had been willing to challenge that bland conclusion and open the household to the outside scrutiny of a murder investigation.

Albrizzi had the look of a man who was not willing to fudge his conclusions.

"And the second doctor the Casimiri summoned did precisely that. But you, I take it, did not go along with the theory that the count's injuries were all caused by falling into the tree?" he asked Albrizzi.

The doctor had picked up the crystal skull again and was turning it over in his hands. It caught and reflected the light, which flashed and gleamed through the orifices and created dazzling shafts of fire inside the gleaming bowl of the skull.

"You see, Mr. Callender, this beautiful but apparently useless object, hopelessly outdated though it may be, is a metaphor, if you will, for the grand desire of all physicians. To be able to see into the human mind— now that would be the greatest of achievements! But I have only the traditional methods of medicine. I have to use my eyes and study the outward appearance, the physical body. And I tell you, when I examined the corpse of the count, I saw two stab wounds so deep they might well have been the cause of death. One was delivered through the eye and another through the mouth. There were many scrapes and scratches, but those were not only superficial, but mostly *postmortem*—there had been virtually no bleeding. He was almost dead when he was flung onto the branches of the thorn tree."

"Almost?"

"He was a strong man. He may have lived for a short while."

"Hanging there on the tree, caught on the thorns?" It was a horrible thought.

"Yes." Albrizzi set down the skull and looked at Callender. "You are a merciful man, signor, I can tell it by your face, but let me give you a hint; there are times when your pity should not be wasted. But let us not speak of the past, Signor Callender, when we have an urgent task in the near future to perform. That place has a great evil in it, that I can tell you."

Callender did not need to ask which place, nor did he, as he might have done at home in England, find these words an absurd exaggeration, a piece of dramatic hyperbole. Here in Venice, even his cool and rational temperament found it possible to believe in the presence of evil. He thought of the hermaphrodite whom Barton had taken him to see, and of the strange venerations and superstitions that had surrounded that afflicted being. The city had a secretiveness which might conceal anything, including ancient survivals of cruelty.

But Clara—she was surely a woman from the modern world, a strong and independent voice. What was she doing, caught in the intrigues and secrets of her family, dragged down by them into ancient evils? He feared her inheritance and at the same time was certain that he had sensed within her a desire to escape from it. She had been born into the Casimiri, but did she belong with them? There was a world outside their palazzo, but a large question in Callender's mind over whether Clara Casimiri could be brought safely into it.

"Will you meet me?" he said to the doctor. "Will you help me?"

"Yes," said Albrizzi without question, and in American fashion, he put out his hand to the Englishman. "Shake! Here's my hand upon it!"

30

He had begun to paint before the early evening light, and as it fell he found his palette darkening, becoming overcast with drifts of slate and fluorite violet, misty damp shrouds that hung in the air over the stretch of water that separated the peering, weak-sighted artist from his elusive quarry.

The object of this strange pursuit changed from moment to moment, although it might be in reality composed of solid matter, graywacke, serpentine, and alabaster that obeyed the laws of weight and gravity. Yet the heavy vapors in the air rendered the building insubstantial, as evanescent as the world of a dream, where walls and arches melted and dissolved with every shift of a dreamer's unconscious vision. The shades that now were falling over the façade were silverpoint, mauve, purple madder, and the yellowish moon gray of Oriental rugs. As the tones deepened, fig blue, black, and indigo crept into the shadows, and the artist felt an unease that seemed to correspond with the dark complexities of the architecture. Were there movements within, or was it a trick of the light? There seemed to be pinpoints of flame within the palazzo, as though the inhabitants were hurrying from room to room carrying lamps or torches. This city of bright, glittering water, ruffled turquoise, and sunlit gold now looked like a dark and sinister place, and even as he tried to capture those somber veils that fell over its waters, he found himself shivering. A consciousness which could only be described as that of the presence of evil crept into him, and he fancied it emanated from the building across the canal, like a mist swirling across the stretch of water which now seemed frighteningly narrow. Sometimes, he thought, old cities, old buildings, seemed to have reached a point when they exuded an uncleanliness, almost called out for destruction, such as had happened in the French Revolution, perhaps.

Not that France had really changed, even though the Bastille and many of the structures of the *ancien régime* had been swept away. He found himself thinking of another grand house, undecayed, one of the new palaces belonging to the untitled nobility of the world of commerce and industry who ruled in modern cities such as London and Paris. It was a class of people which appeared to have made no impact at all on Venice, yet in other places they lived just as grandly as any of these titled Venetians of the Golden Book. In fact, they were probably much richer. The Rémy family of five, Auguste and Cecile and the three young people, had ten servants to wait on them in the Rue de la Pépinière in Paris. He had never liked that house; it always had an oppressive atmosphere, as if its heavy blocks bore down on the rest of the world, crushing the fragile lives around it.

And on their return from Venice, he and Alice would have to face the horrors it had generated. A new fear had been raised, an uncertainty which he could not share with her, because he suspected that she might be complicit in it, if only by saying nothing, allowing a tacit consent to what was happening in Paris, remaining passive in this Venetian interlude. He had not liked the sound of what the Englishman, Callender, had said.

IN another part of the city, Leonora Tenbaker removed her stays with a sigh of relief. Venice was much cooler now, but still, all these undergarments clogged one so. To leave them off would have been unthinkable, though Miss Tenbaker could not help noticing that there were ladies in

Venice who evidently did so, even in respectable society. One could quite see—well—almost everything, under those loose, thin silks! Still, one never knew here quite what was respectable and what was not—that was the trouble with being abroad.

She tiptoed to the communicating door which led to the room of her charge and peeped in. Clementine Marshall lay in a deep and untroubled sleep, her blonde hair spread out over the pillow. Leonora Tenbaker sighed with relief. This was perhaps the only time in the entire twenty-four hours when she could relax with regard to Clementine, whose alluring combination of good looks, wealth, and gullibility drew admirers like filings to a magnet. But exhausted by sightseeing and with no further social engagements, the two ladies were now enjoying an early night.

This was quite unusual. Take the party on the previous evening, for example, given by Messrs. Sullivan, the English bankers, and hosted by Mr. Sullivan himself. It had been one of the few occasions when "old Venice," as Miss Tenbaker thought of the noble families, and the new Venice of modern commerce had come together. And what had happened? Why, of course, Clementine had been the center of admiration: not five minutes after she had entered the salon, a cluster of dark-haired young gallants had gathered around her, and Miss Tenbaker had the greatest difficulty in keeping an eye on her charge, having to peer through the massed ranks of admiring males as best she could. Still, there was safety in numbers, and she had had such a pleasant discussion with Mr. Sullivan himself, though he had perhaps been too pressing on the subject of the Marshalls' wealth. Leonora Tenbaker had a good measure of shrewdness, and she sensed that Sullivan was fishing for information, very delicately, of course, merely asking agreeable questions about Clementine's lifestyle: What sort of a horse did she ride at home? Did her father own a shoot?

As Miss Tenbaker gazed up with her innocent pink face, she saw the desire for information in his eyes. She thought that what he really wanted to know was how much money the parents had. Sullivan, of course, could not hope to be a suitor, but perhaps he hoped to get some investment or deposit from the Marshalls.

He had asked for her card, and Leonora Tenbaker had felt it impossible to refuse, and of course unable to stop him when he wanted to jot down the name of the *pensione* where they were staying. She had not forgotten his reaction.

"But that is quite a modest place! I am surprised you are not at the Danieli or one of the better hotels!"

Stung with the implication, Miss Tenbaker answered, "Oh, I assure you, it is not for want of being able to afford such a place! But Mr. Marshall does not believe in throwing his money around. Plain and sensible, that is his way in all his dealings, and that, I believe, is how he has made his pile!"

"Hmmm!" It seemed a murmur of appreciation, and Leonora Tenbaker thought she saw a figure scribbled on her card, a sum of money ending in many zeroes, as well as the name of the pensione. Her unease increased, as she felt that perhaps she had been manipulated into betraying her employer's confidence. It was unusual that anyone should get around her defenses, but perhaps the banker was as skillful as she. It occurred to her that his motive might not be so much the obvious one of finding out about the Marshalls, but that he wanted to know what her own connection with the family might be.

"I must go and speak to Miss Marshall now, if you will excuse me, Mr. Sullivan," she had said rather breathlessly, as Sullivan bowed and slipped the card into his waistcoat pocket. Eventually, she had detached Clementine and shepherded her into a waiting boat.

Now, there seemed to be a night of peace and quiet ahead. Leonora Tenbaker was in her nightdress and almost ready for bed: she fetched her one indulgence, which was a lilac silk dressing gown, stroking its folds carefully, and slipped it over the plain, heavy cotton sleeping garment. Flannel next to the skin in winter, cotton in summer—that was her way in England; it was her way in Venice, too. All the same, the silk was lovely. She didn't wear it in front of Clementine. Not that the girl would laugh, exactly—she was too good-hearted for that—but she would take such *notice* of it, and Leonora Tenbaker hated being noticed. It was undesirable in all sorts of ways.

Furthermore, thought Miss Tenbaker, it might even be necessary to tell a few people the truth. How very tiresome! Perhaps she should pay the consulate a visit in the morning.

31

Returning to the consulate, Callender tensed and stopped dead when a shadowy figure emerged at the top of the first flight, but relaxed when he recognised Fiametta Corradini.

"Signor Callender," she whispered, "The servant let me in. I have a message for you."

"How did you know where to find me?"

"I followed you after your dinner with the charming Signora Marino."

He realized with a shock that the follower of whom he had been aware as he left Helena Marino might have been female. He had assumed that it was a man, but here of course, everyone was familiar with boats. Venetians were skimming across the water practically from birth, and a light craft could well have been rowed by a woman.

Without speaking he bowed and indicated the way to his room, following her as she mounted the stairs, her leather slippers tapping on the boards. At the top, she waited while he opened the door for her, and then lit the candelabra on his table. The room was still in some state of disorder, but he noted with relief that at least the blood and mess from his previous encounter in this room had been cleaned up.

"Were you rowing after me, signorina?"

She smiled ruefully. "I must admit it. Obviously, I cannot have been very skillful."

"On the contrary—I have no idea when you started on my trail. It was only as I left the island to return here that I really believed there was someone behind me."

"I followed you to the Lido, but I didn't get a chance to speak to you privately there, and when I saw the lady, I managed to slip out after your boat. When I realized that you would be engaged with her for dinner at the taverna, I returned to the Lido and amused myself at the baccarat tables for an hour or so. Then, when I judged your meal might be finished, I came back after you and discovered your abode!"

"You must be an excellent oarswoman!"

"I have always loved boats! I'm a good sailor, too, I assure you. Your poet Shelley would not have drowned in a storm if I had been there."

"You would have saved the ship?"

"No, I would not have let him set sail in the first place with the signs of such a tempest brewing. Everyone who lives on the sea learns to respect it or perish. But there's a purpose to this visit. I was not following you for my own amusement."

She drew out an envelope from under her cloak.

"I'm afraid I cannot offer you a chair, Signorina Corradini." It seemed unnecessary to add that the only chair in the room had flown into pieces when an intruder wearing the Casimiri livery had burst in.

"It doesn't matter; I've only come to bring you a message."

She held out the envelope, and with a shock Callender recognized the crest that surmounted it: the dragonlike creature and the knight with his lance impaling it. He opened the letter and read the one line contained in it.

"How is she?" he said, and at the anxiety in his voice Fiammetta smiled in spite of the desperation of the situation.

"I take it you mean Clara Casimiri? She is well—for the moment. But she needs a friend, as well as a lover, if you understand me, signor?"

He looked at her and said with gratitude, "Yes, I understand. Will you help me?"

It took a few minutes for them to arrange matters, the dark head and the fox-red one bent together as they whispered.

Fiammetta disappeared.

Callender pulled open the window shutters and looked down on the water beneath. A small, determined figure with flowing hair and a long dress emerged from the shadows and stepped into a boat moored just against the landing stage. Fiammetta Corradini hitched up her skirts unconcernedly, stepped in, and cast off, then took hold of the oars with strong little hands and began to row silently away.

He held the note so that the moonlight fell on the sheet of paper and looked at it again. A single line was written on it.

"Signor Callender, I ask you to come at once." There was no signature, but a tiny sketch of a carnival mask adorned the foot of the page, and as he held up the paper an unmistakable perfume scented the night air.

For her part, Fiammetta Corradini had a pleasing thought as she slipped away, guiding her boat through the silent waters of Venice at night, her arms moving swiftly and silently with the strokes of the oars. Not only would she be able to tell Clara that she had safely delivered her message, but that Signor Callender, though he had taken dinner with a glamorous woman the previous evening, had left that lady behind to her own devices and returned to his own room at the consulate, where Fiammetta had observed a single chaste and narrow bed. She would certainly relay this interesting news.

But then she faltered, and the boat slowed for a few moments, as she wondered when she might again see her lifelong friend. The atmosphere in Palazzo Casimiri was chilling and undoubtedly hostile to outsiders.

32

Albrizzi!" called Callender softly, and swore at the thickness of the
door that barred his way and silenced his voice. It had been difficult
enough to leave the consulate without being seen: now he might risk
everything by having to make a noise fit to rouse the dead before Albrizzi
heard him. Common sense prevailed after a few moments: medical men
were often summoned urgently at strange hours. This led to two deduc-
tions: one, that it might not be thought odd if he were pounding on the
physician's door at midnight, and another, that there was probably some
special provision made for rousing the doctor late at night. He ceased
pounding for few moments, and, using the electric torch he had brought
from the consulate, peered round the doorway. It was heavily barred, and
the iron grille was fastened over it, but there was a small brass plate to one
side. He bent down and peered at the inscription.

"Night bell in recess," he translated. Recess? There was a niche set in
the wall at the side of the ponderous door, and within it was a little brass
handle which he seized firmly and tugged. A sound echoed somewhere
above his head, the sweet jingling of a small bell.

A moment later and Albrizzi, wrapped in a cloak, appeared at a balcony above Callender's head. Callender moved into the moonlight so
that he could be seen.

"Callender, what is it? Are you ill?" The doctor kept his voice down, and Callender answered him in the same tone.

"No, but I need your help."

In a few minutes, he heard the sound of the bolts being drawn back, and the grille was opened. Albrizzi stood in the entrance and ushered him into his study, lighting an oil lamp as he did so.

Without a word, Callender showed him the note.

"I know this crest," said Albrizzi, looking up from the paper in alarm.

"Will you come with me?"

"Now?" There was a pause, and the two men stared at each other. Callender wondered if he detected a wavering in the gray eyes opposite his, but after a moment more Albrizzi shrugged his shoulders and burst into an unexpected smile. "I'm a fool, Callender. My father and my grandfather would have said so and kept their heads down in such a situation, but I've got a different attitude. I'm damned if I'll bow the knee to another generation of Casimiri and watch them lie and destroy and corrupt like all their ancestors. It's time we acknowledged we're not living in the sixteenth century anymore. Yes, I'm with you!"

And, as Callender made to move towards the door that very instant, he said, "Wait a minute, though, hothead! We have to make some preparations. Let's see if we can't adjust the odds in our favor a little, at any rate."

THUS some quarter of an hour later two figures left the house of Dr. Albrizzi, both cloaked and muffled, and stepped into the doctor's small boat, ready moored at the rear of the physician's premises. If any neighbor had happened to look out over the moonlit backwater and had seen this event, he or she would have thought merely that the doctor and his servant were attending a patient and bearing medicines for the sick on their mission of mercy, for one of the cloaked figures bore a leather bag under his arm.

The neighbor might, however, have marked one particular feature about this mission of mercy if he had been able to look more closely.

There was a third person already in the boat, a rower, small but skillful, hunched over the oars. The doctor's apprentice boy, perhaps, though a long lock of hair was escaping from beneath a hood. And the rowlocks of the boat were muffled with strips of soft oiled cloth. It would have seemed really extraordinarily considerate of a patient's welfare to take such care ensuring that the little vessel glided soundlessly along in the darkness.

THE Palazzo Casimiri lay in the center of a deep pool of bluish shadow, though the canal was gleaming in the moonlight. But the deep window embrasures had watchers within. Although the little boat slid up silently to the piers and its rower shipped oars without a sound, it was seen.

In a great bedroom on the *piano nobile*, the sleepers, entwined in one another's arms, were startled from sleep as there came a hammering on the door. The woman started up and pulled the rumpled covering over herself, her hair hanging down her back, her eyes startled. The man rose naked and muscular out of the bed and reached for the unsheathed dagger lying on the floor.

"Don't make a sound," he whispered as she was about to speak. He indicated the balcony that overlooked the Grand Canal and, pulling the covering around her body, she slipped across the room, where the bluish white moonlight that struck in through the long windows glinted on old satin hangings, and entwined herself in a drape of velvet.

This was the chamber of the dead contessa, mother of Clara and Claudio. On her dressing table still stood her dusty hairbrushes and hand mirrors, a tail comb with an elaborate silver handle decorated with golden bees, and the woman hiding behind the curtain might have felt haunted by her predecessor. Might have, if she had a conscience.

The hammering stopped, and there was a long minute of utter silence before the door swung open, and two men entered the room.

Callender saw in a split second that there was someone moving behind the door as it swung back, but that was time enough for the blade to flash upwards and strike, though he had managed to slip sideways quickly enough to avoid the worst of the blow. Nevertheless, he saw that a long streak of blood flowed through his shirt as he fell sideways, taken off balance by surprise and the burning pain that sliced down his arm, and he feared another attack.

But Albrizzi had reached the middle of the room, and spun round, a pistol in his hand. He stared at the distraught apparition who appeared from behind the door, clutching the bloody weapon.

"Drop the dagger!"

After a few moments, which seemed to last a lifetime, it clattered down.

Albrizzi kept the pistol firmly trained on his target. Callender had managed to tear off his sleeve, and binding his wound, was gasping a desperate question from the floor. "Where is she?"

The naked man turned towards him, and now defiance seemed to give way to a kind of contempt as he said, " 'Where is she?' I suppose you mean Clara—I gather you have become besotted with her. You won't get her, you know. She's not for you."

Callender had tied the makeshift bandage round his upper arm. He pulled himself painfully to his feet.

"Don't waste my time with these stupid dramas," he said. "We know what went on here, and we're going to get Clara out of it. Such things aren't permitted anymore, you know. You belong in the past, Count Claudio."

"Oh, yes, you're a calm, cold Englishman; you think you'll always win out. Well, not now, I tell you. So you know what happened, do you?"

Callender was coming across the room now with slow determination. "About the murder of your father, yes. And the reason for it, too. *The Cenci*, that was it, wasn't it? The Cenci family all over again. This is the twentieth century, Claudio, and there will be a different ending this time."

"You're such a fool!"

Claudio was smiling as he said this, and Revel had a fraction of a second to wonder why before he saw a shadow glide across behind Albrizzi. The doctor's body suddenly seemed to jerk forward, and his pistol discharged into the floor with a loud report that filled the room with smoke.

When it cleared, there was a woman behind him, with something thin and gleaming in her hand. Albrizzi stumbled to his knees, and Callender, looking frantically to see what had happened, glimpsed a long silver and gold object gripped in her hand. It was the comb from the dressing table, the comb with a tail as thin and sharp as needle, and it had been slipped into the doctor's shoulder, carving into the flesh like a boning knife.

But even as Claudio advanced with a cry of triumph, there came another crack and spurt of flame, and he fell forward across the bed.

Fiammetta Corradini stood in the doorway, a revolver in her hand.

"Look behind you, Callender!" she called, and Callender was just in time to see the naked woman circling him, her long hair hanging tangled over her breasts, with her strange weapon once more poised to strike. He could smell her almost feral scent as her bare feet shifted soundlessly across the floorboards towards him. Sliding sideways as she made a lunge towards him, he grabbed her as she struck out a wild, unaimed blow, feeling the softness of her body against him, and forced her arms down. He was aware of her skin, slippery with sweat and patchouli, before she collapsed.

"*Aiiee*, this is nasty!" exclaimed Fiammetta, who had rushed forward and in a moment was rolling the woman in a sheet plucked from the bed so that her writhing limbs were bound fast. "God, she's trying to bite me! Give me some help here!"

Callender did so, and they finally pinioned the struggling arms.

Dawn was breaking, and the light struck the face of Fiammetta's prisoner.

"Where is Clara?" Revel's question had a note of desperation.

Clara's stepmother, the widowed Countess Mariella, spat at the name of her adoptive daughter. "I'll die before I tell you. Let her suffer—she wouldn't help us. Why should I help her? I'll say one thing—Prepiani's got her. He'll kill her rather than let her go to anyone else."

She looked up at them as she spoke, and Callender thought he had never seen such concentrated hatred on a human face.

Why did I take no notice of Mariella? he thought. *She was always in the background, always silent. Like a snake waiting to strike.* He felt horror that Clara's life might depend on this vicious and unpredictable creature.

Albrizzi had risen to his feet and torn a strip of linen from one of the bedsheets, which he had bound round his bleeding shoulder. He came over to the group and, staring down at the prisoner, said, "I think she's telling the truth. She would in all probability die before she came to her senses and tried to help us save Donna Clara. So we'll just have to search every corner of the palazzo and hope she is here somewhere. Signorina Corradini, do you have any idea where she might be?"

"No," Fiammetta shook her red locks. "I've already looked in her own room. There was no sign of her. In any case, Prepiani might have taken her somewhere else away from here."

Callender felt despair growing within him, but as he looked across the room, he was distracted by a movement. Claudio Casimiri had dragged himself upright to a seated position, leaning his head against an old chest painted with faded figures in court dress.

Albrizzi crossed the room quickly and held Claudio's head in his arms. "I cannot stop the bleeding, Count," he said. "You are going to die very shortly, probably in the next few minutes. If you know where your sister is, tell us."

Claudio raised his eyes, which seemed huge and glazed over like those of a dying animal. For a moment, Callender thought he had gone beyond that room in Venice and was far away from them all, but then he seemed to make an enormous effort to concentrate.

Turning his eyes to the painted chest, he said weakly, "It was our mother's marriage chest. Made especially for her." He seemed to contemplate this for a few moments, while the watchers in the room did not dare speak, but waited, hanging on to his every word.

Perhaps the painted chest stirred some vestiges of feeling within him, for he suddenly started up and gasped, "In the attics. *La Veglia.*"

There was a huge gush of blood from his mouth, and his head fell forward.

Albrizzi looked across at Callender, letting Claudio slip to the floor. A stink of blood and shit from the dying man had filled the room.

The Contessa Mariella had witnessed what had happened, and the sight of her stepson's death appeared to sober her violent passions, for she stopped calling out and struggling and stared with shock at the body of Claudio, then shuffled on her knees towards him.

Albrizzi had crossed to the door, in the lock of which was an old iron key. "We can lock her in here," he said, and Callender and Fiammetta Corradini followed him out into the corridor. The doctor closed the door on the spectacle of Mariella Casimiri leaning against the dead body of her lover and stepson, and turned the key in the lock.

33

"Mr. Barton, I assure you I do have some cause for anxiety! That is why I have waited to see you for several hours."

Leonora Tenbaker was paying another visit. She gazed earnestly at the British consul, who was trying to mollify her. Leonora sat upright on her chair, and since the consul was slumped despairingly on his, their eyes were level. Really, thought Barton, she had seemed to have such harmless old-lady eyes, rather misty and gentle, but they were now gazing at him so sharply that he had the sensation that cold water was being thrown at him, and he suddenly remembered the washbasins in the dormitories of his very expensive public school, where the boys sometimes had to break the ice before they could wash in the mornings. Involuntarily, his shoulders shuddered, and he gave his visitor his full attention.

"When I was asked to undertake this task," Miss Tenbaker went on, "I merely thought I was performing a patriotic duty of a quite unperilous nature. During my time at the Foreign Office, I was not infrequently given small commissions of this kind, Mr. Barton. No one notices a middle-aged personage of my description, and I was able to render several services—of course, I cannot disclose, even to you, their exact nature. So when I at last decided to fulfill my desire to travel, and was recommended to Mr. and Mrs. Marshall as a companion for their daughter, it was quite natural that I should be asked to carry out certain tasks in Italy—as it were, to combine a little professional work with the pleasures of sightseeing. In Venice, to keep an eye on any matters that might affect the interests of one of the most powerful banking families in Europe, and through them, of course, those of the British Crown itself."

Barton sighed openly at the thought of their profligate, debt-ridden king. Miss Tenbaker continued unabashed, "But I did not expect to become involved in anything that involved such danger."

"But surely, madam, there is no risk to you!"

Miss Tenbaker drew herself up, shoulders drawn back, and stared at Theseus Barton frostily. "Mr. Barton, you are quite right. But I tell you, serious dangers are threatening a British citizen, and it is your duty to act. What did Saint Paul say when imprisoned by the power of ancient Rome? *'Civus Romanus sum!'* 'I am a Roman citizen!' I say to you, Mr. Barton, Mr. Callender is a citizen of the British Empire, and he must not be threatened by foreign intrigue and malice!"

"Miss Tenbaker," began Barton feebly, "are you sure . . . ?"

"Quite sure, Mr. Barton. You must do something *now.*"

THESEUS Barton and Miss Tenbaker made their way to the Palazzo Casimiri, accompanied by the commissario and two policemen. At the Rialto they boarded a police launch, which cut a sharp wake through the old canals, slapping against the walls of houses and palaces.

None of the men was happy about this excursion. Barton managed to keep his grumbling to himself, since it would not have done to let the Venetians know his low opinion of an English lady, and the policemen were too low-ranking to risk exposing their resentment at being hauled from their beds, but the commissario was not operating under any constraint, and said loudly, "Signor Barton, if we find nothing, that is our friendship finished, with my career as well. I and my men, going to search the house of one of the oldest families in the city!"

Miss Tenbaker had a quiet voice when she, not Barton, took up the response. Yet it was surprisingly authoritative. Even in the cabin of the police vessel, against the pounding of the engine, every clear syllable could be heard.

"Commissario, is this not the oldest republic in Europe? Is Venice not proud of its resistance to tyranny over many centuries?"

"Yes, but that was when there were many enemies to be fought! The Turks, the French—we defended our city against them all."

"But tyranny is not just about the state and the government, is it? There is a matter of domestic tyranny, of misuse of authority within one's own household? And that, believe me, can lead to crimes that are well worthy of your attention. Is it not time that the justice of the state prevailed in this city, and not some species of private misrule?"

The commissioner stared at her. "It is true," he conceded, "that the families of the Golden Book have gone too far. They are truly living in the past. But Prince Marzano—"

"Has allowed terrible crimes to go unpunished. When that is known, he will find it difficult to retain his position in the city. He has no legal government here—it is purely a matter of tradition and personal authority, is it not? The civil authority will become correspondingly more important. And that civil power, Commissario, is represented by you."

Bravo, Miss Tenbaker, thought Barton. *If you were a man, you would have made a superb diplomat.*

The commissario leaned forward, looking at the city which flickered and blurred as spray dashed up against the windows. "It is true, there have been occasions when I felt we should intervene. In the case of the old princess, for example, the English banker, Mr. Sullivan, asked us to ensure that there had been no irregularity with her finances. But Prince Marzano said—"

"No doubt," said Barton, intervening, feeling that as His Majesty's official representative he should now take some control over the conversation, "no doubt he said that the affairs of the *famiglia* Casimiri were no business of any outsider."

"Yes. And if the old families could regulate themselves—well, we have allowed them to do so."

"I understand. It must have made life a lot easier."

The commissario was not a stupid man and was effectively spurred by this goad of Miss Tenbaker's. "Yes, it was easier, I accept that. But I do believe in justice; I do have principles." He pulled his shoulders up, and holding his head high, stepped out of the cabin and stood at the prow of the boat, not caring that the spray was wetting his handsome uniform as they neared the Casmiri landing stage. For the first time, he saw his city clearly, and not through the eyes of the long line of famous artists who had painted her, nor in the hazy gold light of her history. Venice seemed to him like a place hung round with old, musty curtains, shrouded with veils that clung around like spiderwebs. Prince Marzano might try to persuade some of the Golden Book families to come into the twentieth century, but what was even his power, compared with modern banking merchants such as the Maloneys? They were the future, thought the commissario, as the police boat was moored to a post.

IT was still dark, almost complete blackness. Albrizzi had seized a lantern, and its unstable light showed the staircase twisting up into the darkness above them.

From a cacophony of sounds—the deafening pistol shot, Mariella's enraged shrieks and screams, Claudio's bubbling groans—the palace of the Casimiri seemed plunged into the profoundest silence. And yet there was no absolute quiet: there were the tiny sounds given out by an ancient building where insect jaws are working in the darkness, where wood is perpetually decaying and shifting by millimeters as it does so, where the foundations are slipping gradually yet inexorably into the slime which lies beneath them. When they are old enough, when they have absorbed enough human breath and palm-sweat, the very stones of a building such as this seem to give forth exhalations, to be still-living cells of some sprawling creature dying by inches.

Callender was conscious of this audible presence, this persona, al-most, of the Palazzo Casimiri as he ascended the stairs to the top floor, the long attic beneath the roof tiles. It extended under the huge beams cut down on some country estate three or four centuries previously, vast treetrunks dragged by oxcarts and floated across the lagoon to this in-substantial city in a dream.

Was there a faint murmuring, a dragging sound, once even a muffled cry? His mind was imagining horrors at the same time it tried to work out the puzzle presented to it. He fancied as he went higher, stumbling in his haste, that he could hear other sounds as he and Albrizzi, lantern held high, made their way to the very top of the last precipitous flight of stairs and then along the roof space. A rat suddenly broke from the darkness. It scuttled across Callender's feet and ran back into oblivion, and as Albrizzi raised the lantern higher, they saw the rat making for a gap in the panel-ing from behind which came a faint mewing noise. Callender managed to get a leverage on the edge of the panel and pulled it back. Behind was a narrow gap, a concealed cupboard within the thicknesses of two walls, and lying on the ground with the rat running over her skirts, lay a woman. The swinging light showed her face: it was old Daniella, bound with ropes and a rough cloth tied round her mouth.

"Ah, signori," she said, sobbing, her face soaked with tears as they cut her free. "They did not trust me—maybe Rinaldo saw me speaking to you. They locked me up and took my young lady away."

They dashed on, and were crouching under the eaves now, stum-bling, unable to see into the darkness that lay before them and hampered repeatedly by old tapestries, bales of material, broken furniture, all those things that had been put up in the attic one fine day many years previ-ously and forgotten forever.

At last, having made their way along almost the entire length of the building, they came out into the space that had been cleared for the ser-vants' quarters. Here was a row of narrow beds and a few pieces of us-able furniture, including a rickety table bearing some candles stuck in saucers.

Looking round, they could see nothing more but a few clothes hanging on hooks.

"I think Claudio sent us on a fool's errand," said Callender, his voice echoing against the roof tiles above his head. He was feeling close to despair at the wild profusion of possible hiding holes in this rambling warren of a palace, yet something inside him was insisting that he mustn't give up, that this was for Clara.

He took up a candle and began to pace along the walls. At the far end, there should be the solid masonry of the outer northern wall.

It had been limewashed and looked suspiciously fresh.

He rapped upon it.

"Hollow, Albrizzi!"

There was a mahogany wardrobe which had partly collapsed, and he kicked a plank out of it and used it as a battering ram to charge the wall. It re-echoed with a sound like a roll of drums, but did not give way.

"Here, try here." Albrizzi had been examining the surface more carefully. "This looks like a set of hinges. I think there's a break here."

Charging at the fine line down the wall which the doctor indicated, Callender crashed his plank through, and the whole structure of false walling came down.

Albrizzi examined the walling with interest. It was a strange barrier, two thin layers of wood with a thick padding between them, like the horsehair of mattress stuffing.

"Soundproofing," he said.

Callender's fears took on horrible new dimensions. He could not bear the workings of his imagination—any kind of reality seemed better—and he pressed on further.

There was a room beyond, and within it a dreadful sight.

Hanging from a beam was a set of chains, and caught within them was the body of a woman, her arms twisted behind her back. Her legs were stretched out in front. Set upright just beneath her was a long slab of marble, the top edge honed to razor sharpness. Blood had evidently poured down from the rough iron shackles around her wrists and soaked her thin dress.

"*La Veglia,*" said Albrizzi with horror on his face.

Clara Casimiri seemed to have fainted, but as they looked, she revived, seemed to recognize them, and began a low, moaning cry. Her feet were hanging above the ground, so that her dislocated arms bore the whole weight of her body.

They cut her down carefully, Albrizzi supervising the gentle handling of the limbs.

"One of the great traditions we Venetian physicians have learned from Arabic medicine is the manipulation of joints," he said, feeling the musculature gently. Even so, there were some moments of acute pain, and Clara fainted again several times as he grasped her arms and shoulders and turned the balls of the joints back into the sockets. "I had to do it straightaway—before the tissues become even more inflamed," he said, seeing the look on Callender's face.

34

"It was Antonio. He said that if we were not to be married, he would give me his wedding gift anyway. So he took me up there."

"Where is he now?"

"I don't know. He said he would return soon enough and left me there, in that agony . . . I heard his footsteps going away and I thought he wouldn't come back and I wondered if anyone would ever find me. But then, it was worse, thinking he would come in any minute . . ."

Clara was speaking in a faint but clear voice from the depths of an armchair in the long gallery. The stained ceiling of the room flickered with watery reflections as the light of dawn rose over Venice.

Albrizzi had bound up her wounds and given her a small dose of laudanum. "There is no permanent damage, thank the angels in heaven," he had said, after examining her carefully.

"Antonio said," she murmured, "that since our family seemed to be following the history of the Cenci, he would ensure that the story of Beatrice Cenci was fully reenacted."

"Oh, God!" exclaimed the doctor, understanding what she meant. "And we know what happened to Beatrice, after she was taken into custody. They submitted her to the most feared of all tortures, 'La Veglia.' It means 'the vigil'; I think that's how it would be translated into English.

There are illustrations of it in some old books of woodcuts. That was that hideous contraption he had built in the attic."

"Perhaps it would be better not to go on," said Callender, filled with anxiety, his arm around Clara. But she said, "No, I want to hear this. I know Antonio had some strange old books, with pictures that he used to spend a long time over, and let no one else look at. He tried to order a book like that through Gozzi, but the old man refused to get it for him. Antonio ranted for days. I think that was why he had a grudge against Gozzi in the first place. I think he probably gave Claudio the money to pay young Gozzi's murderer. Please go on, Dr. Albrizzi."

"Very well, if you are sure, Donna Clara. 'La Veglia' was a vigil kept in the utmost secrecy—that's where some of its evil reputation came from. The room would be sealed off with cloths and boards, and a curtain drawn across the door. Once the torture was set up, only the judge and a notary would be present, and the room would be lit only by a couple of small lamps."

He paused, and his listeners pictured the scene, the flickering lights in the stifling room, the fear that filled that small space, the bureaucracy that was prepared to record this agony. Albrizzi continued, "The prisoner was seated on a tripod stool, with his or her feet lashed to a bar in front. The arms were bound behind the prisoner's back, and a system of ropes and pulleys could haul the victim up so that they were twisted backwards in their sockets. A sharp stone was placed under the prisoner, so that when it cut into the victim's muscles, which were already stretched to the most agonizing point, it caused spasms of unbearable pain. The old accounts say that no one failed to confess when they were subjected to this."

"Yes, that is what Antonio did to me," whispered Clara. "Not just for pleasure, perhaps. He might have tried to get a confession out of me, to exculpate him, if there should be any suspicion of his involvement."

"And I suppose it is what they did to Beatrice Cenci, to make her confess to the murder of her father," said Callender.

"Poor Beatrice," said Clara. "One would say anything when subjected to such agony. Evidence obtained by torture is no evidence at all. But also, I think, Antonio enjoyed it."

Her head was lolling against Callender's shoulder. The effects of the painkilling drugs Albrizzi had administered were becoming apparent. Later, when she had recovered a little more and they were alone, she told him something of her childhood.

"After my mother died, my father was too preoccupied to see how brutal Claudio was becoming. He and Antonio Prepiani used to play vicious games as children. Antonio always seemed to be trailing along behind, and I thought that he was the less dangerous one. There was even a time when I thought I would escape my brother by marrying him. But Antonio's vice was hidden, and it was cruelty."

Clara stopped short. "Once, Tanta gave me a little dog like hers, a puppy. She thought I would have the same pleasure and companionship from it as she had found. I found it hanged from a hook on my balcony. I thought it was Claudio who had killed it that way, but now, who knows? The police have arrested our two servants, Pietro and Matteo, but I think there are other people close to me who are far more capable of murder. But apparently they found Mariella's ruby necklace under Pietro's bed."

Callender sat upright, remembering a conversation he had in Paris, where stolen jewels had also helped to condemn the family servants.

"I wonder if they have tried fingerprinting?"

"What?"

"I'll explain another time."

LATER Callender said, holding her tightly, "We heard some terrible rumors, Clara."

She looked up at Callender with great, serious eyes. "Yes, I know about the kitchen maid, Ginevra Rocalle, who disappeared. The sewing woman told me, old Teresa."

"Do you have any idea what happened to Ginevra?"

For answer, Clara got up weakly and walked towards the painted chest in the bedroom where her brother had died. His blood had been wiped away, but there was still a smeared handprint on the lid.

"They spent a long time in here, Claudio and Mariella and Antonio."

Callender approached the chest and reluctantly lifted the lid.

Under the smell of cedar wood an undercurrent reached him, something that stank of rotten meat. He pulled aside a tapestry lying on top of the contents of the chest. There seemed to be a pile of parcels, but when he lifted one, it was horribly heavy in his hands, and he realized that it was wrapped in a soft silvery gray metal.

They stared at each other in horror. There was no escaping the terrible conclusion.

"Lead from the roof?" Had the family literally been stripping the roof of their own house to conceal the murder of an innocent?

They stared at each other.

"I think they must have had Rinaldo seal them up with lead," said Clara. "He did what they wanted. Mariella let him go to bed with her sometimes."

She said this quite calmly. "It was after Mariella came here that things became truly terrible. Though in a way, it was easier for me, because my brother did not bother so much with . . . with his unnatural feelings towards me. He and Mariella became lovers almost as soon as she entered our house."

"Did your father know?"

"I think it was because he discovered it that he was killed. There was a night when he returned unexpectedly. Claudio and Mariella were together—they couldn't resist each other, they took any opportunity, you understand? It was that kind of passion. But there was something else— not just lust. I think it was about money, too, Claudio was furious with me after I had sent you the papers I found in Tanta's rooms—the bank accounts. I couldn't understand why because they were just old statements."

"But they prove she, had been defrauded—and you would be, too, since you should have inherited what she left."

"I am sure it was not my father. He always said the Maloneys were very powerful. We never had any money, you see, but once Claudio said we should get some from Tanta, and my father told him she had to be shown respect."

Sitting on the side of the bed, she looked up at him. "I think I would like to go away for a while. Would you take me to England?"

And as he nodded and gathered her up in his arms she said, "Only for a while. I shall always want to return to Venice. I know that, somehow."

Revel knew even as he was holding Clara that there were impossibilities ahead, even though the specters that hung over her had been lifted. A living, breathing Venetian would still be as improbable in the dark surroundings of Damson Castle as a bird of paradise, and perhaps as unlikely to be able to survive there. The paintings of Italy hanging on the walls at home were merely oil and canvas, lifeless reflections of reality.

But all the same, he and Clara would somehow claim for a while their own brief time and place: they were entitled to that much, surely. Afterwards: well, she would return to her own element.

And he? Something else, another love adventure? His appetite for such things was dulled.

THERE was a commotion on the floor above, a banging that seemed to resound throughout the palace, followed by a cry and a horribly swift sound of something plunging suddenly into turgid water, a sucking sound, almost without a splash. Then there came other noises, familiar in this city, of straining oars and water smashing up against wood and brick. Callender rushed to the balcony.

A woman was being dragged out of the water of the canal, green slime covering her face and naked body. Two policemen, one of them with his heavy uniform dripping with water, were holding her, and helping them was a panting commissario, soaked by her struggles.

A small female figure hastened forward from the cabin, accompanied by the small but agile form of the British consul. Miss Tenbaker wrapped a policeman's cloak round the Contessa Mariella, whose struggles ceased as her bodily instincts took over and she vomited a mass of slime.

"Commissario, hold on to her, you have caught a murderess!" said Callender from the balcony.

"I have always insisted that my men should be able to swim!" shouted the commissario with some satisfaction. And he shook the wet feathers of his helmet over the side of the boat.

"You may not be too late to catch hold of another prisoner," Callender called.

"Prepiani will be coming back here," he added. "He surely won't be able to resist seeing his victim again."

Mariella started to shriek, "Yes, Antonio, he was involved in the old man's murder! Why should I take the blame alone? It wasn't just me and Claudio!"

"But what was Prepiani's motive?" asked the commissario. "Surely he had nothing to gain by the death of the count?"

She quietened down and gave him a look of contempt, as if he were a creature from a more innocent universe.

"He was the one who suggested doing it that way!" she said. "Claudio told him we were in danger because my husband had found out we were lovers. Antonio had read in some old book about covering it up by throwing the body into the tree and so forth. He said that if it ever came out that it was murder, then everyone would believe my husband had raped his own daughter and deserved what he got."

Albrizzi said, "But why should Prepiani get involved in the murder?"

Mariella said simply, as if it were the most obvious thing in the world, "He wanted to watch."

A murmur of horror came from the listeners, but she pressed on, "That was enough for him."

She looked round the group and said, "Very well, if you are going to be shocked, I will tell you everything, you, the English Puritans, and you, innocent little sister Clara. Here is the truth. With that murder, Antonio experienced the ultimate pleasure of the flesh. He had an orgasm as we killed the count."

There was an exclamation from Leonora Tenbaker, but Mariella said angrily, "Let's not have any of your hypocrisy here! I saw he was becoming excited—we had all arranged to be naked, so that we could easily wash the blood off. Afterwards, when it was all over, he helped Claudio tip the body over the balcony—that was the most difficult part. And Claudio and I . . . we still had the blood on our skin . . . I think Antonio watched us, too. There are only certain ways he can . . . if you understand me."

"Only too well, Contessa," said Albrizzi.

"You want to know where he is now?" She looked at the commissario. "It's better for me if I tell you, yes? There is one place especially where he goes. That damned chilly virtuous stepdaughter of mine won't be enough for him—his tastes are getting more and more extreme. He'll have worked himself up on her and then gone to satisfy his other lusts."

She shivered and said as if to herself, "It's so strange, bathing naked in the canal at night. Cold, yet it makes your body burn. I can't explain it."

"You have explained enough," said the commissario, and he moved forward to arrest her.

THE place was an old house in the Canareggio quarter, a poor, rough area. Mariella had told them clearly enough how to find it, a tall house with blackened bricks just opposite a church covered with wooden scaffolding.

"The house has a door knocker in the shape of a satyr and a nymph," she had said. "You can guess what they are doing."

The door did not open for a good few minutes, not until the commissario had one of his men thump on it with a long stave. When it opened, they burst past the woman who stood in the long passageway with a lantern in her hand.

"We are looking for a certain client of yours," said the commissario. "Not the kind who usually comes here—this one is an aristocrat. And one with peculiar tastes."

She was a tall, thin woman with bony arms and a shell necklace. She held the flickering light higher.

"No point in searching here, Commissario. If it's Prince Prepiani you mean, he has already left, just this minute."

"We didn't see him coming away. Try the back door," called out the commissario to Inspector Dario, who was at his side. As they ran through the house, past open cribs with frightened prostitutes and a few red-faced men starting up, the airless stench of musk and dirt in their nostrils, the policemen saw an open door at the far end of the passageway. It gave onto a narrow *rio* with a raft of debris that had drifted against the footing of a small bridge. Unsavory objects bobbed up and down in the frothy scum. The commissario made out the bloated belly of a dead dog, some wooden packing cases, and a long fold of something that was just disappearing under the water.

The woman who had let them in had tried to get out of the front door of the brothel, only to find that an officer remained solidly planted there.

At the back, the commotion continued. There was a rough-looking fisherman the other side of the bridge, who produced a pole with a metal spike when Dario called for his help. Manipulating this awkwardly, they brought the long object to the steps of the house before it could sink. It rolled over, and a pale face stared up at them.

When they had pulled Prince Antonio Prepiani into the kitchen of the brothel, the only place where there was a table long enough to lay his corpse, there was a huge gash across his throat. The wound was clean, however. The blood had washed out into the filth of the *rio*.

"Just the one deep cut. It looks like a razor slash," said the commissario, who had seen many such in his youth, which had been spent in Naples.

Upstairs, they found a room with ropes and blood, and a cutthroat razor glinting in a corner.

"He went too far," said the woman who had let them in. "I don't care how much he paid—I heard screaming and went up to see what had happened. The boy had just taken too much. Prepiani tried to slash him with a razor, apparently, and he managed to get hold of it and cut himself free."

She stopped.

"And then?" asked the commissario.

The woman looked tired to death, he thought. Her hair was piled up high in blonde curls above a yellowish, hollow-cheeked face.

"Where is the boy?" he asked.

"She's in the hospital."

"She?"

"She—he—it's what you might call our speciality here, sir. A eunuch, dressed up as a girl. Prepiani said it pleases him more than a woman."

The commissario made an exclamation of disgust. The young policeman, Inspector Dario, stepped forward, holding up a candle, and bent over the razor.

"Don't pick it up!" said the commissario sharply. "Listen, what is your name?"

"Eugenia."

"Well, Eugenia, we can tell who handled this razor. We have a new way of doing this, I promise you. Give me your hand." It was a small hand, stained with nicotine, with rouged nails. He took it gently.

"These lines and whorls on your fingertips are different from those of any other human being on the face of the earth. And with a magnifying glass, I can see if your fingers left marks on that razor. Do you understand me?"

She gazed into his face and began to believe him. Tears came into her eyes as she said, "Prepiani came rushing in here and said he had to have a boy right away; he was frantic. He already had bloodstains on him—I shouldn't have let him in. When I heard the screams and came up here, I was sickened by what he was doing. Even whores like me have things they can't take anymore, Commissario. I acted just on instinct, picking the razor out of the boy's hand and—"

"And thereby protecting you both from further attack by the deceased," said the commissario. "The law will allow such a defense at your trial. Dario, take her to the boat."

IN the police prefecture one of the officers opened a window as wide as he could. On the table was a pile of objects from which leaked a smell of old blood. They had a strange weight, a heaviness that was dreaded, yet familiar as the weight of joints from a butcher's shop. The policeman had hefted one of them, long and in a thin lead wrapper tightly pulled around the contents. He knew what he had lifted, and it was then he had opened the window.

"Get a sheet!" The commissario sounded irritated. In fact, he was apprehensive, fearful, even. He, too, knew what the smell of decay was like.

It took a few minutes. There was no such thing as a sheet at the police station, of course, but one of the policemen used his initiative and went to a nearby hotel, from where he commandeered a big stretch of fluffy blanket with edges bound in pale blue satin, used on the beds of the luxury suites.

It was on this cruelly absurd object that the mortal remains of Ginevra Rocalle, the butcher's missing daughter, tumbled into the light of day, a limb at a time, as the soft strips of lead that had constituted a semiairtight layer of preservation were unwound. The limbs had been crudely hacked from the trunk, and the greenish, discolored skin of the upper legs showed still a series of long, red slashes.

"Whip marks?" hazarded the commissario, contemplating the top of a thigh, which stank like rotting mutton.

"Where is the head, sir?" asked one of the policemen, surveying the heap.

There was nothing which looked as if it could have been a human head. Nothing skull-shaped, anyway. "It would be pretty unmistakable," added the man helpfully.

"The head is probably in the bottom of the canal," answered the commissario, contemplating a black and rotting hand which had just been unwrapped like an object from a reliquary. It was like a ghastly parody of the saints' bones in their silver cases in San Marco.

"Perhaps they were afraid to put her in the water all at once," suggested his assistant. "Someone might have seen them doing it. They were probably disposing of her piece by piece. And wrapping them in lead so they would sink immediately. Easy enough to get it from the roof. The building is falling apart anyway."

This policeman had not been sufficiently overtaken by nausea to be unable to put forward his own ideas. *You will go far,* thought the commissario, *you will go far, my boy.*

But one of the man's colleagues, young Dario, was also able to speculate. "Or perhaps, sir, perhaps they didn't want to get rid of it all at once."

"What do you mean?" said his boss sharply.

"Perhaps they enjoyed it, sir. Having the . . . the remains there. In the bedroom, sir." Dario looked up nervously, wondering how his suggestion might be received.

You will go even further, thought his boss. *Oh yes, you will go further.*

"Dario, I want you to get an ink pad and some fine dusting powder," said the commissario, rocking back on his heels and slipping his thumbs into his belt, a posture which relieved the tightness around his belly. "I am going to teach you how to take fingerprints. It is the very latest technique in modern methods of police work."

Dario's eyes rounded with excitement, and he gazed at his chief with undisguised admiration.

"How wonderful, sir!"

"Yes, well, I plan to make use of it in the Casimiri affair. It is my innovation." The commissario saw no reason to tell young Dario that it was really the Englishman's idea.

"NO!" said Clara urgently. "The history of the Cenci is not my story!"

They had reached the point where she had to make a formal statement to the police.

"But your father's death—it was contrived to look like that of Count Cenci, wasn't it?" asked Albrizzi. "Although we know thanks to the contessa's confession that you played no part in the murder. But all the same, we need to know the truth of the . . . the circumstances."

Clara was sitting in one of the shabby velvet chairs in the long gallery, Fiammetta nearby. The commissario was standing respectfully in front of her.

"Yes, but I am not Beatrice!" she answered Albrizzi.

Callender felt a huge lightening of spirit. There had been a moment when he had been forced to acknowledge with his reason, if not with his heart, that Clara Casimiri might be a victim of incest and a murderess. And not only a murderess. A parricide.

Then her innocence had become clear, but he was still anxious about her past life, the damage she might have suffered in this horrible place.

"I had nothing to do with the murder of my father, you must believe that! I had no cause."

Callender sensed she was speaking not only to the others, to the commissario and Albrizzi, who stood nearby, but to him, to Revel Callender, on a different level altogether. One level of understanding lay out there in the world of trials and judges. Another was the inner life of judgments of the heart.

"Claudio and Mariella became lovers almost as soon as my father married her."

"But when you were younger—" The commissario searched for a way to say this. "Count Cenci, back in the sixteenth century, was guilty of incest. That was what provoked Beatrice into contriving his murder."

He called out bluntly, tired of all the circumlocutions, "He raped her."

"Oh, no!" said Clara, shocked into response. "My situation was not at all the same."

Callender felt deep relief. A fear that had underlain his anxieties was lifted, a question he had not dared to ask Clara directly was answered.

Fiammetta intervened. "It was her brother, you see. Not her father. I knew about it when we were children. But Claudio only attempted it at first when Count Casimiri was away, and then Clara would run to our house, to my mother. And after she died, to Principessa Tanta."

"Tanta always sheltered me!" said Clara.

"Didn't you try to do anything about it?" the policeman asked.

"I told my father, but I was just a child. He was angry with Claudio, but he thought it was not serious, just a game, just one time. That was what Claudio told him, and it would have brought great dishonor on the family to do anything that would make it public. I think our father didn't want to believe it. And Claudio had never—well, he had never actually caught hold of me, if I may put it like that. As for dear Tanta, she was getting so old, she didn't really pay attention to these things anymore. You know, I think she had been so persecuted herself, she thought it was almost normal. She wouldn't let Claudio and Antonio come chasing me into her rooms, but I don't think it would have occurred to her to actually alert anyone."

"What about the money?" asked the policeman. "Didn't she notice the money was missing from her account?"

"That was later on, and she didn't spend much. She had been extravagant in her youth, but she had very few pleasures in old age. I think she just thought it must be mounting up."

She looked up sadly. "But Papa was always kind to me. I grieve for him still, as I do for Tanta."

THE luggage was being loaded into the water taxi. This was a proceeding of some difficulty, since Clementine's dresses had necessitated two large trunks of the size more normally seen in the baggage hold of a luxury liner.

"I think," said Miss Tenbaker, whose modest valises had easily been stowed, "that perhaps we ought not to wait while this is being done."

"Oh, but how can I be certain they don't splash my cases?" Clementine watched anxiously as a burly Venetian boatman heaved at one end of her cabin trunk, and his side of the boat dipped correspondingly low towards the swirling waters of the Grand Canal.

"I'm sure they are experts at this," said Miss Tenbaker. "And besides, would it not be pleasant to take our last stroll through Saint Mark's Square?"

"Oh, and see dear Florian's for one last time!"

"Yes, but we won't be able to stop for coffee!" Miss Tenbaker, remembering the eager gentlemen who clustered round Clementine in Florian's, attempted to prevent a fresh hazard from looming on the horizon. *Between the devil and the deep blue sea—well, between the devil and the Grand Canal!* she thought to herself.

But Clementine was quite meek about this, and Miss Tenbaker arranged that the porter from their pensione should accompany their luggage to the station, where the ladies would soon join him, following on in a gondola.

As they walked across the square, a familiar figure was approaching from the Saint Mark's side. He swept off his hat to greet the ladies.

"Ah, delightful to meet you again, Miss Marshall, Miss Tenbaker."

It was Mr. Sullivan, the banker. He beamed at the two of them, a far more relaxed figure than when Miss Tenbaker had last encountered him. Now that she was not preoccupied by business, she could see that he was really quite a good-looking man, with thick white hair, and he was most presentably dressed. His thick camel coat had a black velvet collar, and he carried a silver-headed walking stick. She thought there was a look of admiration in his eye, but that was no doubt the result of encountering Clementine.

"Mr. Sullivan, we are leaving Venice. In fact, we are on our way to the station and just enjoying a last stroll round the piazza," said Miss Tenbaker.

Clementine gave the banker her dazzling smile, and Miss Tenbaker waited for the usual reaction from men of all ages, a look of happy fixation, often followed by an almost instinctive predatory movement to Clementine's side.

It did not come.

Mr. Sullivan moved forward. "Then may I offer you my arm, Miss Tenbaker?" he said. "I myself am returning to England next week. Perhaps I might call on *you?*"

Dazed by this emphasis, Leonora Tenbaker allowed him to take her arm.

Thus they walked across Saint Mark's Square, as the pigeons flew like white doves all around them.

35

His eyesight was definitely blurring. The water was turned into a smoky gray, and not only by the rain. The cataracts were increasing, the film thickening, and he dreaded the operation that would remove them. Apart from the suffering that would be inevitable, he wondered what he would see then. Would his vision be so sharp, so clear, that the cruel lines of the world would be inescapable?

Revel Callender said, "M. Monet, I am sure that a terrible injustice is being done. That man, Renard, is innocent."

"But they were convicted at the trial. Courtois confessed!"

"You should have seen the conditions in the prison where he was held. It was torture, believe me, it certainly amounted to that. And evidence given under torture is not worth a row of beans. Men will say anything for one moment's relief from the pain and misery—you must understand that!"

The old man stared out at the Adriatic.

"Sir," said Callender, "I have had a telegram from Paris. Courtois is dead, and I have no doubt it was because of the appalling conditions in La Petite Roquette. He was a sick man when they took him in, and they shut him up in solitary confinement, in a cell running with damp. So he can never recant—he is beyond it all now. But Renard is still alive, and his appeal will be heard soon. After that, he will face the guillotine. And the only evidence against him is the confession of a dead man."

Revel leaned forward. "M. Monet, you must know of matters within the family that have to do with this murder. Who hated the old man sufficiently? Who had an unstable and violent personality, of the type that could commit such a crime?"

The artist's eyes turned towards him. They had a bluish film over them.

Callender felt unnerved by the directness of the gaze but forced himself to continue. "Monsieur, may I give you these notes on the subject? This is my analysis made of the facts, the notes I brought away from Paris. And the conclusions I arrived at, which one must logically come to, if one looks at the matter rationally. I beg you, sir, your intervention could put an entirely different complexion on the case and release an innocent man."

Revel held out the notebook in which he had recorded the details of the Rémy case, the notes he had made on the train from Paris back to Venice. The artist did not take it, so he placed it at his side and rose to leave. He looked out at the wintry sky, the curling rims of early frost on the roof of Saint Mark's and reflected on the results of the investigation here in Venice.

It was not just that the Contessa Mariella had confessed to the murder of her husband, with the aid of her stepson and Antonio Prepiani. There was proof positive. The razor in the brothel where Prepiani was killed was not the only item where the commissario made use of the fingerprinting technique. The big, smooth rubies of Mariella's necklace turned out to bear the fingerprints of her lover Claudio, who had planted the necklace, and of the policeman who had found the piece of jewelry, but not those of poor Pietro, who was alleged to have stolen it.

Revel had helped to save Pietro and Matteo, the servants of the Casimiri who had been arrested for murder, but would he be able to achieve the same for poor Renard in the Rémy household? There seemed little point in continuing this conversation with a man whose thoughts seemed to be elsewhere. He got up to take his leave.

"There is the matter of your fee, M. Callender," said the artist, as Revel went to the door.

"If Renard is convicted, I have not earned my fee," he said. "I am returning to London tomorrow."

He would be returning with Clara, but for how long? Revel thought of the frail fabric of this city, of the thin paintwork of Saint Ursula's blue gray gown. Insubstantial, changing with the light—it showed him the fragility of the bond between himself and Clara.

Claude Monet sat in continuing and heavy silence.

Revel walked out of the room.

The artist sighed as the door closed behind the Englishman. The fact was that Monet had not been able to read easily for some time. Alice had to be his eyes as far as that went, since the cataracts had become so severe. Should he ask her to read this notebook aloud, this analysis of the murder of her own brother-in-law?

God knew, there had been enough members of that respectable bourgeois family who hated old Auguste enough to kill him. He thought of Alice's nephew, the debauched young fellow who had hated his Uncle Auguste. Of Alice's sister, who had put up with the bullying of a husband who had kept mistresses into his old age. Of her other nephew, Auguste's son Georges, who had quarreled bitterly with his father and had a proven record of violence against his wife.

But if he intervened, Alice would have to endure all the consequences, a new investigation, the renewed agony of her sister, Cecile, the exposure of all their secrets. Alice was sick now, he believed, suffering from that inner illness the young doctor had diagnosed. Monet could not bear to inflict any more pain on her.

He picked up Callender's notebook and crossed to the balcony.

In front of him, the light had returned, and the sun was setting in a blaze of russet gold, with an extraordinary violet color that shaded the mauve of campanulas and was caught in the shadows of the waves. In the distance to the left was the bell tower of San Giorgio Maggiore on its island. The building seeming to float in the evening air, the tower reflected in a long, patchy streak of bloodred that discolored the water. On the right, the huge, heavy dome of Santa Maria della Salute, almost lost in a darkness of ivory black, ultramarine, and slate gray.

Yes, if he could set up an easel near here, perhaps it would be the perfect place. There was little time left: they would be leaving soon.

Staring out into his vision of Venice, Claude Monet began to plan his last work in this city. A fear lay within his mind as he worked: that this might be the final time of happiness for himself and Alice, Venice the last place they would visit. This painting was a farewell to their own vital strength, as well as to the city; the brilliant sunset of the canvas would be the last fiery leaping embers of their life together.

The carmine and orange discords of the setting sun fired up again for brief moments that he tried to catch.

Callender's notebook eventually fell unnoticed from the ledge of the balcony. It floated amid the flotsam for a few minutes before the waters of the Adriatic carried it away.

Author's Note

Alice Monet died of myeloid leukemia in 1911, two and a half years after their trip to Venice. She had endured a lengthy illness. Monet's letters mention her being treated by radiotherapy with X rays.

The mysterious circumstances surrounding the murder of Monet's brother-in-law as described in the above pages are based on fact. Auguste indeed died in the way I have described. Monet and Alice visited Venice between the trial and the appeal of the two servants. The appeal of Pierre Renard, the butler, was not allowed. He was spared the guillotine but was sentenced to twenty years hard labor. He never confessed. The valet Courtois was not alive to attend the appeal hearings. He had died in the dreaded La Roquette prison after the trial.

Inspectors Blot and Hamard were also real persons. I would like to thank the Archives of the Préfecture of Police of Paris for allowing me to consult documentation there.

My account of the murder of that grotesque character, Francesco, Count Cenci, and the subsequent torture and convictions of his family is also based on historical fact. The "translation" from an old account is my own compilation from early sources. I have taken some details from Corrado Ricci's *Beatrice Cenci* (1925) and Antonio Bertolotti's *Francesco Cenci e la sua Famiglia* (1879). There is an excellent modern account, which deals mainly with male attitudes towards the Cenci story, by Belinda Jack, *Beatrice's Spell* (2004).

DISCARD

7/06

EAST BATON ROUGE PARISH LIBRARY

3 1659 03016 9334

EAST BATON ROUGE PARISH
LIBRARY
BATON ROUGE, LOUISIANA

BLUEBONNET REGIONAL